I0655322

Spiritual Mischief

Copyright © 2013 Michael Patrick Cleary
All rights reserved.

ISBN: 0-6157-8344-9
ISBN-13: 9780615783444

Spiritual Mischief

by

Michael Cleary

2013

Dedication

To my wife, Mary Ann. A beautiful woman wherein joy and happiness reside. She is spirited and spiritual, a cock-eyed optimist, courageous, selfless and artistic. I am so blessed and always grateful that I am her other half.

"A well put together unreality is pretty hard to beat."

Mark Twain

chapter 1

MY NAME IS Theodomicles. If you enjoy reading aloud or you are simply a stickler for pronouncing names correctly, the accent is on the third syllable. I am God's personal secretary. Now, if I were in your shoes – but, of course, I have no need for footwear – I would probably be a tad suspect of someone who makes such an outrageous claim. I wouldn't blame you for thinking I am, as the saying goes, blowing smoke. However, if you are the type who is quick to embrace spiritual notions, I can imagine one of your first thoughts is that my existence is further evidence that you are indeed an immortal soul. That blissful fact aside, you may wonder why there isn't a far more recognizable and, perhaps, better-suited saint or angel name painted on my office door. Well, for you nonbelievers, I offer nothing in the way of proof except my word which is golden in these here parts. Of course, everyone's word is golden in these here parts. For those of you who do wonder how I landed such a prestigious position, let me first say this is not one of those jobs one finds posted on Craig's List. And, yes, if you must know, there were many, many applicants. As to why they did not get the assignment, my lips are sealed. Of course, I don't have any lips but you get my meaning. It's off the topic, but have you noticed how many metaphors there are built around your temporal body parts?

Suffice it to say, I am what I am. Or, borrowing from Corinthians; sum id quod sum. Even though the language has been dead for centuries, Latin puts a more vigorous tone to this life-affirming aphorism. I might add that I have been at this post for some time. In fact, if I had opened an aggressive 401k when I signed on, I would be awash in the green stuff. On a serious note, though, what I have amassed in that space of time is a dizzying collection of odd and fantastical stories.

The saga of Peter Allen Ramsey and Lillie Langtry with its mischief and merry mayhem is one I've been dying to share... No, that's definitely the wrong expression. You see, we don't die. Explaining that will take forever which is just fine from my vantage point because I have all the time in the world. You, however, are living your mortal moment and time is of the essence. I'd like to say I'm anxious to share this particular tale with you for no other reason than I find it so darned amusing. Truth be told, though, there is another reason. As one of the principal players in this madcap adventure, it was my doing that more or less... Oh, who am I kidding? If I hadn't weakened and given the old "Go ahead, my dear" to Lillie, this story would have not taken the bizarre path it did.

Now, there is the chance that this tale might prove inspirational. I don't meant it to be. My reasons are twofold. Firstly, and I might add, selfishly, I just enjoy storytelling, particularly when I play a role. Secondly, I was advised by You-Know-Who to not be heavy-handed. I could sense early on that my All-Forgiving Employer wasn't that keen on the project when He warned me that once the story is published, even though I am the real yarn-spinner here, it is my earthly amanuensis who will get all the attention as he quite understandably sees himself as the true author. Knowing His creations as He does, God assured me I will be written off as nothing more than inspiration from on High, an expression the writer will use repeatedly while tossing snappy, spiritual sound bites hither and yon on TV talk shows, radio interviews and book signings.

You may have noticed by now that when I use a personal pronoun to refer to my Boss, I opt for He or Him. My guideline is the second definition of the pronoun "he" in the American Heritage Dictionary which states: "Used to refer to any person whose sex is not specified." Please don't read anything more into it. My Employer cannot be defined by such narrow restrictions as he, she or it implies.

So, at this juncture, let's leave it at this regarding this whole inspiration business: If there is something you take from the story that betters you or improves your lot, so be it. And bully for me for having helped.

Before we begin, let me introduce you to my accidental protagonist. His full name is Peter Allen Ramsey. He is weeks shy of his sixty-fifth birthday. That particular number doesn't bother him in the least as he's already had half a decade of dealing with sexagenarianism (Is there such a word?). All the anxieties, fears and apprehensions one usually associates with reaching those kinds of milestones are pretty much behind him. He does muse about his future, though. Plus, he's been entertaining spiritual thoughts of late and that always gets our attention. In fact, that's how I came into the picture. Unbeknownst to him, his life was about to change in a most radical fashion. Little did he know when every morning he went supine on his bedroom floor to pray and stretch away the body's tightening from a good night's sleep, we were listening.

Peter Ramsey has for the last thirty years hosted an early morning radio show in San Francisco. His voice is warm and sincere with just enough of a Scotch-Irish lilt in it to make waking up to him a pleasant addition to one's morning ritual. Much to the chagrin of his employer, the monstrously huge Figg Broadcasting Company, he is not edgy enough, controversial enough nor profane enough. He only remains on the payroll because he has a very large, faithful audience who not only listen to him but they marry amongst themselves and produce more happy little Peter Ramsey listeners, thereby replenishing those older listeners who moved on to join us here in... So, what shall I call my home for the duration of this tale? How about Cleveland? No, I can't really do that as you already have a Cleveland. My problem is mortals have over thousands of years given this place any number of appealing names; Nirvana, the Elysian Fields, Valhalla, Seventh Heaven, Happy Hunting Grounds, just to name a few. Now my Employer, when he gave me the final but hesitant okay for this book, set strict guidelines as to how much information I can dispense. Letting you have our Zip Code is not one of them. Therefore, we'll just stick with the tried and true Eternity.

Peter with his good health, Celtic complexion, blue eyes and tall, slender frame is not a disappointment physically. This crisp description will suffice for now. His eccentricities, his character pluses and minuses and his odd habit or two will all be revealed in due time.

So, my beloved air-breathers, let us begin: It was noon, Friday, January 19th, 2010 when I first took an active interest in Mr. Ramsey. He was on his way to lunch in North Beach, a diverse, vibrant and eccentric neighborhood in San Francisco liberally dotted with dozens of cafes and restaurants. His destination was Ciccarelli's Bar and Grill. With a celebrity bartender behind the bar, Chick's, so-dubbed by those who frequent it, is a hallowed hangout for assorted members of both the private and public sector, many still on active duty and others retired. A batch of the latter usually filled the south end of the bar through the weekday lunch hour. On that particular Friday, they had abandoned their rounds of Liars' Dice to observe one David Augustus Flannery who was seated at a corner window table in the dining room. This was not the first time they put their drinks and dice on hold to watch him. In fact, it had turned into a game of wagering.

Flannery was one of San Francisco's finer slobs. Widely recognized as having earned a black belt in slovenliness, the executive editor-in-chief of the city's morning daily can when he chooses take the art of frumpiness to amazing heights.

On this particular day, he was at the top of his game clad in an ill-fitting, frayed Herringbone sport coat, rumpled khakis, wrinkled shirt and food-stained striped tie. His only nod to style was an Hermes pocket square his wife gave him for Christmas; a bright orange, yellow and green silk affair that grew out of his pocket with the extravagant arrogance of a blossoming peony. His graying hair was uncombed and his nut brown eyes glowered, giving a hint that he was in a foul mood. However, well into his second 10 year-old Laphhroaig, he was actually full of warmth, bonhomie and single malt.

However, it wasn't his physical appearance that earned him all the attention from the bar. Flannery was one of San Francisco's more ill-tempered characters. A moody, irascible man with a short fuse, Flannery – while widely recognized as a topnotch newspaperman of the old school – often ended up making news rather than reporting it.

Larry Rosario, a retired Financial District bartender, began the betting. He remembered when he correctly predicted Flannery and a political consultant to the mayor would end up trading punches. While neither gladiator displayed a talent for inflicting any real physical damage on the other, it was enough of a boxing match for Rosario to win ten dollars. Today, he once again demonstrated his talent for

Flannery-watching: "He looks put out. But he always looks the way. Five says he's in an okay mood and nothing's going to happen."

On a neighboring barstool, Stanley "Stella" Kowalski, a newly retired police inspector who grudgingly had to put up with that nickname for all of his thirty years on the force, took the bet. "He's drinking scotch for lunch. That is not a good sign. I say he quiets the dining room at least once with one of his political rants or maybe some of his damned Irish poetry."

Spotting the star of my story walking into the dining room, Flannery waved him over. It should be noted here that Ramsey was exactly on time, give or take a second or two. His promptness didn't go unnoticed by the editor.

"Order well. My deep-pocketed boss is buying lunch," he barked as Ramsey took his seat.

"I had to make an ATM stop." Peter explained, wondering why on earth he had to have an excuse at the ready because he wasn't the first to arrive. I told you earlier his eccentricities would eventually surface.

"Actually, you're right on time. Scarily so."

"It's a radio thing."

"You know that bunch at the bar?" Flannery asked.

"I do. I recently emceed Kowalski's retirement dinner. All his cronies from here were in attendance. Most of them slept through the speeches."

Flannery glanced around and gave the group a curt nod. "This must be the only assisted living saloon in town."

"We certainly have their undivided attention."

"They're convinced I'm some sort of emotional time bomb and there's always the possibility I will explode. So they put money on it. I'm sure somebody's got five or ten riding on something happening during lunch."

The broadcaster smiled and surveyed the visual mess of the journalist across from him. He wondered if he might be one of those intellectual sorts who, because their brains are so filled with marvelous abstractions and weighty formulations, haven't a nook or cranny left in the old cranium to give any consideration to mundane topics like one's personal appearance. Or then again, maybe he was just a slob.

Ramsey was, for the record, Flannery's polar opposite. Outwardly, he was well-dressed, well-groomed and well-pressed. Inwardly, he seldom entertained a bad mood and anger was an emotion that rarely showed itself.

Flannery, while admittedly there at the behest of his publisher, was actually looking forward to the lunch. As a regular listener to his morning show, he was curious to know if the real Ramsey was as pleasant as the on-air Ramsey. Peter, you see, was born with an inexhaustible supply of niceness which to my way of thinking is a positive, but to the cynical newspaper editor it was a major character flaw.

"Maybe a line or two of some fine Irish poetry," Flannery mused aloud.

"I beg your pardon?"

"The bar crowd is just itching for me to act up. How about some Dylan Thomas?"

"It's fine by me." Remembering the story of his dustup with the political consultant, Ramsey thought a poetry reading was preferable to watching a Flannery fist come flying across the table aimed at his never-been-broken nose. "By the way, you know he isn't Irish?"

"He isn't?" Flannery was genuinely surprised by the revelation.

"Nope. Born in Swansea, Wales in 1914 and died thirty-nine years later in New York."

Flannery sat back in his chair and considered this new information. "I don't really know much about him. I just assumed he was Irish."

"A Welshman all the way. He did, though, marry an Irish woman named Caitlin Macnamara."

"Well, there you are. There is an Irish connection." Flannery grinned, took a final sip of scotch and signaled for a server. "How do you know so much about him?"

Peter wondered what the odds were of Dylan Thomas becoming a topic du jour twice in one day. That morning he had interviewed a local actor who was promoting a one man show built around the poet. Several web sites dedicated to Thomas supplied Peter with all the information he needed to make the interview sound interesting. He explained it all to his lunch partner.

"Do you know his works?" Flannery asked.

"*Do not go gentle into that good night, old age should burn and rave at the close of day. Rage, rage against the dying of the light.*" His recitation was soft-spoken and halting.

Now there are some, and I am one of them, who will say one shouldn't just blurt out a verse or two of the good stuff. If you're going to get into it, do the poem justice and see it through to the end. That certainly must have been Flannery's way of thinking as he intoned, "*Though wise men at their end know dark is right, Because their words had forked no lightening they do not go gentle into that good night.*"

Peter sat in wonderment while Flannery lost himself in the rest of the work. He didn't recite the remaining verses, he became them. He was the poem itself, at times ranting and, dare I say it, raging against the dying of the night.

Flannery held nothing back when it came to the last couple of rages. Indeed, he quieted the room. Most diners simply looked over at our table. But not Alpha Mae Connell. A retired Maiden Lane manicurist, she spun around in her chair and lifting her vodka Martini in a toast said loudly, "You're a horse's ass, Flannery, but I love you." At the bar, Kowalski snatched Rosario's fiver and took a small bow.

Peter, uncomfortable with the attention, glanced around the dining room before reacting to Flannery's poetic outpouring. "You don't mind if I don't ask for an encore?"

"I think that did the trick," Flannery explained, unfazed by the attention his performance received.

"Well, it being Friday and all, maybe something that lifts the spirit and is recited less forcefully would have worked better."

Flannery laughed at the criticism. "I'm not really into poetry. That bunch," he said, "thinks I am because they've heard me talk my way through some Irish songs when I'm drunk. Truth is I can't sing a note. When I take on 'Galway Bay,' the tide goes out. Anyway, I came across that poem a few months ago and was taken by it enough so that I learned it. Memorization strengthens the brain, you know."

"Obviously the poem must mean something to you."

Flannery placed both hands on the table, studied them for a few seconds and then looking across at his dining partner, replied, "Yes, it does. It means death sucks. It is inevitable, so give it no thought. Just concentrate on living as intensely as you can."

Ramsey countered, "Maybe Thomas is saying to rage, rave and burn against the dying of the light because there is no death. That life and light are one and the same and eternal."

"Could be." Flannery's dismissive tone meant that for him the topic was now fully explored. Picking up the menu and scanning the room for a server, he said, "Order well, as I mentioned earlier my esteemed leader is paying for this. Hell, order the abalone. It's priced about the same as a barrel of oil."

While my friends are ordering, let me provide you with a little background on Flannery's boss. The esteemed – at least among the members of San Francisco's social elite – publisher of the morning paper was Sanford "Sandy" Symington, who sadly suffered from sibilance and probably wouldn't even attempt the first part of this sentence. He would have been at Chick's to personally pitch his latest promotional idea to Ramsey if his wife, Mitzi, hadn't ordered him to be present and accounted for at her charity fundraising luncheon and auction at the new DeYoung Museum benefiting Restless Leg Syndrome research. He was glad he came as he could personally muzzle his society reporter who would no doubt jump on the fact that his wife booked a tap dancer as the featured performer. Now Flannery wanted no part of his publisher's new pet project, and because he made that perfectly clear to one and all at yesterday's editorial board meeting, Symington – acutely aware of his editor's disdain for sales and marketing – ordered him to meet with Ramsey. The publisher saw it as a perverse form of punishment and took great satisfaction in handing the assignment to Flannery.

In a tone that showed no enthusiasm whatsoever for what he was saying, Flannery began to explain the nuts and bolts of the publisher's plan to his lunch partner. "Symington is turning sixty this year and he's convinced ever other fucking Baby Boomer is just like him, weighted down with disposable cash to lavish on dream vacations and getaways. So he wants to expand the Sunday travel section and direct it toward other sixty-somethings. So we're going to put out a four-page supplement devoted to travel topics and ads that will attract his contemporaries."

Frowning, he added, "Listen to me. I sound like an adjective-sated editor of a glossy fashion magazine instead of a newspaper. Oh well, whatever."

"You do a very good whatever," Ramsey remarked.

"I have a sixteen and fourteen year-old. God knows, I've heard it enough."

"So, how do I figure in all of this?"

"Symington is eager to team up with a radio station and a local personality, preferably someone his age or older, to promote a group cruise to Alaska in June. That's where you come in. No offense, but you're probably the only old guy left on the air in this town. Anyway, for promoting the trip through radio spots and talking it up on your morning show and then hosting a few parties on board, you get the cruise free and clear. Hold on, there's more," he said, digging into his pocket and retrieving a crumpled Post-It. "Oh yeah, Symington said your accommodations would be on the penthouse deck and your incidentals – I'm assuming that means booze – would be paid."

"It's a very tempting offer."

"As long as Symington isn't in the penthouse next door to yours."

"Are you going?"

"I don't know. On the plus side, there's that sixteen year-old and her fourteen year-old brother that I wouldn't mind getting away from for twelve days. The downside is if I do go, Symington will probably put me in a stateroom the size of a cell at county jail and I'd have to buy my own drinks."

Because we got what we came for, this is where we pack up and leave Ciccarelli's Bar and Grill. We might have stayed on and watched Flannery drain one more Laphroaig or listen to Ramsey expound on how loopy the radio business has become, but it will serve no purpose.

One question remains, though. Did Flannery come away from the lunch thinking the real Peter Ramsey matched his on-air persona? The newspaper editor concluded he did. He also thought that, while Ramsey was a pleasant enough chap, he was too timid and a little stiff. As the two splashed about in the conversational pool, Flannery thought Peter stayed in the shallow end. Of course, that may have a lot to do with the his reluctance to answer questions like "As a single guy at your advanced age, do you get laid a lot." No doubt an inquiry put on the table because longtime married Flannery wasn't.

Departing this luncheon scene was a touchy process. I found myself at odds with my amanuensis who was resistant to leaping ahead in the story. It seems he was a regular at this venerable North Beach saloon in real life and thought the longer we kept the lunch going, the more promotion for the restaurant which, in turn, would result in a lot of free Guinness and Martinis. I would have tolerated this gratuitousness but I knew the restaurant would permanently close its doors in early March. Oh, don't worry about the regulars. Within days the celebrity bartender with the bar crowd in tow relocated to Dante's Trattoria, an Italian restaurant just two blocks away. Sadly, betting on Flannery's antics came to an end as the newspaper editor, after a dinner of really bad gnocchi at Dante's in early 2006, never set foot in the place again.

chapter 2

By late May over two hundred happy souls with their mortal frames securely attached, had signed on to sail north to Alaska in the company of Mr. Ramsey and, as it turned out, Mr. Flannery. My reason for mentioning both body and soul is one guest showed up wearing nothing but her soul. It is I who must take credit for that particular booking.

In all the months since January I paid scant attention to Peter especially as he seemed to be in good working order, spiritually speaking. He dutifully began each day with his usual request for a slice or two of daily bread. His trespasses were for the most part trivial and were as quickly forgiven as he forgave those who trespassed against him. My apologies for playing loose and fancy with your classic Pater Noster which, I might add, is one of my favorites of your myriad entreaties. Now you're probably thinking that being eternal means never having to say your sorry. Not quite. It's difficult to explain, but acclimating to this enchanting world of Forever After isn't something that happens overnight. Many of your fanciful foibles arrive with you much like barnacles on a ship's hull. As a result, for the short term, you're still capable of the occasional goof, gaffe, faux pas or lapse in judgment. Take my horrible mistake of letting Lillie go off on her madcap adventure. And I've been here for centuries. You'd think

I'd know better. It is for that very reason that we here in Eternity are masters of etiquette. In fact, we are so good in the manners' department, when you get here and sample our graciousness, you'll feel like you died and went to... Which, of course, you did.

Speaking of prayer, as you well know, it is that wondrous device which puts you into direct contact with my Boss. Unlike e-mail, there are no filters to prevent your special petition from getting through. There is also no such thing as spam and nothing, absolutely nothing gets deleted. We do, however, see more than our fair share of appeals regarding lottery outcomes, sports' scores, school grades, salary hikes and such. You can imagine what it's like in the days preceding a Super Bowl. Also, the wrongful appeals from testosterone-charged boys on Prom night is downright scary. Is there a proper way to pray? Let me assure you there is none. Physically, all positions work. You can be supine, on your knees or in one of those odd-looking yoga poses with their funny names. You can be hang-gliding, house-painting, horseback riding or holding court. And language isn't all that important. Latin still works, and words like unto, doeth, thee and thou are all perfectly acceptable. But if you're not in the habit of using them in your everyday speech, you can certainly pass on them. Prayers can range from your basic prepackaged variety that often come with grandiose ceremony, elaborately designed garments and lighted candles to the most basic of all which is a wordless invocation. Wordless? Oh yes, indeed. Don't worry if you become tongue-tied. Your heart and soul speak a language which is often more expressive, meaningful and eloquent than any words your mind can send our way. I do have my favorites of your many prayers. Voices rising as one is a personal show stopper, so I always enjoy anything sung or chanted by children or adults. Do prayers work? Ah that, my beloved air-breather, is a question that is answered over and over again.

Peter's life during those months since January could best be described as a period of delicious dullness. All that ended in June when, putting the finishing touches on a Friday morning radio show, he spotted the station manager on the other side of the studio glass clumsily pantomiming that he'd like to see him in his office.

His boss, Howard Aaron Newton is a fiftyish, bow-tie-sporting nebbish whose broadcast resume is bone thin but his references are topnotch. First on the list is his mother-in-law, Philipa Crumley-Figg who owns a sizable chunk of Figg Broadcasting Company. It should be noted here that radio is not one of Howard's passions. Sea birds are. It is a love he shares with his wife, Naomi Newton, nee Figg. With a maiden name like that, you can under-stand why she wisely chose not to hyphenate after mar-riage. Naomi takes Howard's love for sea birds up a notch by painting them. Her gallery, so to speak, is her husband's office which is adorned with her earnest but amateurish oils, watercolors and pen and ink drawings. Compliment-ing these hangings are assorted other birdie bric-a-brac that perch atop shelves, tables and his desk. Among the world of sea birds, Howard's favorites are the Sooty Tern and the Snowy Plover, while Naomi positively swoons over the Blue Heron and the Brown Pelican which, at least in my humble estimation, is one of God's really clever designs. The Newtons wish for nothing more out of life than to spend it studying these winged creatures. Even though Howard gave little attention to his managerial duties at the radio station, Peter thought him a better than average boss. Howard's keep-it-simple approach meant sales' people sold, programming people programmed, engineering peo-ple engineered and on-air people aired, so to speak. And to his credit, he somehow managed to keep the bean counters and the New York corporate suits from messing with that utterly sensible policy. Peter admired him for that and the pair over the years enjoyed a good relationship.

"They want you to retire, Peter," he said as his morning personality entered his office. Howard avoided eye contact by aligning a large painting of a short-tailed Albatross which hung over his desk.

"Buy out my contract. I will instantly vanish." This had been their routine greeting for over a year. This morning, though, both put a little extra something into the exchange.

Howard pointed to a chair. "Sit down, please. I got an e-mail from New York last night. Corporate is planning to syndicate mornings on all the AM stations and they want to do it quickly."

"Who will replace me?"

"You guessed it, " Howard replied, clearly delighted with Peter's question.

"What kind of answer is that? Seriously, who will replace me?"

"I am being serious. That's the guy." Howard was clearly enjoying this verbal volley.

"Who?"

"Yes."

Suddenly the Abbot and Costello baseball comedy classic popped into his head and Peter laughed. "Howard, are you telling me that the FBC top brass are going to syndicate someone called Who?"

"What's so weird about it? We already have somebody in this market called No Name? Look, I know it sounds unbelievably stupid, but New York said the idea tested well in focus groups. Plus, the consultants love it. Their plan is to do a big promotion introducing Who, and then after three months or so, the network will have a contest to give the mystery man a real name."

"And the guy they pick for this insanity is probably a shock jock with a name like Dog Breath who holds regular on-air fart contests, insults callers and daily reduces the cute traffic reporter to tears by comparing her breasts to traffic cones. Oh, and he probably makes jokes about his own slavish devotion to onanism."

"Peter, take the cash and get out now. This industry is not what it was."

Ramsey watched as his boss began to move a small ceramic snowy plover from one side of his desk to the other. He reflected on how uncannily similar in appearance and personality Howard was to the general manager who first hired him in San Francisco forty years ago. Fresh out of the Army, Ramsey had been gathering on-air experience in a medium-sized California radio market when a former coworker arranged for him to interview for a midday shift at a popular San Francisco Top Forty station. Like Howard Newton, George Lamstahl ran things because a relative, his father in this case, owned the station. Like Newton, Lamstahl was short, bald and diffident. While Howard's heart and soul were given over to the study of sea birds, George's heart and soul was totally devoted to the intimate study of his secretary; research that found the lovebirds sneaking off to a hotel room every chance they could. Ramsey's interview lasted for less than a minute. He was never invited to sit down.

Lamstahl: "How tall are you?"
Ramsey: "A little over six-two."
Lamstahl: "When can you start?"

Afterwards, a bemused Ramsey huffed and puffed his way up Nob Hill to look at the city from the breezy corner of California and Mason Streets. His heart pounded and not just from the walk. While thrilled to think he would be working in a market the size of the Bay Area, he couldn't quite grasp the logic of being hired to do a radio show based solely on height. Later, Ramsey learned the station sponsored a charity basketball team and his future boss was obsessed with winning every game. Unfortunately for Lamstahl and the team, he forgot to ask Peter if he could play basketball.

Now here he was forty years later and a quarter inch shorter, staring at another short, bald man who just told him the party's over and he's being replaced by some obnoxious youngster who will be given the name Who. "Howard, you don't have a problem with me announcing my retirement?"

"Not at all," he answered with apparent relief. Leafing through some e-mail printouts, he added, "In fact, corporate is willing to pay off the rest of your contract and tack on an additional four months if you agree to retire. They don't want the headache, nor do I, of dealing with the feedback we're bound to get if it gets around that you've been fired."

And so it was agreed his last show would be the Friday before the cruise which was just two weeks away. Peter told Howard he'd get things rolling by broaching the topic of leaving the show on Monday. He also put in a request to leave without the security guard escorting him to the door, a demeaning practice that had became a standard industry practice.

"Don't worry. I'll see you to the door myself," Howard said. Staring down at his desk, he added nervously, "I, uh, have a favor to ask. Naomi's mother will be on your Alaska cruise. Could you keep an eye on her? She will be traveling alone. If you can, maybe arrange to have her sit at your table in the dining room?"

Ramsey, the gentleman that he is, happily agreed to see to the well-being of Mrs. Philipa Crumley-Figg. "You know in all the years I've worked here, I never met the woman."

"I'm not surprised. She has zero interest in the business. She never went near the New York radio station when she lived in Manhattan. But that's all about to change. She's written a memoir and it's due to be released next week. No doubt, she's going to want radio time and then some to promote it."

"What has she done to warrant a published memoir?" Peter asked.

"Before she married into the Figg family, Philipa was a buyer for... Oh, I can't remember exactly but a Saks Fifth Avenue kinda place. While she was there, she designed what she called her Picasso jacket. She claims she was inspired by how Picasso would select a subject, deconstruct it and put it back together in his own idiosyncratic style. She did much the same with one of those pinstriped, double-breasted suit coats that men like Jimmy Cagney wore in the gangster movies. She deconstructed the coat, moved a collar here, buttons there and stuff like that. Anyway some female rock star wore it at a concert and after that stores couldn't keep it in stock. The jacket sold well in the early seventies and made her a player, albeit a minor one, in the fashion design world. Although she thinks of herself as being as important a contributor as Coco Chanel."

"What's the title of this potential bestseller?"

He opened a bottom drawer to his desk and pulled out a copy. "Here it is," he said, handing it Peter.

Ramsey read aloud, "'My Double-Breasted Life' by Philipa Crumley-Figg. Publisher is PAP Publishing. Please tell me they aren't a mainstream publishing house."

Howard laughed. "Not a chance. My mother-in-law financed the whole things. PAP stands for Philipa and Pablo. She's got about a thousand of these and I'm sure will bring a few on the cruise. I wouldn't be surprised if she doesn't push you to have some kind of event to push her book."

This did not sit well with Peter. "Howard, I'm sorry I agreed to see to this women's well-being. Foisting her off on me is one hell of a going away gift. What's wrong with a gold watch and a quick good-bye?"

Howard put his hands up and said, "Peter, you have my permission to toss her overboard if she gets.... Oh, I shouldn't have said that." Pausing ever so slightly, he explained sotto voce, "You see, she thinks I'm trying to kill her."

Well, there you are. No sooner had Peter quickly digested the Philipa back story and was now planning to slip away to mull over more important matters like his upcoming retirement than Howard slips in that tasty little morsel.

"Of course, I am not trying to kill her," he added quickly.

Ramsey, now aware that he had twice commented on killing his mother-in-law, felt some kind of show of support was necessary. "Howard, you are a man who loves Sooty Terns and Snowy Plovers. Hardly the stuff of a potential murderer."

"Even so, Philipa has it in her head that I am plotting to do her in so Naomi and I can move to Hawaii and pursue our collective interest in sea birds. And, of course, she has concluded that our defection would be financed by her daughter's sizable inheritance."

"How on earth did your mother-in-law get it in her head that you want to murder her?" "Before I answer that let me tell you some more about her. Philipa Crumley-Figg is a nasty force of nature; foul-mouthed, bitchy and demanding. And here's the rub. This category five hurricane currently resides with us, even though she obviously has means of her own. She's staying with us despite the fact that she can't stand the ground I walk on and she's thoroughly disappointed with her daughter for having married me."

"But why does she think you want to murder her?"

"It's silly, really," he said. "I haven't said anything to you about this, but Naomi and I are very serious about moving to Hawaii. We've been looking at various island properties and checking on financing, taxes... That kind of thing. Anyway, I got an e-mail from an old college pal who lives on Oahu and is in real estate. It contained a lot of information on some properties he thought were worth looking into. I forwarded the e-mail to Naomi and added a note telling her how excited I was to know that once we finally get rid of her monster of a mother, we can make Hawaii a reality. Philipa was on the computer the other day and read it. What a scene that night at dinner."

"Howard, this is laughable," Peter said. "Obviously, there are more appropriate ways of expressing yourself, but it's quite a leap for her to think you're conspiring to do her in. I'd like a dime for every time landlords and hosts of unwanted house guests have said they want to get rid of someone."

"I agree. Look, I wrote it because I knew Philipa reads our e-mail. I'm embarrassed to say both of us let ourselves be bullied by her. And trust me, her harassment is unrelenting. I guess sending that e-mail was a way of striking back."

"But that still doesn't explain why she thinks you're trying to kill her."

"There were two recent incidents that suggest there really is someone who wishes her harm. Philipa came home visibly shaken last week. She claimed she was pushed into oncoming traffic while waiting to cross at Market and Embarcadero. She said that as she fell forward a bike messenger grabbed her just in time. Then at the beginning of this week, she said somebody approached her from behind while she was shopping at Bloomingdales and hissed, 'You were lucky last week. Next time you won't be.' She felt certain it was a man's voice, but when she turned there was no one there except other shoppers and they were all woman. Then two days ago she read the e-mail I forwarded to Naomi."

Now Peter had certainly read his share of murder mysteries and watched his share of movies and TV shows where sinister chitchat like this is par for the course. But this was uncharted territory for him. This much he knew, though. Or thought he did. Firstly, matters probably weren't as serious as Howard was making them out to be and, secondly, he was confident they would sort themselves out. As a result, he had absolutely nothing more to contribute fearing he would just end up sounding like an actor in a television crime series.

"Oh, I wish I was making all this up," Howard groaned, sinking further into his executive chair. "For God's sake, I'm not plotting to murder the woman. But I am concerned that somebody might be." Pausing, he added, "It's terrible to say, Peter, but she's so odious a woman, if something is really afoot, there are moments when I wish the bad guys all the success in the world."

Peter moved toward the door. "Howard, I'm absolutely clueless as to what you should do. Look, I've got to go. I'm meeting Liz for lunch at the Big Four at noon. If you want I can give you Frank Burke's home number."

"You mean the former chief of police?"

"Maybe he can help."

"No, no, I'll work it out. Meantime, have a good weekend. And say hi to Liz." Howard rose and extending his hand, added with almost a gushing sincerity, "I hope we'll have occasion to see each other after you leave." Noticing a subtle twitch in Peter's upper lip and knowing from experience what it meant, he added, "Oh shit, I forgot I'm talking to a professional cute guy."

"Howard, you disappoint me. I'm delighted you want to keep in touch. And I'm sure we will. By the way, visiting days at San Quentin are Wednesdays and Saturdays. I'll probably be able to make either day."

"That is not funny, Peter."

chapter 3

WHEN AN OCCASION called for a special location, both Peter and Liz preferred having their celebrations at the Big Four Restaurant in the Huntington Hotel on Nob Hill. The dimly-lit, low-ceilinged, wood-paneled restaurant and bar paid homage to that raucous and adventurous period in San Francisco when Collis Huntington, Leland Stanford, Mark Hopkins and Charles Crocker, a quartet of bearded, deep-pocketed gents who developed California's railroad system, all lived gold-lined cheek by silver-plated jowl in their impressive mansions atop Nob Hill. The restaurant's walls were lined with historic railroad advertisements and train schedules, land deeds, early California maps, wanted posters and political cartoons. Peter enjoyed the clubbiness of the place and thought the restaurant was as fine a place as any to share with Liz the unexpected news of his retirement. Knowing that Liz, also a stickler for punctuality, would be right behind him, he headed for the usually quiet bar to wait for her. Look up the word quiet in the dictionary and you'll see a picture of this classy tavern. In all his visits he could only recall one scene that could be described as feather-ruffling and even that was remarkably suited to the Nob Hill culture. It involved a slight, well-dressed, overly made-up octogenarian named Mrs. Adele Marie

Bennington-Remington. She was a Big Four regular who credited her good health and chipper spirits to a healthy, four-ounce Tanqueray Martini with two blue cheese-stuffed olives served up promptly at five o'clock every single evening of the year including all holidays. It was well known that while she was enjoying her nightly libation, Bernard de Coffeur, her social escort and caretaker for the last couple of years, prepared her dinner in her next door pied-à-terre. One evening, fifteen minutes and fifteen sips into her Martini, Bernard dashed into the bar and with the dramatic flourish of an out-of-work actor announced to one and all that he and an old flame, Reggie Wheatley, who had suddenly found himself on the receiving end of a tidy inheritance, were headed to the Gay Rodeo in Reno and after that who knows where. Next came a litany of complaints about the abuse Mrs. B-R had routinely heaped on him. Then, turning his attention to the Nob Hill matron, in a single breath he informed her that the pot roast was done to perfection, her table was set, her lavender candles were lighted, Truffle, her bitchy Bichon Frise fed and walked and he, Bernard Lance de Coffeur was packed up and out of there. Then with a slight curtsy to the attentive crowd and a quick stop to kiss the now giggling pianist good-bye, Bernard was off on his new adventure with Reggie. Her turn to play offense, Coffeur's former employer screeched, "How dare you do this to me, you bleached out old fag." She then worked her way through a number of insulting comments along that general line, her language getting saltier and saltier. The usually soft-spoken, almost fragile Mrs.Bennington-Remington was finally asked to exit the premises. I won't even comment on her reaction to being formally eighty-sixed.

Even in the dim light, there was no mistaking David Augustus Flannery sitting at the far end of the bar. While still looking like a candidate for one of those extreme makeover shows, he appeared to Peter as looking more put together than their last meeting.

Boarding the stool next to the editor, Peter said, "I'll stay if you promise to keep *"Do Not Go Gentle Into That Good Night"* and anything else by Dylan Thomas to yourself."

If the newspaper editor was taken by surprise, he didn't show it. "Don't worry. I can't even remember the fucking thing. Besides, that over-the-hill gang that used to bet on my unruly behavior can't afford to drink in a place like this. Matter of fact, neither can I. You're welcome to join me, but you gotta buy your own drink."

"Let me buy you one. I hear you're going on the cruise," Peter said.

Flannery's smile, rarely seen by the general public, did wonders for the curmudgeonly journalist's mug. With his shock of gray hair and stern brown eyes shaded by untrimmed eyebrows, he normally looked like the judge you'd never want to appear before. His smile, however, turned him into a genial gent who would be right at home surrounded by happy nieces and nephews all begging to hear "Uncle Davie" stories, minus, of course, the Flannery profanities.

"Oh, I have you to thank for that, my friend," he said, his rare smile neutralized by a tone of voice that left Peter wondering whether he was truly being thanked or blamed. "Symington had it in his head that the travel group would be forty to fifty people max. When you sold the hell out of it and it went over 200 hundred, he was ecstatic. He decided the paper needed to have a representative host on the cruise. And you're looking at him." Flannery drained the rest of his drink and signaled the bartender for a refill. "Symington said you'd know what I would have to do. Now you've saved me a phone call."

Peter at once saw how having Flannery on board would work in his favor. "It's a walk in the park. The first morning at sea we host a Bloody Mary and Mimosa welcoming party. It'll last exactly forty-five minutes. Then we have to come up with a couple of presentations which will be scheduled for our days at sea. The ship will provide us with a theater or a show lounge and for exactly forty-five minutes, while the crew serves up sparkling wine, we talk to our group about our respective professions."

"Why exactly forty-five minutes?"

"The cruise line claims that experience has taught them that after that stretch of time, people start getting fidgety. Some start to leave. Some doze off."

"Considering the age of some of our crowd, I wouldn't be surprised if one or two don't die off as well."

"If you sense we're losing them, you could always relearn the Dylan Thomas poem and scare the hell out of them."

Peter first caught a whiff of her familiar perfume. Next he felt the perfunctory peck on the cheek. Then came her hurried announcement: "Hello, you darling old bimbo, traffic was a bloody, I mean really bloody nightmare. Have to go to the loo. Oh, and give me five minutes to make a phone call to the department. Hey," she added, giving him a quick once over, "you look... Well, happy! Something happen? Tell me when I get back."

And with that, Elizabeth Marie Handlery set off for the rest room. Wearing a tight brown khaki skirt with a simple white blouse and heels, the vivacious thirty-one year-old was as striking going as coming. Flannery was riveted to her every move. "My lord, Ramsey, no wonder you're still single," he said. "How long have the two of you been together?"

"Twenty-three years."

While Dave Flannery is busy doing the math, I will use the time to supply you with more of the Ramsey backstory. At quarter past five on Saturday morning, June 12th, 1985, forty-three year-old Peter Allen Ramsey received a phone call from a U.S. embassy employee in Costa Rica informing him that his sister, Amelia, and his brother-in-law, Edward Handlery, were killed when the bus they were riding in took a curve too fast and crashed on a mountain road. Both were well-respected, and well-liked professors in the College of Environmental Design at the University of California in Berkeley. They had been vacationing in that country following a conference in Panama. Peter, who was watching their eight year-old daughter, Elizabeth, while they were away, waited a full hour before waking her to tell her the tragic news. Somehow he thought those sixty minutes would be enough to find the right words. Then he realized there were no right words. He would just tell her what happened and then hold her for as long as it took to make the pain go away. I remember the two angels who worked this case. They were particularly proud of their efforts. With his beloved sister gone, Peter became the last remaining Ramsey. At least on the West Coast. He knew there were some distant relatives scattered about the Boston area but they had had no contact for years. On the Handlery side, Edward's relatives all resided in England. Further, he had been estranged from them for years. Edward and Amelia's trust and will stipulated that Peter be executor and Elizabeth's legal guardian until she came of age. So as of that tragic and sad June morning, they became a family of two. Thinking Liz would be much better off staying in familiar surroundings, Peter moved out of his apartment in San Francisco and into the Handlery's comfortable home in the Berkeley Hills. He became such an excellent parent, Liz insisted she honor him on both Father's and Mother's Day.

Flannery did more than the math. He remembered the story as it was big news locally. "That's your niece, isn't it? You used to talk about her a lot on your show."

"Yes, that's Liz. A little bit more dressed up than usual and a lot more grownup."

"What threw me was her calling you a darling old bimbo."

"It comes from Brideshead Revisited. We were watching it last night." Peter explained: "When I became her legal guardian, Liz asked me what she should call me. Obviously, father or one of its variations was out of the question. Edward Handlery would always be her father. Neither one of us had ever liked uncle. Liz grew up in a bilingual household so her Spanish is as good as her English. When she was about three or so she began calling me uncle in Spanish.

"Tio." Flannery responded as if being quizzed.

"That's right. So we decided I would remain Tio. But Liz has a playful nature, and whenever she read or watched something and found a character whose name she liked, I would be called that for awhile. I can't remember them all but I have at various times and for short duration been called Papa Bear, Geppetto, Father Goose, Mr Fezziwig, Jean Valjean and even Titus Andronicus. That last name lasted one day as she had a couple of missing front teeth and had a hard time pronouncing it correctly. It was a silly game we played when she was growing up. Anyway, Brideshead brought it all back last night. We joked about it and now I'll probably be that darling old bimbo for a few more days. Liz has always had a keen imagination and an offbeat sense of humor."

"Add theatrical to the mix," Flannery commented.

"And that, too. Most certainly."

"Is she coming on the cruise?"

"No, you're stuck with just me. I'd like her to go, but she's hoping I might meet someone and she doesn't want to get in the way."

Signaling the bartender for his check, Flannery said, "Look, I've got a meeting upstairs. A pissed-off city official wants to tip me off to something weird that's going on at City Hall regarding Muni. Sorry I can't stick around to meet your niece. Look, we'll get together before the cruise to go over what we're going to do." He stood there for a second and then exclaimed. "I got it. You do all the talking during those two lectures and I'll just sit there and scowl."

As he slid off the stool, he asked if Ramsey knew any of the people in the group. Peter said he recognized several names of people who were longtime listeners. Then he told him about Philipa Crumley-Figg. Flannery shook his head and muttered, "Why am I not surprised."

chapter 4

PETER WAS A PICTURE of perfect posture. Sadly, it came with a price, leaving him feeling stiff, achy and awkward. However, Liz had been getting on him about his slouching and he was determined to do something about it. As her phone call had gone on much longer than expected, he wondered if he could sneak in a quick slump before she returned. He was seated at a table in the back corner of the Big Four dining room. It was their favorite and, thanks to the frequency of their visits, the maitre d' would never consider putting them anywhere else. A quiet spot, perfect for conversation, the location also provided a sweeping view of the low-ceilinged dining room making it ideal for people-watching, an activity that never failed to entertain given the colorful and diverse crowd that the Nob Hill restaurant attracted. Peter wished Liz would return, as he knew the early goings of this particular lunch were going to be uncomfortable for both of them and he wanted that portion of it over with as soon as possible. He knew she would kick off the conversation with a litany of reasons why she did not want him to proceed with what she called his cockamamie plan. You see, Peter had decided it was high time he move out of their Berkeley home. He thought he might give San Francisco a go. This move – cockamamie or otherwise – was an emotional issue for both of them as Peter and Liz had resided compatibly and comfortably under the same roof for the past twenty-three years. On a positive note, his being fired would not be a hot topic. Liz had been pushing for him to give up the morning show for some time, so she was totally delighted when he called her on his cell right after the meeting. Their relationship with the restaurant was also a lengthy one. When Liz's eighth birthday was just days away, Peter had suggested they go out to celebrate. Liz put in an immediate request for the Big Four. Peter remembered the feeling of relief knowing that, thanks to this young lady's mature dining preferences, in all likelihood he would get through life without ever having to walk through the doors of a Chuck E Cheese. His niece had selected the upscale Nob Hill eatery because that was where her parents had taken her after attending a matinee performance of the Nutcracker the previous Holiday season. Liz had been thoroughly captivated and highly entertained by the dressed up, stylish world of adults. That August birthday dinner was the first outing for Peter and Liz since the death of Amelia and Edward. Both put on brave faces, delighting in the special service and tender loving care they received from the restaurant staff who knew their story. They even managed a genuine laugh when their server – an exceedingly chirpy chap – sang Happy Birthday in pig latin. By evening's end, Liz had made Peter promise to take her to the Nutcracker and then dinner again at the Big Four in December. That experience was better all around. While the ache of their mutual loss was still with them, they were in excellent spirits and the joy and happiness both exhibited cheered the restaurant staff.

Peter's thoughts of how to format their conversation came to an end when he spotted Liz weaving her way through the dining room to their table. What a striking creature he thought. You might say she was one of God's real works of art, however I won't because it is a fact that all of us are God's perfect works of art. Still, it's a lovely compliment and, when it suits, you ought to keep on using it. Liz couldn't help but draw attention to herself. And Peter, more than anyone, knew the legitimacy of her appeal. More than her obvious physical attributes which were many, it was her self-assured, confident manner that compelled people to look up from their menus, stop their conversations and even pause in their dining – forks in midair – to observe her as she passed. While Peter waited for her arrival, he considered how the child-rearing portion of his life – unplanned as it was – had passed by all too quickly. The child he'd seen through grammar school concerts, parent-teacher nights, braces, basketball games, puberty, middle school mischief, myriad boyfriends, one broken bone, a multitude of stitches (none disfiguring), two proms and many noisy sleep-overs was now two semesters away from earning her doctorate in anthropology at Cal. She had already been working for the department for the previous two years and planned to do so after graduation. His final thought before she sat down was how remarkably easy it had all been. And he knew why. Which made him love her more.

"Sorry, Tio. I told you Henry sent me over to work with the people in folklore archives. It's a department that really does some fascinating stuff and I was looking forward to it. Anyway, I showed up for work and this bitchy, bossy, How-Berkeley-Can-I-Be biddy..."

"Wow, that's a guaranteed A in alliteration."

Liz frowned, not willing to let go of her anger just yet. "Let me finish. This woman put me to work doing tasks you wouldn't ask a freshman to do. She even had the gall to ask me to run to Elephant Pharmacy to pick up her meds. That call I just made was to Henry who, thank God, is moving me back to his office."

Peter tried calming her down. "All right, you're headed back to the comforts of Henry's world. It's behind you. Don't let that woman interrupt your harmony."

"Harmony, shmarmoney," she said with a just a hint of a smile. "Let me stew for a moment longer. And let's get into something else that bugs me. Namely, this bone-headed idea of yours to leave your loving niece who worships and adores you."

Before Peter could respond, Liz picked up the menu and asked if he knew what he was having. "I am thinking about the venison and black bean chili with the crispy onions," he replied, his stomach reminding him that nothing substantial had been sent in that direction for hours.

"I don't think so," she said. "The last time you had chili you got terrible heartburn."

Peter leaned in toward her and whispered, "You realize when I move into this hotel, I can phone room service and have them deliver gallons of the stuff and there'll be nobody around to warn me of incoming heartburn."

Looking pained, she asked, "Is that really what you want, Tio?"

Realizing she was stung by his response, he took her hand. "No, of course not. I appreciate your concern. My stomach, though, has an entirely different opinion."

"I think maybe I deserved it. Seems like I've been advising you on diet and wardrobe for too long a time now," she admitted.

"And don't forget my posture."

She smiled and scanned the menu that she almost knew by heart. "I haven't planned anything for dinner. I thought we might drop by Cesar for tapas tonight. Then I'm thinking I might go on to meet Kevin at Blake's. There's a group called The Phrenetic Frog and he thinks the world of them."

"What kind of music does a band named Frantic Frog play?"

"Fusion. But they spell fusion, frantic and frog with a 'P' and an 'H.' And there are two 'G's on the end of frog. Anyway, it looks good on posters," she remarked, blushing a bit after realizing how silly she sounded.

"How fascinating. And I mean fascinating with a plain old everyday you know what."

Liz smiled. "Kevin says it's a mix of eighties disco, chill-pop and gypsy music."

Peter picked up his menu. "Look, if you're serious about going for tapas tonight, then I'm having a cup of the white corn bisque and a small Caesar salad for lunch."

"And I'll have the Cobb," she said, taking his menu and hers and moving them across the table. "Okay, let's talk about this move."

"I'm going to have to go sometime, Liz."

"Why?"

"I suppose to let you get on with your life."

Liz grimaced. "I am getting on with my life, Dr. Phil."

"What's been the biggest complaint among your past boyfriends?"

Liz, knowing where this was going and deciding to play coy, said in a breathy voice, "I don't know that any of them had any complaints. All except Morty, perhaps. But we were only nine and I was taller and much better in sports."

"All right, with the exception of Morty, at some point in the relationship all the rest decided to break it off because they were uncomfortable with the idea of your dear old bimbo of an uncle living under the same roof. And look at it from my side. How many women have I dated over the years who were intimidated by you and, as a result, beat a hasty retreat."

"Four in 23 years and, really, Tio, the truth of it is not one of them was right for you. Carla was way too possessive. Jeanne Marie was incredibly needy. Then there was that

Channel Ten Action News' anchor with the big boobs. The one I used to call Sara Solip."

"Because you thought she was solipsistic. I think you were the only twelve year-old in the world who knew what that word meant."

Ignoring him, Liz continued, "And I forget the name of that awful woman you dated when I was fifteen. The one who was so snarky."

"Her name was Ellen and she wasn't snarky," he argued.

Liz laughed. "Tio, you don't even know what the word means."

"Okay, Miss Temporary Folklore Archives, what does it mean?"

Liz's voice was a marvelous device, husky but still fetchingly feminine. "Snarky can mean irritable, crotchety, impertinent or critical. Ellen was all of those in aces and spades."

This might be a good time to explain how these two became so unusually close. First one has to understand that missing in Liz's life right from the start were kinfolk. This lively sprite had no grandparents to speak of. Her mother's parents were dead and, as I mentioned earlier, Edward's family in England had no interest in anything he produced, even a child. Also missing were aunts, other uncles and cousins. As result, Peter became the all-in-one relative, often babysitting on those occasions when Liz's parents were off to some exotic locale. This was admittedly a duty made easier by Maria, their live-in nanny, who was ever present to tend to those more challenging aspects of monitoring and controlling an energetic and precocious youngster. Upon the death of Liz's parents, Peter, as her legal guardian, never considered anything other than moving into their Berkeley home to dutifully and lovingly raise her. And she, who right from the start displayed a remarkable maturity for someone so young, took it upon herself to be the one in charge of seeing to Peter's well-being. Their bond, understandably, was something quite extraordinary.

Peter watched as Liz removed her black scrunch, freeing her light brown hair with copper highlights. Now don't go giving me extra points for that expository sentence. I know her hair color because that's what is printed on a flashy bottle that stands on the shower shelf in her bathroom. To be honest, most of the time you'll be called upon to envision these characters solely by their actions and dialogue. When it comes to physical descriptions, I'm left wanting. We don't make a big deal out of looks and appearances here in Eternity for the simple reason that we don't have any. And, yes, it is a blessing. And if you're still thinking about my knowing about her shower products, the answer to your question is yes, everything you do is observed.

Anyway, Peter knew from experience when Liz freed her mane she was about to finally broadcast something she'd obviously given a lot of thought to, and the odds were heavily in favor of it being something that would come out of the blue.

Liz didn't disappoint. "Tio, I want you to adopt me."

The resolve went out of Peter's spine and he slid into a comforting, instantly ache-relieving slouch. "I don't know what to say. I don't know that I'm up to fathering a frenetic thirty-one year-old."

"I'm serious. Actually, I don't even know if an adult can legally adopt another. But, if it's possible, I'd like to do it... Have you adopt me, that is," she said, her cheeks reddening.

Up until now, legal guardianship had worked just fine. During their years together neither had ever brought up the topic of adoption. Peter assumed, quite rightly, that in Liz's mind and heart his sister and Edward would always be her only mother and father. Both seemed content with their respective roles of uncle and niece. Peter asked why now.

"I've been thinking a lot lately about marriage and a family. There's one thing I would really like my child or children to have and that's a living grandparent.":

"They'll probably get two on your husband's side," he pointed out.

"I know that. I just want one on our side." She squeezed his hand and added with a twinkle in her eye, "And wouldn't you love to be a grandfather?"

"Liz, is there something you're not telling me?"

She laughed and shook her head. "No, I am not pregnant. It's just that someday I am going to be married and I'm going to have children and I want you to be their grandfather. That's that. And I figure it might take awhile to move through the adoption process."

Peter knew he wasn't getting the complete story from Liz on this grandiose grandfather plan of hers. "Liz, like I said, your husband will probably come equipped with two breathing, doting parents."

She offered no response. The server, spotting a break in the conversation, arrived to take their orders. Peter asked if she was up to sharing a bottle of wine. She begged off, saying she wanted to run in the afternoon before dinner. Peter ordered an Anchor Steam and then waited quietly, knowing Liz would eventually come around and reveal all.

"Tio, I haven't been totally forthcoming," she admitted.

"Oh?"

"About this grandfather plan. I really, really do like the idea. But there's something else. I would like a father to walk me down the aisle when I marry. I don't think my biological dad would mind if his place was taken by the man who has raised me, and I might add successfully, since the age of eight."

"Seven and a half," he corrected.

"I forgot you work on a monthly basis," she joked. "Anyway, that's what I'd like."

"Liz, I'm ecstatic. Really. Nothing would please me more. Wow, this is turning out to be quite a day. No sooner do I learn I have been... What's that British term for being canned?"

"Made redundant," she answered.

"Right. So no sooner am I made redundant than I learn I am going to be a father. Liz, I would still like to be called Tio."

"Oh, that's a given."

Peter watched as Liz took a deep breathe. It meant her version of a filibuster was about to begin and would probably last until the salads arrived. He knew better than to interrupt.

"It's such a keen idea, Tio. I mean, you've been like a father to me, and I a daughter to you. It just makes so much sense. I don't know why we didn't do it earlier. And here's my thought. We consider it done even though there's all the legal malarkey we'll obviously have to go through with lawyers and social services and such. If companies can backdate stock options for their CEO's, we can certainly backdate our father and daughter relationship before it's all formalized. And here's what I like about it; it makes our living under the same roof together more... Oh, what's a good word for it? Respectable? No. We're already that and more. Fitting! Yes! That's it, fitting. And I don't mean it in the sense that we have any explaining to do to anyone. But because it's not unusual for an adult child to live under the same roof as their parent, now you don't have any reason to move out."

The salads arrived on cue. When the server asked them if there was anything else he could get them, Peter asked if there was a lawyer in the house.

"Tio?"

"Yes."

"Would you consider staying until I graduate?"

"You know, it's usually the children who move out."

"Please, Tio," she implored. "I have so much to do these next two semesters and knowing that my home life is predictable, comfortable and steady is important to me."

And so it was settled. Their North Berkeley hillside home would continue to be the home address for both of them for a while longer. That resolved, lunch moved quickly, the two of them dancing through a number of topics. One involved Liz asking what Peter was going to do with his upcoming free time. She probably shouldn't have.

"I'm going to memorize Shakespeare and learn how to do a decent pushup."

"Oh God! You're serious, aren't you?"

"Yes, I am. I just read somewhere that memorization strengthens the brain so there's a sonnet I like – I think it's 138 – and I've always wanted to do Harry the King's halftime speech to the English troops at Agincourt in Henry V. As for pushups, we all know the benefits from them. I don't have any upper body strength and I plan to change that," Peter explained. Then he decided to make one more attempt to invite his niece to go on the cruise. She frowned at the offer.

"Look, you told me you have a light schedule coming up," he said. "There are still some staterooms with verandahs available." Feeling expansive, he even sweetened the invitation: "You know I'm getting a healthy piece of change from the radio station for going quietly so if you wanted to take a girl friend or, for that matter, Kevin, I'll cover it."

"Tio, that's very generous, considering the grief I gave you when you first told me about it." Liz was convinced no self-respecting thirty-one year-old would voluntarily sign up for a luxury cruise to Alaska, thinking it would be analogous to spending a hard-earned vacation in a retirement community. "Can I have one day to think about it? I want to make sure I have everything covered as regards school."

"Let me know by Monday morning. And, Liz, I'm told by those in the know that the days of passengers coming exclusively from the ranks of the nearly dead and newly wed are over."

Liz's eyes widened. "Oh, I almost forgot. On the way to work the other morning, I ran into Samantha Whitby at Cafe Strada. She teaches English lit. Anyway, she told me that she and her older sister, Isabelle, who lives in New York signed up for the cruise. Seems Samantha's travel agent is the same one who is handling your cruise and he recommended it to them. They're really excited as it's the first cruise for both of them."

"No one's trying to kill one or the other of the Whitbys, are they?" Peter asked.

Non-plussed, Liz asked her uncle why on earth he would ask a question like that. So, for the second time that day, Peter found himself replaying that part of the conversation with Howard Newton regarding his not-so sainted mother-in-law and her threatened future.

Liz was clearly amused. "Tio, forget waiting until Monday. Sign me up. If that's a preview of the human drama and comedy that awaits one on the good ship... By the way, what's the name of this floating hotel?"

"The Ocean Glamour. It's a six star luxury cruise ship belonging to MagicSeas Cruise Line which in turn is owned by a huge shipping company called Stemwinder O'Hanson Shipping. I personally find it a bit unsettling boarding a vessel owned and operated by a company whose initials are SOS, but there you are."

"Anyway, I wouldn't miss this cruise," she said with enthusiasm. "I'll work things out at school."

"Do you want to bring Kevin?"

Liz shook her head. "No. I do like him, but it's too soon in the relationship to share a 136 square foot stateroom for twelve days. Checking her watch, she signaled the waiter for the bill. "Mind if I leave you to pay up?"

"Of course not. What are future fathers for? I'll either see you at home or at Cesar for dinner."

Liz leaned across and kissed her uncle good-bye. "You know I never have played matchmaker in all the years we've been together."

"That's probably because you thought there was no other woman in the world who could take as good a care of me as you."

"Well, there is that and also growing up I didn't like the idea of sharing you. But I just had a thought. Samantha Whitby is single. She's charming, attractive in an intelligent way and loves Trollope. I think you two might get on. Don't make that face, Tio. Just think about it. Okay?"

Without waiting for a response, Liz slid off the chair and moved gracefully through the dining room, leaving Peter to process all that happened in just a little more than half a day. He decided he'd earned a glass of port, a small portion of Stilton and the time to enjoy it.

chapter 5

PETER ALLEN RAMSEY is a bright, decent chap who, by all appearances, inhabits an extremely pleasant and uncomplicated world. One can imagine if anything upsetting, distressing, messy or problematic dare invade his daily life, it would be venial. In fact, one or two of you might even conclude that your own vicissitudes are far more daunting than his you-know-whatitudes. But that would be a mistake. Like all mortals, Peter has not gone from here to there without his share of those unwelcome brickbats that life often throws at you, usually when you least expect it. What makes him less scarred, if you will, is that he has to date done a pretty nifty job of dealing with what has been tossed his way. Also, our Mr. Ramsey seems to be one of those rare birds who, when faced with the unexpected, can carefully reflect instead of reacting rashly. And that's what makes this tale so fascinating. Here we have a mentally and emotionally sturdy, two-feet-on-the-ground gent who, once I got involved, will suddenly see that pleasant and uncomplicated world of his turn topsy-turvy. Now I know it sounds like I was getting up to some mischief with him, but honestly I had the most honorable of intentions.

Here is how it unfolded. One fine day – by the way, they are all fine days here in Eternity – Lillie Langtry and I were having a chat. The former professional beauty paid me a visit as she was curious to know more about our very popular Angel Academy which dates back to when there were actually angels around who never did any mortal time on your third planet from the sun, or for that matter anywhere else in the Universe. Angels are in huge demand and classes are quite popular among our general population. Part of my many duties includes being the school's registrar. As my Boss prefers well-seasoned spirits for admission, I informed Lillie that, as she had only been with us such a short time – not even a hundred years by your calendar – she's still considered a spiritual novitiate and would have to wait awhile longer before enrolling.

What are angels? Now I have heard some of you think they are simply a metaphor for good thoughts. Well, give yourself a pat on the back. You're not bang on, but pretty darn close. An angel's principal mission is to help their mortal client draw wisdom and acuity from their own deep, spiritual wellspring. Angels don't solve problems. Rather they assist you in finding your own way. For example, have you ever had a moment where in conversation with someone you found just the right words. I mean *the* perfect words! In fact, you were so downright inspirational and helpful that you even amazed yourself. Well, you can thank whatever angel was picked to perch – I do mean figuratively – on your shoulder to help you and your little gray cells work things out in your own individual fashion.

During my chat with Lillie, I learned there was something that was causing her some concern. I was not bothered by her apparent diminution of joy. As I mentioned before, it takes awhile for a newcomer to acclimate to a spiritual environment that is rooted in eternal bliss and harmony. Death is just step one of a magnificent transference and most embrace it completely and, yes, happily. However, there are always a few burdened with extra heavy baggage who have a difficult time of it. It is standard practice to send them back for awhile to see if that it might help them sort out what needs sorting out. What justifies a return visit is too complex an issue to go into here. In retrospect, I probably shouldn't have sent Lillie on her journey. But I so enjoyed her and, upon hearing her story, realized that she and Peter, if I timed it right, would be a perfect match as they could help each other in myriad ways, including solving the mystery of – drum roll here, please – the missing painting!

You, of course, have all sorts of names for these returnees; ghosts, specters, spooks, phantasms and wraiths to name a few. One of my favorites is doppelgänger. Call these spirits what you will, they do indeed abound. And they are, for the most part, Eternity's newer arrivals. For instance, you might drop into a winery tasting room in the Sonoma Valley and be informed there's an early 20th century ghost named Camilla who likes to roam among the wine barrels at night, sticking pretty much to the reds for some reason. What you won't hear is someone claiming, for example, that the ghost of Nero can be found on a Rome balcony most Wednesday nights. He's way to old to be ghosting. And besides, who among you really wants an old ghost hanging around who doesn't have a more timely connection to you and your immediate surroundings. Perhaps a violinist like Andre Rieu might appreciate a visit from a fiddle-playing Roman emperor, but that's about it.

Now that you have a loose sense of how this all works, let me share with you my conversation with Lillie Langtry a.k.a. the Jersey Lily.

"Theodomicles, it is the strangest thing, but I have just learned a painting of me by Sir John Everett Millais has gone missing," she said.

"Ah," I replied in that tone that indicated I was up to date on all matters aesthetic. "Tell me more."

"Its permanent home is the Tate Museum in London and that is where it should stay," she said with a fierce determination. "Someone who is newly arrived here told me that it was recently stolen from a museum in St. Louis, Missouri. It was part of an exhibit touring American museums called *Nature, Fidelity and the Pre-Raphaelite Brotherhood.*"

"Ah," I repeated. It is such a useful two letter utterance. "Yes, I can understand your desire to see it returned to its rightful home."

"Theodomicles, when the painting hangs in a museum, everyone can enjoy it. Now it will probably end up in the hands of a collector who will share it with no one."

"And I assume the police have their hands full with all kinds of heinous crimes that trump an art theft." At this point, it was quite clear that if, indeed, *A Jersey Lily* were to hang again in the Tate, it would be up to me to do something about it. "Lillie, my dear, I have an idea. You, of course, are familiar with San Francisco."

She brightened. "Yes, indeed. I was in a play called *Ashes* at the Orpheum Theater on O'Farrell Street. I did so want to bring another play to San Francisco called *Ours* written by my friend, Tom Robertson. I received several rave reviews for my performance at the Haymarket in London. It was a wonderfully witty comedy about the Crimean War. Well, I was told quite bluntly by a rather gruff San Francisco producer that there's wasn't a big demand for plays about that particular conflict." Shifting gears, she sped along, "I don't know whether you know this, but I once owned a beautiful ranch and vineyard just north of...."

Jumping in, I said, "Lillie, I know the rest of the story." Trust me, I did. "I'm sorry to interrupt but we don't have much time." We had plenty of time, but if I was to implement my plan, I now had to work with your mortal time, Pacific Daylight Saving Time to be exact.

I carefully explained to Lillie that I was going to send her back and put her in the company of Mr. Peter Ramsey who would then assist her in recovering and returning her painting to its rightful home in London. I also told her that while she was there she would, in turn, try to help him sort out a few other problems that were about to fall into his lap.

"Will I be going back as an angel-in-training?"

"No, Lillie, you will be going back as a return visitor which means there are strict limitations," I explained. "There's no need to give you a detailed dossier on Peter because when you arrive you'll have no knowledge of anything I tell you. For that matter, you'll have no memory at all of the past eighty years."

"I'm to be a ghost?"

"Yes, and I'm sure a very good one. Now there are a few things you should know. You will be able to hear and see anyone and everything, but you will only be seen and heard by Peter and, because I think it wise, his niece, Liz."

"What about being able to smell, taste and touch?"

I laughed. "Lillie, you'll have no need of those senses nor will you miss them. I remember Henry VIII asking me the same thing. I reminded him that we weren't sending him back for the roast beef. No, my dear, you will be appropriately equipped to do what needs to be done. And, once your mission is accomplished, it's back here for an eternity of supreme happiness. Now, we need to consider your appearance."

"My appearance?"

"Yes. We don't have much of a wardrobe department here." I joked. "All our returnees are clad in basic aura. It leans toward opaque. I must decide on the degree of aura in which to bathe you. My thought is to kick it up several notches. This way, you'll be pellucidly identifiable to Peter and Liz."

Lillie was intrigued and excited. "What will they see?"

"The best way to describe the aura I see working best for you is one that resembles an abstract-impressionist work. Gauzy, filmy and, perhaps, breezy with a hint of lavender and a suggestion of the human figure. I assure you it will be very fetching."

"Theodomicles, I don't know what to say. This is extraordinary and, I suspect, there's a little rule-bending going on. Thank you, thank you," she gushed.

Lillie's marching orders were just about complete. I did make certain that she understood that once she's back on earth, she will have no particular power, supernatural or otherwise. Oh, there would be the standard spectral abilities like hovering, going through doors, etc.. But if asked by Peter and Liz what she's been doing and where she's been since passing on, she will not be able to offer anything that hints at an eternal existence. She also will have no knowledge as she does now of the myriad changes in the world since February 12th, 1929 when she drew her last mortal breath and was suddenly dazzled by a brilliant white light. I did remind her that it's perfectly fine to talk about the light. For some reason, many of you find it a comforting thought when discussing the mysteries surrounding death.

chapter 6

ON HIS DEATH bed, the actor Edmund Gwenn quipped, "Dying is easy. Comedy is difficult." Quipping when your mortal flame is about to extinguish is a marvelous and memorable thing. However, when it was her turn to spin something special, Philipa Crumley-Figg could only shout: "Oh shit!" As you can see, as last words go, Philipa's were not particularly inventive or inspiring, but considering the manner of her demise, it is an understandable utterance. I dare say that under similar circumstances even Mr. Gwenn might not have been so glib. The popular expletive exploded from her mouth at 11:47 p.m. Her final mortal breath, a soft, peaceful exhalation, came a second later. This occurred while the Ocean Glamour, atop behaving seas and under a canopy of bright stars, lazily consumed the remaining fifty or so nautical miles that separated the cruise ship from the charming city of Victoria, B.C., its first port of call. For the previous six hundred miles, Philipa had been something of a walking nightmare. It began with her making Peter Ramsey's first few minutes in his stateroom uncomfortable and challenging. Details of that testy encounter will follow. Here, though, for your entertainment is a random sampling of some of Philipa's finer moments. During the first evening's dinner, she dominated the conversation, shocking her table partners with her unique take on sex, politics and religion, all delivered in language salty enough to redden faces and force a honeymooning couple to depart before trying one or two of the ship's excellent desserts. The following morning she was served a continental breakfast in her penthouse. Instead of eating her fresh-from-the-oven, buttery and flaky French croissant, she threw it at her butler for being late. Meeting with the hotel director, she threw one of the better temper tantrums the ship had seen in recent times. This was inspired by the officer's adamant refusal to arrange a book signing party for her, citing company policy. That afternoon, she treated herself to a Lavender pedicure and an overpriced Silk and Soy Booster Facial in the ship's spa where she tipped no one. Later, a Martini not made to her liking in the Alcove Court – something about the chewiness of the olives – gave her an excuse for a full out verbal assault on the friendly bartender. The second evening was formal and this tyrant didn't disappoint. Dressed to the nines in an Amanda Cleary original designed especially for her, Philipa did a boffo job of insulting the wine choices, the food and the other seven guests at table 8A. The table was hosted by the cruise director who, by the time the entree was being served, began to seriously think about moving up his date of retirement. Not much was known of her movements after she left the dining room..

If it is determined that her death was more than a misadventure – I have to keep some things a mystery – the list of suspects would be mind-bogglingly lengthy. They would include her butler, Bartal from Budapest, Hungary, her stewardess, Halyna from Chernivtsi, Ukraine, and her assistant stewardess, the ever-smiling, always quiet Anna-Nina from Quezon City, Philippines. A shadow of suspicion must also be cast over all of those who attended the required life boat drill at muster station number 7 on the starboard side. Let's also toss in her dinner table companions from both evenings and the Alcove Court bartender, spa attendants and cruise director. In other words, just about everybody and anybody who came in contact with Mrs. Crumley-Figg would probably have entertained a murderous thought after dealing with this cantankerous woman. And, although he obviously has an airtight alibi, we can't rule out our chief suspect, the son-in-law and Snowy Plover lover, Howard Newton.

But, I have jumped ahead. Some fifty-six hours earlier, on a sparkling June afternoon, the area surrounding Pier 35 on San Francisco's Bay front was crowded with people, many of whom would soon be joining Peter Ramsey on the Ocean Glamour. The setting was a sightseers' delight. Across from the cruise terminal loomed Telegraph Hill with its iconic Coit Tower, a hint of downtown high-rises in the distance. To the west was Fisherman's Wharf and beyond that the Golden Gate Bridge. Alcatraz was just a short, cold swim away. Nary a person, though, stopped to take in this enchanting view as this particular collection of travelers, ship's crew, shore agents, dock workers, police and passersby were too busy dancing in and around a mass of cabs, limos, supply trucks, busses and luggage. While the street scene was noisy and chaotic, the cruise terminal was an oasis of calm. There, a capable staff made sure the check-in process went smoothly. They were so good at it that if you took a quick survey of the almost eight hundred people who would board the Ocean Glamour that afternoon, you'd find that to a number they all thought that this was one of the classiest and welcoming procedures they'd ever experienced. Well, almost all of them. Somehow, the two bubbly photographers with thick Manchester English accents who take pictures of the guests before they board the ship were just too much for Philipa Crumley-Figg who had to wait in line while the two fussed over four couples in front of her. It was not a pretty sight once it came her time to smile for the birdie. Actually, her revulsion with the entire embarkation process started when her limo pulled up to Pier 35.

"You, yes, you," she yelled from the limo window, pointing at an older gentleman who wore a MagicSeas' blue blazer and nautical-themed tie, the uniform of those in charge of the arriving passengers. His name tag identified him as one Randolph Vanderploge. He and his amiable contingent were responsible for the guests from the time their shoes touched down on the concrete of the Embarcadero to the aforementioned check-in process in the pier's lobby. They, too, were an equally patient and helpful lot.

"For god's sake, man, over here," Philipa bellowed, now half in and half out of the limo.

"Yes, ma'am," he said, rushing to help her free herself from the limousine's rear passenger seat. Transportation as you know it on earth is nonexistent here in Eternity. We do, though, enjoy watching you all get about. It has always puzzled me as to why people pay great sums of money to be driven around in one of these luxury chariots that are stretched to the length of an aircraft carrier, only to be forced into entering and exiting through an opening roughly the size of a submarine hatch.

Randolph had given up being a gentleman dance host aboard the Glamour because of women like the one he was now trying to extricate from the limo. To be fair, most of the single ladies he met, while sometimes clumsy and heavy-footed on the ship's dance floor, were almost always gracious and well-mannered. However, there were the occasional Philipas of the world one had to deal, or should I say, dance with. It delighted him to know that he would only have to put up with this guest's antics for a moment or two. He smiled knowing that for the next twelve days, he would be snug in his Telegraph Hill condo with his books and jazz and single malt Scotch and not aboard the Glamour having to pay for his cruise by tangoing, waltzing or cha cha cha-ing with the likes of her. "Let's get this over with, Randolph," he muttered as he approached the limo. Ready to handle anything she had to dish out, he gave the slight-of-frame Philipa an easy tug and the rest of her popped out of the car along with a mouthful of instructions: "My luggage is in the back. I want them in my penthouse awaiting my arrival on board. See that that happens. Now, there must be a VIP entrance. Take me to it."

"All guests go through security right over there," he said, pointing to the queue of excited voyagers.

"I am not ALL guests," she snapped. "Now look, you seem official enough. Guide me to the front of the line," she barked.

Spotting a woman in a wheel chair, he quickly excused himself, "I'm afraid, ma'am, that I must ask you to wait just a moment. That lady over there is in need of some help."

"Nonsense, she's already in a chair. I'm not."

Randolph made a mental note to remember this exchange as he would play it over and over for the MagicSeas' ground crew that would gather for drinks at the Fog City Diner after all the guests were safely aboard.

Kevin, noted Phrantic Phrogg fan and Liz's current love interest, spotted an opening and swung his five year-old Jeep Cherokee into the parking spot that had just emptied behind Philipa's limo. He had volunteered to drive Liz and Peter to the ship, thinking this would be a good opportunity to introduce himself to her uncle who sat in the back wedged between the door and some of their luggage wondering why on earth he hadn't hired a car and driver. The rest of their bags, mostly Liz's, were piled up behind him sharing space with Kevin's diving equipment. Peter liked the sandy-haired, ruggedly handsome Australian-born teaching assistant right off. Kevin's musical would, however, take time to appreciate. While on the way into San Francisco, he was not only introduced to the experimental sounds of Kevin's favorite group, but was subjected to a four-song sampling from a group called Demolition Bras and a Norwegian transgender folk rock duo named Ovaltune.

"What a madhouse," Liz said, peeking her head out the window to get a better look at the happy hustle and buoyant bustle. "Tio, I'll bet a lot of these people are in your group."

Peter was thinking along the same lines. Checking his watch, he realized they had plenty of time to check in. Diving into his hosting duties right then and there on the Embarcadero didn't hold much appeal. "Look, we have time before we need to board and we're just minutes from the Buena Vista. How about I treat us all to some Irish Coffees?"

Now they had arrived at the ship just as Randolph Vanderploge was explaining to Philipa that he was off to help a woman in the wheel chair. Philipa stood by the door of the limo, her angry gesticulations drawing their attention. Without an accompanying soundtrack, one could easily misinterpret these movements. Liz did. Suddenly, she was out the door of the Jeep in a shot, thinking she could pick up where Randolph left off and take care of this elderly, well-dressed damsel in distress.

"Excuse me, is there anything I can do?" she asked, moving toward the black town car.

Philipa looked askance at the attractive young woman. "Are you with the cruise line?"

"Uh, no. We just pulled up behind your limo and it looked as if you needed some help."

"What I need," Philipa hissed, "is assistance and attention from this cruise line."

"Are you sure I can't...."

"Oh fuck off," Philipa snapped. Then noticing her driver was unceremoniously tossing her bags on the curb, she transferred her vitriol from Liz to him. "Damn it, those are Louis Vuittons, you clown. They are not meant to be manhandled." Realizing then that she rarely saw her bags being moved from one place to another, she muttered, "At least, not in my presence."

Liz hastily retreated to the safety of Kevin's Cherokee. "Oh yes, yes! Please, let's go to the BV. Do they make double Irish Coffees?"

The BV, as it is known to locals, looked out at the Hyde Street cable car turnaround and Aquatic Park where hardy San Franciscans daily slipped into the Bay's chilly waters to do their laps. Adhering strictly to the adage, "If it ain't broke, don't fix it," the owners of the Buena Vista did little to the century old establishment except to occasionally paint and dust. Irish Coffees, made from a recipe brought over from the Shannon Airport in Ireland some sixty or so years ago by a local columnist were the house specialty. Our trio had barely set foot in the place when they heard Charlie the bartender's effusive welcome. The place was filled with tourists, a situation that seemed to alter Charlie's otherwise cheery nature. Thus, the sight of three locals, two of whom he knew by their full names, entering the place lifted his mood. He pointed to three barstools at his end of the bar and set about making a trio of the house's finest for them.

While they waited for Charlie to deliver this concoction that is noted for containing all four important food groups, Liz continued to fume about the churlish treatment she received from Philipa. When the drinks arrived, she put her rant on hold long enough to toast and sip. Then she started up again. Seeing her uncle smiling didn't help matters.

"Damn it, Tio, that horrible woman was just awful to me and you sit there with this big grin on your face as if nothing happened."

"You have an Irish Coffee cream mustache," he said, pointing to her upper lip.

Licking it off, she said, "Well, I am not smiling, thank you, because of that hideous woman, and besides, I have the cramps." Interestingly, instead of lowering her voice which is what a statement like this usually requires in a social setting, she raised hers making it more of a public pronouncement.

Solidarity is a flower that can grow anywhere and at anytime. When it does bloom, it is remarkable to behold. And blossom forth it did in that front part of the Buena Vista. A pudgy woman sporting a Chicago Cubs' baseball cap loaded down with Major League Baseball pins started it all. "You go, girl! And just for the record, so do I," she yelled, while glowering at her husband whose face was buried in the morning paper's sports section. Then from a table near the entrance came a shy but equally supportive voice: "So do I." Then, almost as if it were an echo, from the same table came another soft "Me, too." They were twins celebrating their birthday. Their boyfriends looked on bemusedly. Finally, a comely server named Katherine, standing at the bar waiting for a trayful of Irish Coffees, snapped at the bartender, "So do I, Charlie. So don't give me a hard time today." Katherine might as well have been talking to the mirror behind the bar as he paid her no mind. Charlie had been too many years behind the scarred, scratched and worn Buena Vista bar to let something like this rattle him.

And what about Kevin? His reaction was one of amusement. You see, the tanned Aussie was besotted. In his mind, Liz could do no wrong. If he had cheerleaders' pompoms handy, he would have jumped off his barstool and invoked the crowd to give him an enthusiastic L, I and Z. And what does that spell? Just the name of the love of his life, that's all.

Experience had taught Peter that sometimes it was best to sit out situations like this, so he concentrated on the magic tastes of his Irish Coffee. Charlie, though, decided some kind of action was warranted. Approaching the trio, he leaned across the bar and said in a low, friendly voice, "Love having you here, guys, but please tell me you're not having another round."

Peter paid up and the three headed for the door. While Peter held it for Liz, she suddenly turned around and said in a clear, chirpy voice, "It's been fun, girls, let's do this again next month."

Minutes later in the Cherokee with Pier 35 coming into view, Liz turned to look at her uncle who was once again pinned between their luggage and the door and announced: "I'm feeling so much better."

chapter 7

LIZ OPENED THE first of two large suitcases, their zippers stressed to the max. A neat and organized woman, she first carefully surveyed the narrow, cramped stateroom to locate all those cubby holes where one stashes one's stuff while at sea. Only after that scouting expedition was complete did she begin to unpack. Cut from the same tidy cloth, Peter would follow pretty much the same process once he made his way to his penthouse. Their penchant for an uncluttered life did earn them their fair share of abuse, albeit, good-natured. Their friends teasing didn't bother them, though, as neatness was something that came effortlessly and, as a bonus, it made their life more manageable. Now, if you are messy, unorganized and clutter is part of your everyday existence, please don't think that by my going on about Peter and Liz's orderliness, I am giving them the Theodomicle's Good Housekeeping Seal of Approval. Though, I must say if you have to maneuver your mortal mass around a cruise ship's tiny standard stateroom for twelve days, having a keen sense of order seems practical.

Liz had now arrived at that phase of the unpacking ritual that didn't require much concentration. It was an opportune time to chat. After hanging up a red slinky something — those were her words to describe a floor length dress, not mine

— she glanced over at her uncle who sat on a small sofa paging through the Embarkation Day issue of the "Ship's Log," a six page newspaper detailing the vessel's myriad activities. "Tio, do you realize when we get back from this cruise, you can sleep in to your heart's content instead of having to get up at that insane hour of three-thirty. I'd ask if you were going to miss doing your show, but I already know the answer."

"Oh, you do, do you?" He looked up from the paper. "Am I going to miss it?"

Pulling two blouses from her suitcase, she looked around for the right drawer. "If I'm right, what do I win?"

He picked up the spa brochure off the coffee table and scanned the treatments.. "Let's see. If you are correct, I will treat you to a... Oh, yeah, here we go. How about a Rose Petal Body Polish which, with its gentle exfoliation, will open your heart and make you radiant And I will throw in my undying respect for your uncanny ability to know my every thought and feeling."

She looked over at him and said confidently, "All right. First, before you speak, you will pause dramatically and get a really serious look on your face. By the way, Tio, you don't do serious well. Instead of appearing sober and thoughtful, you end up with this sort of a Poor Pitiful Peter look.

"So you've told me many times," he muttered.

"Yes, I have, but you insist on trying," she remarked. "Anyway, after looking all hang dog, you'll drop into that announcers' voice of yours which I can't do. Then you'll tell me you're tired of doing the show, that the fun is gone. And you'll add that you're also disappointed in how radio has changed for the worse these last few years. So no, you won't miss it." Holding up her hand to keep him from responding, she added, "But then after taking a breath, you'll quickly point out how much you really, really love radio and being on the air."

"Ah, a man of contradictions," he intoned. "Well, you nailed it. Word for word. That's what I feel and that's what I'll say when asked. But I'll pass on looking serious. So it looks like I owe you the body polish, unless you want to trade it in for the Mandarin Orange and Pink Grapefruit Body Scrub." He glanced again at the brochure. "Do you think the spa and breakfast menus are interchangeable."

Liz asked seriously, "Have you thought about what you're going to do with all your free time? Besides doing pushups and memorizing Shakespeare."

"Have I told you I was doing that?" he asked with mock surprise.

"Tio, I live with you. I now see you doing pushups and I hear you spouting Shakespeare."

"Liz, you don't 'spout' Shakespeare," he remarked. "I suppose this isn't the time or place to show you what I can now do with Harry the King's speech to his troops at Agincourt?

"No," she answered sharply. "It's bad enough that I hear you emoting through the bathroom door when you're in the shower."

"Well, the lines are meant to be delivered lustily," he argued. "After all he was addressing his soldiers out of doors, and good audio engineers were hard to come by."

Liz closed and zippered the empty suitcase and moved on to the next. "Tio, I'm being serious."

"All right. First, I know what I don't want to do. Seeing as we're okay in the money department and I don't have to work anymore, I'm not at all interested in signing on with another radio station. I might do some freelance commercial work if it comes along, but for the time being I am not going to actively pursue it."

"But what do you want to do?" she asked again.

"Well, now that I'm sixty-five, I understand I can audit classes at UC free of charge. I thought I might see if there's an English lit course and...."

Excited, Liz broke in, "Tio, you can take Samantha Whitby's class on nineteenth and early twentieth century English writers. Remember, I told you about her. She and her sister, Isabelle, are part of our group. You and she both love dead authors. You're a match made in literary heaven. We can tell her of your interest when we meet her at the welcoming party tomorrow morning. So, what else are you looking at?"

"Theology," he replied.

"The study of God?" she said haltingly, her voice cracking as she was clearly surprised at his choice.

"Yes, as opposed to your field of anthropology where... What is it you actually study?"

Ignoring him, Liz was ready to shut the second case. "Please tell me there's a place for these bags. Do they take them away or do I spend twelve days stepping over and around them?"

"Leave them right there. I'm sure the stewardess will make them disappear when she comes in to clean tonight. What about those dresses on the bed?" Peter asked, pointing to a stack of five outfits she'd put on hangers. "Oh, let me guess. There's no room in your closet so they're going with me."

"You're a darling," she said, picking them up and putting them in Peter's lap. "Now you need to get to your unpacking. I really do want to know why you picked a class on theology. Let's talk about it tonight at dinner?"

Peter looked around the room. Except for the dresses he was holding, if it weren't for her purse, laptop and books, there was no evidence that anyone even occupied the stateroom. He marveled at the fact that she packed for an around-the-world cruise and almost managed to find a place for it all. Tossing the clothes over his shoulder, he walked by the bed where Liz now sat admiring her tidy cabin. Looking up, she smiled. "Time for you to jump into the madding crowd. Good luck. Watch how you carry those. I don't want them to wrinkle."

"Don't worry, I'm told a butler comes with the penthouse and I'm sure ironing is one of his many skills."

"Tio, you are way more the ascetic than I am. Why don't we switch staterooms? I'll enjoy the penthouse more. You'll spend the entire trip feeling guilty about being surrounded by all that luxury.".

Peter kissed the top of her head and moved toward the door. "Nice try. You know, I've been thinking. These last few days, there's been a part of me that has dreaded this trip. I can't give you any specific reason. Just a feeling I've had. Well, now we are here and so far so good except for your run in with that foul-mouthed woman. Well, there's no sense in my forecasting what will or won't happen. You know we've been really fortunate when it comes to group promotions like these. You've been on a few. For the most part, people are pleasant and friendly. I can't remember any really big problems. So there is no reason to think this trip won't be the same."

While I was delighted to hear him address the futility of forecasting events, as it is truly a waste of one's valuable time, I do wish he hadn't left Liz's stateroom feeling confidant that the trip would be a skip through the dew. But then how could Peter know he was just minutes away from the beginning of a most disruptive and challenging time.

After spending time in Liz's stateroom, Peter walked into his penthouse and was amazed by its hotel room size. Truly, both their cabins were well-appointed, rich in color and decor. The penthouse, though, was spacious as well as sumptuous. He hung Liz's dresses in the walk-in closet and was just about to attack his suitcase which sat atop the bed when he noticed a bottle of champagne in an ice bucket in the sitting room area. He decided to call Liz and have her come up for a glass before the life boat drill. Then the phone rang and the fun began.

"This is Peter Ramsey?" It was a voice that insinuated that once he said yes, everything would go rapidly downhill. He did anyway. "Yes."

"I am Philipa Crumley-Figg and I am not happy with my penthouse. Please move me."

"There is a travel agent aboard representing our group who handles..."

"That may be for everyone else in your group. My son-in-law said if there's anything I need, I am to call you direct. Now I am calling you. I wish to move."

"The penthouses are all the same," he pointed out. "Why do you want to move?"

"I am directly across from the laundry room. The noise bothers me."

"How do you know it's noisy? We've only been on the ship for a couple of hours. I doubt there's anyone who has a load of wash to do."

"Mr. Ramsey, I do not like the location. I want to move. Do something about it now. Call me when you know the number of my new penthouse." This was followed by a loud click as if even the telephone was upset with him.

Peter found a list of ship's personnel who would play a part in handling his group's various onboard activities. Luckily, he caught the hotel director, Fritz Henning, in his office. Unfortunately, the penthouses were all sold out. But word had already reached the hotel director about the difficult Mrs. Crumley-Figg. The crew, who takes great pride in making crotchety grumps like Philipa do one-eighties, had already tagged her as this voyage's prime challenge. Thus, he was sympathetic to Peter's plight and offered an easy solution. He suggested they trade penthouses.

"I will alert the front desk. They don't like doing this, and probably would give you a tough time. It's a good thing you called me. Temporarily, you can use each others card keys, but because these cards act as identification for you, you must go to the front desk and get new ones. Please do that before dinner. On another subject, I notice here that you and a Ms. Liz Handlery are seated at table 8-A with Mrs. Crumley-Figg. Would you like me to move the two of you?"

I love this man, thought Peter. "Yes, please, if you could put my niece and me at a table for two. I think with the large number of people we have in our group, it's probably best not show any favoritism. At least that will be my story."

"I understand. I have a nice window table on the port side for you. Goodby, Mr Ramsey."

When Peter called Philipa, she was surprisingly civil. Not friendly, but agreeable. She had a few questions but all were answered to her satisfaction. Peter's penthouse was mid ship, close to an exit near to the elevators and on the starboard side. She then announced that, as she had never unpacked, she was ready to go. Peter said he'd dispatch his butler forthwith. He almost laughed aloud at his last remark, realizing that of all the sentences in all the world, the last one he thought he would ever hear himself say was "I will dispatch my butler forthwith."

Not a moment later, his butler, Bartal from Budapest, introduced himself. Clean-shaven, lanky and wearing one of five different butler outfits that ranged from everyday formal to evening formal, he asked if this was a convenient time to instruct Peter on the basics of how to live with a butler at your beck and call. Peter told him about the room switch and Bartal beamed. "This is convenient, Mr. Ramsey, as I also take care of penthouse 1050. She is most unhappy lady. This move, you think, will help improve her mood?"

Peter thought otherwise but didn't mention it. Instead, he instructed Bartal to take his bags and Liz's dresses to his new digs. "Do you remember if there was a bottle of champagne in 1050?" Peter asked.

Bartal moved around him and lifted the chilled bottle from the silver ice bucket. "There is, but nothing like this. You must be very important person to get a bottle of Krug."

"In that case, take the champagne along with you and bring Mrs. Crumley-Figg's bottle back with her bags. I'm going to take a quick tour of the ship while you move us. I prefer not having to cross paths with her until all this is sorted out."

Peter began the five story descent to the Bienvenue Deck which boasted an impressive, atrium-style open space that was home to an impressive two-story water feature, the ship's spacious lobby and front desk. Aft of this glamorous public area was the main dining room and one of the many cocktail lounges scattered about the ship. Peter had promised himself that the elevator would be off limits for the cruise as stairs were such a great exercise. Rounding the turn halfway between decks eight and seven he found himself having to take evasive action to avoid a man in his direct path. The elderly gentleman had one hand on the railing while the other held an open book on the artist Goya. Climbing slowly, one careful step after the other, he was totally absorbed in the book and paying no attention to what was in front of him. Suddenly, sensing the presence of another, he realized something was amiss. Looking up from his book and seeing Peter, he quickly apologized, "I am so sorry. Awfully bad habit, I'm afraid, of sticking my nose in a book and not having the good sense to remove it when in transit." Peter said no problem, he'd done it himself many times.

"I recognize that voice. You are Peter Ramsey. I'm with your group. Malcolm Fitzroy," he announced, shoving his book under one arm and extending his hand. Bone-thin, but certainly not frail, and elegantly attired, Malcolm Fitzroy was straight from Hollywood casting. If you were looking for an art gallery owner who also happens to be a noted historian and restorer, that is.

"Mr. Fitzroy, I saw your name on our guest list. I wondered whether you were the same Fitzroy who owns Gallery Malcolm on Post Street. I'd say, judging from that book on Goya, you are."

"Nice bit of detective work, Peter. I may call you Peter?" he asked in a charming, old school sort of way.

"Of course. You probably hear this a lot, but I have visited your gallery."

"Did you purchase anything, thus helping me keep myself in the style to which I have become accustomed?"

"I might have helped make a monthly car payment. When you had the Imogen Cunningham exhibit... Oh, this is years and years ago. I bought a print of a self-portrait she'd taken in a store's dirty window on Geary Street."

"Yes, Imogen began doing street photography in the 1940s as a side project. An amazing woman. We were good friends, you know," he said, glancing at his watch.

"I took an interest in her when I received a postcard advertising that particular exhibit. It came with a letter. In it, she took me to task for complaining on the radio about turning thirty. She wrote that it was nothing to ponder, that she paid no attention to her birthdays and she was turning eighty-five at the time. I framed it."

"As you should." Returning one hand to the railing, Malcolm prepared to continue his ascent. "By the way, I, too, am turning eighty-five and I'm afraid, Peter, I do ponder it. I look forward to our party tomorrow."

Locating a house phone near the front desk, Peter called Liz and informed her of the penthouse switch and the special Krug champagne. They agreed to give Bartal another fifteen minutes to complete the move before meeting up in his new penthouse. Liz was convinced her potty-mouthed lady-in-distress and the terse, demanding woman her uncle encountered were one in the same.

"I knew I would find you!" A pudgy, red-cheeked woman in a powder blue sweatshirt and tight-fitting pink slacks with white sandals sporting large pinkish plastic flowers delivered this line in an excited, high-pitched tone that suggested she had just won the ship's scavenger hunt. Now that she found Peter, she was not about to let him slip by her. She reached out, taking firm hold of his arm just as he was rounding the corner to be begin his ascent to the penthouse deck. Behind her stood a somber, pear-shaped man in loose-fitting khakis worn low as to allow his belly to hang over his belt. He was in a golf shirt that sported a logo promoting a recent Elks Club tournament.

"Peter, we're the Florians from Pleasanton. Remember us?" she asked, keeping a firm hold on his arm.

He was usually pretty agile in instances like these, but caught so unawares by the florid Mrs. Florian, he was left speechless for just enough time to let her answer her own question. "In the summer of 1983, you did your morning show from the Pleasanton Hotel one Friday. I brought our son, Freddie Junior, to the broadcast and you interviewed him. Well, you didn't actually interview him on the air as he was too shy to talk to you on the radio. But you were so nice to him and most people in those days weren't. He thought the world of you."

Peter certainly remembered Freddie Junior. A younger knockoff of Mom, he was overweight, slightly effeminate and painfully shy. The remote broadcast was the last place in the world Freddie wanted to be. Peter guessed, correctly, that Freddie probably didn't have any place he really wished to be, except possibly for his room. As he felt for the boy and his obvious discomfort, Peter remembered putting some extra effort into putting Freddie at ease, if only to stop Mrs. Florian from talking nonstop. He did manage to get Freddie to smile and chat a bit, surprising even his mother. "It was some time ago, but yes, I remember you and your son, Mrs. Florian. Freddie must be in his late thirties now."

"He's thirty-eight and lives in Winona, Minnesota. Went to college there and is now a dentist. He's a partner in the Smiley Face Dental Group in downtown Winona. His fellow dentists nicknamed him Fluoride Freddie." Tightening her grip on Peter's arm, she continued, "I do wish he'd meet someone soon." Nodding in the direction of her husband, she added, "Freddie Senior and I are looking forward to being grandparents someday. You know, I used to listen to you talk about your niece on the radio and I would think to myself, wouldn't she be just perfect for my Freddie. She's, of course, younger by a few years. But that can be good. Is she traveling with you?"

"Yes," Peter answered, grateful Fluoride Freddie was in Minnesota happily root canaling someone.

"Right now Freddie lives with his friend, Ben. They bought a house together, but..." Her voice and smile faded.

Freddie Senior came to Peter's rescue. "Gertie, I'm sure the gentleman has more important things to deal with."

Her smile returned and she let go his arm. "Now, Peter, save us a lunch or dinner. I'm looking forward to a long, long chat."

Freddie Senior stayed back, waiting until she was out of earshot. "Don't worry. I'll see that Gertie stays out of your hair. She's been listening to you for decades, you know. I suppose now she wants to do some of the talking."

"She's not out of line and I'll find some time for us to visit."

"By the way, Freddie and Ben are more than..."

"I figured."

"What Gertie doesn't know is that Freddie and Ben are on the ship. We're going to meet them for dinner. It's going to be sort of a coming out party." Sensing Peter's concern about the impact such a surprise would have on his wife, he quickly added, "Gertie will be okay with it. It's the grandchildren thing, you understand." With that, Freddie shuffled away, leaving Peter to finish his ascent to the penthouse deck.

chapter 8

AT PRECISELY FOUR-thirteen, an upbeat and exceedingly cheery Peter Ramsey strolled into penthouse 1027 while a mystified Lillie Langtry, resplendent – if I do say so myself – in her muted lavender aura, arrived in penthouse 1050. Yes, the aforementioned cabin switch did mess with my original plan as my intent was for Mrs. Langtry and Mr. Ramsey to discover each other in Peter's original penthouse, the one that now housed Mrs. Crumley-Figg. My thinking, even though I understood the inherent difficulty, was for the couple to somehow try as best they could to grab hold of the incredibly bizarre reality of their situation before the Ocean Glamour hoisted its sails. This way they could mutually drink in the many aesthetic pleasures of embarking from San Francisco, one of them being sailing under the Golden Gate Bridge.

Allow me a break in the action here to tell you that I get a huge kick out of this storytelling business. What makes it wondrous is the realization that you, my marvelous mortal, must stick around to learn of the story's denouement. Of course, you don't have to. At any time you can skip to the last page to confirm that they lived happily ever after and call it a day. Now if you're one of those who feels strongly that Armageddon is already on the calendar along with the scheduled Day of Reckoning where you will be judged by the rights and wrongs of your actions, have no fear that ditching my story midstream is something that I will bring up or hold against you. I only mention the personal joy I derive from this tale-sharing because here in – as Shakespeare so eloquently put it – "the Treasury of Everlasting Joy," we spiritual residents have a munificent perk called Divine Awareness. I'm sure you can see how this Know-It-Allness puts a definite crimp in yarn-spinning, gossiping and, of course, joke-telling. There are exceptions, though. Some spirits at times occasionally opt out of Divine Awareness for a temporary state called Blissful Ignorance. It's a particularly popular thing for college alums to do who still love NCAA March Madness and BCS Bowl games. If I'm lucky, I will encounter someone in this blissful state, inspiring me to suddenly throw caution to the wind and shout out, "Hey there, fellow spirit, did you hear the one about the politician, the bartender and the seal?" Anyway, I hope now you can understand why this is such a treat for me.

And now back to our story: Peter wandered into his new digs to find Liz sitting demurely on the sofa while Bartal busied himself with the Krug champagne. Had it been Peter sitting there, the butler would have had the premium bubbly opened and poured in seconds. However, a beaming Bartal, finding himself attending to an attractive young woman, was determined to stretch out the experience as long as he could. Upon Peter's arrival, though, he wisely decided that it might be best to step up the pace.

"Ah, Mr. Ramsey, welcome to your new penthouse," he crooned, careful not to take his eyes off the receding bubbles in the slender champagne flute as he prepared to top it off before handing it to Liz. "I have moved Mrs. Crumley-Figg and she seems satisfied with her new penthouse. Is there anything else I can do for you?"

"I still need to learn the ropes about penthouse living, Bartal. How about we meet here right after the lifeboat drill? And seeing as my niece will no doubt be spending a considerable amount of time here, I will see she's also around to hear your instructions."

After Bartal, who put his trademark smile on high beam after hearing the word niece, backed his way out of the penthouse, Liz exclaimed, "Tio, this is way, way too cool. You have a butler. He's even in real butler clothes, just like Jeeves. And not bad looking either."

Immediately after all the passengers were dismissed from standing in slipshod military formation near their lifeboat stations on the Promenade Deck, the Ocean Glamour did indeed sail away. Most of the guests, now stripped of their bulky orange Mae Wests, gathered on the Du Soleil Deck for champagne, music and the chance to soak up the transformative views of San Francisco, Angel Island, Alcatraz and the hillside village of Sausalito. Windsurfers, braving dangerously high speeds in the choppy Bay waters, came as close as they could to the Ocean Glamour before being shooed away by Coast Guard and police boats whose mission was to escort the ship to the frothy waters west of the Golden Gate Bridge, a stretch of sea popularly known as the Potato Patch. Once this flotilla reached the southern tip of the Marin Headlands, the pilot transferred to his small craft for the bumpy ride back to port while the cruise ship turned in a northerly direction to sail first to Victoria, British Columbia, a two day journey, and then on to Alaska.

By the time the ship was passing by the coastal hills of North Marin, Peter and Liz were enjoying a Martini in one of the ship's myriad drinking establishments. They had by accident chanced upon an intimate bar that reminded them of the Big Four bar at the Huntington Hotel. The Covey was a wood-paneled, dimly lighted hideaway next door to the ship's computer center. For some reason, most passengers strolled right by it and that held enormous appeal to Peter. This early evening, their only company were two men at the bar and the piano player. Peter finally got a chance to explain to his niece in more detail his desire to audit a theology class. For most of his adult life, Peter had strolled harmoniously along his own spiritual path, a road paved by bits and pieces from his early formal religious training and his borrowing a dash of this and a soupçon of that from other sources. If you had to reduce the Ramsey credo down to bite size morsel, it would read: "A unwavering belief in God and the healing power of His love, the unquestioning effectiveness of prayer and keeping goodness forefront in your life." I would add six more words: "At least, most of the time." You see, Peter experienced periods of doubt. Liz early on had decided that if this tenet worked for Peter, it was just fine for her. Thus, she was somewhat puzzled by Peter's new interest. Removing the olive from her drink and replacing it with two ice cubes, creating what she called a Wimpy Martini, she asked, "Tio, are you having some kind of spiritual mid-life crisis? And just whose version of theology do you wish to study? I'm not going to lose you to some monastery where no one speaks and you just till the fields from dawn to dusk and then rap Gregorian from dusk to dawn?"

"I think my calling it a theology class may have been a poor choice of words. My interest is in learning more about the world's religions and their histories."

"Well, you're in luck. Cal has a pretty substantial religious studies department. They can bring you up to speed on every sect, cult, denomination and religious faction ever known to humankind.

Peter grabbed for the ice cubes to make his own Wimpy Martini. "Well, I'm not at all sure how much auditing at Cal I want to do. We'll deal with it when we get home. Meantime, on to other matters, like what shore excursions are we signing up for? Do you want to kayak, try a zip line, go dog-sledding or maybe salmon fishing in Sitka?"

Before she could tell her uncle that she wanted to do it all, they both spotted Dave Flannery approaching their table with his wife. The newspaper editor looked like he had dressed in front of a wind machine. "What the hell are you two doing here?" he barked. "I got dibs on this place. I found it early this afternoon and staked my claim. Nobody from our group will ever find me here. And there's nothing like a safe haven with a well-stocked bar." Pointing to the mirrored shelves behind the bar, Dave sighed, "Did you see the single malts they've got back there?"

"We're of the same mind, Dave. Don't worry, no one is going to learn about your personal hideaway, at least not from us." Peter stood to introduce himself and Liz to Flannery's wife.

Oh, sorry," Flannery mumbled, realizing his social gaffe. "This is my wife, Mary Pat. Dear, this is the preternaturally affable Peter Ramsey and his niece, Liz, who, if we're lucky, is nothing like him."

Mary Patricia Flannery, nee Cavanaugh, was one of those rare creatures who no doubt rose each morning and, while small birds and butterflies fluttered merrily about her, splashed a little rain water on herself, shook her shoulder-length brown hair this way and that and then deemed herself ready to face the day. "I'm delighted to meet you both,' she said in a decidedly San Francisco Irish lilt. "We wouldn't be here, Peter, if you hadn't been such a success in selling the cruise."

Her husband pointed to the two empty chairs. "Mind if we join you?"

And join them they did. For a drink at the Covey, dinner at the second seating in the dining room and, finally, back to their now private bar for an after dinner drink. Dave stayed in character, occasionally offering up his singular brand of bombast whenever he felt the need. His wife, obviously long immune to his huffing and puffing, paid him no mind. Rants regardless, it was an extremely pleasant evening. Liz and Mary Pat were both high-spirited types who clearly enjoyed each other's company. During dessert, Peter gave everybody a refresher course in how to handle the following morning's Bloody Mary and Mimosa Welcoming Party, the first of their three public events. Dave promised to be on his best behavior.

"I think that may disappoint many of your fans," Peter observed.

"I forgot to tell you. My boss is on board," Dave announced.

Surprised, Peter said, "I didn't see Symington's name on any list I have."

"Sibilant Sandy and his wife, Mitzi, found out some of their society buddies were on the cruise, so he signed up through his own travel agent. None of them are part of our group." Suddenly Dave was the proud bearer of a devilish smile. "Hey, that means they can't take part in any of our activities, doesn't it?"

Peter laughed. "Can I be there when you tell him? Seriously, though, there is a chance he might not know about the parties or lectures. Invitations are only sent to the staterooms of our guests. That said, though, if they stroll in we will make them feel welcome." Flannery frowned and cussed under his breath. To further stoke his ire, Peter added, "All of them."

"Well, I only hope I can go twelve days without crossing his path, or God save me, Mitzi's." Lifting his glass, he toasted, "So, here's to a great cruise. And for me, that includes logging a few hours here in my beloved Covey Bar and..."

Echoing that last conjunction, Mary Pat finished the sentence for him: "And taking dance lessons with your lovely wife."

With a defeated look, Dave leaned in toward Peter and Liz and whispered, "That information is not for broadcast."

By the end of their second day on the Ocean Glamour, Peter Ramsey had lots of reasons to smile his way through his bedtime ritual, the last duty of which consisted of pounding a buckwheat-filled pillow into a shape that would comfortably welcome his head. Peter belonged to that growing population who believe once one has found the perfect pillow, one's head must never rest on anything else. As a result, this weighty, Egyptian cotton-covered pliant mass went everywhere with him. Once supine, Peter began his own review of these first two sea days. They were all so altogether pleasant, he was convinced that the following ten days would be a skip through the dew. An odd metaphor of choice, he thought, as the closest he ever came to dew-skipping was sliding once on a wet driveway in his slippers while going for the Sunday paper. Admittedly, a silly thing to ponder, but experience had long ago taught him about the challenges of trying to mentally stay on a logical track during these few minutes before sleep arrives. It was as though his mind at this point would just wander into any territory it darned well pleased, paying no attention to whether any of it made any sense at all. This evening, though, he decided to take a firmer stand and stay in charge of the old thought process so he could properly reflect on how smoothly everything was going. And everything was going smoothly, indeed. The Bloody Mary and Mimosa party came off without a hitch. Their group was, for the most part, a congenial bunch who and seemed pleased with his welcoming comments. Even Dave Flannery, displaying a rare charm, was well-received. Perhaps he was comforted by the fact that the Symingtons, their crew of San Francisco socialites and Philipa Crumley-Figg never made an appearance. Unfortunately, for Liz, who was eager to get a shipboard romance going for her uncle, the Whitby women were also missing in action. Both had left New York on the day of the cruise on a flight that was scheduled to arrive in San Francisco in plenty of time for them to get to the pier. Plans do go awry, though. It seems that they were sharing the Airbus with a beefy, bullying young man wearing a New York Jets football jersey who, even though he was belted into 23B, spilled over into 23A and C. This oafish individual decided to throw a temper tantrum after learning that peanuts would not accompany his Bloody Mary as another passenger had complained of allergies. Nobody, meaning trained flight attendants, the copilot and even a muscled, armed air marshal, could calm him. A minor brawl ensued, forcing the captain to return the plane to JFK. MagicSeas Cruise Lines came to the rescue, finding a new itinerary that would take the Whitbys first to Seattle and then by ferry to Victoria where they would pick up the ship at its first port of call. If all went well, everybody on board these future transports will be allergy-free.

So, Peter concluded, his eyes getting heavy, all is going well. Almost well, that is. There was a disconcerting few minutes in the dining room that evening. He and Liz were assigned a table for two by the port side window. It was formal night and both cut fine figures; he in a vintage, double-breasted tuxedo, she in a simple black sheath dress. Their conversation was lively and cheerful. Now quite often people who saw them together concluded they were a May-December couple rather than uncle and niece as their familial affections could easily be misinterpreted. Whether that was the case with three of the guests at a table of eight next to theirs, they could not tell. The two men and one woman seemed to spend a socially unacceptable amount of time observing them. The trio also made no attempt to hide the fact that they were discussing them in some detail. However as their mutterings were in one of the Turkic languages, Peter and

Liz were clueless as to why they were so interesting. The scrutiny stopped when he and Liz lifted their wine glasses in unison, looked in their neighbors' direction and, catching their attention, silently toasted them.

Sleep arrived. Peter's last conscious thought was a prayerful request for a more agitated sea, as he found the ship's rolling movement had a way of turning his comfortable bed into an adult cradle.

The phone's ring jarred him out of a deep sleep and a surreal dream where he was a crew member of a three-masted frigate that looked remarkably like the USS Constitution that was sailing along the San Diego Freeway in Los Angeles. Because of the crew size, the ship was entitled to be in the High Occupancy Vehicle lane. Still in this silly dream but awake enough to pick up the receiver, he heard a heavily accented voice ask, "Mr. Ramsey?"

Peter replied, "Yes, Peter Ramsey here. Let me guess, you need me topside for the night watch?"

"We have the night watch all taken care of. Mr. Ramsey."

Shaking off the last vestige of sleep and now alert, Peter answered, "Of course you do. Sorry, I was dreaming."

"I'm very sorry to wake you. This is the hotel director, Fritz Henning. Could you, please, come to penthouse 1050 as soon as possible. I will explain all when you get here."

chapter 9

As Peter neared penthouse 1050, he spotted a small knot of ship's officers still in their fancy dress whites from that evening's formal dinner. As he neared, one of them moved forward. "Sorry, sir. Please return to your stateroom." Before Peter could explain he was there on orders from the hotel director, Fritz Henning stuck his head out the door and signaled approval for Peter to come through and join him in the stateroom.

Entering the small, narrow hallway meant having to step over the now unworkable legs of Mrs. Philipa Crumley-Figg. The rest of her lie on the cold tile of the bathroom floor, her head in a pool of blood, close to a blood-stained bidet. Peter looked in horror at her corporeal remains. It is a cruel term, I admit, but that is exactly what he beheld; nothing more than corporeal remains. The substantive Philipa Crumley-Figg, I assure you, had exited her mortal premises many minutes before the scene I describe now. To his credit, Peter accepted that notion and took spiritual comfort in it.

Even though he had lost his fair share of family members and close friends over the years, Peter surprisingly had only one postmortem viewing to his credit before this unfortunate encounter with Philipa Crumley-Figg. It was more than half a century ago when his grandfather, a popular city bureaucrat, had been put on public display during a wake that normally would have been held at his own home but due to his popularity was moved to a downtown funeral parlor. A quiet eight year-old, Peter remembered approaching the half opened casket, his sister on one side, his mother on the other and seeing Grandpa Joe in a striped, double-breasted suit with his favorite tie and white pocket square. Peter couldn't take his eyes off his ashen face, a face that a mortician's makeup couldn't brighten. He remembered not feeling particularly sad, as he was so distracted and fascinated with the myriad noises around him; the loud sobbing, the hushed and not-so-hushed comments and the occasional cheery greetings between attendees who hadn't seen each other since, perhaps, a previous wake. He also wondered what could have happened to the lower half of his grandfather that they kept that portion of the casket closed. An aching grief took hold a few days later when on a sunny afternoon he suddenly yearned for the company of his grandfather and realized it could never be. There would be no more Cub games at Wrigley Field and, afterwards, a foamy root beer for him and two or three stronger somethings for Grandpa Joe at O'Leary's on Madison Street. Of course, the stop for refreshments was their secret. Grandmother Nonie was never to know.

"I called you, Mr. Ramsey," said Fritz Henning shaking Peter out of his reverie, "because Mrs. Crumley-Figg was part of your group. I, of course, will notify the travel agency's onboard representative, but as you and I have already had dealings with the deceased, I thought it best to contact you right away. I thought it appropriate that someone who knows her should be here."

"How did you come to discover the body?"

"Just before midnight, Mrs. Shen in 1052 called the front desk. She said she'd heard what surely was a woman's scream coming from next door. Evidently the doors to their verandahs were both opened. The clerk tried calling but received no answer and sent security to check to see that all was well." The eerily calm hotel director glanced over at the twisted figure on the floor and added, "I can't remember anything like this happening. Given the age of many of our guests, we've certainly had our share of deaths during cruises and, of course, our fair share of accidents, but nothing as horrific as this. Anyway, the doctor and captain are on their way. We will handle everything from here and, of course, with complete discretion so as not to upset or disturb our other guests."

Curious, Peter asked, "What *do* you do in a situation like this?"

The hotel director explained that, while the captain would give him a more detailed explanation, there would be an investigation as to the cause of death, then by morning's light the penthouse will be thoroughly cleaned, the guest's bags packed and stored and Mrs.Crumley-Figg transported from penthouse 1050 to one of the three vacancies in the ship's morgue. Then it would be back to business as usual for the Ocean Glamour.

Peter thought he was throwing a huge wrench into the works when he said, "Mr. Henning, I think you better hear what I have to say before anybody moves the body or for that matter moves or touches anything in the penthouse."

"What do you mean?" he asked, clearly puzzled. "You're making it sound like a crime scene."

"It's possible this is more than an accident."

This is not what any hotel director of a luxury cruise ship wants to hear. In this particular case, Fritz Henning wished he could just put his hands to his ears and holler, "Waa Waa Waa Waa" at the top of his lungs to prevent him from hearing Peter.

"Mr. Ramsey, please, take a close look at the deceased. It's apparent she was going into the bathroom. For what reason, I don't know. She trips, falls forward and strikes her head on the bidet. It is such a traumatic blow, she dies." Fritz threw his hands up in the air as if to say "Voila."

Peter replied, "That very well could be, but there's no sense in me taking a closer look as I don't have the expertise, nor do you, I think, to draw a realistic conclusion as to how she died. What I need to tell you is that she feared someone was trying to kill her. Her son-in-law told me that there had already been one attempt on her life and another incident where she was threatened."

Before Peter could say more, a flurry of movement at the door caught their attention. The captain had arrived with the ship's doctor. Both were of Norwegian registry. The captain, Marius Erikson, was custom-built to go to sea. Tall, swarthy with a full dark beard, he was a powerful, threatening presence. His demeanor took Peter by surprise. The captain he now saw before him looked like he'd be more at home flogging ill-behaved guests than the courtly gent with the practiced smile whom he met earlier that evening at his welcoming reception. Behind him, several inches shorter and many inches rounder, stood Gunnar Ibsen, the ship's doctor. A gynecologist in Bergen, Norway, he viewed the occasional tour of duty as the ship's surgeon as a wonderful opportunity to see the world. And as an Ibsen, he fashioned himself a daring, push-the-envelope playwright As such, he was putting the finishing touches on a two-act entitled *"A Womb With a View"* that the *"No-You're-Not-Seeing-Double Players of Nygardsgaten Street,"* an avant theater group wholly comprised of four sets of twins, promised to stage in the dark winter months. E.M. Forster, whom I met in passing recently, found it all terribly amusing.

The sheer bulk of these new arrivals forced everyone to move further into the penthouse. After an odd second of silence, the captain glared at his hotel director and nodding in the direction of Peter, snapped, "Who is this? Why is he here?"

Peter felt these were questions he was quite capable of handling himself. However, just as he began to speak, he noticed a faintly colored, gaseous cloud in the hallway. Then, suddenly, out of the corner of his eye, he saw it dart to the closet, then to the opened verandah door. The apparition finally settled somewhere near the stateroom sitting area.

Henning answered instead. "This is Peter Ramsey. Mrs. Crumley-Figg was a member..."

The Ramsey name seemed to break the ice. The captain thawed and the smile Peter witnessed earlier in the evening returned. "Ah, Mr. Ramsey from the radio station group. Of course. I can understand why Fritz felt the need to call you."

Before Peter could respond, he heard: "My heavens. What has happened here?" Unquestionably feminine and possessing an English theatricality, the resonant voice appeared to come from what Peter earlier described as that faintly colored, gaseous cloud. His response was automatic: 'It appears she slipped entering the bathroom and struck her head on the bidet."

The captain grinned. "Mr. Ramsey, I'm not accustomed to people answering my questions before I ask them. Thank you."

Peter looked at the three gentlemen to gauge whether they saw or heard the vision in the corner of the room. Apparently not. Henning was busy telling the captain about Peter's concerns regarding the deceased while the doctor busied himself by nervously rummaging through his medical bag. For a second, Peter entertained the thought that the pink hued whatever-it-was might be the ghost of Philipa but he quickly dismissed that idea. A ghost? Surely not. Then two questions came at him at exactly the same time. The captain asked, "So, Fritz tells me you think this may be more than a horrible accident?" And Lillie asked him, "Do you hear me?"

Peter felt comforted knowing that his two word response would satisfy both parties. "I do." In fact, he felt a need to confirm that and said again with more enthusiasm, "Yes, I do."

"Oh praise be! I have been roaming the ship for hours trying to find someone who might acknowledge me," Lillie exclaimed.

Peter opted to ignore her for the moment, thinking this is no time to let these gentlemen know he's maintaining a communication with an apparition. It certainly wouldn't sit well, considering he was trying to explain to them the possibility that Philipa's death was anything but accidental.

The captain and hotel director listened to him with obvious interest. Gunnar Ibsen, the doctor, hoped the captain might be swayed enough from what he heard to put everything on hold, at least, until Victoria. He didn't relish personally tending to the lifeless Mrs. Crumley-Figg as he likes all his patients to be alive and preferably not ailing. In fact, his idea of an ideal cruise was to do no more than occasionally affix a patch behind the ears of a seasick guest. But after hearing the captain's response to Peter, he reluctantly reached into his bag and searched for his gloves. There was work to be done.

"Mr. Ramsey, I will explain how this is handled. Cruise ships these days are well-equipped to deal with all sorts of, shall we say, dire situations and that includes death, be it natural, accidental or suspicious. Our security team which, by the way, includes a former forensics expert from the Baltimore police, will be here in seconds to begin a thorough investigation. Your concerns, of course, will be made known to them. What they report back to me, I will share their conclusions with the FBI and the authorities in Victoria as we will be there in a matter of hours. If our security detail determines that it was a tragic misadventure, which I am inclined to believe, and the authorities are satisfied with our report, that will be the end of it. Meantime, we will place Mrs. Crumley-Figg in our morgue and await instructions from her family. If they would like her moved from the ship before we return to San Francisco, we can make arrangements for that. We will first find out if that port of call has the capacity to handle her. The wisest and most expedient course of action is to leave her on the ship until we return."

Just then one of the concierges came forward and signaled for the captain's attention. After a respectable round of mutterings, the captain announced to the group, "Well, it appears Mrs. Crumley-Figg gave us a fictional person to contact in case of an emergency."

"I'm not surprised," said the hotel director.

"And why is that, Fritz?" asked the captain.

"She surely is, or was one of the most difficult and contentious guests we've ever had to deal with. During her short stay here, according to reports that reached my desk, Mrs. Crumley Figg managed to offend spa attendants, bartenders, waiters, her butler, photographers as well as a wide range of guests. As an example of her handiwork, after this evening's dinner, I heard from all seven of the people at her table who demanded to be moved. And that included our own cruise director."

"I didn't think anything or anyone could get Kelly's ire up." The captain turned to Peter.

"Do you have any information that can help us, Mr. Ramsey?"

"Her son-in-law was my former employer. I have his phone number in my stateroom," Peter replied while watching Lillie move about the room.

Noticing Peter's wandering eye, Fritz Henning asked, "Is there something you're looking for?"

"Uh, no. Well, actually, yes. I just wanted to make sure I didn't leave anything behind when we traded rooms. It appears not."

Over his shoulder, Peter heard Lillie whisper, "The top page of the notepad on the bedside table is of immense interest. Obviously, you can't take it. But don't worry, I will see to it later."

I am delighted to report that Peter Ramsey was holding up rather well, considering that here in the dead of night he was standing just five feet away from the body of his former manager's mother-in-law talking to three of the ship's officers and dealing with a vision only he could see and hear. Such circumstances will rattle anyone's cage. However, he seemed to take it all in stride, demonstrating a remarkable coolness.

The security team's arrival meant the present occupants of the penthouse, minus one, had to move out into the hallway. The captain, after dispersing the hallway crowd, took Peter by the arm and the two moved in the direction of Pete's penthouse.

"Mr. Ramsey, as you no doubt know, passenger safety, crime and mysterious deaths on cruise ships have been much in the news. Knowing that, I want to assure you that while it obviously is in our best interests that Mrs. Crumley-Figg's death be deemed accidental, I will not shy away from any investigation if it is determined that there is evidence of foul play. Authorities will be welcomed aboard and will receive the utmost cooperation"

Peter felt reassured by the captain's comments. "I will call you with her son-in-law's phone number. Do you have any problem with me calling and letting him know what has happened?"

"Those kinds of calls can be difficult, Mr. Ramsey," the captain warned. "But, please, feel free to call. Be advised, though, it's always tough dealing with a grief-stricken person."

Remembering his most recent conversation with his former boss about his less-than-loving mother-in-law, Peter wondered just how grief-stricken Howard would be.

chapter 10

PETER SAT ON the edge of the bed scanning the penthouse interior hoping to locate his new friend. He even ventured a tentative "hello," but received no greeting in return. So just where was this walking, talking aura? Mind you, he was not questioning Lillie's existence, just her location. He saw what he saw. Of that he was certain. He was also convinced he remained sound of mind and needn't think otherwise. The fact that the captain, doctor and hotel director couldn't or didn't react to the ghostlike apparition didn't bother him in the least. She was as real to him as was the harsh reality of Philipa's death. I was quite impressed with the way he was handling it all.

Next on his agenda was informing the Newtons of Philipa's untimely demise. He reached for the phone and then just as quickly put it down. The captain was right. This was going to be tougher than he originally thought, regardless of what Howard's reaction might be. He considered how he would handle the call. Recalling the time he took his first and what ended up being his last swim in the frigid waters of San Francisco Bay, Peter wondered if he needed to employ the same strategy that eventually got him into the Bay. Wearing only a nylon cap, Speedo trunks and goggles, he stood for the longest time on the small, rough sand beach of the South End Rowing Club staring out at the swim lanes of Aquatic Park. An old timer approached. "First time, huh? You know the longer you look at the water, the colder it gets. My advice is waste no time getting in. Once you're in over your ankles, dip your hands in, splash a little water on your face and then just keep moving forward until you are fully submerged. And remember hesitancy can be punishing." As a bonus, the aged swimmer added, "You know a Bay swim is a terrific cure for a hangover."

Armed with that wise counsel, Peter wondered if he should put the swim on hold, hike a block up the hill to the Buena Vista, down several Irish Coffees and then take his swim the following morning. However, he did as instructed and it worked out marvelously well. Now he knew how he would handle the phone call.

Howard answered on the first ring. Considering the lateness of the hour, he sounded alert and chirpy. Perhaps too chirpy, Peter thought. Hearing his voice, Howard reacted with the enthusiasm one reserves for a surprise reuniting with a long-lost, much beloved relative. "Peter, hello! What a surprise. Let me guess. You want your job back," he chuckled. "Wish I could but I'm stuck with this clown corporate forced on us. But you, my friend, are really missed around here. So what's up? Why the reason for the call, particularly at this crazy hour? You know you woke me up from a deep sleep."

"Howard, why is it you sound so wide awake."

"Practice," he answered. "Do you know how many times this phone rings with some frigging Figg suit from New York on the other end?"

Remembering his Bay swim instructions, Peter figured at this point in their conversation he was not only in over his ankles, but over his head and ready to come up for air. Steeling himself, he began, "Howard, I'm calling about your mother-in-law."

"Oh shit, now what has that woman gone and done?" he asked with that same comical chuckle that intimated he was tickled pink his mother-in-law was Peter's problem and not his.

"Howard, Philipa is dead. I just came from her stateroom. She took a very bad fall entering the bathroom and hit her head on the bidet."

"On the what?"

"It's a toilet that thinks it's a water fountain. Ask Naomi. She'll know."

The chuckle gone, he asked, "She's really dead?"

"Yes, I'm afraid so."

There was considerable silence. Peter thought it best to wait until Howard spoke again. "Hey, I'm back. I just told Naomi the news. She's on her way to the kitchen."

"Why is she going to the kitchen?" Peter inquired, knowing he really, really shouldn't have asked.

"It's how she deals with things. For example, if there's bad news or she's sad or down, she digs into a big bowl of Mabel's Magic Magnificent Munchie Crunchie ice cream. If things are rosy, she gets herself a huge serving of Sassy Suzy's Swirly Strawberry Delight frozen yogurt. Hey, hold on a sec." In the background, Peter could hear his former boss holler, "Honey, bring enough of that Munchie Crunchie for me, too. After a slight pause, Howard added with his odd chuckle, "Or the frozen yogurt. Your call, darling."

"Excuse me, Howard. Pay attention here," Peter interjected. "You're going to get a call very soon from... Actually I'm not exactly sure who it is that handles matters like this, probably the captain. Anyway, whoever it is will have all sorts of information and will be able to answer any questions you may have. By the way, your mother-in-law gave them a fictitious name and number as an emergency contact. I had to give them your number."

"She was always doing that," he said. "Say, Peter, you don't think someone killed her and then staged it to look like an accident. You remember our conversation about..."

"I remember. In fact, I told the captain of the threats."

"Oh please, please, tell me you didn't tell them Philipa thought I was behind them?"

"Don't be ridiculous. Of course not. And I won't. I simply told them that prior to the cruise, there had been two incidents in San Francisco that had her convinced someone wanted her dead. That said, Howard, I must tell you that your mother-in-law's death appears to be an awful accident and nothing more."

"Look, I, uh, better go. I hear Naomi coming. Thanks for calling, Peter. I'm sure this hasn't been easy for you."

"Don't worry about me. I'm fine."

"I'm glad you are. Frankly, I'm all over the place. It's probably horrible to say but a part of me feels an enormous sense of relief. Like I've been set free. Come to think of it, I have."

"Howard, it wouldn't surprise me if there aren't a few people on this ship who will feel the same way once they hear the news," Peter said. "For two days now your mother-in-law has been a one woman scourge."

"I'm sure she was. Let's talk later in the day."

Peter pictured Howard and Naomi snuggled up together in bed looking out at a bedroom full of their kitschy birdie art, eating either their Magnificent Munchie Crunchie or their Swirly Strawberry Delight and consoling each other in their eccentric fashion.

Now that the phone call was behind him, he wondered whether he ought to wake Liz and bring her up to date. Deciding to let her sleep, he shed what clothes he had on and started for the bathroom. At the doorway, he looked down and noticed the two inch riser. Funny, I'd never paid any attention to that before, he thought. I just instinctively step over it. Could it be that Philipa had somehow missed the step-up and subsequently tripped? More than likely, he thought.

"Aha, you are no doubt thinking along the same lines I am, Mr. Ramsey," Lillie said. She was in front of the mirror, a sink on either side of her.

Startled and realizing he was naked, Peter broke the current world's record for stepping into the hallway, shutting the bathroom door and reaching into the closet to grab a robe. "Sorry, I didn't know anyone was in there."

Lillie laughed. "Mr. Ramsey, I'm not just anyone. I'm sure by now you have found a robe to put on. Please come in. At this point in my life, I have no personal need for a bathroom."

Peter slowly opened the door. The lavender-hued abstraction was still in front of the mirror.

"I came in here because I was curious to see what I looked like," she began to explain. "During the time I was wandering about the ship, I never once noticed my reflection or shadow. The mirror confirms it. I can't see me, although I can see and hear everything else. How odd it is," she said matter-of-factly.

Modestly wrapped in one of the Ocean Glamour's terry cloth robes, Peter said, "So far, I seem to be the only one who can actually see you. What there is of you anyway."

Peter, as I mentioned, had quickly and easily come to terms with the realization that he was now communicating with a ghost. What else could the apparition be, he reasoned. Interestingly, he was not frightened. Awestruck? Flabbergasted? Yes to both. A little rattled? Definitely. But that was brought on by carrying around a mind stocked with questions. First, though, he needed to know with whom he was dealing. As he asked for some identification, he told himself the only reply he did want to hear was "I'm Philipa Crumley-Figg, you moronic imbecile."

Instead, he heard, "I am Lillie le Breton Langtry de Bathe, born October 13th, 1853, died February 12th, 1929."

Peter's surface cool evaporated. Stunned, he sputtered, "Lillie Langtry? As in Oscar Wilde, Judge Roy Bean, James McNeill Whistler..."

"In the flesh," she said, interrupting his roll call of her colorful colleagues. "Well, perhaps not in the flesh anymore, but in every other way, yes, I am she."

"What are you doing on a ship sailing to Alaska?"

"I wish I could answer that. You see, I can't account for a single second of the last 79 years. I remember vividly on an abusively cold February 12th, 1929 closing my eyes for the final time and instead of descending into blackness, I was suddenly engulfed in the most luminous and brilliant white light. That, Mr. Ramsey, is my last memory."

I'm so glad I let Lillie go back amongst you with her recollection of the white light as it is such a welcoming and pleasant notion. Death is always a dark topic and throwing a light on it – excuse the pun – is often appreciated.

"And you have no idea what happened to you after you saw that light?" Peter asked, hoping to hear more positive news about her post-death experience.

"Oh yes, I certainly do know what happened," she said. "Nothing! Absolute nothingness until a little after four yesterday afternoon when I suddenly found myself fully conscious in what I have come to learn was your original stateroom."

Lillie moved away from the mirror. Now she was visible in a corner of the bathroom near the shower. "Now that I've explained why I am in the bathroom, please sir, tell me what it is you see. I hope it is an approving look to you. My beauty sustained me when I was alive, you know."

Peter's knowledge of Lillie was enough that he knew she was one of the Victorian era's professional beauties, a forerunner to today's high fashion models. He assured her she did have a uniquely appealing look.

"Mind you, it's not a question of vanity. I am merely curious, so if you could be more precise."

"Well, starting from the top where your head ought to be, you're about six inches wide. Then you flare out on both sides like a flowing ball gown to about four feet or so. You stand, if that's the correct term, about five and a half feet high. You resemble a soft, diaphanous lavender cloud. All in all, I'd say you are quite fetching."

"Thank you for the approbation, Mr. Ramsey," Lillie said. "You make me sound quite pleasing to the eye."

"Well, you are in an abstract sort of way."

"Now, turn about is fair play," she said mischievously. "As I just saw you des habille, I shall describe you. Sans robe, of course."

Peter laughed. "That isn't necessary. Unfortunately, the mirror works just fine for me."

"Well, you wouldn't be displeased with my description. In fact, I wish my gentlemen friends had maintained themselves in their advanced years as well as you have. Of course, paunchiness was quite acceptable at that time."

"Do you mind if I use the bathroom. Those of us in our advanced years find ourselves needing this room more and more."

"Of course. It's a silly place to carry on a conversation anyway. I'll wait outside. We have much to discuss."

Peter sat on the penthouse sofa watching Lillie flit about the room, first to the bed, then to the verandah door and finally stopping at a chair near him.

"Mrs. Langtry, are you trying to sit down?" he asked.

"No, Mr. Ramsey, I am not. I am simply trying to create the illusion that I am sitting as it seems an appropriate position to be in while we chat," she replied. "By the way, I think it's high time we begin to use our given names. Don't you?"

Oh, what a marvelous step forward in their relationship. Had this all been happening in the time of Queen Victoria and then King Edward, they would have been Mrs. Langtrying this and Mr. Ramseying that for an interminable length of time. Instead, in just a matter of hours, here they were as intimate a pair as you'll likely find.

Even though he was eager to chat, Peter could not stifle a yawn which prompted Lillie to glance at the clock. "My heavens. Look at the hour. Peter, you need your sleep."

"What will you do?"

"I think I will wander a bit as I continue to be overwhelmed by all the sights and sounds around me."

"Well, I will be right over there," Peter said, pointing to the bed. "I really can use the sleep. I suppose sleep or rest is immaterial to you.'"

"It seems that way. Frankly, I'm not sure. I'm still trying to figure me out." And just as quick as that, Lillie was at the penthouse door. He rose to see her out or through or however she chose to exit. "Peter, there must be a reason we've been thrown together. Perhaps, I'm here to help you. It's possible you're here to help me. More likely, we're here to help each other. But why? There are so many, many questions."

"Now I'm really tired. But you're making me feel guilty for going back to bed."

"Don't be silly. You need rest and so far I don't."

Peter smiled at the wispy lavender cloud with the seductive voice. "You know, I'm actually looking forward to whatever awaits us. Truly, Lillie, my life is blessed, but so far it's been a relatively escapade-free one."

"And this is in your mind an escapade?"

Peter thought it the perfect word. "Yes. Suddenly, thanks to you, I have an opportunity to join you on an adventure that could have elements of mystery and intrigue. Please note – and don't think me a coward for it – I left danger out of the equation. As for an adventure, let's not forget my quick immersion into the world of the paranormal."

After a thoughtful pause, Lillie whispered, "You know, Mr. Ramsey, I find you utterly charming."

Peter thought if she had eyes, they would be winking naughtily. He surprised himself by asking, "Mrs. Langtry, are you flirting with me?"

"I suppose I am. What of it? You're obviously a single gentleman. Wouldn't you enjoy a shipboard romance with a professional beauty who has a colorful international reputation?" she asked breathily.

Peter knew he was blushing and there was nothing he could do to stop it. Indelicately, he responded, "No offense, but you might be a tad old for me."

"Nonsense," she scoffed. "Admittedly, the records will show that I am one hundred fifty-five years-old. But if I have been for all intents and purposes nonexistent for the last seventy-nine years, that makes me seventy-six. And you are, sir?"

"Sixty-five."

"Well, there you are," she exclaimed. "I am a mere eleven years your senior. I see nothing inappropriate about it at all."

Nonplussed about the direction the conversation had taken, Peter, nevertheless, enjoyed the silly, romantic give and the take and didn't want it to end. He said, "I think it would take on more of a real shipboard romance if you had – no offense – some substance."

In an instant, coquettish Lillie became scolding Lillie. "I assure you, Peter, I am substance itself. Don't ever mistake the physical body for substance."

What a difficult notion that is to get your arms around. For example, you stub your toe on the corner of the bed frame and begin to hop around the room in sheer agony. The last thing you want to hear in the middle of all that pain and suffering is that your true substance is entirely spiritual, that your toe is nothing and therefore can feel nothing. But there it is. When you arrive here in Eternity, you come as a complete being. There's nothing you left behind that you need here. While you were earthbound, you might have appreciated that aquiline nose that gave you such a dignified profile or those hypnotic, ocean-blue eyes that everyone commented on, but they serve no purpose here. I should add, however, that while you are on the planet tripping the light fantastic, it is of the utmost importance you take excellent care of your mortal equipment.

Her point made, Lillie said, albeit, lightheartedly, "Peter, disregarding some obvious obstacles, just imagine the purity of a romance involving the two of us."

"Our virtue would remain intact."

Lillie decided to bring their bill and cooing to an end. "All right, I am off. You get some sleep. Tomorrow we have much to do."

"Lillie, is there a chance I will awaken tomorrow and find out it's all been a dream; that Philipa lives to pillage and loot another day and you were just a romantic notion of mine?"

"I suppose it's possible. Let's see who wakes you tomorrow." With that Peter was alone. The visual manifestation of Lillie Langtry was gone.

chapter 11

WHEN YOU EVENTUALLY shed your mortal attire and check into this All-Inclusive Resort I affectionately call home, besides arriving with an inestimable amount of joy derived from simply realizing you continue to be, you may in addition experience a certain giddiness. This feeling is brought about by the sudden realization that you never again will have to deal with those myriad annoyances that can so often send your blood pressure soaring. Come to think of it, you don't even have to worry about your blood pressure anymore. Or cholesterol, for that matter. A sampling of these pesky botherations can include root canals, telemarketers, airport security, tax audits, traffic snarls, bombastic radio talk show hosts, tech support calls, everything and anything to do with the DMV and bagpipes. Yes, even the much maligned bagpipe. However, let me insert here a good word for this odd musical device. To be appreciated, this instrument must be heard under the right circumstances, for example, when it's put to use during a Military Tattoo. Position a tartaned, caped piper by a corner balustrade of the Tower of London and frame him in a single spotlight while ominous, Hamlet-like evening clouds hang low over the River Thames. Then have him pipe a patriotic air from a bloody conflict centuries past and tell me you won't tear up.

Now I included the bagpipe in the list of potential annoyances because Peter Ramsey was rudely awakened by one at exactly eight o'clock in the morning, an hour when by law all bagpipes should be deflated and packed away in their cases. You can imagine Peter's shock when an amateurish rendition of *Blue Bonnets o'er the Border* invaded his penthouse. He bounded out of bed, remembering Lillie suggested she might take charge of reveille. Alas, after stepping out onto the verandah he realized that she would not be around for this morning's rise and shine. That had been left, instead, to a kilted, bearded piper standing several decks below on the Victoria pier. On either side of this noisemaker were two plump lady Victorians wearing ear-to-ear smiles and 19th century Jolly Olde attire. They were holding baskets of souvenir pins to give the guests from the Ocean Glamour who were single-filing off the ship to catch their assigned vans, busses, cabs and horse-drawn carriages that would transport them to their various shore excursions.

It was a spectacular morning. The British Canadian air was fresh and unspoiled; soft breezes and an early sun beckoning one and all to come outside and carpe diem. It was such a welcoming scene, Peter couldn't find it in his heart to curse the piper. Shaking off what drowsiness remained, he marveled at the day's promising beginning. Last night's strange activities must have been part of a dream, he thought. And if indeed it was, it was certainly the corkiest of the many corkers he'd had over the years. Stepping inside, he heard a knock.

"Oh Tio. You're not even dressed." Liz stood at the door wearing black running shorts and a white tank top. She stared up at him from behind a visor with a Cal Bear logo.

With all that happened, Peter forgot they had planned a long, leisurely run through Victoria, a jog that would eventually land them on the doorstep of a restaurant that called itself a gastropub. Both thought gastro had no business affixing itself to a cute word like pub. It was a prefix best left to reside in a medical dictionary. Even so, they agreed a Canadian brewpub was just the ticket for a lunch on dry land after a long run,

"Liz, I really do have a good excuse. I'll explain on the run. Would you page Bartal and order some coffee and juice while I jump in the shower? I need the coffee and delivering it will give him a cheap thrill when he sees you in that getup. I promise we'll be out of here in twenty minutes."

Liz decided it would be quicker if she headed up one deck to the Du Soleil cafe for his coffee and juice. While she was gone, Peter called the hotel director who confirmed that Philipa's death was not part of a dream. Fritz Henning explained that they had already contacted the proper authorities who were satisfied her death was accidental and saw no need for further investigation. He assured Peter they included his comments in their report. However, their security team, finding nothing that remotely indicated foul play, concluded it was an unfortunate misadventure and nothing more. Fritz added that the captain had called Howard Newton who insisted the body be taken off the ship in Victoria. He and Naomi were flying in that night to take charge of transporting Philipa back to San Francisco.

"We'll miss them then?"

"Yes, we will. They arrive in Victoria shortly after we sail for Ketchikan. By the way, we did advise the Newton's of the expenses involved," he said.

"I don't think money matters," Peter noted.

"I gathered that was the case. I don't mean to speak out of turn, but the captain told me he thought her son-in-law was an odd duck."

"He's more a Sooty Tern," Peter remarked.

"I beg your pardon?"

"Sorry, it's an inside joke. Yes, Howard Newton is, indeed, the oddest of odd ducks."

"Evidently, the captain and he had a very peculiar conversation. It seems Mr. Newton is most anxious to see for himself that his mother-in-law is really dead. It's as if he doesn't believe us."

"She made life very difficult for him," Peter explained, anxious now to jump in the shower and get his day underway. "Fritz, thank you for catching me up on everything."

"Not at all," Fritz said. "I assume you'll be going ashore this morning. Have a wonderful time in Victoria. And I promise I will do my best not to have to rouse you out of bed in the middle of the night again."

One block into their run, Peter told Liz about Philipa's death. His *oh-by-the-way, did-you-hear* tone of voice annoyed her enough that she stopped running. Pointing to a nearby bench, she indicated the two of them were to plant themselves for an impromptu family meeting. She, of course, would set the agenda. And she did with a tone that was stern and scolding: "Tio, most of the time, it is a distinct pleasure to be under the same roof with an unexcitable person. However, on those rare occasions when excitable things happen, you disappoint. Let me explain how you should have handled it. As soon as I knocked on your door, you would open it and say not dispassionately, 'Liz. I have some disturbing news. Remember that woman who told you to fuck off when we got to Pier 35? She's dead. Come in and I'll tell you what I know.'" She concluded her chastisement by adding, "Anyway, that's how most people would deal with it."

"There's a lot more to last night than just Philipa's death," Peter said in his defense.

Since Lillie's shocking and sudden appearance last night, Peter had taken to frequently glancing hither and yon in search of her. It didn't go unnoticed by Liz. "Tio, what on earth is going on? You look as if you're expecting someone."

"No, I'm not. Well, yes I am. Actually, I'm not sure,"

"Ah, multiple choice. Should I go with A, B or C?"

"Look, if Philipa's death was the only thing that happened, I would have told you first thing. But last night other things happened. Or didn't happen. Or maybe some of it happened and the rest was a dream."

Liz's smile spread across her face and she shook her head. "Listen to you. What on earth are you going on about?"

Peter stood and took Liz's hand to bring her off the bench. "It's complicated and unreal and I don't mean unreal in a cliched way. Come on, let's walk and I'll unload the whole eerie adventure on you."

So they walked and he talked. He left nothing out, beginning with the midnight phone call from the hotel director and ending with Lillie's quasi-romantic departure from his penthouse. Everything was so fresh in his mind, he was able to replay the evening's events almost word for word. His detailed account took the pair from the ship's pier along the scenic Inner Harbor shoreline path through downtown Victoria and past the impressive Empress Hotel. He wrapped things up about midpoint on the Blue Bridge.

Liz was by nature not a quick responder. Thus, they walked in silence while she mulled. By lunchtime he knew there would be an earnest discussion. He would have liked to tell her that the bridge they just walked over was designed by Joseph Strauss, the designer of the Golden Gate Bridge in San Francisco. However, it was probably best not to distract her from her cogitations. He'd wait for the return trip to play tour guide.

Peter and Liz shared a platter of local cheeses and smoked fish. In front of each of them was an array of small glasses containing sample tastings of the brewery's beers.

They'd been given a window table with a view of the busy harbor. Jet boats filled to capacity with tourists outfitted in matching orange jumpsuits lazily headed out to the open water where, if everything went as planned, they'd get soaking wet when the jets kicked in. Float planes took off and landed. Whale watching boats and cute water taxis came in and out of their view as well as kayakers closer to shore. In the distance, across the harbor, they could see the full length of the port side of the impressive Ocean Glamour. It struck them how far they'd come for this lunch that had been recommended to them by Liz's new friend, Kevin.

"Lavender?" Liz decided that as a topic opener this one word inquiry was as good as any of the other countless questions she had at the ready.

"Yes," he answered. "Do you remember that abstract painting your friend, Rebecca Cesci, did of her and her grandmother that you admired so much?"

"Oh, I do. Two very blurry images with no physical features, yet you could easily see the two of them strolling together arm in arm. They looked like they were floating and, yes, they were bathed in lavender."

"That's what I saw or dreamt I saw. Except just one image."

Liz finished a taste of the stout and grimaced. "I'll trade you my stout for your pale ale." The deal struck, she asked, "Tio, do you think Lillie Langtry exists?"

He frowned. "There's a part of me that would like to think she doesn't. If it was all just a dream, then my safe, comfortable and very predictable lifestyle continues without interruption. I know that may sound dull and boring, but it's a modus vivendi I have become accustomed to and deeply cherish."

Liz put her hand on his arm. "Do you know you still keep looking for her? You're driving our server crazy."

"I think I will probably keep looking for her for awhile yet, Liz. The truth is I am having a difficult time consigning her to a dream. Philipa's death happened and I was there. That's all true. Why not the rest?"

"So, you do think she's real?"

"Yes, I do," he said resolutely. "I am certain that everything happened as I described it. It's about time I stop trying to consign it to a bizarre dream and deal with it. My problem, though, is I don't know where she is or if she's returning." He looked across at Liz and saw what he took to be a skeptical frown. "You think your dear old uncle has lost it."

Liz reached across the table and took his hand. "No, Tio, I don't think you've lost it. I was just wondering how it was that you saw what you saw and heard what you heard while everyone else in that stateroom didn't."

"Don't think I haven't thought about that," he said, signaling the server that they would like the bill. Of course, the server who had already made several false starts toward the table mistaking Peter's Lillie-searching glances paid no attention to him. "There are so many questions. Why Lillie Langtry? Who am I to her? Wouldn't you think I'd be visited by someone I know or knew? Somebody like Eugenie Dominski"

"Who is Eugenie Dominski?"

"My first big love. Third grade. Sat in front of me, Long, black curly hair, huge eyes and a porcelain complexion. I was smitten and remain so to this day."

"Tio, be serious. Besides, Eugenie may still be alive."

Peter again signaled for the check and this time the server took notice. "Let's put the 'Peter and the Ghost' story on hold and have a tourist's stroll back through lovely Victoria. Who knows? Perhaps, my paranormal event was a one-off. Maybe the powers-that-be who direct where these spirits go realized they'd made a mistake and sent her off to find some living Langtry family member."

Whoa! A little too close to home with that powers-that-be comment. But that's the way it is with one's beliefs. Sometimes, you can be bang on as regards a spiritual structure or dimension. Then there are times when you miss the mark completely. So don't get me started on astrology. Anyway, I'm sure you realize Lillie will enter stage left shortly. I certainly wouldn't shift the story and its players after bringing you all the way to Victoria with a shipload of mostly Northern Californians.

chapter 12

VOYAGE! THE WORD just charms the spirit dust off me, conjuring up thoughts of romance, intrigue, mystery and danger. While Peter's voyage has a well balanced mix of all four of these fascinating ingredients, I think it's high time I spice things up by adding a dash of nuttiness.

The finish line for Peter and Liz's Victoria wanderings was the Grand Atrium on deck five, the gleaming centerpiece of the Ocean Glamour's busy lobby. This seagoing tribute to marble glass and brass features along one wall a two-story high waterfall with a large, rather bizarre gold-plated sculpture of Poseidon and Athena trying for the life of them to look like they were ballroom dancing. Obviously, the artist's knowledge of Greek mythology was skimpy as old Posey was never successful in winning the affection of the virgin goddess.

In the Atrium's center was a winding, blue-carpeted stairway that curved its way to deck six with its wraparound gallery of expensive shops and an airy European retreat called the Portside Bistro. And this is where we find the star of our show and his plucky niece.

"What are your plans for the rest of the afternoon?" Peter asked.

"I'm going to sit on the verandah and catch up on my studies. Since we have cell phone reception, I might also call Kevin. What are our plans for dinner?"

"I made a seven-thirty reservation at Va Bene. Italian food sound good?"

"Always. By the way, I am going to wear my turquoise blouse with the puff sleeves, black slacks and my peeky toe shoes."

"Why do I need to know that?"

"Because, Tio, I don't want us to clash. Wear your black sport coat and that lavender shirt I gave you for Christmas," she commanded. "Besides, that way, if Lillie should pop in while we're having dinner, you two will be color-coordinated."

"Amazing how you're always looking out for me."

Liz had for some time been the official dresser for the both of them when they went out. Peter had no objection, but he sometimes wondered how Liz might handle a husband in similar circumstances. As if she read his mind, Liz said, "Thanks for going along with me. I only wish I could get Kevin to stop dressing like he was starring in a Judd Apatow movie. What is it with that?"

"Most guys his age dress like that."

"Maybe I have to find an older guy. Any of your crowd single?" she teased.

Peter asked his niece if she wanted to join him for a coffee at the Portside Bistro. She declined but exclaimed so over the iced mochas that Peter decided he needed to try one. Wanting a few undisturbed minutes, he took a seat at the bistro's empty bar. Still in the habit of searching for Lillie, he looked out at the mostly unoccupied room. He noticed a thickset, older gentleman slaloming through the tables on his way to the bar. The man's idea of fashionable, daytime cruise attire was an open-collar white dress shirt, wrinkled gray slacks and leather sandals with heavy dark brown socks.

"Ah, Mr. Ramsey," the man said. "I am Petra Dosynk."

Peter recognized him as one of the three from the table next to theirs in the main dining room who took such an interest in them. "How do you do?"

"I do very well, thank you. Now I will join you." The accent was one Peter couldn't place. Given the man's heftiness, he took his time maneuvering himself onto a neighboring barstool. Eyeing Peter's iced mocha, he ordered one for himself.

Petra Dosynk's bulky frame, round bald head, steely dark eyes, misshapen nose and fierce mouth gave him a menacing presence. Of course, our goodhearted Peter, a firm believer that books should not be judged by their covers, thought it best not to be too quick to judge him. Who knows, he thought, maybe he wins the Mr. Congeniality award every time he sets foot outside his home.

"How do you know my name?" Peter asked.

"Aha, a little detective work on my part," he laughed. "I simply asked the hotel director. He tells me you are a very distinguished person."

"If I am it's because I brought a rather large group on board. Cruise lines like that sort of thing."

"I'm sure they do," Petra said. "Now I tell you about me. My wife, grandson and I are from Kwyrkistan. Do you know it?"

"Not really. I thought I knew all the countries that end with *stan*. The word translates to land of, doesn't it?"

"Yes, it does. In our case it means the land of the Kwyrkis. We are a very small country on the eastern side of the Aral Sea. Maybe a little larger than Monaco. Our neighbors are the Kazakhs and the Uzbeks. They don't bother us and we don't bother them. In fact, most countries in our part of the world leave us alone. We've been pretty much ignored for centuries." He shrugged off that last comment and continued, his tone still indifferent, "But it does not matter. We are self-sustaining and happy. Unlike the other countries we are a close-knit, homo.... homo... How do you say it when we are all the same people? From the same tribe, so to speak?"

"Homogeneous," Peter offered.

Petra smiled. "Yes, that's the word. We are all Kwyrkis. Except for Barbie Mae Hettleberry who is originally from your New Orleans. She's the only non-Kwyrki. But she is very well accepted and now treated like a real Kwyrki.

"How did she come to settle in Kwrykistan?"

"A year ago she was on an organized Great Silk Road Tour through Uzbeckistan when one day the group went right and she went left. She ended up in small Kwyrkistan border town where she met a handsome Kwyrki baker on vacation. She had bakery in New Orleans. So she made some beignets for him and that was that. They had torrid romance that involved a lot of powdered sugar and he brought her back to Zneferuk, our capital city, where she now owns very popular bakery called Barbie's Big Beignets. There is nothing in the world we Kwyrkis love more than sweets and sex."

Wondering if the conversation could get sillier, a bemused Peter got an answer when he took a sip of his iced mocha, a gesture which didn't go unnoticed. "Aha, you are left-handed," Petra exclaimed happily.

"Yes, I am." Peter glanced over at Petra holding his iced mocha and added, "Looks like we have that in common."

"Everyone in Kwyrkistan is left-handed." Petra remarked casually. Leaning in, he added in a low voice, "It is not a good place to be right-handed."

"You're kidding me?"

"I know it is laughable, Mr. Ramsey, but these kinds of eccentricities exist in all countries. For example, I know that in Spain people say Barthelona instead of Barcelona because once there was a king who lisped and everybody joined in to make him feel better. So it is with our left-handedness. Centuries ago, a Kwyrki King named Krystoz the Inept was left-handed. He decreed that if everybody was left-handed, it would be a happier kingdom."

And a clumsier one, Peter thought.

"Anyway, the tradition continues to this day. I swear it is the truth," Petra added, holding his left hand in the air.

Peter decided this was not the time to inform him that the Spanish lisp story was, if you'll excuse the expression, a myth. "You are a long way from Kwyrkistan, Mr. Dosynk. What brings you to this end of the world?"

"My new wife, Inka, is a famous television news anchor in Zneferuk. Before that she was a pole dancer at a club called Happy Chaps. That's where we met. She has time off so this is like a honeymoon trip for us.

"Mrs. Inka Dosynk." Peter said her name aloud for no other reason than to just hear it. Petra quickly corrected him, "No, she decided to keep her maiden name, Dynka. That's how she's known on television. But off the air, she is now Mrs. Inka Dynka Dosynk."

This was not a man to laugh at so Peter bit his tongue and congratulated them on their wedding. "And the young man with you is your grandson?"

Dosynk nodded. "Yes. His name is Yurk. He is a very good athlete. Very strong. After the cruise, he will be meeting with Oakland Raiders football team."

"Do you play American-style football in Kwyrkistan?"

"Similar. We do not use that oval ball. Ours is more of a disc."

"Like a Frisbee?"

"Yes, it like a Frisbee but more like a discus."

"Mr. Dosynk, a discus weighs almost five pounds."

Dosynk nodded. "It is a very physical short passing game."

"Probably sponsored by 1 800 DENTIST," Peter muttered.

"I beg your pardon?"

Peter decided this was as good a time as any to cut short his visit with his new and strange Kwyrki friend. Pushing his stool away from the bar, he said, "Mr. Dosynk, I have a meeting scheduled in half an hour and I have to change. I'd best be on my way."

Dosynk grabbed his arm, and not gently. "I almost forget the reason I want to talk to you. My grandson, Yurk, wants to have sex with your niece. How do we make that happen?"

Isn't it odd? When you're on the receiving end of a verbal fast ball, rather than expressing immediate indignation, most people simply request another one be tossed their way. And that's exactly what Peter Ramsey did: "What did you ask me?"

Dosynk removed his heavy lips from the straw and with the same casual air repeated, "My grandson wants to have sex with your niece."

"Now look, Mr. Dosynk, that's...."

Dosynk cut him off. "Don't worry, I can assure you it will be very good sex. He is like a bulniki. He will make her smile silly."

"Let me guess, a bulniki is..".

"Yes, a bull. She will be in for rodeo ride of her life."

Peter surprised himself at how fast he came up with a way to respond to Petra's offbeat request. Taking a second to look one way and then the other, he leaned in and whispered three convincing words in Dosynk's ear. The beefy gent immediately let go his arm and returned to his iced mocha. Seeing the disappointment in his face, Peter knew he hit pay dirt

"Yurk is going to be very disappointed. Oh well, there are other attractive women on the ship who aren't that way."

Peter thought it best to advise him that his direct approach might not be appreciated by fellow shipmates. "Mr. Dosynk, those of us not familiar with Kwryki sensibilities might be put off by that question."

"What do you mean by this put off?" Dosynk even made a expression of puzzlement appear threatening.

"They may find it offensive. Your helping Yurk find a lover.

"A lover," he barked. "Yurk doesn't want lover, Mr. Ramsey. Only someone to have sex with." He was dumbfounded Peter couldn't grasp the difference.

"May I make a suggestion? Tell Yurk to find a male crew members who is close to his age. Maybe a bartender or waiter. Have him explain where he's from and that he'd like to know how to best approach a woman on the ship that he's interested in."

"I will think about it," he said.

"As I said, I better be on my way," Peter said, moving away from the bar.

"I enjoyed our conversation. I will tell Yurk what you said. Meantime, he will have to stay away from the pancakes and waffles for awhile."

Well, there you are. A simple "Nice to have met you" would have been both a pleasant and appropriate parting shot, but then Petra had to go and toss in the waffles and pancakes thing. Peter returned to the bar. "All right, I have to know. What on earth do waffles and pancakes have to do with Yurk's wanting to meet a woman?"

Peter by this time thought he was way past being astonished by anything Dosynk told him. How wrong he was. The Kwyrki elder went on to explain that on their property just outside Zneferuk they have an orchard of Emba trees. The tree's Latin name is Arbor Bonus Connubium Vita or Tree of Good Sex Life. Oddly, it is indigenous to a very small area near the capital city and it is all Dosynk-owned property. The Emba produces a sap that Petra makes into a syrup. It seems Dosynk's homemade syrup, besides being a delicious topping for a well-made waffle or a stack of pancakes, can sometimes act as a powerful sexual stimulant later in the day.

"I told you earlier we Kwrykis love sweets and sex. I don't make much of the syrup. Just enough for family and friends."

"But it doesn't always work," Peter remarked.

"Well, it always does as a breakfast treat," he boasted, patting his ample stomach. "But early on, I needed to know about that wonderful side effect. I decided to do test it on unsuspecting people. Yurk is a volunteer fireman at firehouse number seven. He took some with him and served nine firemen. It worked on two. Then Inka asked me to let her bring some syrup to work at the television station. She saw that everybody had a taste during their editorial breakfast meeting"

"How did that go?" Peter asked.

"Saw it with my own eyes," he replied. "That night during the evening news, the weather girl, Heska Fedkos, ran onto the set and starting tearing the clothes off the sports' anchor. That's when I knew it could work on women as well as men. When it works," he felt compelled to add.

"There haven't been any reports of four hour erections?"

Dosynk studied Peter for a moment. "That is an odd question. But the answer is no." Peter managed to find the right words to bring his visit with Petra to an end, thanking him for his utterly fascinating company. As Peter weaved through the scattered tables, Petra shouted after him,"Mr. Ramsey, I look forward to more conversation. By the way, I am sorry about your niece. It must be very difficult for you."

Without turning around, Peter waved and said, "We manage."

At exactly seven-thirty, Pico Enea, the jaunty, ever-smiling maitre d' of Va Bene showed Peter and Liz to a table in the center of a dining room that was alive and warm thanks to the many robust colors of Italy. Pico, who once studied fashion design in Milan, was of the mind that well-dressed people deserved to be seen and, as the dress code for this evening was casual, he guessed Peter and Liz might be the only guests he'd seat that evening by how well they were attired.

After ordering two glasses of pinot grigio and before Peter could stick his head inside the Va Bene menu, Liz remarked, "Tio, do you know whenever I leave you alone on this ship something really really weird happens to you." Peter had already told her everything about his Portside Bistro encounter with his new Kwyrki friend, Petra Dosynk.

"It seems that way, doesn't it? Anyway, the good news is you won't have to worry about a syrup-charged Yurk chasing you all over the ship."

"I can't believe telling him I was right-handed did the trick. What if it didn't work?"

"I had a backup."

"I'm married?"

"No, you're gay."

"Well, it wouldn't matter much on this ship," she observed, watching an assistant waiter put an assortment of breads on the table. He then offered each of them half a roasted head of garlic.

Do I, Theodomicles, have any thoughts regarding this bulbous herb? I do not. That you might think so is testimony to the transcendent power of this Allium Sativum.

While garlic remains one of mortal life's extraordinary pleasures, alas, you can't take it with you. Somehow Peter and Liz grasped that notion requesting the waiter to return with more.

Once their order had been placed, Peter began to talk seriously about how they should handle the next gathering of their group. But, he didn't have his niece's total attention as she was too busy watching Pico in his Holy Communion-white dinner jacket and a diminutive, swaggering chef outfitted in a starched, spotlessly clean black chef's jacket marching toward them. When the smiling pair were almost table-side, their waiter smoothly cut in front, deftly placing two plates in front of them.

Pico began the introduction: "Ah, Signor Ramsey and Signorina Handlery, I want to introduce our consulting chef for Va..." Before he could get Bene out of his mouth, the chef gave him a poke and whispered something in his ear. After being corrected, Pico continued, "I mean to say our *celebrity* chef. How lucky we are to have him on this cruise. This is chef Umberto Flagiola from Trattoria Innamorata in Santa Monica. I'm sure you have heard of him and his restaurant." They hadn't.

Standing as close as he could to Liz, Umberto was a shade over five feet, six inches tall, a height attained thanks to a pair of Crox that had been fitted with raised heels. He was a handsome man with dark wavy hair, heavy eyebrows and blue eyes. He resembled, if you squinted, a miniaturized Dean Martin. That Umberto knew this was one of his many flaws.

Pico continued with his introductory remarks: "Chef Umberto wanted to deliver the amuse bouche himself."

Without taking his eyes off Liz, Umberto waved one arm toward the plates. "I have prepared a very special amuse just for you. This is salmon with cucumber skin, a portion of eggplant, sea salt, shaved carrot, one pea, caviar egg, lemon rind and a special pepper from Rimini with a splash of pesto from Portovenere and aioli that I only make in the dark after midnight in a cold place. It is, quite frankly, a masterpiece. One of my many." With that Umberto bowed to some wild applause only he heard.

The amuse was no larger than a quarter. Peter downed it before Umberto had finished giving the ingredients. No one noticed.

"Signorina Handlery, it is my pleasure to give you a dish that celebrates your beauty. You know, I am often told I look and sound like Dean Martin. So while you enjoy my humble little amuse, I will provide you with an Italian serenade. Music and food, Signorina, is a match made in Heaven." No it isn't and I, Theodomicles, can say that with authority.

Umberto first looked about the room. There was no sense in wooing a beautiful woman without an audience to watch you in action. He began to croon: *If our lips should meet, Innamorata. Kiss me, kiss me, Innamorata.* Because his lips would purse when he got to the word kiss, he looked to Liz like a just-caught flounder. After so many bars of *Innamorata,* he braked, glanced around at the room and said in a loud voice, "Like the amuse, you only get a little sample. But there's more where that came from. Perhaps, I can finish the song for you later tonight?"

Caught off guard, Liz stumbled a bit with her response. "That's very nice of you to ask, but I, uh... I..." She looked at Peter hoping he might toss a lifeline across the table. Getting no help, she blurted out, "I can't. You see, I'm right-handed."

For a second, Umberto was puzzled by her answer. Then he decided the signorina just had a quirky sense of humor. "I see. You are being coy with Umberto. It is understandable. Perhaps, I come back during dessert and we talk more about it over my special tiramisu."

Liz looked across at Peter and whispered, "It worked for you. I thought I'd try it."

"There's always the backup," Peter reminded her.

It was then that Umberto saved them both the trouble of coming up with a diplomatic reason to brush him off. Looking with disdain at Peter, he said to Liz, "So, my pretty thing, you need permission from this man to stay out late? Maybe you are younger than you look and not ready for a night with Umberto."

Peter knew that an angry Liz is a fascinating thing to observe. Even her hair seemed to turn red. Certainly, her cheeks were flush and her eyes smoldered. Sitting back in his chair, Peter awaited the inevitable volcanic eruption of Mount Handlery. Hot molten lava was sure to flow.

Liz indeed exploded, but she had enough sense to keep her voice low. No one in the dining room had a hint there was anything amiss at their table. "Listen, Mr Fellatio, or whatever your name is, that man is my uncle. My thoughts are that he probably doesn't want me to meet you later because he thinks you are an insufferable ass. I certainly think so. And if we order tiramisu for dessert, it better be brought out by a waiter. If you come with it, you'll be wearing it back to the kitchen."

Liz sat back in her chair, folded her arms and waited for the chef to slink away. An anxious and embarrassed Pico tried to nudge his chef away from their table as he'd been told by corporate that Flagiola had a nasty temper that he often couldn't control. However, all Umberto did, even though he was seething, was to say loud enough for the room to hear, "Prego, enjoy your amuse, Signorina."

It would seem this is the perfect moment for me to weigh in on the topic of anger. I'm sure you have already worked it out that this strong emotion is nonexistent here in Eternity. It's one of those many things like the aforementioned garlic that stays in the mortal world. Now my personal observation is anger seems to be a huge waste of time and energy. Expressed anger can have all sorts of dire consequences, everything from a loved one not talking to you for a day to all-out war between countries or peoples. I will wrap this up by suggesting that it probably does a person good to work on controlling that emotion. However, without the expressions of anger and all those other good to bad emotions, we'd have to say ciao to good old-fashioned storytelling. I mean what dramatic muscle would *Hamlet* have if they all acted like the Ozzie and Harriet Nelson family. I can't imagine Shakespeare giving Hamlet this dialogue: "Hi, Mom, I'm home. What did you do today? Killed Dad, huh? Okay, I'm good with that. What's for supper?"

Their dinner was excellent. Under different circumstances Peter and Liz might have invited the chef out and kissed him on both cheeks for creating such a feast. Instead, they were able to thank Pico who had become extremely solicitous after the amuse fiasco. "Please, Signor Ramsey and Signorina Handlery, I insist you visit us again. The good news is that Mr. Flagiola is getting off in Ketchikan and then flying home after doing some fishing. You won't be troubled again." Pico served them each a generous helping of their acclaimed tiramisu. Then leaning in, he said in a hushed voice, "I can't wait to tell the staff how you told him off and called him by that funny name."

When Pico walked away, Liz asked Peter, "What funny name?".

"You called him Mr. Fellatio."

Liz went wide-eyed. "No! Tio, please tell me I didn't"

Anxious to try the tiramisu, Peter took a large spoonful and said, "Oh, but you did."

Then a third voice entered the discussion: "Oh my, it sounds as if I should have arrived earlier. What did I miss?" And just like that, Lillie Langtry appeared out of the blue. Or, more appropriately, out of the lavender.

chapter 13

AMONG THE MANY pluses of living where I do is every last one of us is gifted with Divine Enlightenment. And so will you when it's time. As alluring an idea as that is, I completely understand if you don't want to rush things. Interestingly, as a result of this DE, there is no need for signs, not even name tags. We happy souls manage quite well without them. However, in a dimensional world such as yours, life wouldn't go so swimmingly sans signage. You require them for all sorts of excellent reasons. For instance, there are signs to control the flow of movement so you don't keep bumping into each other. Then you have signs that help promote a more civil society. For example, those cute table placards you see in restaurants suggesting you not use your cell phone otherwise the waiter will confiscate it and the kitchen will add it to the soup stock. Perhaps the disruption caused by Liz Handlery's noisy, supersonic exit that rattled the entire dining room population might have been avoided if Va Bene's management had posted a sign reading: "It is recommended all ghosts kindly refrain from haunting, scaring or spooking our guests while they are dining."

Now Mrs. Langtry had no interest in haunting, scaring or spooking anybody when she chose to hover in her lovely lavender abstractness just to the left of Peter and in full view of Liz. Peter, of course, was thrilled with her return. It didn't matter to him that she dropped by during the first spoonfuls of the delicious tiramisu. For him, her appearance was a welcoming affirmation that he wasn't off his head. For Liz, though, it was another matter entirely. Lillie's unexpected appearance came as a nerve-tingling, heart-pounding, mindspinning, soul-shaking, hair-raising, eye-popping shock. This was never supposed to be. When Peter told her about the famous and beguiling spirit who had visited him, she was thoroughly convinced he had somehow fixated on a vivid dream to the extent that it had become all too real for him. As a dutiful niece, she lovingly patronized him whenever he talked about her, but at the end of the day if somebody handed her a questionnaire asking if she believed in Lillie or any of her paranormal crowd, she'd have marked a big X in the NO box.

After discovering that Lillie did indeed in some postmortem fashion exist, Liz bolted. Standing at the front desk, Pico watched in amazement as she shot out the Va Bene door like a rocket, a contrail of screeching noise in her wake.

"My heavens, Peter, your niece is certainly hyper," Lillie remarked.

Not wanting to draw attention to himself, he asked through closed lips, "How do you know a word like hyper?" All Lillie heard was *"wummsmsmsosmeporfghglg?"*

"You are mumbling, Peter. It is not a good idea. I remember Edward mumbled. It is not becoming to royalty at all. Anyway, we'll talk later. Let's go find Liz," she said, adding enthusiastically, "I have so much to tell you."

Midway between their table and the Va Bene exit, ready to spring into action when Peter came within snagging range was Gertie Florian of Pleasanton. It must have been a struggle for Pico to find an appropriate place in the dining room for this disparate foursome. Their dentist son, fleshy and plump Fluoride Freddie and his partner, tall and slender Ben, were handsomely and fashionably attired. However, Gertie and Freddie Senior looked like they were dressed for a tailgate party before a football game.

Gertie sprang from her chair, grabbing Peter just as he thought he might make it past them with a small wave and howdy-do. "Peter, is your niece okay?" she asked, her concern genuine after witnessing Liz's panicky departure.

"Just a bad reaction to the tiramisu. She had to get away from all things Italian. She'll be fine," he assured her.

There was no getting away quickly. Gertie introduced him to her son. Gone was the shy, retiring teenager. Considering his girth, Freddie bounded out of his chair and came round to greet Peter. He was friendly enough but Peter felt something was not right. He glanced over at Ben who sat there unsmiling and distinctly uncomfortable. Peter muttered something about interrupting their dinner and excused himself. Gertie walked a short distance with him. At the front desk, she stopped him and said, "Peter, I have wonderful news. Freddie Senior and I are going to be grandparents. Freddie and Ben are adopting a child. We have decided to sell our house in Pleasanton and move to Winona to help them out. I am so happy. You must come visit us sometime." There was pure joy oozing from every pore of her substantial body.

Entering the penthouse, Peter and Lillie spotted Liz lounging on the small sofa robotically paging through the spa catalogue. To Peter's relief she appeared relaxed and calm and he felt he did not have to warn her about screaming. Tossing the brochure aside, Liz rose and advanced toward the ghostly apparition that had sent her scurrying from Va Bene just minutes earlier. She extended her right arm. Then realizing Lillie had no hand to shake, she hastily returned it to her side. Her voice was cheery and animated: "Mrs. Langtry,

I want to sincerely apologize for my behavior in the restaurant. Seeing and hearing you gave me the shock of my life. I felt if I got out of there... How do I put this?"

"You would return to your safe and secure world where such phenomena do not exist," suggested Lillie.

"Yes, I think that may well have been the reason. I don't know if I can explain this correctly, but I have always felt I would get through life without ever communicating with the dead, dealing with a ghost, encountering zombies in a cemetery or werewolves in London. I also figured the odds were slim to none that I would ever have an out-of-body experience, be abducted by aliens, kissed by a handsome vampire or channel a past life. Now, you come along and shake everything up."

"It may be that..."

"Please let me finish. Now that I've had a chance to catch my breath and give this whole crazy situation some serious thought, I..." Liz paused. Then Peter's niece flashed that brilliant smile of hers and continued, "Anyway, I just want you to know I am more than fine with the circumstances, weird as they are. In fact, I find it all pretty darned exciting. May I call you Lillie?"

"You may. And I'm delighted to hear you feel that way," Lillie said.

Returning to the sofa, Liz bounced down and said, "You know I have lots of questions."

Lillie laughed. "Unfortunately, I don't know that I have answers for the kinds of questions I think you are eager to ask." She had followed Liz into the penthouse, choosing a spot on the edge of the bed to settle. "However, if your inquiries have anything to do with my seventy-five years and four months minus a day on this beautiful planet, then by all means ask away. My memory is flawless"

Liz couldn't believe her good fortune. She had always had a fascination with Victorian and Edwardian England.

Now here she was sitting across from a major personality of that period who could speak with authority on the culture, people, politics, art and gossip. As a future doctor of anthropology, she wondered how she could ever present such research. Citing extended conversations with Mrs. Langtry obviously wouldn't work. She wondered whether others before her had had similar experiences but knew it was futile to credit their ghostly sources. Could it be, for instance, that noted cultural anthropologist Ruth Benedict who wrote *"Chrysanthemum and the Sword: Patterns of Japanese Culture"* actually interviewed a Takugawa spirit. Certainly, she'd never admit it. Trying to convince your fellow academic anthropologic air-breathers that your exhaustive research was enriched by a paranormal acquaintanceship would no doubt elicit a healthy round of snickering and endanger your tenure.

Peter decided if he didn't dive into this conversation soon, the evening would turn into a girls' gabfest involving one long since deceased Professional Beauty and one very much alive doctoral student of cultural anthropology. "Ladies," he said, unaware he had dropped into his announcer voice, "time to call this meeting to order."

Liz, hearing the all too familiar voice change, gave him a puzzled look which Lillie noticed. "Your uncle is right, Liz, there is much to talk about."

Peter walked over to the sliding glass doors and pulled the curtains back to reveal the final moments of a late Alaskan sunset. "I'll start with two questions. Why are you here? And why are Liz and I the only people who can see you or hear you? At least, so far."

Before Lillie could answer, Liz opined, "My guess, Lillie, is you've come back because there's something that happened in your lifetime that needs resolving. I mean, isn't that what ghosts do? Resolve things that occurred in their past."

Lillie was quick to reply. "I, too, thought about that, Liz. Given that my actions were at times scandalous, sometimes even notorious and that I often acted in a less than virtuous manner, I wouldn't even know where to begin the complicated business of resolving matters. But, if that is the reason I am here, what I am doing on a cruise ship in Alaskan waters? No, my dears, I assure you I am not here to *resolve* a thing. Rather, I think I am here... No," she said, correcting herself and adding confidently, "I *know* I am here because something needs *solving*."

"In that case then, we must be your accomplices," Liz exclaimed, pointing to herself and her uncle. So excited was she at the prospect of being part of some mystery romp, if the ship's sundry shop stocked deerstalker hats and long-stemmed pipes, she'd be there in a shot. "So tell me what game is afoot?"

Before Lillie could explain, Peter jumped in, "Excuse me, Liz. Lillie, before you answer that question, there's something I've been meaning to ask you. You and I first met in Philipa Crumley-Figg's penthouse. Why there?" Peter asked.

"Peter, you forget you and Mrs. Crumley-Figg switched penthouses. I believe I was in 1050 because that is where you were supposed to be."

Itching for adventure, Liz said, "Tio, that makes sense."

When Lillie first came to her senses – well, two of them anyway – she was predictably bewitched, bothered and bewildered. And wouldn't you be if you suddenly emerged from nothingness to the bright lights of a conscious world? Now I always thought Descartes nailed it when he said aloud for the first time, "*Cogito, ergo sum.*" Lillie's first thoughts were pretty much along those same lines when she awakened in penthouse 1050 in the late afternoon of embarkation day. Philipa Crumley-Figg, the stateroom's human occupant, was unaware that she was sharing her luxurious square footage with an historical 19th century professional beauty. Initially, it was a disappointment to Lillie that she could see and hear Philipa but not be seen or heard in return. However, after observing this mean-spirited and foul-mouthed woman in action, she concluded it probably was for the best. Leaving Crumley-Figg to her unpacking, Lillie went exploring. She knew the date, thanks to a note on one of the bedside tables and was certain that outside the penthouse door was a considerably different world than the one she left more than eighty years ago. Thus, she wisely thought it efficacious to acclimate herself to her new surroundings as soon as possible. In the process, she would also try to find out if there was anyone whose eye or ear she could catch during her crash course on life in the early goings of the Third Millennium. Meantime, penthouse 1050 would remain her home base. Why? She felt strongly there had to be a raison d'être for her coming to life in that particular stateroom. This kind of smart thinking paid off late on the second night when she learned that Peter could see and hear her. It was a magical moment even though it involved the death of her much despised roommate.

Lillie explained this all to Peter and Liz. "My dears, this has been an extraordinary experience for me on some many different levels. I was and, frankly, still am utterly dazzled by absolutely everything; they way people dress, the way they speak, especially the way they dance." That thought elicited a charming giggle. "And I still can't fully grasp the magic of all your many devices. But, I suspect, neither can many of you. And, of course, the best part of my exploration was finally learning why I am aboard this ship."

Liz edged forward, almost slipping off the sofa. "And that is?"

"Art theft!"

Peter and Liz repeated the words in unison: "Art theft?"

"Indeed, but let me get to it in my fashion, please. When I discovered the ship's computer center, I reasoned that it would be there where I could acquire more quickly than anywhere else a literacy of modern life. It is such an amazing place. I watched people correspond with what is called e-mail. I watched them play computer games. Did you know you can play Solitaire and you don't even need a deck of cards? Of course, you do. I observed several people checking their stock portfolios. There are some very wealthy people on this ship. Although, you'd never know it from the way they dress. Of course, that's never been a true determiner of wealth. Look at darling Wilde. Poor Oscar was always so extravagantly – some would say flamboyantly – turned out but sadly his wallet was always empty. Anyway, in the computer center there was a gentleman who was connected to the BBC news website reading an update on a story about an art theft. It seems a painting went missing from a museum in St. Louis, Missouri. It was part of a traveling exhibition of works from the Tate Museum in London. The show was called *Nature, Fidelity and the Pre-Raphaelite Brotherhood.* I ask you who thinks up these silly titles? Well, you can imagine my surprise when I read that the painting is of me. You may know it. It's called *A Jersey Lily* and was painted by my dear friend, Sir John Everest Millais."

"And you are on a cruise ship sailing the Alaskan waters because of a painting stolen in St. Louis?" Peter asked, astonished at the thought of it all.

"Not just any painting, Peter. A painting of *me*," she said. "Do you think I would be here if, let's say, it was the Mona Lisa that was stolen?"

Liz laughed and remarked, "Can you imagine if that were the case, Tio? We'd be sitting here talking to Leonardo Da Vinci himself or maybe the woman who sat for him, whoever she was."

"Actually, most authorities agree she was Lisa Gherardini, the wife of a Florentine merchant. However, there are many theories. Some art experts even speculate he was his own model while others argue his mother sat for him. It was, in fact, Mrs. Gherardini," Lillie said in an authoritative voice better suited for a museum director than someone engaged in casual chitchat.

"Why are you so certain?" Liz said.

A mystified Lillie answered, "I don't really know."

I do. Let me explain. Before sending Lillie back as a ghost rather than an angel, I erased her Eternal Hard Drive. It is a tricky maneuver and bits of data always end up remaining on it. As a result, Lillie will, while she's with Peter and Liz, surprise herself by coming up with the most arcane facts. However, it is not enough information for her to deduce that she is and has been for eighty years a paid-in-full resident of Eternity.

The temperate weather and sinking sun lured Peter, Liz and Lillie to call a recess and move to the verandah to watch the sun's butter-golden glow spread across the horizon. The three stood at the railing quietly admiring one of nature's better shows. For Liz and Peter who had never been this far north, experiencing a sunset at such a late hour was a special experience.

"I always adored sunsets. Sunrises as well, but later in life I was rarely awake early enough to enjoy them," Lillie remarked. "I think back then even our better poets leaned more heavily on the aesthetics of a sunset. Perhaps, that's because they drank a lot and were too hung over to fully appreciate a dawn's magical power."

Peter leaned forward and looking right and left noted that the staterooms on either side appeared empty. Even so, he felt it best they go back inside to finish their discussion.

"So, Lillie, tell me your thoughts regarding all this," he said, taking the small chair near the sofa where Liz promptly spread out. Lillie returned to her favorite spot which was the left edge of the foot of the bed. Peter suddenly wondered where Lillie should stay the night.

"I am assuming the painting and the thief or thieves are either on this ship or will be in one of our ports of call. I am hoping we can work together to recover it."

"Isn't it middlemen or brokers who try to fence stolen art? I would think we'd be more likely to encounter them than the thieves," Liz observed.

"You're probably right," Peter said. "I assume stolen art can surface in the most legitimate of environs. I did read that often the thieves themselves receive only a small percentage of the value of the loot. So they've probably been paid and now the hunt for buyers is on. However, we should remember that valuable art is often used as collateral for drug deals or other illegal activities."

"So you're saying the painting is on this ship because they are going to sell it or transfer it to someone. Or it will be used as collateral for some possible drug deal. I don't know why but the latter sounds more dangerous than the former," Lillie said.

"I'm not sure what I'm saying. This is all new to me," Peter said.

Lillie decided this was the time to move the conversation toward another thought she'd been entertaining while admiring the sunset. Considering she was at the very beginning of her earthbound mission, it was remarkably perceptive of her to work it out. "Peter and Liz," she began with a serious tone, "there is something else we must talk about, and that is reciprocity. I have come to the conclusion that my role here is far more involved that just recovering my painting and returning it to its proper home in London. Obviously, I can't do it alone. That must be why we are able to communicate. You see, I simply can't succeed without your assistance. I also feel strongly my presence here means I am to help you in some way."

Peter and Liz looked at each other. Neither of them had a response.

Lillie asked bashfully, "So, do you think we can discuss what it is that I can do for you?"

Liz was first up with a request. "Now that I am dealing with this new reality where I am conversing with a woman who has been dead for about eighty years, I probably could use some help in figuring it all out. And if it's not asking too much, maybe when you have a free moment or two, you can talk to me about the exciting times you lived in."

Lillie was thrilled with her response. "Yes, Liz, we shall do that. Now, what about you, Peter? Is there anything I can do for you?"

Peter shrugged his shoulders. "I can't think of a thing, but thank you for asking.."

Liz surprised them both when she said, "I can."

Peter frowned. "You can?"

Liz leaned forward to reach across and pat his knee. "Tio, you know how much I love you?"

"Lillie, that's my niece's way of saying I'd better fasten my seat belt. God only knows where we're headed."

Liz sat upright, staring at the lavender-hued spirit whom she now comfortably and easily accepted. Then she began. Peter and Lillie listened intently. The gist of it was Liz worried that once she graduated from Cal Berkeley and Peter moved out of the house, he'd be helpless without her. In a previous chapter, I believe I explained that since she was eight, Peter was the one responsible for the care, feeding and proper upbringing of this headstrong, perky young woman. During those same years, through her adolescence and into early adulthood, Liz felt equally responsible for Peter's care and upbringing.

"Lillie, my uncle has a few peculiarities."

Peter remained silent.

"Do you mean eccentricities?" Lillie asked.

"Those too."

Peter, of course, could have thrown his hand in the air and hollered time out, thus allowing himself the opportunity to defend his good name. However, he decided to let his niece continue without contradiction or interruption. He knew she spoke only from the heart and a genuine concern for his well-being.

Lillie asked if Liz could provide her with a sample or two of Peter's peculiarities or eccentricities. "Well, he absolutely baffles me with this routine. Occasionally, my uncle will invest five dollars and buy a Lotto ticket if the jackpot is really into the millions. But he will never buy one for the Wednesday game, only the Saturday drawing," she said.

Lillie had placed a wager or two in her day and knew that people who entered the world of chance came with all sorts of silly superstitions. Liz seemed to sense it was a bad example, so she quickly added, "Well, there's that, of course. Plus he's way too neat."

Alas, on that count, Peter knew full well he couldn't defend himself. He was neat. Very, very neat. In fact, if he were a town in the English countryside, he would win Britain's Prissiest Village award annually. Of course, this penchant for tidiness was also embraced by Liz who failed to share that small fact with Mrs. Langtry.

"My dear, I fail to see how Peter's peculiarities as you call them are cause to worry that his world will collapse without you. Methinks, you just don't want him to go."

Liz bit her lip and sat silent for moment. "The truth of it is, Lillie, and what concerns me most is that I read stories about men his age who retire and because they can't shake the feeling that they are no longer useful, they retreat into themselves. Then after too many golf games..."

Peter could no longer sit idly by. "Liz, I don't even play golf. And I am not retired. I just haven't decided yet what I'm going to do with my time. However, I assure you I will not wither away. My biggest concern right now is getting off this ship in nine days time with my sanity in tact."

chapter 14

SHERLOCK HOLMES ONCE asked Dr. Watson, "Where do you hide a leaf?" Because the good doctor knew the detective enjoyed answering his own questions, he waited patiently, ready to dutifully enter Holmes' answer in his little black notebook. After the appropriate pause, Sherlock shouted, "In the forest, Watson. Hah!" Several passersby of the 221b Baker Street residence, familiar with the occupant's eccentric manner, glanced up and shook their heads when they heard his trademark snort of self-satisfaction float down onto the street.

As Peter was bidding adieu to his female company, Liz came up with a variation of the Holmesian query. "So where do you hide a piece of art on a ship?" she asked no one in particular.

Unlike Watson, Peter didn't wait for her to answer. He walked over to the built-in desk where he had neatly stacked in a corner all the ship's promotional literature. Rummaging through them, he pulled out a wildly colorful brochure and, after straightening the pile, held it high. "Maybe you hide it in an art auction."

The three agreed that that was as good a place to start as any and they should meet up again in the morning to dish out individual assignments. Then Liz, confessing that ventriloquist acts were one of her guilty pleasures, scooted off to catch Archie Arbuckle and his redneck frog, Redeep, who were headlining the late show in the Monaco Lounge. Lillie told Peter she was headed back to penthouse 1050. "I don't really know why, Peter, but I feel strongly there might be something in the room that can help us." Peter was about to remind her that she didn't have a key when he realized breaking and entering for her was a no-brainer.

His guests gone, Peter prepared for bed; every step, every action an exact copy of the previous night's movements. He wondered if this strict routine qualified as a peculiarity or an eccentricity. And just what was the difference in Liz's eye? However, before he could really chew on the matter, the phone rang. It was Liz.

"I thought you were watching some redneck frog puppet."

"Couldn't handle it," she said. "Not many laughs for a born and bred Berkeley liberal. Conservatives, though, were falling out of their chairs. And, boy, are there a lot of them on the ship. I had to get out of there. Anyway, I'm tired and ready to call it a night. Just called to tell you I love you and..." Her voice trembled slightly.

"Liz, are you all right?"

"Tio, my mind is so unsettled. I'm a little freaked about what happened tonight. I mean it did happen, didn't it?"

"Oh yes, every fascinating second of it."

"I don't even know how to approach thinking about Lillie and... Well, everything else."

Peter wondered why he wasn't as nonplussed as his niece. "Liz, you told Lillie you were, despite the weirdness of it all, willing to accept her and deal with it. Go to bed comfortable with that thought. We'll delve deep later."

The next call came but a second after Liz hung up. Yet another feminine voice, this one husky and nervous.

"Mr. Ramsey, it's Jenni Ramirez. I apologize for calling so late, but is there any chance you could meet me?"

"Tonight?" he asked, wondering what it was that the group's travel agency representative thought so important they had to meet right away.

"Please," she said. "It's taken me three daiquiris just to work up the courage to call. I really need to talk to you. I'm one deck up at the bar in the Oasis Court. It's quiet here this time of night."

"Give me five minutes."

The Oasis Court was the ship's sanctuary. The spacious, airy retreat featured floor-to-ceiling windows, two large skylights, palm trees and sitting areas with comfortable white wicker patio furniture. On the port side near the front was a small lounge area. Jenni Ramirez was alone at the bar. The co-owner of Triton Travel and Tours in San Francisco was a compact, attractive woman with short dark hair in her mid-fifties. With her white slacks and navy blue sailor's blouse with a Glamour insignia over her left breast, she could have easily passed as one of the crew. On embarkation day, Jenni had assured Peter he need not worry about any client complaints, telling him that if anyone approached him with a problem, all he had to do was send them her way. She boasted that after twenty five years of being in the travel business, there wasn't a complaint, gripe or grievance she hadn't dealt with. She explained to him that normally she would send one of her employees along, but given the unusually large size of this group, she thought it best she come along. However, Jenni also had an ulterior reason for being aboard and Peter was about to find out what that was exactly.

He noticed she was not wearing her usual perky smile and she had moved from daiquiris to coffee. He told the bartender he would have the same. "Let me guess, you finally met a guest whose bellyaching got to you."

His question at least produced a sardonic grin "Oh, if you only knew, Peter. But, of course, you're going to know because that's why I want to talk to you. Look, maybe you ought to change your drink order. Considering what I have to tell you, you might want something stiffer."

"Coffee's fine. If the going gets rough, I can always have some brandy tossed into it."

Aware of the bartender's close presence, she leaned close and whispered, "I was in Philipa's stateroom on the night she died."

"I think I'll have that brandy," he said, catching the bartender's eye.

Shaking her head, she hastened to add, "I mean I *was* there, but I left before... Actually, I was shown the door by an irate but very much alive Philipa. That was about ten-thirty."

"Jenni, start from the beginning."

She turned to see where the bartender was. "I was talking to Fritz Henning today and he told me all about the circumstances of Philipa's death."

"Did you tell him you were there that night?"

She shook her head with vehemence. "No, because Fritz started talking about you and how you mentioned Philipa had been the recipient of death threats. After I heard that I didn't dare."

"Why not?" Peter asked, puzzled.

"Because I was the one who told her I was going to kill her."

Howard Newton had always kidded Peter that he had the perfect face for radio. While Peter could convey a wide range of emotions with his voice, he didn't have a huge arsenal of facial expressions. Thus, Jenni was unable to read into what Peter was thinking or feeling as he just sat there quietly.

Noticing the bartender approaching, she whispered, "Peter, it's why I asked you to meet me. I want to tell you what really happened. And I need your advice."

Peter pointed to a table in the distant corner and suggested they take their drinks and conversation there. This way they would be out of earshot of the bartender and Peter, whose use of headsets over the years had damaged his hearing, wouldn't have to struggle to hear her.

When they'd settled, he asked, "Jenni, are saying you pushed Philipa into traffic on the Embarcadero?"

She was clearly shaken by the question. "Good lord, no! What happened to her was an accident. But I was there and I saw it all. There was a crowd of us waiting for the walk sign. A man on a cell phone stood a little to the left behind Philipa. He was carrying on a heated conversation and paying no attention to anything. Suddenly, he must have thought the light changed and he started moving forward. He bumped her and she started to fall forward. In a split second, a bike messenger grabbed her and pulled her back onto the sidewalk. The man by then had moved away, still on his cell arguing with someone."

"So where do you fit into all of this?"

Jenni leaned back and sighed. Staring at her hands which she'd placed palms down on the table, she began telling them her story rather than looking directly at Peter, such was her sense of shame. "In the seventies, my mother, Gretchen Hoyt, worked as a seamstress at I. Magnin where Philipa Crumley was this hotshot buyer. In her spare time, Mom loved to draw and design. She mostly drew because materials were expensive and we didn't have a lot of money. My dad died when I was very young. Mom was never shy about showing her designs to people. She loved their reactions which were for the most part positive. One of her designs was for a sort of hippie style jacket. I never thought much of it. Anyway, Philipa took the design and, as they say, the rest is history. When my mother went to her and accused her of stealing, Philipa laughed at her, warning her that she would have a hard time proving such an allegation. She told my mom that her best bet was to keep her mouth shut or she'd lose her job and Philipa would make it impossible for her to find work anywhere else."

"That's the jacket Philipa said was inspired by Pablo Picasso."

"That was bullshit," she said. "Mom just drew. If she was inspired by something, she never told me. All that Picasso nonsense was Philipa's idea."

"How did it become so popular?"

"She paid a rock star named Snooty who was big at the time to wear it at her concerts. Do you remember her? She was at the forefront of what was then called Snide Rock."

Peter knew the rest of the story. Her son-in-law, Howard, had told him that Philipa reveled in her short-lived career as a popular designer. So much so that this period of time took center stage in her memoir of which several hundred copies were now stashed somewhere on the ship. "Your mother must have been very angry," he remarked.

Jenni looked up at him. "Oh, no. I was the one who was spitting mad. Mom never got upset. She explained to me that it was God's plan and that was that. She told me that Philipa could steal her design, but she was not going to let that hideous woman destroy her own joy and harmony."

"Your mom sounds like she has a lot of spiritual muscle."

"Had. She died of breast cancer ten years ago." Jenni removed her hands from the table and cupped her ample breasts. "That's why these puppies get a medical look-see every year," she said, her perky smile making a brief appearance.

"So where does the death threat fit into all of this?"

Jenni's hands went back to the table and so did her eyes. "It's not my proudest moment. As you know, your boss and his wife are clients and we speak a lot. When he told me that Philipa came home the night after she was pushed into traffic convinced someone had tried to kill her, I just laughed. I'd been there and I knew otherwise."

"So you told him it was an accident."

"Uh, no. I think I commented about how preposterous the whole thing sounded and then suddenly Howard said he had to take another call. So, the following week I am in Bloomingdales and there is Philipa sniffing away at a perfume counter. When I saw here, Peter, all I could think about was hurting her. I knew I wasn't capable of doing anything physical, but I could put the fear of God in her and that seemed to me to be the next best thing. So I sneaked up behind her, lowered my voice and said, 'You were lucky last week. Next time you won't be.' You hear my voice. If you can't see me and I lower it a notch, you'd be totally convinced I was a man. Philipa was. I didn't even have to walk away. When she heard what I said, she spun around and saw only women nearby. Of course, Philipa had no idea who I was."

"Why do I think this isn't the end of the story."

"Because it isn't. Initially, I came on the cruise because I wanted to tell her to her face what I thought about her stealing the jacket design from my mother. I also wanted to tell her I was the one who threatened her." Jenni shifted nervously in her seat. "Peter, I know it sounds strange but I swear there are times I can hear my mother talking to me. And this time she was telling me to just set things right. While she was alive, Mom never let Philipa get to her. And here I had gone and done the exact opposite. I knew I needed to free myself of the enmity I carried for that woman. So that ended up being the principal reason I went to her penthouse the night she died."

Aha! You are now expecting Theodomicles to weigh in on whether your beloved parents can or cannot insert themselves lovingly or otherwise into your mortal lives even though they have long since departed. Alas, this is one of those ineffable topics that will remain so. I can say, though, that nary a soul in Eternity is troubled in any way by the folly and foibles of their mortal progeny. So, be cheered that no matter what mischief you get up to, all remains steady as she goes on this end. Now, if you chose to believe your mama or papa every once in awhile peek through the cumulus clouds, so to speak, and advise you on right from wrong – and that advice is pure and sound – then by all means listen and learn. And don't forget to say a quiet thank you.

"Philipa's reaction must have been something to behold," Peter said, thinking of his own and Liz's experiences with her and her volatile temper.

"That's the strangest thing, Peter. She was... How shall I put it? She was dismissive. In fact, she laughed at me and said she never took the threat seriously. Then she muttered something about me being a silly girl to think a prank like that could frighten her. That was the extent of her chastisement."

"But earlier you told me that when she kicked you out she was irate."

Jenni explained, "Yes, she was angry, but not at me directly. It was more like she was mad at herself for leaving me standing there while she took a phone call from some man."

"How did you know it was a man?" Peter asked.

Jenni shrugged. "I don't know. I just assumed it was a man from what little I heard."

"What did you hear?"

"You mean aside from the fact that every other word she uttered was the f-word?" Jenni shook her head. "When she first took the call, she started blasting whoever it was about the way they've planned things. Then, she said, 'Of course, I still want it.' That's when she noticed me. She told the person she'd call him right back. Then she approached me screaming and asking me why I was still there? Then she told me to get the hell out of her penthouse and stay out of her life."

"And that was about ten-thirty?"

"Give or take a few minutes. Why?"

"Fritz Henning told me the woman in the penthouse next door reported hearing a scream about midnight."

"Well, I certainly wasn't there. When I left, I went directly to my stateroom to check messages. The Florians wanted to see me, so I met them in the Covey just short of eleven. They introduced me to their son and his partner. Have you met them?" she asked, her eyes widening. Peter nodded. "They're quite a pair. Their behavior is so cautious and hesitant. It's like they've been entrusted with some dark secret and they're afraid everyone they meet is trying to find out what it is. Anyway, it turned out the Florians wanted to bring Freddie and Ben to our group events and wanted my okay."

Peter checked his watch. It was way past his bedtime. "It must have been quite a shock when you ended up booking Philipa on the cruise."

"She's not part of our group, Peter. I didn't even know she was on the cruise until Howard told me."

"That's odd." Peter was confused. "Can you find out who her travel agent is?"

"The ship is careful about us travel agents asking too many questions about guests. They don't want us poaching clients. But, in this case, I don't think they'd assume I wish to poach a dead guest. I'm sure I can. I'll have the information for you tomorrow." She looked at her watch and then at the yawning bartender. "It is getting late. Before you go, Peter, let me ask you something. I am quite fond of Howard and Naomi and over the years we've built a good working relationship. I'd like to keep them on as clients but I also want to tell them what I did. What do you think their reaction will be?"

"I can't speak for Naomi, but Howard will probably pin a medal on you."

Peter and Liz were in their respective beds, their physical frames resting comfortably on obscenely high thread count linen sheets. While their bodies oohed and aahed over the luxury bedding, their minds were busy mulling over this and that. This being the reality of Lillie Langtry. That being the supposed art theft. However, with sleep fast approaching, a weary mortal mind loves to head off in any direction it cares to, regardless of its owner's desire to keep it on track. Thus, Liz found her Lillie and art theft musings interrupted by intrusive, negative thoughts about Kevin who, because he was e-mailing and texting her constantly, was beginning to annoy her. Peter, too, found himself sidetracked by recurring dark thoughts that were sometimes bothersome. Every once in awhile he entertained serious doubts about there being anything that could remotely be called life after one *shuffles of this mortal coil* as Shakespeare so eloquently put it. He recalled one of Jack London's lines where describing a man who had just died, London wrote, *And then he knew nothing.* This night as Peter continued down this yellow brick road of metaphysical reflection, he had one other ingredient to throw into the mental stew and that was the stunning, mind-blowing, idea-altering existence of Lillie Langtry. That most certainly changes things, he told himself, smiling as he gave himself over to sleep.

chapter 15

NEITHER PETER NOR Liz saw the Ocean Glamour cautiously and slowly parallel park alongside the Ketchikan waterfront. Both had slept in. They also missed the arrival of three other cruise ships, all considerably larger than the Glamour. This quartet of floating hotels would in less than an hour announce to their guests that they have been cleared to go ashore. Ketchikan would for that day boast a population three times its normal size. There'll be no complaints from the resident Ketchikanians, though, as the visiting populace will spend the entire day shopping, eating and drinking, not necessarily in that order. After such a massive invasion of shoppers, one can only hope there'll be enough smoked salmon, ulu knives, reindeer sausage, fur mukluks and Alaskan theme-designed shot glasses for the next fleet of cruise ships headed its way.

This morning Lillie made certain her new acquaintances were up, dressed and ready for a solid day of investigative work. She woke Liz whose opening remark after seeing the lavender vision at the foot of her bed was, "Oh, Lillie, we *really, really* need to talk." Peter was not as clear-headed when Lillie tried to roust him. The best he could muster was an unintelligible mumble which Lillie considered a sufficient enough sign of life.

All three gathered in Peter's penthouse for a en suite breakfast that Bartal was busy arranging on the table, his usually efficient movements slowed by Liz's presence. The two young people exchanged smiles and the handsome butler got the distinct impression that her smile was warmer than usual, almost flirtatious. In fact, it was. As previously mentioned, Liz had spent some time last night reviewing her feelings for Kevin who, in his flood of text and e-mails, demonstrated a jealous, needy side that Liz found not to her liking. Then, recalling the despairing and dreary lyrics of his favorite group, Phrantic Phrogg, she came to the conclusion that Kevin was not the man she thought he was. Thus, this morning she was feeling resolutely single and unattached. Outside a light mist fell.

"From what I've read in the guide books," Liz said, reaching for a croissant, "this is considered a good weather day."

"Actually, Ketchikan, which is Alaska's fifth most populous city, has an average annual rainfall of 152.4 inches," Lillie announced.

"How do you know that?" Peter asked, glancing over to see that Bartal was paying no attention to their chit-chat.

"I honestly don't know. I've never been here before. It just seems to be another obscure fact that stuck in my brain," she remarked, somewhat embarrassed by these sudden outbursts.

"Tio, rain or shine I really want to go ashore. I know we don't have any excursions planned for this stop, but I'd still like to see the town."

Before Peter could respond, Bartal spoke up. "I have the middle part of the day off. I would be happy to show you around."

"You don't have to wear that penguin suit, do you?" Liz asked.

Bartal laughed. "Only if you want me to. By the way, you know ships' crews are probably the best guides you can't buy in a port of call."

"Bartal, this is awfully nice of you. Yes, I'd like that." She looked over at Peter and Lillie. "Is it okay with the two of you?" Her face reddened as she quickly realized her head count would not match Bartal's.

Fortunately, the butler's heart had only allowed him to hear her acceptance. At that point he busily went about pouring Peter's coffee, anxious to move on and finish his other morning duties. Before he left, he took Liz out to the verandah. Pointing to a large touristy, log-framed emporium with a stuffed Alaskan bear acting as doorman, he instructed Liz that he'd meet her there at eleven-thirty.

When he'd departed, the three gathered around the table laden with fruit and pastries. Liz was now on her second croissant. "Sorry, guys, I wasn't thinking a moment ago. He didn't seem to notice it, though."

"I'm not surprised. The poor man is clearly besotted. Peter and I might as well be invisible to him when you're in the room," Lillie said.

"Lillie, you are invisible," Peter reminded her. "Anyway, Liz, go ashore and have a good time. At least you'll have a chance to spend time with someone more your age."

"But I'm having such a good time hanging with my sexagenarian uncle and a 155-year-old professional beauty," she teased.

"I'll have you know, young lady, those numbers are worthless. I am ageless and stage-less," Lillie declared. "And it would do you well to embrace that same philosophy." Her tone was gentle and loving.

"I'm sorry. Where's my head? Would you rather I stay and help in the investigation?" Liz asked..

"No, we can manage," Peter spoke up. "Go have some fun. Oh, and if you can, bring back a newspaper or two."

"Why don't you just go to the computer center and read them on-line?"

"I miss getting printers' ink all over my hands."

"And you, Lillie? Are you okay with me going in to Ketchikan?" Liz asked, desiring her blessing as well.

"Yes, do go and have a wonderful time. Peter and I can handle things." Turning her attention to Peter, she said, "Unless you also have some pressing obligations. I know you have certain responsibilities."

Now you can't blame Peter for laughing when she brought up responsibilities. By this point in the cruise, he realized his duties, such as they were, were so minimal that it was almost embarrassing. Of course, there were the frequent chance meetings with members of his travel group but as affability is his middle name, Peter found most of these encounters to be enjoyable and rarely inconvenient. Even their scheduled events required little heavy lifting. In fact, after these last few days, if asked, Peter would shout it to the far hills and beyond that anyone desiring the cushiest job in the world, they should find a way to become a minor celebrity and then offer to host a cruise.

When Liz had gone, Lillie asked Peter to get a notepad. She'd memorized a series of numbers she'd found scribbled on a paper near the phone in Philipa's penthouse. "I don't know if it means anything, Peter, but it's the only thing I could find in the penthouse that seemed worth looking into. It is my belief these numbers might somehow relate to that phone call Philipa received just before she threw Jenni out of her penthouse."

Peter looked at her in amazement. "Lillie, you were there when I spoke with Jenni last night."

"I was careful to stay out of your view. Our relationship, my dear Peter, is still in its infancy and I knew there was a chance you might find my presence in a social setting to be, if not disruptive, certainly distracting, " she explained.

"Seems to me we've gone past the baby stage if you're dear Petering me."

"I have always been fond of terms of endearments," she explained. "Now, here are the numbers and the way they appeared on the notepaper."

She recited and he wrote. As Lillie instructed, he put a space between the first two and the next three numbers. The sixth number was separated by a hyphen. "48 376-3," he read aloud. "Lillie, these numbers could represent anything. Anyway, why all this interest in Philipa? What could she possibly have to do with a painting stolen from the Tate?"

"I am convinced there is a connection," she said. "Call it feminine intuition. I just think we ought to check that combination of numbers."

"Fine. Let's start with her son," Peter said, reaching for his cell phone. Moving to the verandah, he dialed Howard Newton only to learn that he was no longer the station manager. He stood at the railing looking down on the buzz of activity of the Ketchikan waterfront while he listened to Howard's secretary tell him that his former boss had resigned as soon as he returned from Alaska with the body of his mother-in-law. She gave Peter his new cell phone number. While he dialed, Lillie came close to him. He felt uncomfortable. "I just want to listen in," she whispered. Howard answered on the first ring. "Peter, good to hear from you," he sang, his voice as chirpy as one of his beloved Sooty Terns.

"Howard, catch me up. I'm told you left the station."

"Don't let this go to your head, but when you left things changed and not for the good. That idiot morning show replacement they foisted on me was a daily challenge. I just realized it wasn't worth sticking around. Of course, Philipa's death helped speed up the process. So, my friend, why the call? Everything must be smooth sailing now that my mother-in-law is no longer the ship's menace du jour."

"Actually, I had a question regarding her."

"Better get in line then."

"What's going on?" Peter asked, making himself comfortable as the answer would, no doubt, be a lengthy one given Howard's tendency to ramble.

"When we returned from Alaska, Naomi and I... You know we're co-executors of her estate? Anyway, we were anxious to settle all of Philipa's affairs in the shortest period of time so we can hightail it to Hawaii. I was educated as an accountant, so my job was to handle the financial side of the estate. Naomi went off to New York to deal with her mother's personal property. At first glance, it all looked real simple. Most everything is in a trust and we are the major benefactors, although there are a couple of charities that will get some money. One is the Midtown Manhattan Women's Tattoo Removal Center where, if a cash-strapped young lady is experiencing tattoo regret, she can have it removed free of charge. Philipa was passionate about women not defiling their bodies. It's a good thing she never knew her own daughter has a cute Marbled Murrelet on her right butt cheek."

"A little too much information, Howard."

"Maybe so, but for me it's a real turn-on," he said lustily. "Anyway, as I said, aside from the two charities..."

"Please, I don't need to know about the second one."

"So the big news is we hit a bump in the road. Seems my mother-in-law left us with more than we wished to deal with."

"Certainly not the money part?"

"No, absolutely no problem there. The woman had a ton of the green stuff. The president will probably treat us to a night in the Lincoln bedroom after he hears what we're going to have to cough up to cover the estate tax. Nope, it's certainly not the money. The problem is Philipa's art collection which I have to say I always thought was pretty damned impressive. Naomi has been going through it deciding what to keep and what to send to auction. She's working with a top-notch New York auction house called Bidderup and Selloff. Anyway, Clifford Bidderup told her he thought several of the paintings were hot."

"Hot as in great, hot as in really cool or hot as in stolen?"

There was a heavy silence. Peter waited. If Lillie had the power to nudge Peter she would have. Howard finally replied, "Hot as in stolen! He thought there may be as many as four. He advised us to contact the police. Naomi did, but these days the local constabularies don't have the experts who can investigate these kinds of shenanigans. She got shipped over to the FBI where they have this elite art squad. They looked at the entire collection and sure enough they identified four stolen pieces. And get this, all of them came from museums. Two from the states and two from Europe. Can you believe it? My mother-in-law, the art thief."

"Surely, Philipa didn't steal them?"

Howard laughed. "Just joking. Can you picture that foul-mouthed witch in a black jumpsuit rappelling down a museum wall in to snatch a Monet? No, she didn't steal them, but I'm certain she bought them."

"Howard, I don't know much about the art world, but I do know that even museums and galleries can be snookered into buying forgeries and stolen art. Could Philipa have purchased those paintings thinking they were legitimate works of art?"

"Actually, Naomi has receipts for all four of them. Seems they were purchased over a six year time span from Gallery Claude in Sag Harbor. Purchase prices ran from two to five hundred dollars with frames."

"At that price they'd have to be copies."

"Peter, learn your art lingo, please. They are called classical reproductions. The problem is the paintings are the real thing and the receipts are fake. No such gallery exists in the Hamptons or anywhere else for that matter."

"How are the FBI treating Naomi and you?"

"Okay. They seem to understand the strange position we've been put in and they appreciate us being upfront about everything. We've made it clear that we will cover the costs to ship the paintings back to wherever they came from. Of course, they'd love to know how she got her hands on them. Unfortunately she's not around to tell them. Which is a good thing. Knowing her they'd have to resort to physical torture."

Lillie whispered, "Tell him we might be able to help."

Peter put a finger to his lips. "Howard, I've got some numbers I took off a notepad in Philipa's penthouse. Write them down and see if they match anything in your files." Howard did just that, telling Peter he would call him later in the day with the results.

"Before you go, there has to be a reason why your mother-in-law was on this particular cruise. Our suspicions are that it wasn't to see brown bears and bald eagles."

"Our?"

"Did I say that?" he said, glancing at his lavender side-kick. "I meant *my* suspicion. One last question. Did Philipa ever express any interest in Lillie Langtry?"

"Only in the sense that she was utterly fascinated by that period of time in England. She has numerous art books on Whistler and some of his contemporaries. There's also quite a collection of books by and about Oscar Wilde. And, let's see, I think there are four or so paintings by minor artists of the time and three or so reproductions from the better known painters. They are all legit. Philipa often mentioned that she would have loved to live in those times. Why do you ask?"

"Just curious. Call me back when you know something about that set of numbers."

Lillie moved to the other side of the verandah. "Peter, in my opinion, Mrs. Crumley-Figg was on this ship to buy a stolen painting," she said confidently. "It could be the Millais."

Peter walked into the penthouse and picked up the auction circular. "Maybe we ought to take a leisurely walk around the sixth deck. They display a lot of the auction paintings in the hallways. Let's learn what we can before actually talking to the people involved in running the operation. Then we can head to the Portside Bistro and have an iced coffee." Peter looked over at Lillie and grinned. "Funny, I'm beginning to treat you like a real person."

Indignant, Lillie snapped, "Peter, I am a real person."

He threw his hands up. "Sorry, wrong choice of words. Of course, you are real. You're just missing a few body parts and a couple of senses, but otherwise..."

Lillie laughed, "I know what you meant to say. Ours is certainly an unusual relationship. Now, listen to me, what I have to say is important as this is going to be our first time going out in public as a couple."

"Lillie, this isn't a date."

Ignoring his protest, se continued gently, "I just want you to know that I am fully aware that one of us cannot be seen or heard by others, and I realize the social importance of you always appearing to be alone when I am in your company. That said, I am not planning on being a quiet, submissive ghost on your arm. Rather, I will be offering what I can when it seems appropriate. Perhaps, we can concoct some kind of signal that will serve as an acknowledgement when you can't respond to me directly." It was agreed Peter would pull on his left ear lobe, a gesture he swore was something he never did on a regular basis.

Does this mild hectoring on the part of our dear Lillie cause one to think she may have romantic aspirations? Has she set her sights on Peter? She may have. As a ghost, Lillie comes complete with most of the accoutrements of a mortal being. Like you, she has feelings and emotions, so it's entirely conceivable the former professional beauty once again had romantic stirrings.

Our intrepid pair of investigators decided on their way down to the sixth deck to head directly to the computer center. Peter, knowing so little about the business side of art, how it operates and the language it employs, felt a quick tutorial might help. In a matter of minutes, he was googling "shipboard auctions." He and Lillie were surprised by their findings. It seemed these kinds of sea-going auctions have had more than their fair share of detractors. Caveat emptor was the overarching theme on most of them. Several sites, in fact, reported in detail about a nasty class action lawsuit brought against one particularly large gallery and cruise line. Finally they clicked on a web site that offered what seemed to them to be a forthright, intelligent how-to lesson on purchasing art at a shipboard auction. Lesson number one was on provenance and the role it plays when acquiring fine art. Lillie and Peter scrolled through several examples of genuine provenances to demonstrate what information they should contain. They read about fakes and forgeries and their proliferation. They were advised to disregard meaningless phrases like "hand embellished" and "unique variations" and the alluring sale's pitch about art as an investment. They were warned that what they buy on the ship might not be what is eventually shipped to their home. Peter signed off and whispered, "Absolutely fascinating stuff. Ready to go look at what might be some questionable art?"

Leaving the computer center they found themselves surrounded by paintings in ornate frames lining both walls of the hallway. It was a riot of colors, styles and sizes. All in a row were puzzling abstracts standing next to scenes of comely lasses on swings or armed with parasols. These were positioned next to dramatic seascapes and serene landscapes. Peppered into this potpourri of salable art were the inevitable nudes featuring mostly the feminine backside. Peter recognized some names; Picasso, Miro, Chagall, Warhol, Rockwell and Dali. Then he remembered reading that four of those were the most copied artists in the world. Still other works sported artists' names that were unknown to him. He and Lillie worked slowly, perusing each painting. Some they liked, some left them cold, still others were unexplainable.

"Ramsey!"

Peter looked up from a signed lithograph by Gerard Plaznorski that featured the side view of a cow whose body was a huge crossword puzzle. The sky was filled with clues across and down. Next to the cow was a naked woman wearing glasses with a pencil poised to fill in thirty-two across on the cow's hide. Her entire backside was a sudoku puzzle. The piece was called *"Why?"* It was a question Peter found himself asking.

Flannery approached, as usual his voice arriving first. "Ramsey, I am in deep, deep shit. Where can we get a drink?"

Peter once again marveled at his complete mastery of dishevelment. This morning's gear consisted of a wrinkled Brooks Brothers white button-down dress shirt worn half out of a pair of slept-in looking khakis, apparel that perfectly complimented the newspaper editor's five o'clock shadow and uncombed hair.

The two men and Lillie found the Portside Bistro bustling. Peter located one empty table in the corner. Ramsey ordered the beer of the day, an Alaskan pale ale called Sitka

Bear Paw IPA. "If you order some cute coffee drink with a long name, I'm leaving," he barked.

Peter recognized the server as one of the wine stewards in the dining room. "I'll have an mocha-cappucino-latte with twice-roasted Brazilian mountain beans, two and a half per cent soy milk and a sprinkling of non-fat, lo-cal Belgian chocolate chips. Oh, and make it decaf."

"Sir, I, uh..."

"Just kidding. I'll have whatever beer you're bringing my dissolute companion."

Flannery, like Jenni Rodriquez from the night before, preferred talking to his hands that were palm down on the table. "My wife has signed us up for a dance contest."

"Then you should be rehearsing instead of drinking with me."

He looked up. "Don't be such a smart-ass. This is serious."

"You're right," Peter admitted. "So, when and where and what kind of dance?"

"Tomorrow evening at five-thirty in the Glamour Lounge."

"And the dance?"

"The tango," he replied. "What's worse is there's only one other couple signed up."

"Forgive me for saying this, but you don't really look like the tango type."

"Yeah, well appearances can deceive," he said, taking a swig of the oddly named local microbrew. "I have some pretty damned good dance moves. Even the instructors think our tango is technically solid.

"So what's the problem?"

"Mary Pat says there's one important element missing in my tango. She says it will cost us points."

"What's that?"

"Passion," he muttered.

"I beg your pardon?"

Flannery face darkened. "Ramsey, why is that every time I have to tell you something that's important but personal, you always make me say it twice? What I said is Mary Pat thinks I lack passion." He slowly enunciated the last word, turning it into a three syllable word.

"It is a major ingredient in the tango," Peter remarked.

Frustrated, Dave hissed, "I know that!"

"So what can I do to help?"

"Any chance you can order me up some passion between now and five-thirty tomorrow evening?"

Then Peter spotted Petra Dosynk at the bar. "Dave, I think I can."

chapter 16

ERNEST HEMINGWAY once wrote that he could get his writing juices flowing by coming up with one true sentence. That sort of thing comes easily to those of us here in Eternity. We are famous for our truthful utterances. Papa's comment, though, addresses an air-breathing scribe's sometimes difficult challenge in finding mortal truth, elusive as it can be. It is a worthy ambition, though, and certainly ought to be among the top ten tips in any creative writing class. I mention all this because the following few words are a perfect example of Hemingway's idea of a true sentence: *David Flannery's wife could not have picked a worse dance for tomorrow evening's ballroom competition.* Drunk, Flannery might capture gold in an Irish step-dance contest. But the passionate tango? Not in a million years. While the newspaper editor positively brimmed over with a fervency that fueled his irascibility, regrettably he possessed nary a drop of that I-want-you-at-any-cost lustfulness which one needs to successfully navigate the floor in a tango battle.

When Peter first found out about his colleague's shortcoming, he felt bad because he had no idea how he might help. Passion, to be honest, wasn't one of his strong points either. But then, spotting Petra Dosynk at the bistro bar, he realized, even though it was the longest of shots, if anyone had a chance at helping Flannery succeed, it was he. Excusing himself and leaving his companion to his beer and brooding, he headed for the bar, taking a seat next to his eccentric acquaintance.

"Ah, Mr. Ramsey. As you can see, I like this coffee contraption that we had yesterday," Petra said, shifting his bulky frame to more properly observe his guest.

"It's a concoction, Petra. And, please, call me Peter."

"Explain the difference, please, Peter" Dosynk said, taking another sip.

"You see that expresso machine over there," he said, pointing to the bistro's elaborate coffee maker. "That is a contraption. What it makes is a concoction."

Dosynk beamed. "I see. You explain it well."

Peter got right to it. "Speaking of concoctions, yesterday you told me about this syrup you make."

His newfound friend's smile stretched the width of his face and he shouted, "Doshma blava!" If you're curious about that Kwyrki expletive, its literal translation is "Kiss my constipated goat!" Petra and his countrymen use it in a variety of ways. "So you met someone and want to try it. If you need for tonight we have to get some pancakes right away," he said with a sense of urgency.

"No, it's not for me," Peter said. "See my friend over there?" Petra glanced over at the scowling beer drinker and nodded. "He's in trouble, Petra. His wife entered them in tomorrow night's dance competition. They are doing the tango. He has explained to me that he has all the moves down pat. However, his wife told him that he doesn't possess that certain kind of passion that will make the difference between the winner and the rest of the dancers. He's a tough guy by nature but he has a soft spot for his wife, so he really wants to do well."

"I have seen this peculiar dance," Petra said. "The man wears a frown and stares hard at the woman. The woman frowns and stares back. Get him to frown like he's doing now. No one will know the difference."

"I wish it were that simple," Peter said. "But when I saw you here at the coffee bar, an idea came to me. If I had some of that syrup, I could invite him to breakfast tomorrow and somehow get him to order pancakes..."

"Or waffles or French toast," Petra added helpfully.

Peter nodded and continued. "Right. Anyway, I would see that he has something in front of him that requires syrup."

Petra was quiet for a moment. Then he leaned in and asked in a low voice, "You say this man is confident he can do the tango?"

Peter looked over at the plump, disheveled Flannery. "Forget what he looks like. If he says he can, then he can. I believe him. We just need to put a little fire in his belly."

Petra laughed. "What a fascinating expression. I must remember that. All right, I will have some of my syrup delivered to your stateroom this afternoon. It will be a small amount. I wish I could be generous, but I brought along just enough for family use."

"I understand. I truly appreciate this."

Petra dropped his smile. "Peter, I told you yesterday there's always the chance the syrup won't work."

Peter suddenly spotted Lillie on the other side of Petra. She had been so quiet and out of his sight, he'd had forgot about her. "Peter, assure him that it *will* work. I have an idea," she said.

He tugged at his ear lobe to indicate he'd heard her. "Petra, I think I know how I can make it work even if it doesn't actually *do* anything."

"How?"

Peter hoped Dosynk would just take his word and not ask for details. "You asked me how, huh?"

"Yes, how are you going to make it work, please?"

Lillie cued him. "Tell him you'll give the syrup to Mr. Flannery and then use the power of suggestion on him." Peter tugged on his ear lobe and repeated what she said to Dosynk. For someone suggesting he could successfully persuade Flannery that the marginally magical syrup would propel his libido into the red zone, he wasn't at all convincing.

"If you plan to hypnotize him, why would you need the syrup?" Petra asked innocently.

"No, not hypnosis," Peter said, unsure if he could properly explain his inchoate strategy. He gave it a go anyway: "My plan is to take him to breakfast tomorrow. Without mentioning you, of course, I willI tell him of the syrup's super power. I will not even hint that it might not work. It is best for Dave to think that it always does the trick. Then I will in the strongest terms possible, warn him that he must stay away from his wife, emphasizing that any physical contact, no matter how minimal, will lead to more contact and we don't want that to happen. Their first body-to-body connection must occur only when they are on the dance floor and the music starts. And the rest will be dance competition history," he said a little too weakly.

Petra laughed and Lillie giggled. Peter waited for a response from either one of them. Dosynk went first. "Peter, do you think this plan of yours can really work? It is very important to give me an honest answer."

But before Peter could respond, Dosynk waved his hand. "Forget my question. How can you know if it will work? Maybe I should explain why I am most anxious about this." WIthout turning around, he said with a jerk of his head, "Take a look at the couple in the far corner by the window."

Peter did as directed. He saw a woman in a tight, white designer tee-shirt that fit like a second skin, her straw blonde hair pulled backed away from her face and wrapped in a tight bun. Her slender but muscular counterpart wore a skin-tight black tee-shirt, his gelled, jet-black hair combed straight back. They weren't talking. They were there only to be looked at. Or so it seemed to Peter who said, "I don't think they have an ounce of body fat between them. They are a very striking couple, although he looks quite bit older. Who are they?"

Petra put a beefy hand on Peter's shoulder and replied, "Those two are your friend's competition in the tango."

"Oh boy!"

Even Lillie issued a deep sigh.

"His name is Anatoly Plushenko and she is Svetlana Plovanovavichskaya." Dosynk rubbed his face, a mug so malleable, it appeared for a second as if he'd accidentally rearranged his facial features. But in a flash, his nose, mouth and lips were back where they belonged. "They are from Moscow where she is supposedly well known fashion model and he owns a popular restaurant. He is probably a gangster."

"I would have guessed they were professional ballroom dancers."

Dosynk grinned. Mangling an old adage, he said, "Looks are not good tellers of stories. My friends tell me I look like one of those old Soviet leaders you used to see on the reviewing stand in Moscow on May Day. But I am actually a real pussykitten."

Peter let it go. "What's your connection to them?"

"We were at the same blackjack table last night. It was a pleasant evening until he showed up with his girl friend. He started talking loudly as soon as he sat down. He got mad when the casino wouldn't raise the betting limits like he says they do for him in Moscow. And he kept shouting for drinks. Then he brought up the dance contest and began bragging how he and his lady friend were going to show the other dancers how to really do the tango. The final straw was when he asked me where I come from. When I told him, he started making jokes about my country."

"What did you do?"

"I told him I was tired of hearing him talk, that I only wanted to play cards. Then I told him if he was so eager to make a large bet, I would bet ten thousand dollars American that they would lose the dance contest."

Peter's eyes widened. "And he took the wager?"

Petra nodded. "Oh yes. He told the other players they were witnesses. Then he came over to me and said, 'Did you make that bet because you don't like me?' I said it was, and he laughed and said, 'Not liking me is going to cost you ten grand, old man.' So there you are, Peter. It was a pretty stupid thing to do." Petra Dosynk looked over at the two Russians and shrugged. "But, what's done is done."

Peter stole another glance at the well-toned pair. "I'm not saying they are intimidating but they look like they're dancing even when they're sitting down."

Petra took a final sip of his specialty drink and turned toward Peter. "Ah, but now, thanks to you and your dancing friend, I have someone to cheer for," he said, standing to take his leave. "Peter, you must do all you can to put that fire in your friend's belly. Remember, he must stay away from his wife until it is time to dance. You will have to watch him like a hawk."

Warming to his role as self-appointed manager of Team Tango, he said enthusiastically, "Oh, I will, Petra." Looking behind him he saw Flannery had left the bistro. "By the way, I think it best we don't tell him you have ten thousand riding on him,"

Peter and Lillie returned to the area where much of the art that would be auctioned later in the cruise was on display. They closely examined the paintings and any accompanying descriptions, searching for any sequence of numbers that might resemble those Lillie took from Philipa's room.

"Peter, look here," Lillie said excitedly.

Peter looked up and down the hallway. It was quiet and empty of people. "Lillie, what am I supposed to looking at?"

"Look at the right side of the frame of that hideous abstract. There is a small white label taped to the frame with a series of numbers on them. Two numbers together followed by a space then three in a row, and the first two numbers are the same as those on the note in Philipa's room."

Then the others must be appropriately marked as well, Peter thought. Eager as he was to check the paintings, he was wary of being spotted moving or touching them. "Lillie, it shouldn't be a problem for you to check the reverse sides of these paintings."

"It isn't and I have, Peter. They all seem to have identical white labels and the first two numbers are four and eight just like Philipa's," she said.

"It's not much of a stretch to imagine that forty-eight represents the number of this particular shipboard auction. The next three numbers must identify the individual paintings up for sale. Do you see anything with a dash and another digit after the three numbers?"

"I don't. Peter, we have to talk this through and we can't do it here. Let's return to your penthouse where we can have some privacy."

He looked about and saw they were still alone. "Lillie, one thing before we go. Look at the labels again and see if one of them matches the set of three numbers on the note."

Just then Fluoride Freddie and his partner came out of the computer center, headed in Peter's direction. He turned his back to them and pretended to be concentrating on a large unframed canvas on an easel, hoping he would go unnoticed.

"Ah, Mr. Ramsey," Gertie Florian's Pride and Joy shouted. "Not going ashore?"

"Perhaps later."

"How very exciting running into you here. I had no idea you were a fan of the visual arts," he said in a contrived Oxford English accent that caused Lillie to giggle and exclaim, "Is he trying to sound like my dear Oscar?"

"Actually, you caught me trying to sort this one out," Peter replied, nodding toward the painting and ignoring Lillie.

Freddie gave the piece a cursory glance and said, "That might be a mistake. I think you're giving it far more thought than it deserves," he said. "Just out of curiosity, though, what do you think you see?"

Peter looked more closely at the riot of inharmonious colors and puzzling textures. "I have no idea. If the painter is trying to express something or there's some purpose to it all, I fail to grasp it."

Freddie's partner, Ben, who had yet to smile, entered the discussion, his Oxford English accent anything but contrived: "You'll find the artist, Mr Ramsey, would be quite content hearing your candid reaction. You see, this is a perfect example of a new school of artistic expression that is getting some attention in the art world. It is called Vague and the artists are known as Vaguists. This piece, appropriately titled '*Whatever*,' is by Tiffany Ann Timberlane. She is a former communications' major and cheerleader from UCLA who reportedly paints in between auditions for reality TV shows in Los Angeles. Other Vaguists have similar backgrounds. And, yes, she is tall, blonde and very, very vague."

"Please tell me you're making that up."

"I wish it were so, Mr. Ramsey. As you can no doubt tell from my sardonic tone, I am not a fan." Pointing to the work next to it, he added, "My personal tastes run toward this lovely plein air by Dewitt Masterson, a Carmel artist of some renown. Sadly, that monstrosity we're discussing will probably sell for several thousand dollars more than this beautiful seascape."

"Peter, Masterson's painting has the exact same numbers as Philipa's minus the dash and extra digit," Lillie said excitedly.

After tugging on his ear lobe, Peter turned his attention back to the ebullient Freddie and the droll Ben. "You two seem to know an awful lot about art."

"I'm sorry. How rude of me," Freddie said, rolling his eyes. "I just remembered how hurried introductions were when we all met last night. Let me make up for that." Puffing his chest, beaming with pride and staring adorably at this partner, Freddie said, "Peter, this is Benjamin Lytton-Crisp of the Lytton-Crisp Gallery in Winona, Minnesota. The gallery is in the same office complex as our dental offices. As we had so many common interests, it was ordained we be together. How we met, though, does have its hysterical moments. It was a snowy night, the kind that only Winona can produce..."

Benjamin put a hand on Freddie's arm and gently stopped him mid-sentence. "Freddie, we really must go. Remember we have to be in Ketchikan in less than an hour and I simply refuse to go ashore in this outfit."

Lillie and Peter returned to his penthouse. Petra had already had the syrup delivered. Peter was surprised by the small amount. However, Peter knew Petra would give him a sufficient dose as he had so much riding on the Flannerys doing well.

Lillie watched as he carefully examined the small bottle. "Curious to try a little bit? Room service can have a pancake up here in no time," she teased.

chapter 17

"My heavens," Lillie exclaimed, aware of the mischief in her question and the discomfort it brought to the man who stood at the foot of the bed. "I do believe you're blushing, Mr. Ramsey."

"I am not," he snapped. Still, he could not resist glancing in the mirror where he discovered two reddening cheeks located just below and to the right and left of his nose, a feature he didn't consider one of his best. Further, thanks to the coolness of the room, his proboscis was now a glacier blue. "Anyway, I have no interest in trying that syrup. I only hope for Dave's sake it works on him. Or, at the very least, I can get him to think it does."

Satisfied that all was being done for his colleague that could be, Lillie suddenly moved things in a different direction. "Do you believe in God?" she asked.

Now there's a conversational game changer for you. If you're wondering whether this means I am calling the shots from my lofty perch, the answer is a firm no. This was as they say in football parlance an audible. You see, when someone returns as Lillie had, we scrupulously avoid any direct contact with them while they are — for lack of a better term — ghosting. As a result, they must again rely on faith alone when assessing their own circumstances. That said, though, I was delighted with the inquiry as I am a huge fan of product placement in stories, particularly when said product is worth promoting. And it doesn't get any better than my Boss.

Peter, too, was surprised by the query from the amorphous figure who now seemed to be reclining on the left side of his bed. "I do," he said after a time, nodding as if he needed to to give his reply added weight.

Lillie laughed. "You make it sound like I am swearing you in to give some sort of sordid testimony."

"You threw me off balance with that question. In fact, Lillie, you seem to take delight in doing that."

"Doing what, Peter?"

"Throwing me off balance."

"I don't mean to," she said gently, her tone apologetic, "but you are teasable. Is that a word, do you think? I was, though, quite serious when I asked if you believed in God. He has been in my thoughts lately."

"Sorry to say He hasn't been in mine," Peter confessed, opening the sliding glass door and looking down at the midday bustle of showery Ketchikan. "I don't know why, but when things get crazy, and right now they are really, really crazy, I seem to forget I have a spiritual side."

"It is more than just a side of you," she said.

Peter looked at the luminous vision. "You're certainly living proof of that."

"Come sit by me," Lillie said.

Now you might think– I certainly would – that Peter would dismiss this invitation, thinking Lillie was just up to more mischief. But he did not. Rather, he was excited by her request as he was curious to know if there might be more to her than just that lavender glow and her ability to see, hear and speak. By joining her on the bed he thought he might discover something more to her like a physical warmth or a subtle fragrance that can only be detected close up. As regards that, I just made a mental note to myself that the next time I send someone back in that lavender getup, I might as well have them smelling like a Provencal country-side on a summer's day.

Peter moved away from the verandah door and, propping up a couple of pillows, stretched out on the bed. "So tell me about these thoughts of God," he said, turning toward her, his nose twitching as he tried to pick up any evidence of an odor.

"Peter, what is that you are you doing with your nose? By the way, do you know it is blue?"

"Yes, I know it's blue," he huffed. "The cool air is the reason. As to your other question, I wondered if you had a smell."

"I prefer the word fragrance," she said. "So, do I?"

"No, you don't."

"You sound disappointed."

Actual, Peter was. However, ever the diplomat, he merely shrugged and said, "No, not at all. I was just curious."

His behavior continued to vex Lillie. "Peter, what are on earth are you doing now? If you stare any harder, your eyes will fall out of your head."

What he had just realized was that up to now he had always given her her own space just the way he would any person. Now that they were this close to each other, side by side in bed, he wondered what if anything he would feel if he stretched his arm out to touch her. He thought it best that he ask first, which he did, again blushing.

"You are a gentleman for asking and I appreciate that," she said. "Go right ahead and poke away to your heart's content. I possess no parts that are considered off-limits," she laughed.

He watched as his right hand easily moved through the the fascinating chimera who lay beside him and landed on the pillow that would have been her physical support had she needed one.

"What do you feel?" she asked.

He answered with a question: "Did you ever smoke?"

"I don't know what that has to do with anything, but, yes, there were a few occasions when a gentleman friend and I would in a private setting enjoy a cigar with our brandy. As for cigarettes, I tried them but found them lacking. Not much style to them, I'm afraid."

"So I am guessing you probably never smoked in bed after making love?"

"Mr. Ramsey, where are going with this line of questioning?"

"I was just thinking of scenes in movies where a couple are in bed and they are both inhaling up a storm..."

"I beg your pardon?"

"I mean they are both smoking cigarettes," he explained. "A pale grey cloud of smoke hangs in the air above them. Then the woman leaves and the only evidence of her presence is this wispy smoke that hovers over her side of the bed. You're like that smoke."

"Well, thank you very much," she sniffed.

Peter smiled and added quickly, "But less offensive and more colorful."

"Peter, enough of this foolishness," she said. "Let's talk about who I am."

"How would you describe yourself?"

"I would say I am easily explained but not so easily understood. Quite frankly, my dear, I am an abstraction that somehow you can see and hear. And I believe the reason for that is so we can get about doing what I am sure I was sent here to do and that's find my painting. I am now also convinced there is yet another important purpose to this visit of mine but we can discuss that later. For now, just know that I am a spiritual idea and that's that."

"Well, you're certainly my idea of a great idea." It was a remark that would have worked better coming from Groucho Marx. Hearing how banal he made it sound, he wondered if he ought to have coughed up something a little more thoughtful.

Lillie's response confirmed he should have. "Peter, you disappoint me. Here I am going on about weighty notions and your only reaction is that I am your idea of a great idea."

It didn't sound right coming from her either. "Lillie, I apologize, but I truly did mean it as a compliment."

"Peter, no lady wishes to hear that she's simply an idea, great or otherwise."

Peter was once again thrown off balance as Lillie scolded him for what he thought was a sincere mea culpa. He stared at the shape next to him. "You're doing it again, aren't you?"

Giggling, she said, "Gotcha."

Peter shook his head. "Please tell me you didn't use that expression in your day. I can't picture Oscar Wilde putting gotcha into one of his poems or plays."

"Oscar certainly would have found it an unattractive word. But you are correct, it wasn't around to be used. Short for 'I have got you', the term actually came into popularity in 1932 according to most respected etymological sources."

"How do you do that?" he asked, impressed by her collection of Delphic facts and the robotic manner she assumes when she dishes them out. "What's odd is I get the feeling even you are surprised you know these things."

"Ah, the mysteries of me," she sighed. "Peter, I, too, am trying to figure me out. That bit of trivia just popped into my head. Well, my head if I had one. Quite frankly, I'm as puzzled by how I do it as you are."

Let me explain what it is that has them baffled. When one sheds their mortal trappings and becomes a full-fledged, card-carrying eternal spirit, one of the big benefits is Awareness. Not just self-awareness. The whole enchilada. All is explained, all is known, all is understood. When a spirit returns to the mortal world in the same capacity as Lillie, they must once again take on a life of rather severe limitations. But it seems our degaussing technique needs some work. The result is many go back with enough tidbits of information stuck to them that they'd break the bank on the game show *Jeopardy* if Alex accepted ghost contestants. We here in Eternity live with this minor flaw, which is, if you think about it, so much better than organizing a massive ghost recall.

Both heard the card key. A second later, Liz bounced into the room carrying two bags of Ketchikan merchandise. "Guys, I had the best time," she announced, her mood buoyant. Then she took notice of Lillie and her uncle with his outstretched right arm resting on Lillie's pillow. Staring disapprovingly at the pair, she shook her head. "Tio, I really, really hoped you'd have a shipboard romance on this cruise. I even have someone in mind. But in my wildest dreams, I never thought I'd catch you in an intimate moment with a woman who is seven, maybe eight... Oh, I don't know how many decades older. And then, on top of that, she's dead! This has to go into the record books as the ultimate cougar relationship. "

"Whatever does she mean, Peter?" Lillie asked.

"Older women who date younger men are called cougars," he explained, moving his hand off her pillow.

"I'd call them smart," she laughed.

"So just what are the two of you up to?" Liz asked, first tossing her bags on the small sofa and then straddling the corner chair.

Peter explained how they ended up in bed together. From the way, his niece was looking at Lillie, he knew she understood his curiosity. Next, he brought her up to date on their morning, including the challenge of readying Dave Flannery for the tango competition and their suspicions about the ship's art auction operation.

"Funny, I thought that Petra person was selling you a bill of goods when he talked about his homemade viagra-like syrup. Now, I pray it's the real thing and Dave will be turned into a sex-crazed dancing fool." she said.

"We all pray for that, my dear, but not necessarily in those words," Lillie remarked.

Liz ignored the mild rebuke of her choice of words and asked instead, "So you think the shipboard auction people are somehow involved in Lillie's missing painting?"

Peter answered. "They could be. All we know is that a series of numbers on a painting on display match those Lillie found in Philipa's stateroom. And Howard has confirmed that they have discovered stolen art among the pieces in Philipa's personal art collection in her home in New York. So, we think she might have been on this cruise to buy something. As to one of the paintings being Lillie's..."

Lillie finished his thought, "My being here is enough to convince me that it is on this very vessel. It only stands to reason. If the thieves were trying to sell it in, let's say Washington DC, then I would be there scaring the daylights out of one of your politicians instead of being here in these lovely surroundings dealing with you two delightful creatures."

Liz clapped her hands together and laughed. "Lillie, this is sooo weird. Having you here seems so natural and comfortable. I'm really going to miss you when you go?"

"Thank you, Liz."

"So, what's next?" she asked excitedly.

Peter answered. "We were just about to talk about that when you came in. By the way, how was your day in Ketchikan with Bartal?"

Liz shrugged her shoulders. "Pleasant enough. He's very sweet and gentlemanly, but there's nothing there romance-wise. We met up with some of his friends at this really funky bar. They were all very nice. They're going to try to sneak me into one of their crew parties sometime."

"All right, my dears, let us talk about our next step," Lillie said.

Peter bounded out of bed. "First, let me call our tango competitor and nail down breakfast," he said, reaching for the bedside phone. Dave answered on the first ring. He seemed puzzled by the invitation but accepted and agreed to meet Peter in the Oasis Court at eight-thirty the following morning.

Putting the phone down, Peter announced: "Good. Now that that's done, I'm all yours."

In a soft voice, Lillie said, "Unfortunately, Peter, you are not *all* ours."

Now there is a perfect example of the kind of provocative sentence one wishes for when bringing a chapter to an end. There's a marvelous teasing quality about it which leaves the reader with something to mull over while they take a break from reading to, perhaps, sneak outside for a smoke. Unless, of course, you've decided that particular recreation is endangering your precious time on earth and, instead, you opt to hit the fridge for a shot of carrot juice. Interesting how these staying-alive, staying-healthy, staying-young issues are more than middling in your mind. However, should you give my occasional statements about the unlimited benefits found here in Eternity any credence, then one would think the resulting grand expectation of such a glorious never-ending future trumps temporary physical anxieties over such concerns like good colon health. That said, however, this chapter continues.

Saving Peter from having to ask what it was she meant by her remark, Lillie explained, "You see, Peter, I told you earlier I know I am here to recover my painting. However, I also pointed out that I have since discovered yet another purpose for my being. And, indeed, it may be the more important of the two. I believe I am here to – for lack of a better term – mentor you as you enter this next phase of your life. You, my friend, are now in my care."

"Obviously, whether I like it or not," Peter mumbled, flabbergasted at what he'd just heard.

"No, that would mean haunting you. I merely want to..."

"Light a fire under him," Liz said when Lillie stalled trying to find the right words.

"Yes," she said excitedly. "Exactly, Liz."

Liz turned to her uncle. "Tio, maybe you ought to listen to Lillie."

"And just what did I do that requires this kind of special attention?" he asked.

"You didn't do anything. That's the problem," Lillie answered.

"I think I know what Lillie is trying to say, Tio."

"Please, I am all ears," Peter said.

"You're like the eight year-old boy who never ever spoke until one evening at dinner when out of the blue he said, 'These carrots are cold.' His parents were shocked and asked him why he'd never spoken before that. He replied, 'Until now, everything's been okay.' Does that make any sense?" she asked tentatively.

"No, I'm not sure how that applies."

"My turn, Liz," Lillie said. "Peter, you are cautious and conservative in your behavior and manner. I fear you may have lost or never had a sense for adventure and that is something that is certainly going to be required if you want to go along with what I have to propose. As regards other aspects of my caring for you, I think you've been giving a lot of thought lately to who you are spiritually and it's been a struggle. I think I can help," she said with a sincerity that Peter found touching.

Peter turned to Liz. "You think I need a fire lit under me?"

Liz looked lovingly at her uncle and nodded. "Since you left radio, Tio, it's like you stored away that man who was on the air." She went to him and gave him a hug. "Maybe Lillie can help make this transition from a lifetime of working to confronting a future that will be different in so many ways that much easier."

Oddly, Peter was not irked by this negative attention. He knew they were right. He realized he had somehow slipped into neutral. As this was no time to delve more deeply into the tricky topic of self-improvement, he looked over at Lillie, smiled and said, "All right, coach, more about me later. What's this plan you've concocted?"

chapter 18

TAKING HER CUE from Peter, Lillie began to explain how she and her two mortal companions would go about recovering the stolen painting called *A Jersey Lily.* She was two sentences in when the phone rang. Reaching for it, Peter said, "Hold that thought." My, she thought, what a creative way to put everything on hold. As it turned out, she didn't need to do too much thought-holding as the call was over in less than thirty seconds. Peter's only contribution was a crisp, "Five-thirty then." Putting the receiver down, he glanced at his curious audience and said, "That, ladies, was a most unusual invitation."

"Who is this host who is blissfully unaware that you'll be in the company of a lovely lady who will discreetly stay in the background? In fact, they won't even know I'm there," Lillie joked.

"Actually, there are two hosts. Dr. Freddie Florian, Jr. and his partner, Benjamin Lytton-Crisp, have invited me, or I should say us, for cocktails in their penthouse. I have the feeling Freddie is more up for this than Benjamin. You know, I wonder if Freddie's mother put him up to this. The idea of a full sixty-minute encounter with Gertie is downright scary. Nightmarish, in fact. And the way she squeezes your arm, it would be a physically painful hour."

"Gertie or no Gertie, pain or no pain, I look forward to it," Lillie said. "I'm enthralled with the promise of an evening's society. I can be ready by five-thirty."

Peter glanced over at her. "You say that as if you need to make an appointment at the spa to have your lavender atmosphere color-enhanced before the party."

"A little smart-alecky, Tio, but a cute line," Liz observed, giving him a subtle round of applause. Turning her attention to the lavender image, she continued, "So, Lillie, I'm curious to know more about this devious plan of yours."

"I don't remember describing it as devious, dear."

"Well, I just assumed it would be cunning."

"Perhaps, it is. I'm afraid it is also somewhat sketchy," she confessed. "I'll let you two be the judges of that." With that she unveiled the rest of her scheme. Even though it only required four sentences top, she delivered it with unbridled enthusiasm. "Well, what do you think?"

Peter and Liz looked at one another to see who would respond first. Liz gave the nod to her uncle. "You're right. It is short on detail, but count me in," he said enthusiastically.

"So you two are going to confront the auction dealer, tell him you represent the estate of Philipa and that the game is still on?" Liz asked with a hint of skepticism.

"Exactly, my dear," Lillie said confidently.

"But what if there is no game and he hasn't the slightest idea what you're talking about?"

Lillie assured her that would not be the case, explaining the numbers on Philipa's note paper and the painting's numbers are too eerily close to be a coincidence. "My nose tells me this is the right thing to do. If I had a nose, that is. I point out its absence only to beat your uncle to the punch.

"Yes, he is in a frisky mood," Liz observed.

Peter ignored them both. "Lillie, if we go ahead with this, I have to tell Howard. We're going to need his backing and maybe his money."

Liz suddenly popped up and walked into Peter's closet. Over the sound of hangers being pushed this way and that, she hollered, "What are our dinner plans for tonight? Are you hungry for something?"

"I thought I would have Bartal make us a reservation at Zen-Tao for seven-thirty," Peter shouted back, thinking he sure liked this butler concept.

His niece stuck her pretty head out and chirped excitedly, "Tio, that's great! I read Chef Tommy Tomiko from The Limp Chopstick in Beverly Hills and Las Vegas is responsible for the sushi bar at the Zen-Tao. They say he has a salmon skin roll to die for, and I can't wait to try his take on a spider roll and unagi."

"As I see it, I probably won't be more than an hour with the boys from Winona. How about we meet up at six-thirty in the Covey. You can explain to me why any chef in his right mind would name his restaurant The Limp Chopstick."

"Maybe he has erectile dysfunction issues."

Lillie's unexpected speculation elicited giggles from Liz. Peter said, "I can't believe you said that."

"Why are you so surprised? When I was wandering the ship the other day, I saw an advertisement on television for something called Viagra which implied that taking it can instantly take the limp out of one's chopstick. They even warned of a four-hour erection. Dear me, just the thought of it exhausts me. I do think there are times when a woman enjoys a little flaccidity in her lover."

Liz came out of the closet holding a shimmery, red dress. "Lillie, this is a perfect example of why you and I have to talk. There's so much I want to know. I imagine a conversation like this would not have happened in Victorian England."

"Perhaps not in a Victorian parlor over sherry. However, we weren't as modest and close-lipped as you might think. Most of the gentlemen I knew considered themselves to be stallions of the first order and they weren't shy about telling you. Even when their neigh was bigger than their lay," Lillie deadpanned.

"Okay, you two, what do you think about this for tonight?" she asked, holding the dress she'd taken from Peter's closet up against her and making a slow model's turn. "It is an informal evening as opposed to casual, so it should be acceptable."

Lillie responded first. "You will look beautiful in it, my dear, but, I daresay, it is a bit provocative."

"You wore that on your first date with Kevin. I remember you telling me he made a concerted effort to get you out of it that night," Peter said.

Liz tossed the dress over her shoulder and grinned. "And I also told you that that's when he found out what it's like trying to undress a mountain lion."

"In his defense, Liz, I'm sure it stirred his libido," Peter opined.

"So you guys think I shouldn't wear it?" she asked.

"Not at all. Given the median age of the men on this ship, they could probably stand a little libido-stirring."

"Maybe I'll loan it to Samantha Whitby then. I'd really love to see her stir your libido," she teased.

"Won't work," he said.

"Why?"

"I like my libido shaken, not stirred."

Liz closed her eyes and groaned. "Seriously, though, Tio, I really think you and Samantha would make a great pair. And now that I've said that for what, the fortieth time, let's move on. I promised myself I would study every day and that's what I am going to do." At the door, she pointed at Peter and said to Lillie, "Keep his fire going, girl."

After Peter explained the modern use of the words *girl* and *guys* to his puzzled companion, he phoned Howard. It took a while but he eventually made an ally of him. The problem was Peter's former boss was tired of dealing with the aftermath of Philipa's untimely death. He was anxious to put an end to all matters relating to his former mother-in-law. He told Peter he was counting the days before he could hightail it to the Coast and look for Snowy Plovers instead of dealing with humorless estate attorneys and accountants. "Let it go, Peter. Forget stolen art and shady characters. Enjoy the cruise. The good news is you don't have my mother-in-law ruining things for you. Go have yourself a passionate shipboard romance."

"What is it with everyone wanting me to have a shipboard romance."

"Ah, Liz is on your case," he laughed. "Well, take her and my advice and go get laid."

Peter knew he couldn't possibly tell Howard about Lillie's existence and her ambitious goal of recovering the missing painting. Nor could he share with him that he was fully committed to helping her. He wondered what he could say to persuade Howard to sign on. Then, remembering what he'd just gone through when Lillie and Liz decided to do a Peter Ramsey personality makeover, he thought he might try the same strategy on Howard: "Before you hang up, I have one question." He paused for dramatic effect. "Have you no sense of adventure?"

"No," Howard snapped back. "For heaven's sake, Peter, when I want adventure I go on a search for sea birds. That's my idea of real derring-do. Come to think of it, you aren't exactly Indiana Jones, you know."

"Then maybe we both need to change," Peter argued. "What was it Virgil said about fortune sides with him who dares."

Howard snorted. "Oh great! Enlisting the aid of an old Roman poet, are we? Well, two can play that game. Remember Marcus Aurelius? He advised that you should be content to be what you really are."

"And what are you really?"

"A coward! A smug, satisfied, happy, bird-loving coward," Howard answered proudly.

Exasperated and out of Virgil quotes, Peter sighed, "Howard, I am not keen on this either. My bet is that art thieves and crooked auction dealers surely have their nasty sides, and that, quite frankly, scares me."

Now the mortal mind is a marvelous piece of equipment. In a nanosecond, Peter instantly recalled the one occasion where he found himself in anything that could be remotely called harm's way. As a junior in high school, he was drafted to box in the first round of what the school called the Silver Gloves Tournament. He was scared. Wise to the fact that no boy except for the preternatural toughs wanted to go past that round, he agreed to take a fall as his partner whom he thought suicidal actually wanted to advance. Their subsequent circling, dancing and occasional light body taps were noticed by Father Riordan who sternly ordered the pair to start punching or else. This was in the day when a Dominican priest's threat of "or else" stood for something. The fight accelerated with Peter managing to land a few successful jabs, but for the most part he spent the better part of three rounds being a punching bag for his opponent. Subsequently, six decades plus would go by without Peter ever needing to put the gloves on again.

Inspired by that memory, Peter suddenly blurted out, "You know, except for one time in high school, I've never been in a fight, Howard. I don't know if I can even defend myself." He felt embarrassed by his admission.

Howard sounded confused. "Peter, are you worried about getting in a fight on the ship? Look, I'm the biggest sissy going, but I learned early on that most conflicts or arguments never get past the talking or finger-pointing stage even with bullies. Maybe some escalate to chest-poking, but that's about it. Knowing that helped me immensely when I was in management. Besides, I wouldn't worry about getting into a scrap. Chances are if these guys take a dislike to you, they'll just shoot you."

"Thanks a lot."

"Relax, I'm only kidding."

"I suppose I was just taking the long way round trying to explain that I don't even know if I have the courage to deal with what could become a potentially dangerous situation."

"So if this isn't a test of your bravado quotient, what is it?"

"I don't mean to sound abstruse. There is a very good reason why I am deeply committed to seeing this through. I just can't explain it. I know it all sounds terribly confusing, but I really do need your help." Peter had delivered that final plea with a strongly felt emotion that even caught him by surprise.

Lillie, who was listening in, whispered, "You just might have done it, Peter."

And he did. Howard fell silent. Then came a loud exhalation of breath. "All right, run this whole weird thing by me one more time."

Peter did and his former boss came around. In fact, Howard Newton broke the speed record for mind-changing. He was now so keen on the plan that he volunteered to fly to Alaska and join them on the ship.

"I don't know if that's necessary." Peter replied almost too quickly, not relishing the constant company of his former boss.

"It certainly is. Now that you have my adrenaline going, if you think I'm going to sit here while you have all the fun, you're crazy. Naomi has another week in New York what with the estate auction and all, but I'm good to go. I can meet the ship at the next port of call."

"I don't think they take on passengers in the middle of the cruise."

"Nonsense. Money talks and I have scads of it. I'll get our travel agent on it right away. And put me in one of those penthouses," he ordered.

Peter reminded Howard that Jenni Ramirez was on the ship. "I'll have her call you."

"What about the FBI? Should I alert them?"

"No, absolutely not. We need to do this our way and I guarantee they won't take kindly to that. Now look, Howard, after I meet with the owner of ATSEA Auction House and tell him that we're acting in Philipa's place, the first thing he'll do is call you. His name is Charles Van Woort. Your mother-in-law probably told him that no one knew of her little hobby. You will have to tell him otherwise. You know the identity of the stolen works in her collection, so drop the name of a painting or two. Assure him you were looking forward to her shipboard acquisition as well. Do your best to convince him that you and Philipa were birds of a feather."

"Like mother-in-law, like son-in-law, huh?"

"Something like that."

"Something bothers me, though," Howard said.

"What?"

"I don't think it's wise for you to act like you know what Philipa was up to. That might really worry Van Woort. I think it is better if you're just a innocent messenger. When you meet him, act like I called and wanted you to give him a heads up that I'm coming for the auction and that he knows the painting I'm interested in. Then let him see those numbers which will convince him that Philipa shared the information with me."

Peter was impressed with Howard's thinking. It certainly made a lot of sense and he told him so. "Van Woort may prove to be a real challenge. Are you sure you're up for this?" he asked.

"Hey, I spent years talking over, under and around the greedy, larcenous Figg Broadcasting suits in New York. Charles will be a piece of cake. I'll be fine, Peter," Howard said reassuringly.

"I'm sure you will, tough guy," Peter joked.

"Up yours, Peter."

"Up yours," Lillie repeated aloud. "Is that a popular way of ending a phone conversation?"

"It is with him."

"He was right, Peter. Mr. Newton was enormously helpful in helping to refine our less than detailed scheme," Lillie observed.

Peter found Jenni and told her of Howard's plan to join the cruise. She explained getting him on board would be no problem. While it was not common practice, joining a cruise in progress was not unheard of. Peter glanced at the ship's itinerary on his desk and asked her when she could get Newton to the ship.

"We're in Skagway tomorrow."

"That's too soon," Peter said, hoping for a day or two without his company.

"Well. let's see. We visit Glacier Bay the following day and then we're in Sitka. Sitka will work. You say money is no object, so I'll book a private charter out of Oakland and fly him direct. And I'll get him booked on the cruise. Even though they say they're sold out, there's always a penthouse or two available."

"As long as it's not Philipa's stateroom," Peter added.

"Wouldn't think of it. I'll call Howard right now. By the way, Peter, you asked about Philipa's travel agent. I learned she booked the trip through an agency in Manhattan called CVW Travel. What's interesting about this agency is the owner."

"Let me guess. His name is Charles Van Woort of ATSEA Auction House."

"I'm impressed. Anyway, there are about ten people on board who booked through CVW Travel. I can get you their names if you like."

"I would appreciate that, but I don't want you getting in trouble for being too inquisitive."

"No problem. It falls into the category of pillow talk."

"I beg your pardon?"

"I'm sleeping with the hotel director," she laughed.

chapter 19

HE COULDN'T HELP himself. Peter Ramsey was punctual to a fault. Too many years spent in radio studios staring at a variety of imposing timepieces, both digital and analog. For that reason, at exactly five-thirty, he stood at the door to Freddie's penthouse located in the far aft portion of the Ocean Glamour. He glanced down the dizzyingly long, narrow, sea-blue carpeted hallway thinking if the weather ever gets too inclement to stroll around the promenade deck, he could walk it for exercise. Then he thought it might be interesting to walk all the hallways from deck five to twelve. Then he wondered how he could possibly find such a boring idea appealing.

At his side, Lillie whispered, "Before you ring the bell, I can sneak in, look around and let you know what awaits? Our earliness, you realize, might not be appreciated."

"We are not early, Lillie. We are on time. Why is punctuality so frowned on? They requested our presence at five-thirty. So that's the time we should arrive," he huffed.

This particular topic is one that traditionally gets the punctilious among you huffing and puffing, eager to defend the notion that promptness is a virtue. It is an entertaining subject but one which we won't explore here in any great detail. Suffice it to say, from my observations of the social rules concerning matters of timeliness, the only really big sin is arriving early. Enough said on that topic. However, I have splendid news. Once you shed your mortal attire and land on Eternity's doorstep, you will have nothing more to do with time. You leave it behind you. Time is your invention, not ours. Here in Eternity, you will simply be. Forget words like tomorrow, yesterday, hours, seconds, light years, leap years, etc.. Toss them all in the recycling bin so they may be used again by future air-breathers. Unfortunately, your languages are far too limited for me to properly explain this timeless world. Will you miss it? I daresay about as much as you would a root canal.

It was Freddie who opened the door, inviting them in with a sweep of a soft hand that boasted just-manicured nails. Lillie looked at him and then at the dimly lighted stateroom where candlelight cast gauzy shadows on the walls. The closed curtains made Alaska seem a million miles away. "Oh my heavens," she exclaimed.

Both men wore Edwardian smoking jackets with elaborately-designed paisley ascots. Freddie's coat was a rich maroon with decorative black crushed-velvet cuffs and lapels. In the center of the room, Benjamin stood ramrod straight in an Oxford grey version with similar dark cuffs and lapels. They were a perfect fit for their surroundings as they apparently with the merest of props had cleverly transformed the penthouse into a Victorian parlor.

Noticing Peter's interest in the altered decor, Benjamin said, "The only thing missing are real candles, but understandably the ship won't allow them. I hope you don't mind the battery-operated variety?"

"Not at all. It's remarkable how you have successfully turned back the clock. I'm suitably impressed. Very imaginative."

"Thank you, Peter," Freddie said, affecting a British accent. "Benjamin and I are what I like to call part-time

Edwardians. We so love everything about that special time. When we can, in our own humble way, we try to recreate the age and escape into it for our own enjoyment. Not too many people know of our strange predilection."

"Your parents?" Peter asked, wondering what Freddie Senior and Gertie would think.

"Certainly not. They already think I'm delusional enough," he giggled.

Peter, feeling like he ought to make some kind of wry observation, said, "I suppose one person's illusion is another's delusion. Mark Twain's advice is that a person should never part with their illusions. He said when they are gone, you continue to exist, but you cease to live."

Freddie clapped his hands together and forgetting his British accent for a moment said, "Peter, I will remember that. I wonder if Mister Twain, or Clemens if you will, ever met Oscar Wilde and if so what he thought about him?"

Lillie responded excitedly, "I can answer that. Remind me to tell you later."

Now a habit, Peter tugged on his left earlobe to signal he'd heard her. To Freddie he said, "It's certainly possible. I imagine there might have been a healthy rivalry between those two writing giants. You know, with you two dressed in your smoking jackets, I don't wonder that they just might show up for drinks. Twain in his late-in-life white suit and who knows what Wilde would be wearing."

"I do," an animated Freddie chirped. "Something extravagant, flowing and colorful. After all, it was Oscar who said, 'Looking good and dressing well is a necessity. Having a purpose in life is not.'" Smiling broadly, he placed his thumbs behind his velvet lapels and continued, "And by the way, Peter, please take note. We now call these our non-smoking jackets."

"Freddie, that line is getting terribly stale," Benjamin said with an accent defined by family and refined by Eton and Oxford. Turning to Peter, he added, "Mr. Ramsey, Oscar Wilde is part of the reason you're here this evening."

Peter was about to invite Benjamin to call him by his first name, but realized Lytton-Crisp wanted to keep things formal, at least while they were pretending to be in Victorian England and not on an Alaskan cruise. "What's Wilde got to do with my being here?" he asked, exceedingly grateful that it was the Irish wit and not Gertie Florian who inspired the invitation.

Freddie took over. "It will all be explained, but first a drink. We're having Dom Perignon."

"That's more than fine with me."

Freddie directed Peter to a chair. After pouring the champagne, he took a seat next to his partner on the sofa. Peter thought they looked like clean-shaven versions of Gilbert and Sullivan and would at any moment break into, perhaps, *Fair Moon, To Thee I Sing* from *HMS Pinafore*. Lillie had found a place opposite Peter.

Freddie raised his glass and proposed a toast. "And the truth shall set you free. At least, that's what we're counting on,' he added with an audible sigh.

"What an odd toast," Lillie said.

"What an odd toast," Peter echoed.

Freddie's expression was wistful. "It is, I suppose."

Benjamin nudged his partner. "Freddie, this is not an Agatha Christie mystery. Please just tell Mr. Ramsey why we summoned him."

Freddie edged forward, put his champagne on the table and began. "We mentioned Oscar because Benjamin and I are members of a club that consists of nine men, a band of brothers if you will, who are frankly over-the-top in our affection for Oscar Wilde and all things late Victorian and Edwardian. We all met a few years ago at a Gay Pride Function in Oxford. I was there because I had just read in *De*

Profundis that Oscar felt the two major turning points in his life were when his father sent him to Oxford and society sent him to prison. I knew then I had to go to Oxford."

"I hope you don't feel the same way about prison?" Peter joked.

Freddie was clearly shaken by the question. Shuddering, he said, "No, I most certainly don't want to go to.. I mean visit a prison." Sitting back, he nodded to his partner. "Oh dear me, Benjamin, I am making such a mess of this. Perhaps, you had better take over."

And so it was that Benjamin moved forward. Placing his hands on his knees, he began to explain why the truth might set them free. First, though, I will let Benjamin rest his wagging tongue while I, Theodomicles, provide you with a few background notes. When Benjamin and Freddie met their future brotherhood at the aforementioned Gay Pride function in Oxford, included in the batch were the Sprottle twins, Jason and Jaspar. They were handsome, blonde-haired, entitled insolent brats. Jasper, who was the more truculent of the pair, was an art restorer for the Tate Museum in London and Jason was director of the Salzstangen Museum of Art in St. Louis, Missouri. Yes indeed, a curious name for a museum. Explaining it is worth a detour. Years ago, there resided in St. Louis, a pretzel titan named Conrad Kinkelmann whose eponymous Kinkelmann's Salted Twistees made him a considerable fortune. Realizing he could no longer store his personal collection of pretzel memorabilia in his mansion, he built a neoclassic structure of considerable proportion and beauty in downtown St. Louis to house his inventory. The building was the envy of museum devotees everywhere. This is, perhaps, a good time to mention that when considering such grandiose moves, one should always consult others first. In Conrad's case, there was no one to whisper in his ear that most people just weren't into pretzel history. Eventually, the city powers convinced him to let them take over the building and turn it into a bonafide museum of art. He agreed, hinting that he wouldn't be disappointed if they named it Kinkelmann's Salted Twistee Museum of Art. Fortunately, the art commission was able to persuade Mr. Kinkelmann that *salzstangen,* the German word for pretzel, seemed more fitting. As a bonus, they promised him a basement wing to display the best of his pretzel collection, twisted as it was.

And now back to the story Benjamin is nervously telling Peter. Jasper Sprottle, the de facto head of this merry band of Wilde enthusiasts had persuaded the group to purchase a property that would serve both as a clubhouse and as lodging for those members outside London when they came a-visiting. Their good fortune was a mews house in Mayfair had come on the market owned by a Mrs. Abigail Wetley-Rainford, a peroxided-blonde centenarian and retired writer of – as one critic moaned – bloody awful romance novels. As it was her plan to move in with her widowed daughter-in-law who had a large country estate outside Sedlescombe in East Sussex, she included in the sale all her furnishings and most of the art. Ecstatic over the fact that all they would have to do is tweak the already crumbling elegance of the pied-à-terre's interior, the Wilde bunch happily anted up the required amount to close the deal."

I'll let Benjamin finish up. "Now that we had a headquarters, we decided to call ourselves the the Socrates Club, after a club Oscar invented in 1892 to help fight off the ennui of Sunday afternoons."

"Peter, Oscar and the others used to meet at the Cadogan Hotel which was once a former residence of mine," Lillie interjected.

While Benjamin rattled on about their connection to the Sprottles, Freddie went into the closet, returning with a large, loosely wrapped mailing tube. Benjamin had now gotten to a part of the story where he began to noticeably hem and haw. Peter sensed he was drifting from the truth. "So, Mr. Ramsey, just before we left for San Francisco, our friend, Jason, called from St. Louis. Knowing we were going on this Alaska cruise, he asked if we'd do him a huge favor and deliver a painting to the man in charge of the shipboard auction. We, uh, saw no problem with that."

"Did you know what painting you were being asked to deliver?"

"Yes," Benjamin said as he began to nervously rub his knees with his hands. "He said it was some contemporary abstract from a London artist that Mr. Van Woort liked. Well, it isn't. Freddie and I opened it and, believe me, we were shocked by what we discovered we had in our possession."

"That is sheer poppycock," Lillie said. "Tell him so, Peter."

Peter was by nature non-confrontational, but he agreed with Lillie that Benjamin was not telling the truth that would set them free. "How convenient, you being on the same cruise and all. Too much of a coincidence, I think. And why couldn't Jason simply ship the piece to ATSEA Auction. Frankly, it all sounds sort of dodgy," Peter charged, his heart racing.

Freddie, who had been holding the mailing tube in front of him as if it was a rifle and he had been ordered to present arms, placed it on the cocktail table and returned to the sofa. He looked his partner in the eye. "Benjamin, we are at wit's end as to how to get ourselves out of this horrible dilemma. We need help, we're scared and this is no time to make us out to be holy innocents or victims. I am going to top off Peter's glass while you tell him what a frightful mess were in. The truth, please," he pleaded.

Chastised for presenting a version that no one was buying, Benjamin let Peter know the full extent of their situation. "This takes a little explaining. Jasper and Jason were from the beginning the leaders of our little group. Both are take charge kind of people, sassy, confident and aggressive. Jasper more so than Jason. Jaspar is also very intimidating. Anyway, the last time the nine of us were all together in London, we had a dinner party at the house. The house was much the same as the last time we had visited except there was a new painting. It was, we thought, a copy of a painting from Whistler's Nocturne series. I felt it too moody and cheerless, but everyone considered it a wonderful addition to our Socrates Club decor which now boasted three of Jasper's quite efficient reproductions. During dinner, the conversation came around to the Whistler. Jasper stunned us all when he announced that it was the real thing. Tony, a member from Manchester, said that can't be because that particular Whistler is currently on display in the Tate and he knows so because he was just there. Jaspar explained that what Tony saw at the museum was a forgery. His forgery, he bragged."

Freddie returned to the sofa and, putting a hand on Benjamin's knee, continued the story. "Peter, at the time it all seemed so exciting. We were all thrilled silly to think that an original Whistler was ours. No one, not a single member objected to it being there," he confessed.

"But it wasn't to be the last," Peter guessed.

"No. Some time later Benjamin and I received a letter and a photo from Jaspar. Another original had made its way onto one of the dining room walls. This time it was a Ford Madox Brown piece called *Carrying Corn*." In the letter, Jaspar boasted that the Tate was now displaying two of his masterpieces."

Peter stared at the mailing tube that now dominated the coffee table. Pointing to it, he said, "This is the real reason I am here, isn't it?"

Both men nodded. Benjamin continued: "You may have heard on the news recently that a painting had gone missing while in transit from the Tate in London to the Salzstangen Museum in St. Louis. The painting was a part of a traveling exhibit and St. Louis was the first stop. When the Salzstangen took delivery of the pieces, they found one empty frame. The painting had been cleanly and neatly removed. The museum insists it was stolen while in transit. However, because it wasn't discovered until the painting had been unwrapped in the museum, suspicions are that it could also have been taken from the museum."

"What does this have to do with you two, other than there's a Sprottle at each end and that's terribly suspicious? And what work was stolen?"

"First, you should know it wasn't stolen. It never left the Tate. Well, I suppose it did leave the Tate but it didn't go to St, Louis," Benjamin said sheepishly. "That was all a ruse to distract everyone and to let it be known the painting was stolen."

"And that painting is *The Jersey Lily* by Millais?"

Clearly put off by Peter's use of the wrong article, Benjamin corrected him sharply. "Sir John Everett Millais titled it *A Jersey Lily.*"

"Oh, for God's sake, Benjamin, stop being so snotty about such a common mistake. I swear this love affair of yours with Lillie Langtry is driving me mad," Freddie barked, folding his pudgy arms and pouting.

"Well, Freddie darling, you should thank the stars in the sky for my passions or we'd never have discovered what we did."

What was Lillie's reaction to all this? One of enormous elation. She wanted to holler out, "Job well done, Peter," but wisely thought it premature. Better to not divert his attention away from the neo-Edwardians' meandering, somewhat bizarre confession. Then, of course, there was the difficulty of her being unable to visually demonstrate her delight. That, of course, was frustrating for both of them as Lillie did have a capacity for human feelings. There was no sense in sending her back without giving her a shot at once again experiencing the full range of human emotions. Well, an almost full range. Given her paranormal status, she possessed a spiritual governor that kept her heavily weighted on the chirpy side.

Making a show of looking at his watch, Peter said, "I have someone I'm meeting at six-thirty."

"Patience, Peter," Lillie warned.

"Sorry. I'll try to do a better job of editing," Benjamin replied his tone more peevish than apologetic. He stared at the mailing tube as if it contained radiation. "That has been in our possession since it was shipped to my gallery. Our instructions were to deliver it to Charles Van Woort. Does that satisfy?"

Peter moved his chair back from the table, crossed his legs and said, "Okay, take your time. Tell me how this all came to be."

Looking less lugubrious, Benjamin apologized again, this time with sincerity. "Sorry, Freddie and I both are so on edge. We are swimming in dangerous waters and we need someone to toss us a life preserver. As to how this all came to be, here's the story as told us in exasperating detail by Jaspar himself. First you should know that, according to Jaspar, he told Van Woort he was shipping the painting to him via two friends of his; one who happens to own a gallery and who happened to be booked on the same cruise. He told Van Woort that we think we're delivering an abstract by a London artist that Charles ordered from him. Jaspar assures us that Van Woort has no reason to suspect we are aware of its contents."

"That's good if you believe Jaspar," Peter commented. "If I were Van Woort, I'd be suspicious."

Benjamin shrugged off the thought and continued: "Anyway, it seems Van Woort and Jaspar are longtime associates as Jaspar paints reproductions for him on a regular, irregular basis. According to Jaspar, Van Woort had recently called to inquire about a delivery and in the course of the conversation VanWoort told him that he was taking some of his special clients on this Alaskan cruise as a thank you for their past business. Jaspar immediately saw it as a great opportunity to make a lot of money. He knew three things; VanWoort dealt in stolen art and those special clients were no doubt the ones who bought them, that Freddie and I were booked on the same cruise and a traveling exhibit was about to leave the Tate for St. Louis. He contacted Van Woort and told him that he was tired of just creating hotel-motel art for him, that he wanted to deepen the relationship. Van Woort asked him what he meant and Jaspar said he could get him one of the Tate's more valuable paintings. Van Woort said it certainly would add some excitement to the cruise, that he might even have a possible client who was going on the cruise. Jaspar called him back in a day and said he could get the Millais for him. Van Woort told him the only time he could take delivery of the painting was on the cruise. Jaspar explained that would be no problem. That's where we come in. Jaspar told us that Van Woort's final words to him were succinct and memorable: "Don't fuck up.""

"So Jaspar contacted you and asked if you..."

"No, he didn't *ask* us, Peter. He *told* us," said a wide-eyed, frightened Freddie. He pulled at the neck of his paisley ascot and Peter noticed a makeup stain. "We were hesitant to agree to do it until Jaspar reminded us of the originals that hung on the walls of our clubhouse and how we are all in it together. Then he went all sweet and promised we'd be paid handsomely, in fact, enough to cover what we'd put up for our share of the house in London."

"The nasty truth of the matter is our going along with it was based half on fear and half on greed," Benjamin admitted.

Peter shook his head. "How did Jaspar pull something like this off? Don't museums have all sorts of security measures in place to insure that paintings are handled well in transit? I read about special plywood boxes and how they don't uncrate them for a few days after transport while the art acclimates to its new surroundings. Plus, I would think there must be any number of people involved in the process."

Benjamin smiled. "I don't exactly know what Jaspar did. However, Peter, I can say unequivocally that the art world suffers from all kinds of human error, ignorance and general laxity just like any other profession."

"Isn't it dangerous or harmful to the work to simply roll it up and shove it into a mailing tube?" Peter asked.

"Yes, it is. Very damaging. A sin, really. And when I learned that it was Millais' *A Jersey Lily* that was headed my way in such a manner, I was crestfallen."

"Tell him why," Freddie said, pouting. Benjamin let out an exasperated sigh. "Well, if you won't, I will. You see, Peter, like I said earlier, my loving partner for life has this humungous thing for Lillie Langtry. I swear he's more devoted to her than he is for our beloved Oscar."

"What a strange turn of events," Lillie marveled. "Of course, in looking back, he's not the first gay gentleman whom I have swept off their feet."

"So knowing that the Millais painting was in there,' Peter said, again pointing to the mailing tube, "must have really upset you?"

Without answering, Benjamin picked up the package and rising, moved toward the foot of the bed. He removed the painting and rolled it out onto the bed. Peter and Freddie joined him.

"Marvelous, isn't it," Benjamin observed.

The three men and one ghost in the oddly decorated penthouse suite were all in agreement.

Without looking up from the painting, Benjamin said, "It's a fake."

chapter 20

"I STILL CAN'T believe it. Jasper sent us a fucking fake."

"Benjamin, don't be a potty-mouth. What have I said about that kind of language in the company of our guests?" Freddie looked over at Peter and quickly explained, "You aren't the only one visiting us, Peter. Whenever we slip into our Edwardian world, we choose to believe we are in the gracious company of Oscar, Bram, Arthur, Jimmy and the rest of the gang. Yes, we are all on a first name basis. Like theirs was, our goal is the constant pursuit of the bon mot."

"You excluded Lillie again," Benjamin pouted, his eyes still riveted on the painting. "You always leave out Lillie, Freddie."

"What part of the rest of the gang don't you get? Of course, she's included."

To Peter's relief, Benjamin put an end to their silly nagging by returning to the topic of the forged art work. "This truly is an impressive piece," he said to no one in particular. "Sprottle really outdid himself this time."

Peter examined more closely the alleged fake. While the painting might not be the real thing, Lillie Langtry certainly was. She was, indeed, a natural beauty. That was self-evident. However, what really captivated Peter was how Millais successfully conveyed in the painting her strong character, sharp intelligence and seductive personality, qualities that turned her beauty into a transcendent handsomeness. He now understood Benjamin's fascination for her as he, too, was falling under her spell. He told himself whenever he looked at the lavender vision who was at the moment on his left and being very quiet considering she was the topic of conversation, he will remember the face in the painting. "Benjamin, how do you know this is a forgery?" he asked.

Freddie, who had returned to the sofa and was busy fanning himself as if he had a sudden attack of the vapors, said, "Yes, Benjamin dear, do tell Peter why you're so convinced that it's not the real thing."

"As Freddie mentioned, Mr. Ramsey, I do have a thing for Lillie Langtry. I am thoroughly enchanted – perhaps besotted is a better word – by her. I have been in this contrary state of infatuation for years." Benjamin finally took his eyes off the painting. Staring affectionately at his partner, he continued, "Freddie tires of me bringing this up, but I was first attracted to him because in many ways he and Lillie look alike. Honestly, they do share some physical similarities. Look first at the painting and then at Freddie. See how his lips and the curve of his nose resemble hers. They had the same chin until he gained weight."

Amazingly, Freddie readied himself for inspection by turning slightly so Peter could see for himself. He didn't seem at all embarrassed or upset with the comparison. Instead, he gave his partner a gentle slap on the wrist, "Benjamin, really! Peter doesn't need to know all our secrets."

Peter wholeheartedly agreed. Any physical resemblance – chins, lips or otherwise – between Lillie and Freddie was not a seed he wanted planted in his mind. He made no comment.

"Anyway, as a result of this ardor, I am no stranger to *A Jersey Lily*. Just ask the guards at the Tate. Whenever we are in London, I'm there for hours on end. I know every square inch of this piece, every brush stroke. I know the correct count of the tendrils in her hair. Trust me, this is not an authentic Millais. I am also convinced Jasper could never handle a painting of this richness and reputation in such a crude manner. He is many things, admittedly most of them not virtuous, but he loves art and respects artists. No amount of money could make him harm a painting. However, it seems he has enough chutzpah to think he can get away with selling Van Woort a fake."

"He's taking a big chance," Peter commented.

Benjamin spun around and faced him. "When I unwrapped the package and saw the fake, I was delighted and thrilled. However, I soon came to my senses and now all I feel is abject fear."

"Abject fear, indeed. I'm absolutely petrified," Freddie added. "When Van Woort realizes he's been taken, we'll be the first two people he comes gunning for."

"Why didn't Jasper just ask you as a personal favor to deliver an abstract to Van Woort and let it go at that? Why did he have to involve you?"

"First, you have to know there's a theatricality about him. He loves drama, particularly when he's the star of the show. Plus, the more complicated he can make a storyline, the happier he is. Add to that, and this is not so surprising, Jasper Sprottle needs an audience for everything he does. Absolutely everything. I think he brushes his teeth in front of an open window." With a shrug, Benjamin muttered, "It's just his way. He wants us all to know how damned clever he is."

"So conceivably every member of the Socrates Club knows about this strange caper or is somehow involved in it?"

"I'm sure of it," Benjamin sighed. "I wouldn't be surprised if Jasper was at this very minute selling the rights to this folly to the BBC."

"Something else bothers me. Why haven't you already delivered it? We are days into the cruise."

Freddie volunteered to answer that query: "Jasper said we were to wait until Van Woort contacted us. He didn't call until this morning. I must say he was rather devil-may-care about it all. Said if we weren't busy this evening, we can drop it by, and if that didn't work, we could always bring it by tomorrow sometime. We were anxious to get it off our hands so we agreed to meet him tonight at ten-thirty at the Covey. Remember we still thought we were giving him the original."

"But then you decided to open it. Why?"

"Thinking it was the original, I just had to see it one more time," Benjamin confessed.

Freddie added, "We knew right away we were in over our heads and we also knew we had no business getting involved with such a scheme. We had no one to turn to, Peter. I certainly couldn't tell my parents. That's when I thought of you. That's why I invited you over. I thought, perhaps, three heads would be better than two scared-to-death ones."

"What do you think we ought to do, Mr. Ramsey?" Benjamin asked.

"First, give Van Woort the painting," he answered without hesitation.

The two hapless Edwardians appeared shocked at the suggestion. Benjamin laughed derisively. "That's your idea of coming to our aid?"

"There are two other options but I wouldn't recommend them. There's the police. For your confession and cooperation, you might get some kind of leniency. And there's Van Woort. Tell him up front you're delivering a fake but explain you're just the messengers. However, I would definitely pass on that one."

"What a mess," Freddie groaned.

"So we just hand it to him and walk away?" Benjamin asked, joining Freddie on the sofa and taking his hand.

"Can you rewrap that so it looks like it was never opened?" Peter asked.

"I own a gallery, Mr. Ramsey. Packaging is second nature. Van Woort will never know we sneaked a peek," Benjamin answered confidently.

"Good, that's important. Now, I have one more question and your answer matters greatly." Pointing to the fake *A Jersey Lily*, Peter said, "I know from your earlier exclamations, you are impressed with Jasper's work. But that seemed a visceral response. Now I want you to think hard before you answer this. How good a forgery is it really?"

The gallery owner didn't have to take the offered minute as his response was immediate: "It is very, very good, Mr. Ramsey. I'm sure Van Woort has a discerning eye, but in this case, quite honestly, I don't think he would question it."

Peter took a last sip of the excellent champagne and stood up. He was ready to take his leave. "Then I see no other choice than to give it to him. All you supposedly know is that you're doing a favor for a friend by delivering some abstract by a London artist that he, Van Woort, requested. Hand it to him, make nice, have a drink and then, like the innocents you are, be on your merry way. Besides, you'll be doing us a big favor." he added.

Both men looked up at him. "What do you mean by *us?*" Freddie asked suspiciously.

Realizing in their bizarre Victorian world of Let's Pretend, all he had to do was tell the truth, Peter smiled and explained, "By us, gentlemen, I mean Lillie Langtry and me. I'm certain Mrs. Langtry would love to see her painting back on display in the Tate. And like you said, she has been party to our conversation along with the rest of the gang."

Freddie, his usual toothy smile even toothier, bounded up and grabbed Peter's hand. "By Jove, Peter, you truly are one of us. I'm sooo glad I invited you. You get us," he gushed, still holding his guest's hand. It was yet another first for our Mr. Ramsey. Until now he'd never heard "By Jove" used in everyday conversation.

Benjamin rose as well and came round to show Peter out. Curious at his last comment, he asked, "Mr. Ramsey, Lillie aside for the moment, why are we doing *you* a favor by giving the painting to Van Woort?"

"Because you asked for my help and I can't help you until you do," Peter replied with a confidence that even caught him by surprise.

Silent, Peter and Lillie walked the long hallway of the penthouse deck. Lillie, unrestrained by the restrictive laws of gravity, floated. However, you get the picture. The narrow passageway was deserted as by six-thirty most guests were either dining, drinking or putting quarters into slot machines while the butlers and stewardesses were resting up before tending to their evening responsibilities. Finally, Peter spoke. "Lillie."

"Yes, Peter."

"I just left a stateroom disguised as a Victorian salon where I drank expensive French champagne with two men wearing elaborate smoking jackets and ascots. Now here I am strolling down the ship's hallway with a lovely spirit who actually was once upon a time a world-famous Victorian in real life. Come tomorrow, I will try to influence the outcome of a tango competition by force-feeding a respected big city newspaper editor a supposed aphrodisiac, a potion given me by a man from a tiny country where it is politically incorrect to be right-handed."

"Is that a question?"

"No."

"And the question?"

"Am I sane?"

Lillie did not take the question seriously, nor did she feel Peter did. "An acquaintance of mine, a Mr. Samuel Clemens, once said 'a well put together unreality is pretty hard to beat.'"

"I believe it," Peter remarked, truly impressed with its quirky logic. "Speaking of Twain, you mentioned you had a story involving him."

"Not a story exactly. It regards a compliment he once paid me."

"I'm sure you're dying to tell me."

"Of course I am, even though I am already dead. If memory serves and it does in a remarkable fashion, I will quote him. Mr. Twain said of me, 'Mrs. Langtry is good company with her friends, but it would be hell to be married to her. She's too damn bright!'"

"And so you are," Peter affirmed. "Good company, I mean."

"Well, you are going to be without my good company this evening, Mr. Ramsey, as I have made other plans."

"And they are?"

"I am spending the rest of the evening with our two troubled friends, Freddie and Benjamin. I wish to know what they talk about when they think they're alone, and I want to be there when they meet Mr. Van Woort."

"That's a great idea. Lillie. Please, no matter what time your evening ends, promise you'll wake me and tell me all about it."

"As you are, no doubt, going to retire at some ridiculously early hour."

Peter disregarded the dig. "Before you go, what did you think of our hour with the two Edwardians?"

"Where do I begin? I thought the boys delightful and I am flattered by Benjamin's affection. I hope when I return I see them much as they were with us."

"And that was?"

"Fully accountable," she replied. "And I think sincerely repentant about their participation in this folly."

"Did you enjoy seeing Oscar, Bram and all the rest?" he joked, but nevertheless wishing that she had discovered company on the other side.

"Oh, Peter, would that they were there," she said wistfully. "It's regrettable that Freddie and Benjamin must remain ignorant of the fact that at least one of the old gang was really present for one of their soirees."

They each fell quiet as they entered Peter's penthouse. The curtains were opened to a brilliant, early evening Alaskan sun, calm waters and green, tree-filled islands in the distance. It was a welcoming sight.

"Now that we seem so close to seeing *A Jersey Lily* returned to its rightful place in the Tate, I feel a certain disappointment. I'm not sure I want to see an early end to our adventure," LIllie said, the implication clear that she thought it would also be the end of her.

"I know. I feel the same way," Peter assured her. "It makes me not want to know where where the original is."

"But we do."

Of course, Peter knew but he also realized that in this instance ignorance can be bliss. "Lillie, this will sound crazy, but I think it's best I don't know where it is. Look, here you are with all these spiritual powers that I can't even begin to comprehend. However, to bring this all to some kind of satisfactory conclusion, you're going to have to eventually use me or Liz. Therefore, if I don't know where the real Millais painting is, the mystery continues and so does our adventure. And so do we," he added as an afterthought.

"Then forget I even mentioned it," she laughed. "By the way I was impressed with the confident and assertive way you dealt with Benjamin and Freddie. Any more demonstrations of the kind of behavior and there'll be no reason for my being here to guide or direct you."

Peter walked over to the full length mirror and adjusted his pocket-square. "I forgot you have taken on the daunting assignment of being my life coach or spiritual advisor."

"I most certainly welcome the latter title. As for the first one, what is a life coach?"

"A popular term describing somebody who..." Peter paused and looked over at Lillie. "You know, I'm not exactly sure what a life coach is. For that matter, I don't even know what they do. I have no idea if they are regulated, licensed, educated in their field or just confident extroverts who are comfortable in their own skin and have learned they can make a buck by telling someone else how to be comfortable in theirs. That said, I do understand the term spiritual advisor."

"So, I don't tell you where the painting is," Lillie stated.

"And I will remain someone in desperate need of an extreme spiritual makeover," Peter added.

"And, as a result, we both do our part to keep our relationship going," Lillie concluded.

Of course, I let them get away with this mischief as Peter was correct in stating that Lillie needs his help if she wants to see *A Jersey Lily* returned to the Tate. As regards Lillie's desire to play spiritual advisor to our Mr. Ramsey; that was of her making.

chapter 21

BEFORE I WAX POETIC about the beauteous morn that greeted the guests and crew of the Ocean Glamour in Skagway, let me give you another tiny glimpse of one of the myriad amenities awaiting you in the Hereafter, or as the Bard describes it in *Hamlet: the undiscovered country, from whose bourn no traveller returns.* I applaud William for his well-worded description even though he missed the mark as travelers return all the time; Lillie Langtry being a perfect example. That said, when you arrive, one of the first things you'll notice is an environment of climatological perfection, precisely because there is a blessed absence of weather. Is there any place on earth that might give you a tiny hint of the non-meteorological perfection I'm talking about? San Diego comes to mind where its residents claim it is always seventy-two degrees with blue skies.

Now let us return to this particular Alaskan day's awakening as it was one for the record books. It was so welcoming, in fact, that if a bird had refused to chirp or tweet, he'd have been thrown out of his species. Even in the dark of a curtained stateroom, there was enough promise of sunlight sneaking through that a still drowsy Peter Ramsey knew something special was going on. Attracted by the sharp sliver of light, he slowly got out of bed. I'd like to report he bounded, but given his age a certain orthopedic stiffness was now part of the rising ritual. Drawing back the curtains, he stepped onto the verandah and beheld Skagway, a movie-set frontier town located at the keyhole-shaped north end of the Chilkoot Inlet. The Ocean Glamour was docked in such a manner that he was treated to a sweeping view of the historic waterfront city and the distant Coast Mountains, home to the White Pass whose hazardous trail in 1898 provided gold prospectors access to Canada's Yukon Territory and, specifically, Bennett Lake where they then floated to Dawson in their quest for the precious alloy. Peter thought getting to Skagway must have been challenging enough to discourage even the hardiest. He couldn't imagine having to then face the horrific challenges of making your way up and over White Pass. What kept them going? Was it need or greed? Both, he concluded. He made a mental note to reread Jack London's *Call of the Wild*. I'll have the time, he thought, as I'm no longer a working stiff. He laughed at his musings. Had he ever truly been a working stiff? Silly thoughts like this reminded him to never mull over, chew on or ponder anything until after he'd stretched and showered.

After putting a call in to Bartal for coffee, he stepped carefully into the shower. The blast of cold water shocked the Ramsey noggin into action, causing him to suddenly realize one more item needed tending to if Operation Tango was to be a success. Apprehensive about phoning so early, he was delighted to hear he hadn't wakened Petra Dosynk who listened with interest to his shower-inspired idea. With ten thousand dollars riding on Dave Flannery's tango, he happily agreed to be at the Cafe Du Soleil at eight forty-five and, yes, he would bring his grandson, Yurk, with him.

Peter had decided all efforts at retrieving the missing painting were to be put on hold temporarily. His breakfast meeting with Dave and the evening's dance competition were today's top priorities. In between these two events, he and Liz were going to spend the day in Skagway. Besides doing some sightseeing in town, they had signed up for a shore excursion which involved a hike on a portion of the Chilkoot Trail and a float down the Taiya River.

Looking back on last night, Peter felt much had been accomplished. After Lillie left him to monitor the movements of Freddie and Benjamin, he met up with Liz at the Covey for a drink and then on to dinner at Zen Tao. By the end of their martinis, Liz knew all about her uncle's bizarre hour in the faux-Victorian salon. She agreed with him that they shouldn't rush to resolve matters as that very well could end their unusual relationship with Lillie, a paranormal partnership and friendship both valued highly. At the last bite of her perfectly prepared Limp Chopstick special unagi, Liz learned what role she would play in the following day's Operation Tango.

The highlight of the evening, though, was Lillie waking him sometime after midnight to tell him of her successes. She first confirmed that the Winona dentist and art gallery owner were, as he had heard firsthand, genuinely frightened and repentant. She then told him of the painting's transfer. She reported that after receiving the expertly rewrapped mailing tube, Charles Van Woort promptly excused himself for a few minutes. Returning empty-handed, the auctioneer assured them that it contained the London abstract he wanted for the auction. In high spirits, he bought another round for Freddie and Benjamin who by this point were downright giddy, their fears evidently assuaged by expensive cognacs and the auctioneer's friendly and engaging manner.

David Augustus Flannery was already seated in the Oasis Court on the twelfth deck. He looked as if he came straight from bed; tousled, messy, wrinkled and irritable. Peter took a seat across from him. He knew it was not going to be easy. "Good morning. You haven't ordered breakfast yet, have you?"

"Just this coffee," the newspaper editor snapped. "Ramsey, why in the hell are are we having a breakfast meeting? I thought we didn't have to do anything on the days we are in port."

"I invited you to breakfast because I can help you win the tango competition this evening," Peter replied flatly.

Flannery burst out laughing. Then just as quickly he stopped and stared hard at Peter, "And how do you plan on doing this?"

"First you are going to order pancakes for breakfast," he replied. "Or waffles or French Toast. Anything that requires syrup."

"Why am I going to do that?"

Peter signaled the waiter and asked for coffee. "Because I have a syrup here that I will put on whatever you order." He placed the three ounce plastic bottle on the table. "It's a powerful and very effective sexual stimulant. It will put in your tango the one thing that's missing."

"You mean passion."

"Romantic passion," he said. "Like you've never felt it."

Doubting Dave looked at the bottle and then at Peter. "You're crazy. You know that, don't you?"

"I understand your skepticism, but, Dave, trust me, this will work. However, it won't unless you do exactly what I tell you. If you do, you will dance the tango of your life."

"Meaning I will dance with this newly found passion?" he asked sarcastically.

"Absolutely."

"And if I don't play by the rules?

"Then the only thing you'll dance with is indigestion."

Peter thought this would be the moment when his obdurate co-host would up and leave and probably not quietly, given his penchant for causing scenes. However, Flannery remained in place. The reason was the crusty journalist had a soft spot, namely, his wife. He would do anything for Mary Pat and if that meant going along with Ramsey's daffy plan, so be it. So instead of storming out, he ordered a waffle when the server came around with Peter's coffee. In a few minutes, it arrived golden brown. Peter leaned across and distributed the syrup as best he could, watching the amber liquid disappear into the waffle's small, square cavities. "Can I put butter on it?" Dave asked.

"I honestly don't know," Peter replied. Then he spotted Petra and his groggy grandson, Yurk, enter the restaurant. They took the table next to them. Peter smiled a greeting and asked in a low voice, "Petra, can he put butter on his waffle?"

"How's his cholesterol?" the elder Kwyrki inquired.

Ignoring them all, Dave reached for the dish of whipped butter. His first bite and ensuing smile confirmed the sweet, rich flavors of his breakfast treat. Wiping a small drop of syrup from his mouth, he looked at the next table and asked, "Who are these guys? "

"They are part of Team Tango." Peter said, introducing them all around. Petra reached across to shake David's hand. Yurk, who was alternately yawning and checking his bulging left bicep, merely nodded. "All right, gentlemen, here's the plan. Dave, after breakfast I want you to get whatever clothes you're going to wear to dance in and a toilet kit and bring them to my stateroom. After that, do what you wish except no going to your stateroom, no going near your wife and try not to drink too much. Petra and Yurk, your job is to keep an eye on him and see that he plays by the rules."

Petra and Yurk gave the Team Tango manager the Kwyrki version of okay while Dave mumbled something suggesting he'd go along their plan but he wasn't keen on it. When Peter told him he wanted him to report to the penthouse a good hour before the dance competition, Dave scowled like a petulant teenager who'd just been told to be in by midnight. "It takes me five minutes to dress," he complained.

"Indulge me, please, be there at four-thirty."

Dave's fork stopped halfway from the plate to his mouth. He pointed the syrupy utensil at Peter. "You're not planning one of those extreme makeovers? You know, manicure, new hair style, chest-hair waxing... That kind of thing. Please tell me you're not going Oprah on me? Somehow I wouldn't put it past you," he fumed.

"There will be no makeover, Dave. I assure you."

"How come you can't keep an eye on me?" he asked Peter, looking with suspicion at the two Kwyrkis.

"Because you'd drive me crazy," he replied. "Besides, Liz and I are spending most of the day with your wife. We'll be in Skagway on a hike and float for a few hours. Then Liz will keep her company while she prepares for the dance contest."

"This is all pretty damned elaborate and time consuming." Turning his attention to Petra and Yurk, he asked brusquely, "What's all this to you?"

Petra remembered he shouldn't mention the ten thousand dollar bet. Ignoring Flannery's boorish attitude, he replied cheerily, "We, my good friend, are doing it because you are left-handed."

Lillie was waiting for Peter when he returned from breakfast. "Did you sleep well?"

"I did. And you?"

"Actually, I find that I do need to rest. It helps my thinking," she said from the verandah. "After our chat, you went right back to sleep so I came out here and spent the night. You ought to try it sometime."

"I didn't see you when I opened the curtains."

"I left early for the computer center. I do so enjoy peering over people's shoulders and catching up with the news of the day or what seems to be pass for news these days." Peter was amused that Lillie had only just returned to earth as a ghost and already she was a media critic. "Anything on the missing painting?" he asked.

"Not a word, but I can tell you the stock market is up, there's a heat wave in New York and a church-going congressman who espouses traditional family values was filmed in a pink leather thong dancing the night away at a gay bar in Georgetown. They say it is now one of the most viewed videos on something called You Tube. Anyway, enough of this nonsense." she said cheerily, "I want to know what you have planned for us this splendid day."

It is reasonable to say that the splendid day he described to Lillie was not without its odd moments, the first of which was waiting for them on the Skagway pier. A weather-tested van was parked near the ship. Standing by it were two equally weather-tested young people eager to get the show on the road. Five women and one man loitered nearby, all but two dressed in makeshift hiking gear. Peter and Lillie were the last of the hikers and floaters to arrive. They were a small group as it turned out, eight in all counting Lillie who was in excellent spirits, no pun intended. Those standing closest to the van were Peter's niece, and Dave's wife. Two women Peter didn't recognize stood a few yards away. A short distance from them, spraying insect repellent on each other's exposed body parts, was a couple expensively dressed in matching khaki outfits better suited for an African safari than an Alaskan hike. To Peter's surprise it was the newspaper publisher and San Francisco socialite, Sanford "Sandy" Symington, and his equally social spouse, Mitzi.

As Peter and Lillie approached, Liz flashed one of her infectious smiles and waved excitedly. It is rumored it takes a lot to remove a Liz Handlery smile from her pretty face, but Lillie's presence did it. What on earth would a ghost possibly find appealing about a walk in the woods, she asked herself. Liz's dilemma was she had invited the Whitby sisters to join them, her plan being to put Samantha Whitby and her uncle on the same path, namely the Chilkoot Trail. She had not counted on Lillie tagging along.

Peter approached them, gave his niece a morning kiss and nodded a hello to a puzzled but cordial Mary Pat Flannery who said, "Good morning, Peter. Liz tells me you are going to turn my David into a dance champion but in order to do that I have to keep my distance from him for the day which explains why I am going into a bug-infested Alaskan wilderness with you all. Do I have that correct?"

"You do, and I want to thank you for being such a good sport. You know Dave really wants to do well for you."

"Why aren't you with him then?" she asked.

"Trust me, he's in the hands of experts."

After first trying to discreetly shoo Lillie away, Liz guided Peter over to where the two Whitby sisters were standing. Both were taller than average, handsome women. Isabelle Whitby dressed for the hike in worn jeans and a Boston College tee-shirt. A broad-brimmed hat hung from her neck. Her younger sister, Samantha, wore khaki hiking shorts with an oversized Cal Bear football tee-shirt and a bandanna tied loosely around her neck. The pair reminded Peter of the Janus Masks.

Yes, I thought it odd he'd employ such an archaic term for the famous drama masks of tragedy and comedy, but then I remembered he had an affection for the arcane. That Janus was a mythological god who represented, of all things, doorways, was enough for him to store that information away knowing there might come a time when he could work it into a conversation, speech or broadcast. Best he let this tidbit go, though, as I happen to know, while Peter has many more years ahead of him on your strange planet, he will never find the right time to let that information loose among the listening public.

So there they stood, live models of not tragedy and comedy exactly, but most certainly sadness and happiness. To his left Isabelle did a bang-up job of representing the former by wearing an expression whose ingredients included one part anger and two parts melancholy. Her look was frozen in place and did not thaw a bit when Peter and she were introduced. To his right, Samantha did happiness proud by sporting an engaging smile that suggested all was right and well in her world thank you very much. Her smile broadened further when it was Peter's turn to shake her hand. While addressing both sisters but looking directly at Samantha, he said graciously, "I can't believe we have all been on the same ship for this amount of time without meeting. This is way overdue. Liz has told me so much about you."

Lillie and Liz, each for their own reasons, noted there was nothing discernibly different in Peter's gentlemanly manner, except that he was slow in releasing Samantha's hand. After a quick exchange of pleasantries, Peter excused himself to check in with the guides. Lillie accompanied him as he walked to the van. "Well, Mr. Ramsey, it appears your niece has arranged quite a fascinating outing for you. I think you'll fare better without me," she said with just a teensy hint of jealousy. "Odd isn't it? The one individual not going on the hike is the one who doesn't require bug spray. Anyway, have a grand time. I'll see you back at the penthouse." Peter tugged at his ear lobe to signal he'd heard her, but she was already back in the penthouse pondering her pouty exit.

The van, thirsty for oil and brake fluid, creaked and groaned as it moved through Skagway to the trailhead. The two Whitby sisters, Mary Pat Flannery and one of the guides squeezed into the far back seat as Mitzi Symington, citing claustrophobia, demanded the front passenger seat. In the middle seats, Peter and Sandy Symington sat on either side of Liz.

The newspaper publisher leaned forward to address Peter, "Sorry for missing your group functions, old boy. Truth is this is the first day I've felt like leaving our penthouse. A bad case of mal de mer, I'm afraid." With his well-known sibilance, Sandy wisely opted to use the French term for sea-sickness. Besides, he thought mal de mer made him sound more aristocratic. He did so want to create the impression that he was to the manor born. Most of the time, though, he could only muster up a quasi-poshness that rang false.

Hearing her husband address Peter, his wife spun around and extended her left hand which supported a gigantic diamond. Mrs. Symington's smile – more a smirk –was now a permanent fixture on a face whose many features had been carefully and expensively re-tooled by some of San Francisco's best known licensed medical professionals. Mitzi was a slender woman who considered the term social X-ray to be a compliment. Her hand, palm down, was inches from Peter who didn't know whether to kiss it or give it an underhanded shake. He choose the latter.

"We haven't met, everyone," she shouted to the occupants in the back of the van, pulling her arm back and glancing at her diamond to see that it was still on her finger. Pointing to her husband, she continued, "I'm Mitzi Symington and that's my husband, Sanford. You may call him Sandy and it's perfectly fine to call me Mitzi."

Her husband acknowledged the introduction by waving his right hand in a royal fashion. "Perhaps, everyone ought to tell us who you are, and what you're famous for," he suggested. All he got back was a quick recitation of names. Peter went last. "Well, everyone knows your famous for being on the radio," Sandy sniffed, his feathers ruffled by the crowd's resistance to play along.

Mitzi, who obviously loved her husband's Who's Famous game, came to his rescue by pointing out to everyone that her partner was a newspaper publisher from San Francisco and she was one of the city's bigger fundraisers. Even that announcement did little to encourage others to either add their own credits or question the Symington's about theirs.

The ensuing silence gave the college-age guides an opportunity to talk about the upcoming hike and float. They were full of good cheer and important information. Everyone listened carefully, particularly to their comments about bears, mountain lions, poison ivy and insects.

Once they'd finished, Mitzi turned to the group behind her and asked Mary Pat Flannery why she wasn't with her husband. "He's not really the hiking sort, Mitzi, as you well know," Dave's wife answered in a steely tone.

Her husband's boss turned toward her. "Hey, I read in the Ship's Log that the two of you are in a dance contest this evening? The tango, of all things." Mary Pat nodded. "Somehow I can't picture Dave on the dance floor. On a barroom floor passed out maybe, but not on a dance floor."

Before Mary Pat could let her Irish temper get the best of her, Peter jumped in, "Actually, he's a fine dancer. As a matter of fact, I think they can win."

Both Symington's laughed loudly. To be exact, Sandy produced a hearty whistling snort while Mitzi , as a result of her cosmetic surgery, emitted a pitiful little giggle. Offended by their insensitive reaction, Peter added without thinking, "I'm so confidant, Sandy, I'd put money on them if anybody wanted to wager."

Sandy's wheels spun for a second and then he said, "Tell you what, Ramsey, if my editor wins, which, by the way, I don't think he will, I'll pay all his shipboard expenses." With that Symington glanced back at Mary Pat and winked. She ignored him.

Mitzi didn't like that idea at all as there was nothing in it for her. "Sandy, darling, don't let Peter off the hook so easily." She looked at Peter. "How about this: If the Flannerys win, Dave gets his shipboard expenses paid and if they lose, you, Mr. Peter Ramsey, have to emcee my upcoming fundraiser at the Fairmont in September."

"I don't do those sorts of things anymore, Mitzi. I'm retired from radio, you know. How about I just donate something to the cause. Whatever it is."

"Actually, I am raising money to start a drop-in Botox-injection center for executive women who have been laid off or had their jobs eliminated. This way, I can help them, admittedly in a small way, to improve their looks and their chances at future employment. We're going to call the new center *Read My Lips!*"

When she had finished, the van's occupants fell into what can only be called mass stupefaction which resulted in a stunned silence. Mitzi reasoned that the lack of response was due to the driver steering the van into a small gravel parking lot near the trailhead. Looking around the van, she nastily offered one last comment, "Well, it's obvious to me that some of you could use a little plumping."

The hikers and floaters devanned. They continued their silence, but now it was a quietude inspired by the grandeur of their surroundings. The guides were quick to tell them that Skagway and surroundings rarely see a day of such spectacular beauty. After a brief explanation of the do's and don'ts of Chilkoot Trail hiking, the guides advised them to hit the bug spray and sun lotion one more time before departing. They then asked them to assemble at the trailhead sign.

Liz walked along with her uncle. "Tio, those two are absolutely insufferable," she whispered.

"Who? The guides? I think they're doing a good job."

"No, I mean the Symingtons. Mary Pat is fuming and I'm sure everybody else is ready to feed them to the first grizzly they see."

"I don't know, I find them amusing in a weird sort of way. As to Mary Pat, my guess is she's been hopping mad at them from the first day Dave joined the paper. If all goes well, she'll get her revenge for their insensitivity by winning the dance contest and getting their shipboard bill paid. That's a pretty good deal."

Liz slowed so they were out of earshot of the rest of the group. "You instructed me to watch Mary Pat and I intend on doing that on the hike. Would you do me a favor and..."

She didn't have to finish the sentence as her uncle interjected, "You want me to entertain the Whitby sisters, particularly Samantha because you do so want us to spend quality time together."

Liz gave him a peck on the cheek. "You're adorable when you're so perceptive. I'm a little puzzled by Isabelle's stoniness. Maybe you can find out what's bothering her."

Just before they began their woodsy walk, Chip, one of the two guides, shouted for their attention. "All right, a couple of notes. This is what we like to call a stop-and-smell-the-roses hike. We are not in a hurry. This is a very unique place and I want you to take it all in and experience it on your terms. Kelly and I aren't going to do too much talking. If you have a question about anything, the names of trees or flowers or animals or the history of this place, just ask. Otherwise, we won't interrupt your own communion with nature. Oh, and one more thing, the first person who either sings or suggests we all sing *The Happy Wanderer* will be thrown into the first batch of poison ivy we find."

chapter 22

THEY WALKED, OR some version thereof, single file on a steep and narrow portion of the damp Chilkoot Trail, their guide, Kelly, leading the way. Behind her, Liz moved with a jaunty stride, arms swinging, her head turning every which way to try and take in every morsel of the old growth rainforest. She was followed by Mary Pat, a shuffler who tended to keep her head down. Next was Sandy Symington who, instead of walking, marched as if off to some war only he knew about. The publisher was in a funk because he thought having a hearty sing-a-long was just what the doctor ordered and there was no more perfect a song than *The Happy Wanderer* to put some kick in everyone's step. But then Chip, who was bringing up the rear, had to go and throw water on that idea. Three goose steps back was his spouse, the ultra-thin Mitzi Symington, who with her model's strut treated the earthen path is if it were a fashion runway. Isabelle came next. Like Mary Pat Flannery, she was another eyes-to-the-ground hiker. The rear contingent was made up of Samantha Whitby who walked like the veteran hiker she was, thanks to hours spent in the Berkeley Hills, and Peter who, while making every effort to keep his head erect, found himself frequently looking down to not only watch where he was stepping but to also admire Samantha's well-shaped legs.

In the early going of the hike, all was quiet on the trail. Everyone seemed to take to heart Chip's suggestion that they silently commune with nature. After determining there was sufficient space between Samantha and the rest to carry on a quiet conversation without bothering the others, Peter asked her if she was enjoying the cruise. She turned slightly and nodded yes. "I assume from her shirt that your sister teaches at Boston College?" he asked.

They were at a point where the trail widened and Samantha Whitby slowed until she was alongside Peter. "Isabelle teaches Comparative Literature there. Your niece, I'm sure, has told you English Lit is my specialty at Cal." Her voice was cheery and her smile captivating.

Before he could respond, though, Mitzi, whose hearing was so acute, it was rumored that in a noisy room full of the social elite she could hear a hushed conversation twenty paces away, shouted, "Attention hikers, it seems we have two university professors with us. I had no idea we were in such high-brow company."

Symington stepped off the path to allow his wife to catch up. Grinning, he said to her, "Darling, you obviously forgot our esteemed leader called for a moratorium on speaking and singing while hiking."

"Better watch where you're stepping, Mr. Symington," Chip suddenly hollered up the line.

Clearly irritated, Symington snipped, "So now you're telling us where we can and can't step?"

Chip rushed past Peter, the Whitbys and Mitzi to confront the pouting publisher who had come to a stop. The others closed in around them. Chip couldn't stand the man's prissiness, but he knew that how he treated him would determine the size of the gratuity at the end of the excursion, and he needed substantial tip money to pay for his next semester in Colorado. Softening his tone, he said,

"My only aim, sir, is to help you get the most out of this special place."

"Perhaps so, but you did make it clear you don't want any singing."

Chip laughed. "That was meant as a joke," he explained, even though he truly abhorred *The Happy Wanderer* and fantasized brutally punishing any hiker who sang it.

"So why the urgent warning to watch my step?"

"Because you just stepped in bear scat." Chip bent down to examine the excrement. Startled, Symington quickly looked down to check the bottoms of his brand new hiking shoes. The rest watched anxiously as Chip poked at the scat. "The good news is it's been here awhile. He's probably moved on."

Chip noticed the concern on his charges' faces. He'd seen it many times before. Everything is hunky-dory on the hike until the bear word pops up. That's when most of his clients realize they are sharing this beautiful neighborhood with other living creatures including one species who considers a hearty mauling to be heaps of fun and good for their cholesterol. This merry band was no different. Mary Pat Flannery no doubt spoke for the group when she asked, "Chip, you said the bear probably moved on. You're not sure?"

Sensing the need for some expert outdoorsman's comforting reassurance, Chip cleared his throat and replied, "Kelly and I have been taking people on this hike and float for two seasons now and we've yet to encounter a bear of any kind. Haven't seen a grizzly, a black or a brown. Certainly not a polar bear. Too far south for that. Heck, I don't even remember ever seeing a Teddy Bear on the trail." He looked around to see if his humorous explanation relaxed them but most were too busy furtively looking at the wilderness that surrounded them. Did they see movement in the trees or was it just the breeze?

The rest of the hike portion went off without a hitch. Symington, sensing it bothered Chip, spent a lot of his time humming *The Happy Wanderer.* Mitzi was surprisingly quiet as she was still on edge about the possibility of there being a bear in the woods. Mary Pat, Liz and Isabelle walked together, quietly chatting. Dropping back a distance from the rest, Samantha and Peter resumed the conversation he tried to start in the early goings of the hike.

"Isabelle seems to be enjoying Liz's and Mrs. Flannery's company," Samantha observed. "She not smiling yet, but seeing my sister not frowning or looking forlorn or angry is immensely pleasing."

Peter wasn't sure he should pry. Instead, he said, "Well, if anyone can cheer someone up, it's my perky, ain't-life-grand, glass-half-full niece."

"She's very special. And she thinks the world of you," she said.

"So tell me how you came to be on this cruise."

Samantha slowed her pace as did Peter. "I'm here because of Isabelle. Three weeks ago her only child, Emily, graduated from Cornell and left immediately for New York to work in the marketing department of a tech firm."

"So your sister and husband are now adjusting to life as empty nesters?"

"I wish it were that easy. You see, her husband, Jeremy, decided with Emily gone, it was high time he moved on as well." The explanation caused her lovely smile to evaporate. Even so, with her expressive eyes and gentle manner, she still radiated a natural cheeriness. "Isabelle was never what you would call a happy person, and she certainly was not the easiest person to live with. Nevertheless, she didn't deserve what happened to her and the ugly manner in which it happened. Anyway, I decided my sisterly responsibility was to somehow lift her spirits as best I can. I suggested this cruise and insisted she come along." She looked up at Peter, shaded her blue eyes from the sun, flashed that engaging smile again and added, "So here we are!"

"You're a good sister," he said.

"Trust me, I am," she laughed.

The hike portion had come to an end at the banks of the seventeen mile-long Taiya River. Stretching from the British Columbia border to its terminus just outside Skagway, the waterway played a key role in the Klondike Gold Rush as thousands of prospectors opted to bypass the challenging and crowded White Pass trail to take the Chilkoot Trail and the Taiya River to the headwaters of the Yukon River for the journey to Dawson in the Yukon Territory. It, too, was a daunting trek considerably longer and far more arduous than the few miles our hikers would log.

Chip and Kelly were efficient in overseeing the boarding process. Soon, everyone was comfortably settled in a large rubber raft, snug in their life jackets and eager for the ride on a swift, but easy-going current to the van. Their eagerness heightened by the sudden presence of annoying gnat-like creatures that seemed to love their faces.

Chip took a moment before shoving off to tell them about the float portion of the excursion: "Kelly and I hope you enjoyed the Chilkoot Trail hike. Now you get a chance to sit back and relax as we float through the Klondike Gold Rush National Park. There's lots to see here, so keep alert. You might spot a wolf, coyote or maybe an otter. In the sky and in the trees, keep an eye out for eagles, hawks and ravens." He thought it wise to avoid mentioning bears as also being proud members of the local fauna population.

Seeing the incredible beauty of the place from the river had a profound effect on everyone. They were awed by their surroundings, asking lots of questions of Chip and Kelly. By journey's end, they had all seen two eagles and a playful otter. Mitzi, however, swore she saw an enormous beer on the right bank who, it seems, only had eyes for her.

Back at the pier, Peter pulled Chip aside and gave him a larger-than-usual tip, more than enough to cover the Symingtons who, when the van came to a stop, jumped out and headed directly to the ship without saying a word to anyone.

"I noticed you and Samantha in deep conversation on the trail," Liz said, as she and Peter made their way to the gang plank. "Isn't she wonderful?"

"She's..." Peter stopped and faced his niece. "Samantha is warm, exceedingly warm and soft. Yes, soft, too."

"Tio, you sound like you're doing a toilet paper commercial," Liz joked. "And you're getting announcerish on me again."

"Sorry, but those are the first two words that come to mind when I think of her. Anyway, what you really want to know is am I interested in seeing her."

Liz approached the security officer and produced her card key for identification. She looked back at her uncle and said, "Well, do you?"

"Yes, I would like to get to know her better. However, right now, we need to tend to the business of the day which is the dance contest at five-thirty. Until then you're in charge of Mary Pat and I've got to go see what's happened to Dave and his two Kwyrki babysitters. I'm curious to find out if the syrup worked. If not, I'm afraid all we'll have is a tango dancer with dyspepsia."

I am, frankly, amused by the dizzying array of stimulants available to the average air-breather and the myriad circumstances that seem to require added stimuli other than that which an individual produces naturally. In Dave's case, one hopes that Petra's syrup is physiologically doing the job for which it's intended. If not, one hopes Dave can be stimulated psychologically by merely thinking it is working. Ah, the marvels of the harmless placebo. Now I am not proselytizing here, but I do want to throw in a good word for a stimulant called spirituality. The good news is you can take as much of it as you want. There's no chance of overdosing and there are no dangerous side effects. Perhaps, one. You do tend to smile a lot.

Peter arrived at his penthouse with time to spare before Dave was due. There was no Lillie. Having a friend who is a spirit can be frustrating because they are incapable of leaving any kind of note to let you know where they're off to. Peter was hoping they could have a few minutes together before he had to give all his attention to Dave.

At exactly four-thirty there was a loud knock on the door. Wearing hang-dog expressions, Petra and Yurk, framed the doorway with Dave behind them. Their punctuality prompted by the fact that they were extremely anxious to turn their charge over to Peter, as they'd had their fill of him.

"Please, don't tell me he's drunk," Peter groaned, stepping aside to let them enter.

Petra looked at Peter through heavy-lidded eyes and shrugged. "I don't think so, but he should be," he mumbled.

Yurk merely burped.

Dave pushed past the three of them and collapsed onto the sofa. Pointing to his two companions, he said in a gravelly, theatrical voice, "Ramsey, we few, we happy few, we band of brothers had a hell of a day." His left eye was framed in bruised purple. "Say hello to Bedford and Exeter."

"You have a black eye, Henry."

"No, I have a purple eye. I saw it in the mirror in the men's room. Do you have a beer in that minibar?" he asked.

Ignoring him, Peter phoned Liz, explained matters and asked her to come up and do a rush cosmetic repair job on Flannery's eye. Putting the phone down, he looked over at Petra. "What happened?"

"We went to town for lunch. There is a place called Klondike Kate's. It's a saloon that used to be a brothel and a dancehall during the rush for gold days. It is very popular with people from all the cruise ships. We were lucky and found three stools at the bar in the back near the bathrooms."

"How did he get the shiner?" Peter asked, looking over at the man on the sofa and wondering if he could realistically get him in shape for the dance contest that was one hour away.

"Ken hit him," Petra replied, barely able to suppressed a grin.

"Who is Ken?"

"He is a doll."

"A doll? Let me guess. The Ken doll goes to the men's room. Flannery starts hitting on Barbie. Remembering he is not anatomically correct and didn't need to go, Ken returns, sees what was going on and decked Dave." From the corner of his eye, he saw movement and barked, "Dave, stay away from the fridge. In fact, now that you're up and moving, go take a shower and shave."

With the shower running and muffled strains of an atonal version of *I've Got You Under My Skin* coming from the bathroom, Peter showed Petra and Yurk out. Concerned about no apparent evidence that the syrup was working, he asked them their opinion.

"It is puzzling, Peter. Usually by now, I would be chasing Inka around the stateroom. Mr. Flannery shows no sign of being interested in sex. I am worried it didn't have any effect on him. There goes my bet."

"By the way, how *did* he come by that black eye?"

The question elicited laughs from both Petra and Yurk. The elder Kwyrki explained, "Like you said, it did involved Ken and the bathroom. In Klondike Kate's, they have a Barbie doll outfitted as a dance hall girl attached to the women's room door. The Ken doll is dressed in prospector clothes holding a tiny mining shovel and it is about head high on the men's room door. After three beers, Mr. Flannery rushed off to the bathroom. He was about to open the door when a young boy inside swung the door open and the Ken doll found his eye."

Peter thanked them for their help and said he'd see them at the competition. "I don't know why, and this may sound crazy, but I'm still hopeful, gentlemen. You haven't lost your bet yet, Petra."

It was a worrisome hour. Peter studied David Augustus Flannery, watching for any sign, no matter how subtle, that the Kwyrki syrup was working. Nothing! Now, with five minutes to spare before they needed to be in Club Glamour for the dance competition, he inspected the final product. Dave was sober, of that he was certain. He was also clean and shaven. Liz had done an excellent job of covering his black eye, and, surprisingly, he was not sporting his usual tousled, bed-head look. As for attire, though, Flannery was his old wrinkled self; dark grey slacks, white shirt, paisley tie and a herringbone jacket finished off with his trademark Hermes' pocket square. Admittedly, he was dressed more for one of his editorial meetings than a dance contest, but it would have to do. Flannery watched amusedly while Peter gave him the once over. "So, coach, how do I look?" he asked, executing a nimble dance step.

"Lose the tie," Peter commanded. Dave did as instructed. "Now unbutton the first two buttons. Let me see some chest."

"Jeez," he grumbled, but complied. "Now what? You want me to roll up my pants?"

"If I thought it would help," Peter replied, "but as the tango is done in long pants, you're fine. Actually, Dave, you look pretty good. The big question is how do you feel?"

"Nervous." He looked in the mirror and tried opening the top part of shirt even more. "As for that magic elixir, it's had zero effect on me. But the waffle was delicious." Feeling Peter needed some reassurance after all he did to help him, Flannery added, "Hey look, I'm going to give it my best shot. Okay? If I don't win, Mary Pat will still be happy. It's not like we've got big money riding on it. Besides, the only people who are going to be there are the people from the dance classes and they're a pretty sympathetic bunch except for that Russian couple."

Peter wondered what was going through Dave's mind when they arrived at the starboard side of Club Glamour and saw that, instead of a few dance enthusiasts and a couple of people lingering at the U-shaped bar, the entire place was packed. SRO, standing room only! By the way, no SRO in the eternal hereafter. I daresay we're a promoter's dream. Anyway, back to where space is measured in finite terms: the wide-open, spacious circular lounge with its two tiers of tables and chairs surrounding an ample-size dance floor and stage was full to the brim with an audience fully alert to the fact that some kind of spectacle was about to unfold. Escorting a now visibly nervous Flannery through the lounge to the stage, Peter caught snatches of conversation that explained why. Word had evidently spread through the guest and crew population that big money was being wagered on the tango portion of the competition. Peter knew the spreader had to be Anatoly Plushenko.

"I'm outta here," Dave mumbled, as they moved closer to the stage. "I can't do this, Ramsey. Where the hell did all these people come from?"

"Dave, don't worry," Peter said without any conviction, realizing there was nothing substantive or meaningful he could say that would placate Dave or put him at ease.

The newspaper editor reluctantly followed Peter onto the stage where they were directed to two unoccupied folding chairs that were stage left of the band. Dave sat down and looked across to where Anatoly Plushenko and his partner, Svetlana Plovanovavichskaya, were seated on the other side of the band. Anatoly, in his trademark tight black tee-shirt and black slacks, spotting Dave staring at him, shouted across the stage, "Hey, Flannery, I like your new dance partner. Couldn't find someone of the opposite sex to dance with you, huh?" Svetlana looked dazzling in a skin-tight white dance leotard and linen skirt. Her sober expression suggested she didn't approve of her dance partner's trash talking. Anatoly laughed aloud.

Dave made a motion to charge across the stage. Peter who stood behind him put his hands on his shoulders and forcefully held him down. "Don't let him rile you, Dave."

"He was always making insulting comments in the dance class." Dave explained, while continuing to glare at the Russian pair. "I let it slide because the remarks weren't directed to anyone in particular. Now, it's personal."

"Well, harness that angry energy and use it on the dance floor," Peter said.

While the band played some unidentified piece, the ship's dance instructors bounded on stage. Professional dancers by trade, the cute and compact pair were joined by two gentleman and one lady who had been selected to be the judges. Their qualifications were never explained. Peter had always wondered why there were only two couples in the tango dance. What he didn't know was that Anatoly had so intimidated the other dancers in the class, none of them signed up to compete. Just having two couples dancing brought a heightened level of tension to the contest. Peter looked around the lounge and saw a crowd that wanted action. They had already sat through tepid performances of the samba, foxtrot and waltz. The tango was the last act and the most anticipated.

The male dance instructor came over and told Peter it was time for him to leave the stage. He also snippily reminded Dave that his partner was late. Peter found a spot near the stage. It was close to a smaller side entrance to the club on the port side. He stood facing the crowd when he felt a sharp poke. Turning, he saw Mitzi Symington, her inflated Botoxed lips holding a straw whose other end was drilled into an elaborate and colorful punch-like cocktail. She was alone. Deserting the straw and grimacing, she said, "Oh my! Dave looks a complete mess. This is going to be ugly and I personally am going to enjoy every minute of it. And don't forget our bet, Peter, darling."

Peter took another look at Dave. Nerves had taken a heavy toll. He sat round-shouldered, head down, looking much like a boxer who after nine punishing rounds slumped in his corner, bruised, swollen and battered. While there were no visible injuries, Dave's pained expression spoke volumes. It said, briefly, "I will somehow go out there, fall down, let them count to ten and then I will crawl to the first bar I see." Peter's heart went out to him.

Then David Augustus Flannery lifted his head and saw Mary Patricia Flannery.

chapter 23

PETER WAS ECSTATIC over the outcome of the dance competition. It was a euphoria he'd not experienced before, and it got him thinking about, of all things, auto racing. Reaching across the small table, he filled Liz's champagne flute with the Veuve Clicquot Bartal had just delivered. After returning the bottle to the chilly confines of the silver ice bucket, he lifted his glass in a toast. "Here's to us. Now I know what the pit crew of an winning Indy 500 car feels like."

"Possibly, except they'd all be in their fire-retardant jumpsuits in some grease-filled garage spraying each other with this good stuff instead of drinking it," Liz remarked, staring at the mousse in her glass which was still de-bubbling. Noticing her uncle eyeing the bottle, she said sharply, "Tio, don't you dare shake that up! We're not NASCAR or NOCAR or whatever they call those racing associations. So behave."

"I'm only going to top off your glass, Liz. All you got the first time was foam," he said, pouring her a little more. "This calls for another toast. Here's to Dave and Mary Pat and their truly amazing performance."

Clinking glasses, Liz said, "Here, here. Their dancing was so hot, I still blush thinking about it. They both were totally intense and scary good. Dave was a surprise. He really is one bad dancer."

"While I'll never understand your fascinating choice of adjectives, my dear," Lillie said, "I must say I agree with you about the Flannerys' superb interpretation of the tango. It was truly passionate. And, Peter, your comparison to that motor race brought back a special memory."

Liz looked mildly aghast. "Lillie, don't tell me you know about the Indy 500?"

"Know about it, dear? I was there for the first one in 1911. My husband, Hugo de Bathe and I were in America on some sort of business. A friend suggested we join him even though he knew Hugo was more a horseman than an auto enthusiast. I was not entertained at all. I found it to be a hot, noisy, dirty and oily experience. Also, I was of a certain age where spending long hours watching cars making repetitive left turns was tedious to a fault."

Peter and Liz stared in wonderment at the lavender vision that was Lillie. Liz then asked if she remembered any specific details of that first Indy. Her reply came wrapped in that dry, passionless monotone she used whenever the arcane and trivial poured out of her for reasons even she couldn't grasp: "Ray Harroun was the winning driver. He averaged seventy-four miles per hour in his Marmon Wasp, crossing the finish line in six hours and forty-two minutes. You don't require the seconds, do you?"

"No, that's not necessary," Liz said. Peter shook his head in agreement.

Bewildered as they were, she said, "Why I know all this is beyond me. We didn't even stay for the finish."

The three had returned to Peter's penthouse after the dance competition and were chatting about not only the Flannery's winning tango but their personal transformations. David, in what seemed a heart beat, went from a woebegone, unromantic underdog to a self-confident gent possessed of a heady masculine charm and presence. Mary Pat, whose over-haul took a bit more time and effort – a process which will be explained in detail later – went from a cute-as-a-button, fresh-faced Irish lass to a sublime temptress.

Dave Flannery's metamorphosis began shortly after Liz let go of his wife's arm at the far end of the dance floor, thus allowing Mary Pat to walk unaccompanied across the deserted floor to take her seat next to him on the stage. What got his attention? It may have been her all too familiar per-fume or hearing the murmured approval of the spectators or simply a spouse's sense that their mate is nearby. Whatever the reason, he stopped staring at the six square inches of stage floor beneath his feet and, like everyone else in Club Glamour, looked up to gaze upon the ravishing creature headed his way. Mrs. Flannery was striking, outfitted in a body-hugging, coral-red halter dress with a flared skirt that was short in front and long in back. In short, the perfect dress to handle the provocative moves of the tango. Even though she was test-driving an absurdly high pair of heels, she strode gracefully and confidently across the floor, proudly showing off her newly acquired sexiness. Mary Pat Flan-nery quite frankly, glowed. I could add she also glistened and glimmered, but the alliteration police would haul my amanuensis away.

While her dramatic entrance caught most people's eyes, Peter's were affixed on her husband who, seeing his wife approaching, instantly sat up straight, throwing his shoul-ders back and holding his head high. Then he rose. Peter watched as the wrinkles began to fall out of his clothes, his beer belly receded, his hair fell into place and he seemed taller. Or so it seemed to Peter at the time. By the time Mary Pat arrived at the stage, David had shed his coat, placed it over the back of the folding chair and stepped forward to take her hand, escorting her to her seat. Peter was convinced that David Augustus Flannery was ready to dance. Actually, Peter knew Dave was now fired up to do a lot more than dance. He only hoped his co-host understood the tango had to come first.

"I'm going to record this ridiculous spectacle and put it on You Tube," Mitzi announced, rudely aiming a camcorder the size of a deck of cards at Peter. Moving around him to get a better view of the dance floor, she continued, "Flannery's such a jerk. You have no idea. Oh, the stories I could tell. You know he hates me. He really does. Anyway, knowing thousands of people will be able to watch him making a complete ass of himself thrills me no end."

Peter had now seen enough of Dave's positive transformation to know how the evening would play out. He was so certain of the outcome he felt he needed to do something to demonstrate his confidence in him no matter how silly or grand the gesture. Thus, he did both. Tapping Mitzi on the shoulder, he said, "Mrs. Symington, on the hike today, I told you I'd contribute to your Botox charity if Dave loses. How about a side wager just between the two of us?"

Looking up at him and flirtatiously batting her awning-like eyelashes, she whispered, "And just what do you propose, Mr. Ramsey?"

"If Dave loses, I'll emcee your charity fundraiser."

She continued to bat her eyes while her Botoxed lips struggled to form the sort of smile meant to send a sexually naughty message. I must add here that Mitzi Symington was not unfaithful to her spouse. She did, however, enjoy creating sexual tension between herself and men she found particularly appealing, and Peter was definitely one of them. Actually, truth be told, most men fell into that category. "And if he wins, what do you want from little Mitzi?" she cooed coquettishly.

Peter noticed her husband approaching. "Not much. You loan me your camera so I can post the video of them winning. Something I gather you wouldn't do."

"No, I wouldn't," she snapped, shutting down eye-batting and her distorted smile.

"Mitzi, one more thing. Can you include the Russian pair when you record the dance?" Shrugging her bone-thin shoulders, she asked why. "For a couple of reasons. For your benefit, if Dave is as rotten a dancer as you say he is, seeing the Russians on camera will only make him look worse."

She put her hand up, stopping him there. "That's reason enough."

"Reason enough for what, sweetie?" asked her husband who had quietly sneaked up behind them.

"Peter and I were just talking about the details of our little bet on the dance contest, dear," she explained.

Symington grinned. "Ah yes, I believe I said I'd pay his bar bill if he won."

Peter shook his head. "I distinctly remember you saying you'd cover all his onboard expenses."

"Trust me, his bar bill will be ninety per cent of that," he laughed. "Besides, I'm not going to lose. You, however, will be making a sizable donation to Mitzi's charity." Symington glanced over at the Flannerys sitting quietly on the stage. Unlike Peter, he saw Dave's wrinkles, messy hair and beer belly. This is going to be like taking candy from a baby, he thought.

"Sandy, let's fatten our wager. Right now the Flannerys are in a stateroom on the seventh deck that has an obstructed view which really means no view at all. They deserve better. He's my co-host and he's basically in steerage. So here's what I propose: We arrange to have them moved to a stateroom with a verandah on deck nine. If the Flannerys win, you pay for the upgrade. If they lose, I'll cover it."

Symington pondered. When he pondered, his eyes went skyward as if a divine power was ready with the correct response. Then he pursed his thin lips and moved his mouth right to left. "You are a glutton for punishment, Ramsey. All right, you have a bet." He extended a bony hand to make it official.

It was Lillie who reminded him of his foolishness. "I know what you think you saw, Peter," she said, appearing at his side when Mitzi and Symington left to join a couple at a ringside table. "I saw it, too. Dave so reminded me of when I first met Bertie. I saw that same fiery infatuation in his eyes and then, of course, how the romantic infection grew, affecting his every gesture, move and word. I thought it utterly romantic at the time. However, I doubt I could have entered Bertie in a tango contest with an assurance that that burning passion would guarantee his winning. You, Peter, have extended yourself and the Symingtons may have the last laugh."

If one is to be scolded for a foolhardy action, who better to deliver the reprimand than Mrs. Langtry with her caring, velvety glove approach. Peter, feeling properly chastised, began a weak but understandable defense of his actions. First, though, they moved to the hallway where it was quiet and he wouldn't be seen talking to himself. "Alright, Lillie, I'll admit offering to emcee that ridiculous woman's Botox fundraiser was wrong. However, I truly feel bad about the Flannerys' stateroom situation. We're co-hosts of this cruise and I'm in a comfy, spacious penthouse while they have to put up with a broom closet with no view and no outside space. If I lose the bet, I'll be happy to pay for their upgrade, but I don't think I'll have to. When Mary Pat joined him on stage, I looked at Dave and saw a winning dancer."

Indeed, he did, and it didn't take long for the Flannerys to bring home the bacon. Five minutes, in fact, from the time Kelly Fenton, the excessively perky cruise director, walked to the microphone to introduce the two couples to when he returned to crown the victors. After Kelly instructed the couples to take their places on the dance floor, the Russians bounded off the stage like tightly wound springs. The pair skip-danced their way to the far end where they waited for their opponents. Dave, meantime, had stepped cautiously off the stage, careful to watch his step. He then helped Mary Pat while she stepped down. They stayed close to the stage, holding hands and facing each other, their posture straight. Watching with interest, Plushenko hollered across the floor, "You two want me to bring your walkers?" Dave ignored him completely, as dealing with Anatoly would mean taking his eyes off his wife.

"Ladies and gentlemen, we have been waiting for this moment. It's time now for the tango portion of this evening's dance competition. Our very talented dance instructors, Irene and Stefan..." Pausing, he cued the audience to applaud them, whereupon they took a professional bow. "Thank you," he continued. "Now the music Irene and Stefan have selected for this evening's tango is *Hernando's Hideaway* from the Broadway musical *Pajama Game*." With a dramatic pause, the timing perfected from saying and doing the same thing cruise after cruise for the last eight years, Kelly asked, "Are our dancers ready?"

Certainly the audience was. They cheered lustily. So much so, the band leader waited a few seconds before giving the downbeat. When the music finally began, the dancers began to move. The audience fell quiet, stunned into silence by the mastery of the tango both couples were exhibiting. Both the Flannerys and their Russian opponents chose to dance the traditional American Ballroom Tango with its sharp head snaps, open moves and side-by-side choreography. For the first minute, it appeared as if the judges would struggle to find a winner, as both couples danced so magnificently. But then something happened. Anatoly made a fatal mistake. Hearing the rounds of applause and boisterous hurrahs, he became concerned. He had first sensed that the audience's positive response was directed solely towards them. Suddenly, he wasn't so sure, so he let his eyes wander to glimpse the seamless, fluid moves of Dave and Mary Pat. Unfortunately, when he turned his attention back to Svetlana, his manner reflected the anger and frustration that was building up in him. Thus, while the Russian couple continued to dance superbly, any observer could only assume from Anatoly's sullen demeanor that as soon as the dance was over, so was their relationship. The Flannerys were another story entirely. They saw no one as their eyes were locked on each other. Every step they took, every move they made created for each a... Now here's where I can get really silly. Shall I described the physical sensations they were experiencing as paroxysms of pleasure of jolts of joy? Take your pick. Suffice it to say the Flannery's seductive moves advertised to one and all that once the last note was sounded, they were headed directly to their stateroom where the Do Not Disturb sign would be put out for a considerable length of time. The musicians knew this. Liz, Peter, Lillie and the Petras knew this. So did the crew and passengers packed into Club Glamour that historic evening. When *Hernando's Hideaway* was finally shuttered for the night, the crowd came to their feet, whooping and clapping. Some of the more romantically sensitive, pulled out hankies to wipe away tears of happiness.

The tango is a dance of seduction and that's what made the Flannerys the crowd favorite. For them, the dancing, or rather, the seduction began not when the first note was struck but when Dave welcomed his wife to the stage. From that moment on their behavior was electrifying and intensely personal. It was noticed by all.

Fortunately for the winning couple, the award ceremony was short and sweet. After a chirpy word from the cruise director and the presentation of a pair of champagne flutes with the Ocean Glamour insignia embossed on them, the Flannerys were on their way to their stateroom. The lounge emptied quickly as the guests were eager to sample all the myriad shipboard activities Kelly had promoted before bringing the dance competition to a close and ending the show.

As the crowd thinned, Peter spotted Petra Dosynk making a beeline for Anatoly who was getting an earful from Svetlana. No doubt, Petra was anxious to collect his ten thousand dollars. After arranging to meet Liz and Lillie back at the Penthouse, he walked to the table where the Symingtons sat alone, grim-faced. "If you like, Sandy, I'll be happy to deal with the stateroom move. I'll just have them put it on your account with instructions to also transfer over all their onboard charges. Believe me, it will be my pleasure."

The newspaper publisher nodded glumly and made a gesture meant to send Peter on his way. But there was more business to be done. "Mitzi, I'll have that camera, please," he said, holding his hand out.

"Oh shit! It seems I accidentally deleted it," she said, sitting back and treating him to a snide smile.

"Probably for the best. I don't think Dave would have wanted it on You Tube," he said affably. "So, it looks like our business is done. I want to say I really enjoyed our hike today and it was a pleasure getting to know both of you."

"Oh, bullshit, Ramsey. Stop being the gentleman. It's fucking tedious," Sandy Symington barked. "Just get the hell out of here."

Let us now bid adieu to the swearing Symingtons as they have served their purpose as regards my story. Between now and when I decide to slap a happy ending on all this, neither Sandy nor Mitzi will be seen or heard as they will have managed somehow to always be on the port side of the ship while Peter and his gang were starboard and vice versa.

Peter took another sip of the Veuve Clicquot. It was an especially satisfying champagne. "Lillie, I know I acted foolishly as regards the betting. Anyway, the good news is I don't have to contribute to that silly woman's even sillier charity and I'm not out any money."

"Excuse me, Tio, there were some expenditures," Liz said tentatively.

"Expenditures? For what?" he asked, knowing that before he got an answer, his niece will give him the *look*. It was a disapproving glance that Liz had developed over the years that loosely translated meant, "I don't know why you'd even ask that question."

Tio," she said with the exasperating sigh that always accompanied the *look*, "how do you think I got Mary Pat to look so drop-dead gorgeous?"

"Of course, I should have known that," Peter responded. "How silly of me to ask. So, just how much did it cost me to turn Mrs. Flannery into a sex goddess for a three-minute tango?"

Liz pulled a slip of paper out of her slacks' pocket. "Can I round it out?"

"Please."

"Nine hundred dollars."

"Nine hundred dollars!" That's when Liz was treated to Peter's *look*.

Fully understanding its meaning, she rushed to explain, "First there's the dress. Shipboard prices are sinful but it was on sale. We saved on shoes, though, because the sale's' girl loaned her a pair when she heard about the contest. Then there's the various spa charges, including eye-brow waxing, hair-styling, makeup, that sort of thing."

Before Peter could respond, Lillie came to Liz's defense. "I'm afraid, Peter, I played a significant role in this. I knew how vital it was for you that Dave and Mary Pat win the contest. You were doing all you could for Dave. I felt we should do all we could for Mary Pat. After all, it takes two to tango."

"No, in this case, it took about about eight of us to tango."

"Be that as it may, I want you to know that Liz was initially very reluctant to spend your money."

"And you weren't?"

"If I had any, I would have gladly invested in Mrs. Flannery's transformative makeover. Now that you know the outcome, you must agree it was good we did what we did."

Peter thought for a moment about how Dave came romantically alive when Mary Pat walked across the dance floor. "Yes, I agree. Having said that, I can think of a really fascinating question." He looked at them both and asked, "What do you think did the trick?"

"What do you mean?" Liz asked.

"I know what he's asking, Liz," Lillie said. "Your uncle would like to know which of the many stratagems, for lack of a better term, should get the credit for putting the Flannerys in the winners' circle. Was it Mary Pat's stunning makeover? Did Mr. Petra Dosynk's magic syrup really work? Was it the day-long separation? Were our prayers heard?"

Liz volunteered, "How about all of the above?"

They all agreed that was the best answer.

chapter 24

IT WAS 3:42 in the morning when Lillie realized what she was feeling for Peter Ramsey was, as I'm sure you'll understand, problematical. Why am I in such high spirits, she asked herself, laughingly dismissing the idea that she was falling for him. Even so, she had to admit that whatever was going on felt very, very good. Did I know this would happen to her? Of course, I did. Does that imply Predestination? Not at all. I'm the story-teller. I know these things. That said, do I want to weigh in on the P word? Sorry, I can't do that. Nor can I expound on Fortuitism, Latitudinarianism, Dualism and the myriad other Isms. The rules of the game state quite clearly that those doctrines, theories and beliefs are there for you rational-minded, free-willed air-breathers to play with, and, I stress, with no help from Above. They are, after all, your creations. A bit of advice, though: If you should find yourself among a bunch of wagging tongues debating the merits of, let's say, Fallibilism, and it's getting a little too heady, a clever exit is to roll out a few incomprehensible sentences and then finish it up with Oscar Wilde's pithy comment: *"I'm so clever that sometimes, I don't understand a single word of what I'm saying."* Nothing like a well-placed bon mot to leave 'em laughing or, at least, scratching their heads.

It was nearing sunrise and the Ocean Glamour was quietly sneaking up on the entrance to Glacier Bay. A giddy Mrs. Langtry was on the penthouse verandah, her favorite place to park when alone. But now she didn't want to be alone as the early light with the help of a cloudless sky unveiled a spectacle of such magnificence and dazzling beauty that she was eager to share it with Peter. However, this being an Alaskan dawning with the sun announcing its bright arrival before the little hand hit four, she decided it was too frightful an hour to wake a man who had gone to bed just two hours earlier.

It had been a transcendent evening for both. It began just before seven when Liz begged off dinner, claiming she really needed to study. Peter decided to call Bartal and order dinner in. After Liz left, Petra Dosynk rang.

"Congratulations to you, Peter," he shouted into the phone as if he were calling from Kwyrkistan. "What was it? That funny name you called all of us this morning at breakfast?"

"Team Tango?"

"Yes, that is it. Well, Yurk and I were proud to be a part of Team Tango," he boomed. "It was a fine thing seeing that Russian put in his place."

"I saw you go over to him after the contest. Did you collect on your bet?" Peter asked.

"No, I told him I didn't want his money. Just seeing him lose was enough for me."

"Ten thousand dollars is a lot of money, Petra."

"Peter, it is not good money if it comes from him. I don't want gangster money," he said, explaining why he let Plushenko off the hook.

"Petra, you amaze me," Peter said. "By the way, thanks for the syrup. It certainly worked its magic."

After a lengthy silence, Peter asked, "Petra, are you there?"

"Yes, I am," he replied sheepishly, not in his usual loud blustery voice. "Peter, the syrup didn't work its magic."

"What do you mean, it didn't work?"

"I couldn't find my supply. We looked everywhere but it was gone. I knew it was somewhere and I would eventually find it, so I went to the bistro and got a small bottle of their maple syrup and put it in one of my empty containers and had it delivered to your room. My plan was to find the real syrup and switch it before the breakfast."

"And you didn't find it in time and Dave ended up having the ship's maple syrup with his waffle instead?"

"I'm afraid that is so."

"Did you ever find it?"

"Yes, Inka hadn't unpacked all of it and the rest was in our luggage in storage. I am very embarrassed, Peter."

"Petra, David won the contest," Peter said. Now that it was after the fact, he found it all very funny. "That's all that matters. Don't worry about it. Look at it this way, if Flannery asks for more, I can tell him where there's an unlimited supply."

"Thank you for understanding," Petra said. "I must go. We're late for dinner. We will see each other soon, I hope. Maybe have one of those special coffee drinks in the Portside Bistro."

After Petra rang off, Peter ordered dinner. Bartal tried to press a Hungarian goulash with potato dumplings on him as the chef happened to be his cousin twice-removed and wanted to cook something special for him. It seems Bartal, aware of Peter's confidence in Flannery, told the chef to put a chunk of his hard-earned on the editor to win the tango competition. Peter, calculating the dinner would be in the region of seven thousand calories, while gracious in his refusal, nevertheless stood firm on his request for a grilled salmon and small salad. While he dined, Lillie entertained him with amusing anecdotes from her colorful past. After pouring himself a cognac, Peter suggested they move to the verandah where he first checked to see that the penthouses on either side were dark before they settled in and began to talk. And talk they did, until just before two in the morning. In the early goings, the voluble pair exchanged autobiographical sketches of themselves. They spoke of their families, education and religious training. Lillie spoke of her romances, marriages and affairs. Peter in turn shared his romantic resume' even though it paled in comparison. As the evening evolved, they told stories of successes and achievements, disappointments and failures. Their final conversational foray was into the complex world of spirituality. Peter kicked it off when he asked offhandedly, "Lillie, do you remember the other day asking me if I believed in God?"

"I do. I also remember how awkward I felt. The living Lillie would have never asked such a question.

"Why is that?"

"During my lifetime, I made a practice of slipping graciously away from any discussion of sex, politics or religion. It was my experience that when people wade into these topics, many forgot the rules of polite discourse and became too strident or judgmental," she explained. "Thus, I surprised myself when I asked you that question."

Grinning, Peter glanced over at his phantom companion. "Lillie, you expect me to believe you shied away from conversations of a sexual nature?"

"Avoiding discussions of politics and religion was easy as they bored me silly," she admitted. "As to sex, though, that was such a pervasive topic one couldn't escape it if you tried. Goodness, Peter, we were forever talking about each others' indiscretions."

"Plus ca change, plus c'est la meme chose," Peter said in a fractured French accent. He was impressed with himself that he remembered the phrase.

"Oui, Monsieur," Lillie said. "But what marvelous changes there have been. I would loved to have worn the red dress Mrs. Flannery danced in to one of those interminable dinner parties I attended as a Professional Beauty. Imagine the ruckus, the scandal I would have caused. There is so little to it."

"Well, there you are. The only difference between the sexual peccadilloes of then and today is we can get out of our clothes faster."

"Peter, I'm still curious why you brought up my asking you about God."

"I remember treating the question lightly and I gave you a hurried answer. Later, I realized it was something you obviously wanted to talk about, so I made a mental note to..."

"Give me an unhurried answer?" she teased.

"Something like that, I suppose," he replied

"Now seems as good a time as any," she said.

Peter, taking a sip of his cognac, became pensive. After putting a few thoughts together, he began: "It seems a relatively uncomplicated question. Or is it? If you had asked me when I was nine, I would have unhesitatingly said yes. Because of my religious upbringing to say otherwise was unthinkable. But you asked me five decades later, and I said yes again. But, this time it's a shaky yes."

"Whatever do you mean?" she asked.

"I believe, and then there are times when I ..."

"Doubt His existence," she said, finishing his sentence.

"There's more to it but yes," he confessed.

"Speak to me of your uncertainty as to His being."

"I'd like to blame my mind for these thoughts, but I am my mind. However, it does seem at times as if it wants to act on its own. This is really new territory for me," he said.

"I don't understand."

"It's only recently that I have given any serious thought to God or my relationship with Him, the power of prayer, life after death, that sort of thing. There was a lengthy stretch of time between my church-going youth and now where I went about my life raising Liz and working in radio. I was busy. I was happy. I was also thankful for having what I considered a fortunate life. It may sound odd but it was that sense of gratitude and feeling blessed that prompted my soul-searching."

"But you're vexed by pesky thoughts that God may not exist."

"I question not only God's existence but the infinite aspect of ours as well. Do we just have this moment in time and that's it? Do I exist only from my day of birth to the day I die? These kinds of question can certainly mess with your faith in a deity. Then I ask myself why would an all-powerful, all-knowing, all-loving Supreme Being create a single-use, totally disposable human being.

"The odd thing is I'm growing strangely comfortable in dealing with this uncertainty. Or rather, these bouts of uncertainty. Not so comfortable, though, that I want to continue to have two minds regarding God. I just don't consider these musings to be blasphemous any more. Now that I'm older, and I'm not going to add wiser, I have come to the conclusion that if there is a God, He must understand and forgive these mental wanderings, cynical or seemingly disrespectful as they may be to Him. I also hope He gets some laughs out of this clumsy spiritual predicament I find myself in."

"Why do I have a feeling there's more to your unhurried answer?"

Peter, indeed, was anxious to explain further. "There is, Lillie. Having said all that, I do feel strongly that God deserves a constancy, a steadfastness, if you will. I do try very hard not to entertain these contrary thoughts that seem to invade my mind." He looked over at his translucent companion. "Of course, since you've come into my life, everything is topsy-turvy. I mean here I am discussing spirituality with, of all things, a spirit! That's utterly amazing. You are someone who has lived and died, yet still exist. It's fair to say that in my mind that makes you the poster child for life continuing after death."

"What if I am a one-off?"

Peter stared at the vision across from him. "Lillie, how could that possibly be?" he asked, more amused by her comment than anything.

"I don't know. Maybe I'm a cosmic accident. Think about it. There are only three of us who know of my existence," she argued. "I haven't seen, met or talked to any other spirit. Not a single soul. Have you?"

"No, you're my first," he said cheerily, lifting his glass to toast her.

"Now listen to me, Peter. Even though I am here seventy-five years after my death, I am no closer to knowing God or what awaits me than you are. No pun intended, but we're in the same boat. I have no idea what will happen when I leave this puzzling state."

"Maybe you never will. Leave this puzzling state, that is,' Peter speculated.

"Humph! I doubt heaven or whatever you wish to call it is an eternity of taking round-trip cruises to Alaska from San Francisco."

Placing his cognac on the table, Peter moved to the verandah railing and looked down at the dark water and the white-grey foamy wake the ship created. He was comforted by the movement and sound. He loved being on the ship and knew he could comfortably stay aboard longer than their scheduled twelve days. Maybe not an eternity, but he'd be happy at sea for a couple of months. He shared that thought with Lillie. "Only if I had your company, by the way," he added.

"That's a sweet thought. You know, I am astonished at how easily you have come to accept me."

"I can't explain it, and I don't want to waste any of our valuable time together trying to figure it out," he said honestly. "Wait a minute! I do know. It was that lovely shade of lavender that caught my eye. I don't know what would have happened if you arrived wearing steel grey with a voice like a boat horn."

"As if I had a choice," she joked. "Peter, may I say one more thing, as regards these periods of doubt you experience? Are you familiar with Kierkegaard?"

"I've heard the name. Probably from a line in an old Woody Allen movie."

"He was a Danish philosopher and theologian. He wrote: 'Doubt is conquered by faith, just as it is faith which has brought doubt into the world.'"

"Is that another one of those facts that even you don't know how you know it?" he asked.

She laughed heartily. "Not this time. I was a great fan of Kierkegaard, and I read much by him and about him."

"I will add him to my reading list," Peter responded. "You know, I just might be fretting over something I shouldn't. Kierkegaard put his finger on it. Doubt and faith coexist. I suppose my concern is that I believe God is always present, alway near, always helping, always loving even during those times when I'm distant from him. As I said earlier, He deserves my constant attention. In fact, what I should be thinking about is learning how to listen to Him."

"Amen," Lillie said softly.

"Ah, the cue that the sermon's over." Returning to his chair, he sat on the edge to be closer to Lillie. Stifling a yawn, he said, "This has been an extraordinary evening. My head is spinning with a thousand thoughts. I think I'll start working through them until I fall asleep. Are you coming in?"

"No, you rest," she said. "I, too, have much to think about. I think I will stay out here awhile."

"I wish I could kiss you goodnight," he said clumsily but sincerely.

"Just thinking it makes it so," she replied softly.

Peter managed to work through two of his many thoughts before falling into a sound sleep. Lillie, though, energized by their evening together, began to wade through hers. Firstly, she decided to scrap any preconceived notion she had of her strange existence. Now she wasn't so sure about this ghost status and what came next. She remained adamant, however, on one point and that was her conviction that there must be a purpose to her being. And she still clung to the idea that getting the painting back on the Tate wall was that purpose. As regards Peter, she was happy to have him as a partner to achieve that end. She would scrap, however, the idea that he needed a mentor or, as Liz called it, a life coach. Thinking of Liz she remembered his niece calling her the ultimate cougar. Perhaps, there was some truth to it as she was now going to remain there in the brisk night air reveling in her feelings for Peter. And, yes, she happily conceded, there was within her a stirring of an emotion that was, indeed, romantic.

It was one of those rare mornings when Peter awoke from a dreamless sleep. He ignored the bedside clock that advertised a ridiculously early morning hour. Putting his morning rituals on temporary hold, Peter instead ran his hands through his hair, donned a robe and drew back the heavy drapes to let the morning's light creep illuminate the penthouse. His evening with Lillie fresh in his mind and anxious to in her company again, he stepped onto the verandah.

She was where he left here just two hours before. Lillie said a quick good morning and then directed him to look past her to behold the stunning Glacier Park panorama. Peter walked to the railing where he put both hands on the worn, smooth wood and looked out at what, thanks to President Calvin Coolidge, was now Glacier Bay National Park and Preserve. A dramatic mix of rugged mountain peaks, multi-colored glaciers, islands and valleys, this paradisiacal slice of earth shared the space with an equally impressive watery landscape of narrow, ice-strewn fjords and inlets. Blues, greens and grays were the dominant colors of this natural wonder. Peter couldn't get enough of it. But knowing there were nine more hours where they would be surrounded by this grand spectacle, he let go his gaze to turn to Lillie and exclaimed with boyish glee and a sappy smile: "How could I think there isn't a God with all this beauty surrounding us?"

Now that joyous announcement deserves some commentary on my part. I understand in today's world, marketing is everything, and name recognition is all-important. With that thought in mind, I would like point out two very popular ways my Boss's name stays front and center. They are firstly the wonders of nature and secondly thirteen year-old girls. Those two remarkably different entities have done more than their share in promoting my Employer's Name. How, you ask. Let's take Mother Nature first. One can't count the number or times someone is awestruck by, perhaps, a gushing waterfall, a cloudless sky with an orange-gold moon and twinkling stars, a red rose in full bloom, a forest of trees or, in the case of Peter Ramsey, Glacier National Park and Preserve. The lost-for-words feeling of awesomeness is such that one is compelled to salute and vocally affirm the Maker. As to the role thirteen year-old girls play? This seems to be the age when these nascent teens discover three words that they will repeat hundreds of times a day. It is "OH MY GOD!!!!!" It is usually screamed. However, today it is also e-mailed, texted and tweeted. Here's the good news. They have been at it for so long now that it has been adopted by TV game show winners, performers who win awards and recipients of surprise birthday parties. That list seems to be growing. Our thoughts on it? We'll take any attention we can get. Now, back to our story.

Peter, you might remember, had just broadcast in his way an enthusiastic "There is a God!" While it was directed to Lillie, a reaction came from the penthouse verandah to his left.

"If there is a God, then why can't I get some goddam reception for my Blackberry." The angry voice belonged to a man in his early forties wearing shorts and a loose-fitting tee-shirt. He was a thin, muscular man with a small, mean face and a Franciscan tonsure that he obviously came by naturally, much to his chagrin. Spotting Peter who had peered around the metal barrier that separated the verandahs, he introduced himself, "Lopinsky. Jim Lopinsky."

"I'm Peter Ramsey," our protagonist replied, though sorely tempted to do the same James Bond-style intro. "Good morning."

"It would be a better morning if I could get some news on the Europe markets," he growled, not looking up from the small device in his right hand.

Ignoring his grousing, Peter said, "This is breathtaking. It's astonishing."

Mr. Lopinsky, who could not have looked more bored, muttered, "Yeah, whatever," and retreated into the verandah's interior.

"He certainly tried to ruin a perfect moment," Peter remarked.

"Sad, isn't it," Lillie said. "He is so concerned with the ups and downs of the marketplace, he can't see the riches in front of him. But, Peter, don't let it bother you."

Before Peter could assure Lillie that the morning was so excellent in all aspects that he was immune to anything but a sense of joy, Lopinsky, Jim Lopinsky reappeared. He looked over at Peter and said, "It's Ramsey, isn't it."

"It is, but call me Peter."

"I want to apologize for my little tantrum. Look, no Blackberry," he said, holding both hands in the air out over the water. "It is pretty weird to stand out here amongst all this and be pissed off just because you don't know what's going on in London. Thanks for bringing it to my attention."

"What? The tantrum or the scenery?" Peter asked, smiling.

"You seem like too nice a guy to mention my boorishness. Anyway, a pleasure meeting you. I'd give you my card and tell you if you ever need an investment strategist to give me a call but my wife would lock me out here for the rest of the cruise. I'm supposed to be on vacation and she wants me to act like it." WIth that, Mr. Lopinsky turned to head back inside. Still, he couldn't resist shouting, "You can always Google me." Peter realized he'd just heard the revised version of "I'm in the phone book."

"So what are we going to do with the rest of our day,?" LIllie asked.

Peter's eyes widened and he smiled at his spirit sidekick. "Lillie, it's just a little after four. I'm going back to bed."

chapter 25

I HAVE NO plans to walk you through this particular day's minutiae because most of it revolves around the guests oohing and aahing over the beauty of Glacier Bay. Instead, here's a quick wrap of the day leading up to the one event relevant to our case of the missing painting. We'll begin where we left off at four in the morning. After enjoying the breathtaking dawn and the verandah-to-verandah exchange with his investment banker neighbor who was trying his darndest not to morph into Gordon Gekko, Peter crawled back into bed for four solid hours of dreamless sleep. For that period of time, Lillie rested nearby, sublimely happy in his company, even though he snored loudly.

By eight in the morning, they joined the other guests who were milling about on the promenade deck or the two top decks of the Ocean Glamour enjoying the expansive and dramatic views. Cheery crew members scurried about offering cups of refreshing hot chocolate or hot spiced-apple cider to take the edge off the chilly Alaska morn. Today the star of the show was Nature. Spa treatments, lectures, blackjack tournaments, napkin-folding classes, bridge games, treadmill workouts and all the other shipboard activities were put on hold. Instead, guests spent their time staring in wonderment at bluish-white glaciers that when they noisily calved, would elicit finger-pointing, gasps and mass camera-snapping. The guests were enthralled with the park's vibrant lifestyle; the occasional whale breach, an eagle in flight and birds of every size, color and range of cuteness, some perching on the small chunks of ice that surrounded the Ocean Glamour as it moved ever so slowly through the various inlets.

Liz, who was quick to notice a new intimacy between Lillie and her uncle, had joined them early on for breakfast and a stroll around the top deck. Like the rest of the guests they were overwhelmed by the natural beauty that surrounded them. They were also most anxious to see Dave and Mary Pat Flannery, but the newly crowned dance champions remained holed up in their new stateroom.

Peter's to-do list for the day contained one item; seek out the owner of ATSEA Auction House in the early evening and alert him as to Howard Newton's interest in the painting his late mother-in-law desired. As it turned out, Charles Van Woort fell into his lap, thanks to Petra Dosynk. By midday, the elder Kwyrki had decided there should be a celebratory gathering of those who played a role in bringing the dance competition to a successful conclusion. To that end, he issued invitations to join him and his family in the Covey for drinks at five. All were present and accounted for by the appointed hour. Peter was surprised and delighted to see the Flannerys had finally taken the *Do Not Disturb* sign off their door and ventured out. Everyone was in high spirits, even Dave. Lillie tagged along, hovering in a corner of the bar's alcove where the convivial group huddled around two tables pulled together. While they waited for their drinks, Petra asked for everyone's attention. Ignoring him, Yurk continued to play with his iPhone. Petra smacked the top of his head and his beefy grandson quickly put it away.

"Please," the florid-faced Kwyrki gentleman began, "I want to make a speech. It will not be long. We are here to have a party and celebrate the victory of these two wonderful people." He pointed to Dave and Mary Pat who acknowledged the group's enthusiastic applause. "But you could not have done it without us," he told them. "So we need to also clap for ourselves."

Now public speaking can be for some a powerful opiate. Those who fall under its spell can range from the tongued-tied to the verbose. If you've ever been on the receiving end of one of these bloviations, you know just how torturous an experience it can be. Fortunately, Petra was a man of a few well-chosen words. He was also, to everyone's amusement, refreshingly candid.

While drinks were being served, Petra demonstrated his verbal charm. "We came on this cruise to see some of the American West, eat lots of sweets and have plenty of sex." He first winked at his wife and then looked over at Peter who just shook his head. "I have been told that a lot of you feel uncomfortable talking about certain topics in public. Maybe I should not have brought up sweets." There was much laughter. "However, I am serious when I say being a part of this Team Tango and meeting all of you has made this trip very special for us. So I raise my glass in a toast. Thank you all and special thanks to you, Mr. and Mrs. Flannery, for helping me win my bet. I am a happy man."

Petra sat down and signaled the bar manager to bring some hors d'oeuvres to the table. Inka, his wife, leaned in and gave him a peck on the cheek and and patted his hand, the familiar spousal gestures denoting a job well-done. While Peter had glimpsed Inka Dinka Dosyk in the dining room and knew she was attractive, it was only now upon seeing her close up that he realized she was an extraordinarily beautiful and sexy woman. She was almost illegally voluptuous; long-legged, tiny-waisted, big-breasted with huge round dark eyes and full red lips. There was no way Inka could hide or disguise her searing sensuousness. She radiated sex. Peter thought her sex appeal so strong, he was certain that if she were airlifted to one of those mountainside monasteries, the monks would be rethinking their vows of celibacy. He wondered if her powerful and seductive animal magnetism was what kept Petra so physically active and not the magical syrup from his backyard Emba trees.

"I sure had you sized up all wrong, Ramsey." Peter turned toward the all too recognizable voice of David Flannery. He said nothing while Dave took a sip of his single malt. "I had you pegged as a neutral, stay-on-the-sidelines type of guy. Then you go and stick your neck out to help me. You surprised the hell out of me. Consider what you did, Ramsey. First you conjured up this lunatic scheme to fire me up romantically with waffles and maple syrup. Then you arranged to have those two goons keep me in protective custody for the day so Mary Pat with the help of your niece can get ready for the contest. Finally, you go and make what I call a really stupid and expensive bet with the Symingtons."

Might as well let him know, Peter thought. "That's what it turned out to be, Dave. Plain old maple syrup."

"I know."

"How'd you find out?"

"Petra told me when we went into Skagway for a beer. He said he never had a chance to switch syrups at breakfast. I think he has a thing about honesty. He even told me about his bet with Plushenko."

Peter's incredulity was written all over his face. "You knew all this before the competition?"

"I did," he answered, smiling smugly. "And now you're itching to know how a churlish, grouchy old bastard like me ended up being crowned Mister World Class Tango Dancer."

"Something like that, yes," Peter replied.

"Well, a lot of the credit obviously goes to you and Liz and those two characters," he said, pointing to Petra and Yurk. "The four of you went to great lengths to see me win, and I didn't want to disappoint you." He paused and took another sip of his scotch. "However, right up to a couple of minutes before the contest, I wasn't so sure I could win it. Sitting on that stage alone, I got very nervous. I knew the syrup didn't work. I knew Petra put big money on us to win. I knew how good the Russians were. I know I always look like a wreck on the outside but at that moment I was a worse wreck inside." He turned to glance at his wife who was bending Inka Dinka Dosynk's ear. "Then I saw Mary Pat."

With that, he picked up his drink and came around the table. Taking a chair from an unoccupied table, he moved it close to Peter and sat down. Flannery rarely talked about himself or shared confidences but he wanted Peter to know exactly what happened on the dance floor and why. He leaned in and in a low voice began his fascinating narrative: "When Mary Pat and I met, it was love at first sight for me. It took several sightings for her, though, as I wasn't exactly a prize package. For reasons naive, silly and romantic, we decided to wait until our wedding night. You know what I'm talking about?" Peter indicated he did. "Actually, she wanted to wait. I agreed because I would have done anything for her. Fortunately, it was a short engagement. But four weeks of heavy necking and petting took its toll on me. I was so horny, during the wedding service when the priest asked me to take Mary Pat's hand..." Here he leaned in closer and with a heavy whiskey breath, whispered, "I got this hard-on."

"Dave, we're talking about your wedding," Peter whispered back sharply.

Flannery sat back and smiled. "You're right. It was my wedding and I should find a more tasteful way of expressing myself. Okay, smart-ass, how about this: I felt a fierce stirring in my loins."

"Perfect! Right out of a romance novel," Peter joked. "I hope you were alert enough to say I do when asked, and not 'I need to have her right now, Father.'"

Ignoring him, Flannery continued, "Anyway, everything was all right because I came prepared. I knew the wedding dance would do me in in the erection... Excuse me, the fierce-stirring-of-the-loins department, so I switched from my usual boxer trunks to Jockey shorts to keep everything, shall we say, contained."

Peter looked over at Mary Pat who broke from her conversation with Petra's wife, curious to know what her husband was talking about. Dave waved across the table. "Just giving Ramsey a few dance tips, Honey."

"How does all this relate to last night's dance?" Peter asked.

One would rarely describe Dave's face as animated, but it was now. Putting a hand on Peter's forearm, he answered in an excited but low voice, "When Mary Pat walk across that dance floor toward me, Ramsey, the last twenty-one years vanished, just like that." He lifted his hand and snapped his fingers. "It was my wedding day all over again and we were about to have our first dance as husband and wife. A pair of one-word vocabulary teenagers, a shrinking 401-K, a furnace that needs replacing, dealing with an asshole of a boss; that was all part of an unknown future." Dave removed his hand from Peter's arm and sat back, silent.

That's it, he thought. Flannery needed to say nothing more. Peter, however, felt compelled to issue some kind of response, even a banal one. "That must have been one hell of a wedding dance."

"You had to be there," he said wistfully.

"I hope you wore jockey shorts last night?"

"I haven't worn boxers in twenty-one years," he laughed.

Because of the dance competition, the Flannerys were now the most recognized couple on the ship. As guests, thirsty for a pre-dinner libation, poured into the Covey, they first stopped by the Team Tango celebration to personally congratulate the winning dancers. Aside from Yurk who was oblivious to everything as he was captivated by a game application on his iPhone, everyone else enjoyed the interruptions, feeling it added to the gaiety.

Now it is widely known that in most circumstances people love the underdog. It was certainly true in this regard as most of the guests could more easily identify with the Flannerys physically than they could the dashingly handsome, but arrogant Anatoly Plushenko and his zero body-fat girlfriend with the tight hair. One gentleman from Arlington, Texas put it to Dave this way: "My friend, I saw you walk onto that dance floor sporting that beer belly and I said to my wife, Marge... I said, Marge, that's who I want to see win this damned rhythmic rodeo!"

Far more complimentary was the dapper gentleman who approached Flannery after the Texan noisily departed. He was thin, of medium height and elegantly attired in a dark, striped double-breasted suit, white dress shirt with French cuffs, a lavender silk tie and matching pocket square. Both the man and the clothes he wore were wrinkle-free. WIth his soft, boyish features and a full head of wavy hair professionally dyed a dark brown, the 56-year-old looked a good fifteen years younger. He oozed charm.

"Mr. Flannery, I'm Charles Van Woort. I'm a huge fan of ballroom dancing. You, sir, danced an absolutely amazing tango as did your beautiful wife. What surprised me was the crispness of your steps and the use of your arms. Also, I don't think I've ever seen so much passion exhibited in a dance. I was swept away by your performance."

Before Dave could comment, from across the table, Mary Pat exclaimed, "Say, I recognize you! All those paintings we see in the hallway are yours."

"Yes, they are mine, Mrs. Flannery, but I hope that's temporary," he quipped, his manner easy and his voice pleasant. "If all goes well, and I can persuade lovely people like you to come to the auction, they won't be mine for much longer." With that, he deftly spread several small auction flyers on the table, all within easy reach of everyone. I used the word deftly because it was as if he had produced them from thin air or, more likely, from up his sleeve. Peter reached for one and pocketed it.

"I'm trying to talk my husband into going. I fell in love with an abstract landscape by an Italian artist. His name is Florizio Panna.. Uh, Pinna.." She blushed, embarrassed she'd forgotten his name.

"Florizio Pinacchio. The painting is *TechnoTuscany*," he said. "It is a marvelous painting. You have a discerning eye, Mrs. Flannery. The good news is I don't think it will take much to see it hanging in your home. Anyone else see anything they liked?" he asked the assembled.

Inka Dinka Dosynk finally spoke. "I am sorry to say Petra and I haven't paid much attention to your paintings, Mr. Van Woort. I think now we will look more closely at them. My husband is always big spender in our city's annual spring art fair and auction. Last year, he was the high bidder on a life-sized ice sculpture of me wearing only a Brazilian micro-bikini bottom. We bought an extra freezer just for it." She smiled demurely and the debonair Van Woort was rendered speechless.

Peter and Lillie saw their opportunity at the same time. However, before Peter could act, Lillie shouted, "Peter, now! Do it now! Tell him about Howard." Startled, he looked over at her and gave his left earlobe a violent tug. It was his way of firing back, "Okay, okay, I hear you." Van Woort's eyes were still on Inka Dosynk when Peter brought him back to earth. "Excuse me. Mr Van Woort?"

Recovering, he turned and smiled at Peter. "Please, it's Charles," he said, sneaking one more peek at Mrs. Dosynk, no doubt, imagining what she must look like wearing only a melting micro-bikini bottom.

"I'm Peter Ramsey." They shook hands.

"Of courses, you're the host of a rather large group of people. I hope you'll spread the word about the auction."

"I will. Speaking of the auction, I received an unusual phone call last night from my former boss, Howard Newton. He's the son-in-law of Philipa Crumley-Figg."

"Ah, dear Philipa. She died so tragically," Charles said in a doleful manner.

"Yes. Anyway, he informed me he's joining the cruise in Sitka tomorrow. Now that might be good news for you, but I've had to put up with him and his eccentricities for years, so I'm not particularly over the moon about it," Peter explained, trying to make it sound like Howard's embarkation would ruin the rest of the cruise for him.

"Why might it be good news for me?" a curious Van Woort asked.

"He told me to let you know tell he's interested in a painting his mother-in-law was eager to bid on," Peter said, watching closely for any untoward reaction.

There was none. Instead, the auction house owner merely smiled and commented, "Sounds rather silly. Sending an advance notice of his arrival, that is."

"That's pure one hundred per cent Howard Newton. It makes him feel important. It must be a CEO kind of thing," he said lightheartedly.

"He probably learned it from his mother-in-law."

"I had the pleasure of working for both of them, but didn't get to know Philipa until she came on this cruise."

Charles ran a hand through his hair and thought a moment. "You're right, of course. Having a potential buyer come aboard is always good news. It will be nice to know there's going to be at least one serious bidder in the audience. I wonder, though, what painting he's talking about. Philipa had her eye on so many." Giving Peter an look of exasperation, Charles continued, "I have had many dealings with the lady in the past and she was always... Well, let's just say, she was a challenge."

Still keeping it light, Peter commented, "Oh, trust me, I know how difficult a woman she could be. Consider your experiences with her, though, a dress rehearsal for dealing with her son-in-law." Then pausing, he added excitedly, "Wait a minute! I almost forgot. Howard told me Philipa gave him the number of the painting. It's here somewhere," Peter said, making a show of digging in his trousers' pockets. "Ah, here it is." He handed Charles a piece of paper that had written on it 48 376-3.

Again, no change in Charles Van Woort's cool demeanor. He took the wrinkled paper and glanced at the numbers. "It's somewhat similar to the kind of coding I use. I'll check my inventory. I'm curious to know what painting has him so captivated that he's willing to take half an Alaskan cruise to get it." Looking up from the note, he said, "I'll call you if I learn anything."

Peter laughed. "Don't bother. My job was being Howard's messenger boy, nothing more. He's all yours now."

"Will you be coming to the auction?"

"Not if Howard's going to be there. Seriously, though, auctions and art don't interest me. I'm more an antiquarian. First editions, that sort of thing."

Glacier Bay was now a memory. The Ocean Glamour had left the park's watery arteries and was now sailing through sounds and narrows with unusual names to enter

the Gulf of Alaska for its southerly journey past Chicha-
gof Island to Baranof Island where the ship would sail into
island-studded Sitka Sound.

Peter, Liz and Lillie were the first to leave Petra's party.
The early evening was so agreeable, the trio decided to take
a stroll on the promenade deck. They walked in silence for a
while enjoying the crisp air and splendid views. Liz was first
to offer her impression of Charles Van Woort, an observation
that came in at just four words. "He is a charmer."

Lillie was wordier. "Mr. Van Woort is most certainly
that and more. I might add he seems unflappable. I found
him to be surprisingly ingenuous."

It was Peter's turn to weigh in. "You both, I'm sure,
noticed his reaction or lack of reaction when I told him about
Howard. I'm no expert at reading faces or translating expressions, but he's either a first rate actor or he genuinely doesn't
care about Howard arriving. I think it might be the latter."

"Then one must ask why," Lillie observed.

Liz came to a stop midship. "I'm going in, Tio. Would
it disappoint you if I passed on dinner tonight? I'm really
into my studying and... Well, you know how I get," she said.

"I do," he replied, kissing her cheek. "And I admire
you for it."

"Besides, you and Lillie seem to be enjoying each other's company."

Lillie jumped in, "Dear Liz, if that's the real reason
you're leaving us..,"

"No, I really do need to study." She turned on her heels,
but before entering the ship's interior, changed her mind and
returned to the railing where Lillie and Peter were watching
the passing scenery. "By the way, I thought you might like
to know that I briefly entertained the idea of making a move
on Van Woort back at the party to see if I could learn anything. Lillie, of course, would be much better at it than I, but

I currently sport the necessary equipment and she doesn't. Anyway, my gaydar told me otherwise and I passed on it. Bye bye, lovebirds."

Peter explained gaydar to Lillie. "Do you think he is, Peter?" she asked.

"I don't know. It certainly is a possibility if Liz has a feeling about it. However, I don't know how it matters other than we can't use her seducing skills on him."

"Peter, do you realize you snapped at me at the party?" Lillie asked, changing the subject.

"How could I ever snap at you?"

"I saw the way you pulled at your left earlobe. It's amazing you have a lobe left. You might just as well have been hollering at me," she said with a pinch of hurt in her voice.

"I am sorry," he said sincerely. "I did give myself quite a tug, didn't I? I suppose we were thinking along the same lines and I was..."

Lillie interjected, "No explanation is necessary." The lavender vision was now hovering over the frothy waters of Cross Sound. She was directly in front of Peter who stood at the railing.

"Lillie, I know you can't fall overboard, but, then again, maybe you can. I don't know. Maybe you don't know for sure. So, would you mind coming back to this side of the railing."

"Uh, Peter..."

"Oh, I can see it now. First, a quiet splash and then me shouting 'Ghost overboard! Ghost overboard!"

"PETER!"

It was too late. He felt a tap on his shoulder. Turning, he stared at a confused Samantha Whitby. "Peter, who are you talking to?"

chapter 26

LILLIE LANGTRY HAD vanished into thin air without so much as a goodbye and Samantha Whitby had made her presence known by asking a grammatically correct but extremely embarrassing question. While flustered at being caught talking to himself, or so it would seem to a passerby, our protagonist's real concern was Lillie's sudden disappearance. Certainly, ghosts defy gravity, he thought. There was no way she could have fallen into the churning waters seven decks below. His real fear was she no longer existed, gone just as quickly as she came. As for the college professor who stood behind him patiently awaiting an answer, he wondered what he could say that might sound like a plausible explanation as to why "Help! Ghost overboard" was heard coming from him, not once mind you, but twice. I can't blame it on the Bard, he thought, even though it did with its iambic rhythm have a Shakespearean tone to it. As it turned out, no response was necessary. Just when he spun round to confront Ms Whitby, he spotted Liz scurrying down the four steps to the promenade deck floor. He was delighted to see Lillie right behind her, floating as fast as she could.

"Liz has your back, Peter," his favorite ghost shouted over his niece's shoulder. He wondered how on earth Lillie came by that piece of populist argot.

"Sam, what a pleasant surprise," Liz chirped, skidding to a stop in front of the pair. Catching her breath, she bestowed one of her beautiful smiles on her uncle. "Tio, sorry for sneaking away. I had to make a powder room run."

"I'm afraid I was caught red-handed," he said. "Open-mouthed might be a better way of expressing it."

"Talking to yourself again, huh?" Turning to Samantha, she said, laughing, "He's notorious for it. You'd think someone who made his living talking would quiet up in his off-time. Not my uncle. Now he's even spouting Shakespeare. There's a bit of the child in him, I'm afraid."

"I don't know that that's necessarily a bad thing," Samantha said, flashing what Peter considered a worthy rival to the warm smile Liz had extended him.

"Oh, I absolutely agree, and I'm delighted you think so. It made for a very entertaining way to grow up. Anyway, I'd love to visit, but I have to study. You know how it is for us doctoral students, professor. Anyway, I am off. See you two later." With that, she and Lillie headed toward the nearest exit.

Their hasty departure caught her off guard as Samantha wanted to talk to both Peter and his niece. Now alone with just him, she felt like an awkward school girl wrapped in shyness and youthful innocence. She stood facing him, her eyes cast downward, wishing Peter would say something, anything and soon.

He didn't disappoint. Turning to point out the passing scenery, he observed, "It's a lovely evening."

"Yes, it is. Although, a bit chilly."

"I'm not keeping you from your walk?" he asked, even though she was dressed in a gray-black tweed jacket with a black skirt and heels. "What a silly question. You obviously don't look like you're out here to do twenty laps. In fact, you look very nice." Mentally slapping himself for using an adjective he had come to both despise and rely on, he hastily tacked on, "In fact, you look like you're ready for a night on the town, or a night on the ship to be more precise. You look terrific."

Samantha folded her arms more for warmth than anything. "I should just let you keep talking."

"Oh no you shouldn't."

"On the contrary, you have been extremely flattering," she said. Her initial shyness beat a retreat thanks to Peter's pleasant and easy manner. "It's refreshing to hear. All my sister tells me is if something fits or not."

Peter grinned. "Well, we can't have that. I assure you look very smart, sophisticated and extremely attractive. Plus, everything looks like it fits."

"Enough," she laughed, putting a hand up to order a halt to his compliment-tossing. "Actually, I came out here looking for you. I dropped by to congratulate Dave and Mary Pat and I thought I'd run into you and Liz in the Covey. When I asked after you, they said the two of you came out here for some air."

"You know the Flannerys?"

"I met them through the paper. I've written a few reviews for the Sunday book section over the years," she said.

"Well, I'm delighted you found me."

Samantha had hoped he would ask her why she sought him out as she had carefully rehearsed her answer. She decided to pretend that he had asked anyway. "I made a reservation for my sister and me to dine at the Italian restaurant tonight. At the last minute, Isabelle decided she'd rather stay in our stateroom and read. I thought, perhaps, you and Liz might like to join me. Of course, it sounds like Liz has studying to do and you probably already have plans." The last sentence was improvised and rushed. She hoped her nervousness wasn't showing, but she was certain she was blushing. Actually, it was a leftover blush which blossomed after hearing Peter's positive take on her appearance.

"I have no plans. In fact, I just learned Liz was bowing out of dinner tonight," Peter explained. "If the invitation still stands, I'd love to join you."

They arranged to meet in front of Va Bene at eight. Peter made a mental note to call the host, Pico Enea, to request a quiet table and confirm the nutty little chef (Peter's words, not mine.) was no longer on the ship. Samantha excused herself citing the cold of the evening air while Peter decided another lap or two around the ship was just what he needed.

While Peter breathes in more of that clean Alaska air, let's check the playbill to learn more about our newest cast member. Always in good spirits, brimming with kindness and generous with her time, Samantha Whitby was much loved by her colleagues and students. However, if you asked any of them what else they knew about her, they would shrug their shoulders and admit that that was about it. What they didn't know was this university professor with the perky smile, friendly mien and generous nature had for the last fifty-six years lead a relatively adventure-less life. Nowhere was her inexperience more apparent than in the world of romance. Having never married with a list of prudent courtships you could count on one hand, her romantic resume' was even thinner than Peter's. To understand why she preferred sheltering herself from life's more challenging exploits, we must return to her childhood where the seed was planted for this assiduous self-protection. Samantha was the youngest of the Whitby clan that included parents, Gerald and Lorraine May, and older sister, Isabelle. Gerald was an English professor at a small liberal arts college in upstate Minnesota. Lorraine was the school's librarian. Hers was a quiet upbringing because most of the time all four Whitby noses were stuck in books and, let's face it, reading is basically a quiet enterprise. When the family wasn't reading books, they were talking about them. It was her father's intention to introduce Samantha to English Literature chronologically. However, unbeknownst to him, she had already discovered Charles Dickens and Robert Louis Stevenson and had fallen in love with them, their characters and – what's most important – the exciting times in which they lived. Even so, at the gentle urging of her loving father, she waded through the Tudor, Elizabethan and Jacobean Ages coming away with a fondness and deep appreciation for William Shakespeare. Ever the obedient daughter she then marched forward through the Cromwell and Restoration eras. Next it was on to the Eighteenth Century and the Romantic Period. There she fell in love with the poetry of young John Keats. Shelley did not win her heart. While she dutifully read her way through these eras, it took no paternal encouragement for her to finally wrap her arms around the Victorian Age and the Early Twentieth Century. Her passions stirred, this would be where her heart and soul decided to take up permanent residence.

Samantha much preferred reading about the adventures and misadventures of fictional females than actually going out and having some of her own. To her, life was a roller coaster; full of bedeviling twists and turns, ups and downs. It was her devout wish to avoid the inconstancy and tumult both promised. She felt safe and secure, readily admitting without a scintilla of regret that she truly enjoyed the manner in which she chose to live her life. When she occasionally did come face to face with one of life's unsuspecting speed bumps, unlike most people who – if I may borrow a song lyric – *pick themselves up, dust themselves off and start all over again,* Samantha hastily retreated into the world of English fiction.

Make no mistake, though, there was a dent or two on this fine piece of human machinery, the latest damage occurring just before the cruise. It was such a crushing experience that she was still on tenterhooks. After a lengthy period of not dating, Samantha was approached by concerned friends who convinced her to go on a blind date with a psychology professor whom they'd promoted as being in tiptop shape when it comes to wit, interest and personality. Now if there is such a thing as truth in advertising, they should have also informed her that he was a good seven inches shorter, five years younger, crude in his language and allowed food to nest in his beard. They could have also pointed out that he was a nasty, insensitive man who was a master of verbal abuse. This does leave you wondering about the caliber of these so-called friends. Their date began badly. They had been in each other's company barely five minutes when he began ridiculing her for her bubbly enthusiasm. He even went so far as to order her to tone it down, as he couldn't abide excessive chirpiness. Throughout the meal, he chipped away at her with cruel and cutting comments. Having never experienced anything quite like it, she had no defense for these venomous attacks. She just prayed the evening would speed up and she could escape him. To hasten the dinner's end, she declined dessert. Her date merely issued an evil snort and told her that with her mature figure, what would another pound matter. He then signaled the server for the bill, poured himself the last of the wine and, lifting the glass in a mock toast, loudly suggested they go to his place for a drink and sex. It was such a preposterous offer, Samantha laughed. Then, true to her nature, she politely but resolutely refused his impolitic offer. She couldn't know but this was the second time that day that he had been laughed at. After hearing her laughter, he rose, removed his sport coat from the back of the chair and came round to her side of the table. Leaning in close with an odious grin and foul breath, he told her that it was his professional opinion that even at her advanced age she was obviously a sexual amateur whose freshness date had long since expired and that his offer of sex and booze was his way of offering her some sorely needed therapy. All of this was, of course, heard by nearby diners. To add to the indignity, he left her to pay the bill. So it was that Samantha sat there for what seemed the longest time, deeply humiliated and emotionally bruised, the sympathetic stares of the other diners offering her no solace.

Now to the story's postscript: As this short, bearded and poisonous brute walked toward his car, he reviewed the evening and his contemptible behavior. He had arrived at the Berkeley restaurant in a foul temper because a cute, bubbly teaching assistant had earlier laughingly refused his advances. Then when he saw that his blind date was also attractive, tall and perky, his anger over that afternoon's rejection got the best of him. He thought for just a second that he might have gone a little overboard. After all, she wasn't the one who did him harm, but when Samantha laughed that sealed it. She deserved everything he threw her way. He credited himself at being very good at that sort of thing and that made him feel better about the whole evening. It was a feeling that would last only a few seconds, however. Earlier that evening, his mind distracted by the teaching assistant's brushoff, he had parked too close to a residential driveway, thus blocking anyone from entering. So it was that he arrived just as they were towing his car away. Samantha meantime was still in the restaurant figuring out the tip as the server who'd witnessed the attack comped the wine and offered her a dessert on the house. She couldn't know that just a block away, her dinner partner was shouting to the heavens: "WHY ME? WHY ME?" Oh, we heard him, but we paid no attention.

Isabelle and the cruise became her distraction. Devoting herself to her sister's welfare helped lessen her pain. Now here she was off to dinner with Peter Ramsey and for the first time since that horrible evening, she felt a bit more like her cheery self. It was not lost on her that she chose dinner out with a relative stranger over returning to the snuggly security found in the pages of a good book. That leaves just one more thing you need to know about Ms. Whitby. However, I'm going to save it. After all, timing is everything in your strange, temporal world.

"Pico, the table is perfect," Peter commented to the Va Bene host while standing behind Samantha as she took her seat. She couldn't remember the last time anyone other than a host or server seated her. Thus, you can imagine her surprise when Pico returned not a moment later to tell her there was a call for her and when she rose, so did Peter. When he popped up to welcome her back, she noticed the gesture hadn't escaped the notice of nearby diners. Peter paid no attention to them, only looking at her.

When they both sat down, she smiled demurely and said, "Your niece told me you were old school."

Peter knew there were some women who took offense at such gentlemanly manners and many of them reside in Berkeley. "If it makes you uncomfortable, I can..."

"Oh no! Please," she pleaded, this being one of those rare moments when a real life situation mirrored one from her beloved world of English fiction. She wanted more of his chivalrous behavior, not less.

"The phone call. Everything all right?" he asked, his concern genuine.

A waiter interrupted to place her napkin in her lap. "Oh, yes. It was Isabelle being Isabelle. Nothing to concern ourselves with."

The conversation flowed easily, fueled by a glass of Pinot Grigio and then two glasses of a recommended Brunello di Montalcino. When they weren't talking, they were happily enjoying their dinner. Samantha was surprised at how comfortable she was in Peter's presence. She loved the way he looked at her, that it didn't make her feel uncomfortable. That he was a listener thrilled her no end. Now among the many things Liz had told her about her uncle was his love for, as she liked to put it, dead authors. Samantha shared this with him.

"What else did my niece tell you?"

"Lots of things but all affirming, I assure you," she replied. "If you ever decide to run for political office, you have a campaign manager living under the same roof."

For the much of the evening they stayed on the subject of Victorian Age and Twentieth Century literature. She was impressed with how well-read Peter was and soon they discovered they shared favorite authors, books and characters. When she mentioned to him that she particularly enjoyed the women born of the imaginative mind of Anthony Trollope, Peter wholeheartedly agreed. Interestingly, neither showed any enthusiasm for the ladies of Jane Austen.

As the courses came and went, Samantha Whitby became more relaxed and less anxious. Confidant she had an attentive and gentlemanly dinner companion, she was ready to venture out and discuss anything other than her beloved English literature. Remembering a recent chat with her sister that had caused her some concern, she said, "Last night, Isabelle asked me the strangest question. I can't seem to get out of my head. Do you mind if I share it?"

"Not at all."

"I should tell you first that enigmatic questions are par for the course for my dear sister," she said, taking a sip of her wine. "Actually, she's famous for them. My parents and I even gave them a name. We call them Isabellean inquiries."

"And just what qualifies as an Isabellean inquiry?"

"The one she asked me yesterday is a perfect example. It was abstruse, a bit troubling and oddly worded."

"What did she ask you?"

Samantha looked across at Peter and wondered where this was going to take them. "She asked if I thought at our age we are on the other side of dreams?"

"It is an odd question. How did you answer it?"

"As always, with Isabelle, I asked her what she meant and did it just have to do with our getting older."

"I gather Isabelle feels we are on the other side."

Samantha nodded.

"She's right in one regard, you know," Peter said. "Lots of our dreams have expiration dates. I used to fantasize and dream about all sorts of things. I can't remember them all. I do remember thinking playing quarterback for Notre Dame would be neat."

"I, too, had my share. As a little girl, my really big dream was being an Olympic ice skater. Minnesota winters inspire such ambitions," she said smiling.

"I'll bet you still look great in a skating outfit," Peter flirted.

Oh no, she quietly groaned, here I go, blushing again. "I haven't been on skates in years," she said self-consciously.

"You mentioned Isabelle has been in a dark place for awhile," Peter observed.

"She is" Samantha replied. "And I'm afraid she wasn't talking about the letting go of youthful pipe dreams or fantasies when she asked her question."

"Was she referring to dreams as in goals, aspirations and wishes?" Peter asked.

"I'm afraid so," Samantha said, her tone woeful.

"Samantha, those dreams are the ones that keep our spirit fueled. Say good bye to them and you bid adieu to hope, and hope is the key to opening the door to all kinds of wonderful possibilities. These are the dreams of the spirit, the soul, life itself." Peter stopped suddenly. He sat back in his chair and laughed at himself. "Listen to me. Peter Ramsey the philosopher."

Samantha stared at her dinner date. While impressed with his answer, she was more impressed with Peter's spirited optimism. "Isabelle has always been by nature a dour individual," she explained, "but that doesn't mean her little sister is giving up on her." This time she lifted her glass in a toast.

After they clinked glasses, Peters said in a lilting manner, "*On the other side of dreams.* You know it would make a terrific song title. It's very poetical."

"Would it be a song by Elton John or George Gershwin?" she asked, smiling.

"Am I showing my age if I answer Gershwin?" he joked. Noticing they were the only two diners left in the restaurant, he gave the server who was hovering nearby the international sign for the check, reminding himself to fatten the gratuity. "I have a question," he said, leaning forward. "I am thinking about the fascinating cast of fictional female characters from the Victorian Age and the Early Twentieth Century. You have, for example, the rigid, judgmental matriarch of the manor, the porcelain-skinned young lady waiting on her inheritance, the scheming, impoverished widow, the Vicar's haughty, spoiled daughter, the ambulance nurse on a World War One battlefield..." Peter paused. "Stop me," he joked, "I'm having a lot of fun asking this question."

She laughed along. "I can see that."

"Seriously, though, are there any women from all that literature who..." Peter struggled to find the right words.

Samantha obligingly finished the question for him: "Who speak to me more forcefully than others?"

"Yes, something like that," he replied.

Samantha shook her head and smiled. "Ironically, they are not the made-up women that came from authors' creative minds. They are the real women of that time."

"Who, for instance?" he asked, taking a last sip of his wine.

"Well, just from the Victorian Age alone there's Victoria, of course. Florence Nightingale and Elizabeth Garrett Anderson are two I highly respect. Their professional achievements were extraordinary."

"I know the first."

"Anderson was Britain's first doctor. She went on to build a hospital for the poor in London," she explained. "Oh, another is Mary Ann Evans."

"Otherwise known as George Eliot."

Samantha smiled and mused, noted, "To some extent, it's a list of the rule setters and the rule breakers of that period."

"Is there a place for Lillie Langtry on your list?" Peter asked.

"She called me a rule breaker?" Lillie asked.

"She did but it was a compliment," he replied. Lillie was in her favorite spot on the verandah. "When I brought up your name, Samantha chided herself for not mentioning you initially. She particularly admires what she calls your airiness and lack of timidity. Please note that I put everything in the present tense."

"Thank you. Well, I suppose I should feel flattered," she said with a feigned haughtiness. "What I don't understand is why you chose to spend the evening with a Langtry wannabe when you could have been here in the company of the real thing"

"You're teasing me again, aren't you?" Peter asked, frustrated by Lillie's lack of any physical expression. "I really can't tell, you know. I have only the tone of your voice to go by. And, by the way, earlier tonight you told me Liz had my back. Now you just used the word wannabe. How the devil do you come by these terms?"

"To answer your first question, yes, I am teasing you. As for the second, I listen to people and their colorful expressions and if I like them I put them to use. You are aware this is the 21st century? I don't want to sound likes some starchy old Victorian when I speak. Can you get with that?"

Peter shook his head and laughed. "Yes, Lillie, I can get with that."

"Good! Now that that is all settled, there's something I want to talk to you about."

The phone rang. "Let me get that and a drink. I'll be right back." Peter left Lillie on the verandah. Picking up the phone, he said, "You're supposed to be studying."

"How did you know it was me?" Liz asked.

"Because you're dying to know how my dinner went with Professor Whitby. I'll save you the trouble of asking. It went splendidly. She is a fascinating woman."

Liz was thrilled and let her uncle know it. "I knew you two would hit if off. Do you have another date?" she asked.

"I think we both would like see more of each other. If not on the ship, then certainly when the cruise is over. She really has her hands full with Isabelle. And I have my hands full with Lillie."

"I heard that," Lillie shouted from the verandah.

Returning with a cognac, he settled into the chair opposite Lillie who now claimed the chaise lounge as hers. "So, Mrs. Langtry, what's on that marvelous mind of yours?" he asked, lifting his glass in her direction to toast.

"It may or may not be a marvelous mind, Peter dear, but it's been a very busy one and I do have much to talk about.

"I have nowhere else to go tonight," he said.

"I'm delighted to hear that," she said. "To put it bluntly, I have no idea how long I may remain in this ghostly condition. I talk about the fact that my existence must have a purpose but I'm not really sure. Therefore, it is possible I could be gone in an instant, leaving you and Liz behind to wonder if I ever existed at all. Having said that, however, I am at ease with whatever happens next because I firmly believe I will be in God's presence which is the complete opposite of the state of nothingness from which I sprang. Until this happens, Peter, this is my reality and I want to make the most of it. I am alive again, albeit with certain physical limitations and stronger spiritual powers. Once again, I am experiencing human feelings, although they are different this time. I seem to have a certain protection against disappointment. That might just be my age and the emotional muscle that comes with it. It's not for me to define. However, I want to revel in this new and wonderful existence. You and Liz can help me achieve that as you are the best of companions."

"Lillie, we're your only companions," Peter so rightly observed.

"That may be. But if that is the case, then fortune decreed I should have the best of companions even if they are the only two issued me. Now, having said that, and emphasizing I think the world of your niece, it is with you I wish to spend most of my

limited time. For one reason, we are closer in age and maturity. For another, I have always loved a gentleman's company and this time is no exception."

The close in age comment threw him. "So you prefer I wait until after the cruise to pursue Samantha."

"Exactly," she exclaimed. "And you will not have made a mistake. Consider, Peter, you'll be in the loving company of the real and – if I can borrow a term from Professor Whitby – the airy Lillie Langtry. I might add, too, that in this precious time we're given to be together, Ms Whitby can work on her own insouciance."

chapter 27

I HAD WHAT I thought was a decent beginning to this chapter. Nothing over the top, mind you, just a breezy paragraph or two on the Sitka environs followed by a chuckle inducing account of Peter and Liz's salmon-fishing excursion. However, my amanuensis, who sometimes likes to assert himself, assured me that all you, the reader, need do is type the word *Sitka* in the search engine of your choice and you'll find everything there is to know about this Alaskan community whose two syllable, easy-to-pronounce name came from the area's first settlers, the Tlinglits, which is not easy to pronounce. It is an adaptation of Shee Atika, meaning *People on the Outside of Shee.* This extra bit of historical fluff is meant to both educate you and annoy my earthbound assistant who was also keen to point out that only people interested in fishing tales are those who fish. It seems that rule also applies to stories about golf, scrap-booking and your children's academic achievements.

Thus, we will join our fisher-people after their successful three hours of searching for what I think is one of the more fascinating methods of getting one's ration of Omega-3 fatty acids. Between them, they hooked five Silver and two King salmon which Captain Jack of the *Liza Baby*, a battered but sea-worthy fishing boat, assured them would be filleted, vacuum-packed and shipped directly to their Berkeley domicile. Delighted to be off the choppy, grey waters of the Sitka Sound, Peter and Liz relaxed with cold beers in a back booth of Bucky Baranof's Bistro, a casual restaurant near St. Michael's Cathedral. Bartal, the butler, had recommended they try their pelmeni. Lillie would join them but first she wanted to check out the collection of Russian nesting dolls in a shop next door. While they waited for their order, Liz occupied her time thumbing through the photos taken on her iPhone while they were fishing. She stopped on a picture snapped by her uncle that caught her making the most awful of faces as she bravely kissed the first salmon to come aboard, an embarkation the fish did not do willingly. She handed the device to Peter so he could see the photo again.

"At least now, I can confirm that fish have lips, or some sort of fleshy protuberance that passes for lips," she said, shuddering from the memory. "Tio, do you think there really is a tradition behind this goofy ceremony or was Captain Jack just BS'ing us because I was the first one to catch something?"

Peter shook his head. "He seemed too shy to me to get up to that kind of mischief. I don't know if it means anything in this instance, but I heard somewhere that fishermen will sometimes kiss a fish before returning them to the sea."

"What do they call it? Kiss and Release," she remarked, laughing at her own joke.

"Maybe it makes them feel better about the manner in which they go about catching them." Peter returned the iPhone to Liz. "You mentioned you wanted to break it off with Kevin. Why don't you e-mail him this photo and tell him you and the fish are seeing each other and it's getting serious."

Liz frowned. "I beat you to it. I called him this morning. It didn't go well, but at least it's done. I had no idea

Kevin could be so whiny and needy. It really isn't becoming. Of course, now we'll have to figure out a way to get home from the ship." Looking up she saw Lillie and waved her over. Dolefully, she added, "Tio, it was the right thing to do even if it was by phone."

Peter reached across and squeezed her hand. "At least you called him which is a darn sight more considerate than unfriending him on Facebook or de-tweeting him or whatever it is you do on Twitter." Neither Liz nor her uncle were enthusiasts of these popular social media tools.

No pun intended, Lillie arrived in fine spirit, positioning herself along the booth's wall so both Liz and Peter had a good view of her. "The shop was touristy and very busy, but I'm glad I popped in to see those charming Russian nesting dolls. I first saw them at the World Exhibition in Paris in 1900," she explained.

Liz said, "We have a doll that is a cultural icon. Bet you never heard of Barbie."

"It may surprise you to know I have, young lady. Ruth Handler created the anatomically disproportionate figurine a little more than half a century ago. She was inspired by a German doll named Bild Lilli." Lillie stated such in that automaton-like voice she adopted when broadcasting this kind of esoterica. "I wonder, now that Barbie is in menopause, if they will manufacture her with hot flashes." Before either could comment, she asked if they knew when Howard Newton was due to arrive in Sitka.

"In about an hour or so," Peter replied, looking at his watch. "Jenni is meeting him at the airport. We might run into them when we get to the tender pier."

Which is exactly what happened. As they approached the gated entrance to the dock where the Ocean Glamour's tenders tied up to shuttle guests and crew back and forth, they spotted Howard and Jenni in the waiting area. The pair sat on a bench, a small pile of luggage nearby. Peter almost didn't recognize his former boss who was stuffed into a pair of black designer jeans, a black turtleneck sweater and a black leather jacket. Plus, what little hair he had was now dyed a dark brown. Peter didn't know if it were the clothes, the new hair color or a combination thereof, but his former boss definitely had a less furtive air about him.

"Peter," Howard shouted, springing off the bench and approaching the trio, two of whom he could see. "What a flight! Bumpy, uncomfortable and a bit scary, but hey, I'm here. You're not going to believe this but the pilot is a bird fancier. We talked birds from Oakland to Sitka. He told me Sitka Natural Historic Park is walking distance from here and any number of birds call it home this time of year. So my plan is to visit the park and then catch the last tender." Howard paused to take a breath and then, almost as an afterthought, added, "Oh hi, Liz. You look great."

"Thank you, Howard, so do you," she muttered. For as long as she could remember that brief, spiritless exchange was the extent of their communication. Liz decided now was as good a time as any to break from their longstanding tradition. "I kissed a salmon this morning, Howard," she deadpanned.

Flummoxed, he stammered, "That's uh... That's really weird, Liz."

"You're probably wondering if they have lips."

"I never gave it much thought," he said, hoping that would end the conversation.

It didn't. Liz rattled on, "Well, they do. Sorta. Have lips, that is. And you're right, Howard, it was a really, really weird experience. The salmon I've met in the past were all headless and either poached or grilled. Definitely way past the kissing stage. This was a first for me," she said, shoulders back and beaming proudly.

Figuring it was best to ignore her, Howard returned his attention to Peter and asked, "Can you help Jenni get the luggage aboard?"

"The crew will take care of it. Listen, we need to talk, Howard," Peter said with an urgency born of his desire to establish some sort of shipboard schedule whereby he could minimize their daily contact.

"Plenty of time for that. Jenni tells me I'm having dinner tonight with the captain and the hotel director in some Italian restaurant at seven. I think they want to see and hear for themselves that I've not come aboard to cause any trouble, legal or otherwise, regarding Philipa's death. Anyway, we can meet up afterwards." Grabbing his small backpack and edging toward the gate, the transformed Howard Newton added, "I'll call when I get settled in. Fun times ahead, huh?"

That afternoon Peter and Lillie enjoyed just being in each other's company. Let us linger here a moment and examine that sentence as it has more richness in it than meets the eye. Being in each other's company is an art form. It is a key ingredient in any successful relationship, if for no other reason than that's what you do with the bulk of your time together. Tally up the hours spent dancing in the moonlight, walking barefoot on a sandy beach or feeding each other from a fondue pot and you'll discover you've only eaten up a few seconds on your life clock. Being in each other's company is what happens between those ephemeral and occasionally orgasmic events. That some couples are better at it than others is testimony to its elusive simplicity. However, as this was pretty much the sum and substance of our plucky pair's relationship, or so they thought at the time, it was imperative they master the art of it so as to immediately reap the benefits of their unusual coupling.

What with most of the ship's guests wandering around Sitka, the Lido deck was practically deserted. Peter and Lillie easily found a table in the Poseidon Grill that would allow them to converse freely without drawing attention. After ordering a blended Margarita, he opened his Kindle to give the impression of someone who didn't want to be disturbed.

"That gadget of yours, Mr. Ramsey, intrigues me," Lillie said. "Will it be the death knell for books as you and I know them?"

"I don't think so, Mrs. Langtry. There will always be a place for books."

"Perhaps in your heart, my dear, but in the future perhaps not on your shelves. By the way, what are you pretending to read?"

"*The Autobiography of Mark Twain*. This is volume one of three. Twain requested it not be published until one hundred years after his death."

"What marvelous timing. Here I am back just in time to read it," Lillie chuckled. "I remember him being entertaining, charming but at times curmudgeonly. He was, though, a gifted wordsmith even though I thought he took too much pleasure in fattening his comments."

Peter laughed. "I remember you telling me what he said about you. 'You are good company with your friends, but it would be hell to be married to you because you're too damned bright.' Seems succinct enough to me."

"Succinct! My dear Peter, that was his peroration," she countered. "Before that supposed succinctness there was a string of lengthy sentences, albeit, all of them quite complimentary towards me. But that said, the truth of it is I thought him a bit of a blatherskite. Well, to be fair, more of a blowhard than a blatherskite. And if he were to suddenly make an appearance at this table that's what I would tell him to his face." Her threat was softened by a voice honey-coated enough that Mark Twain would not have in the least felt offended.

Peter leaned back in his chair and stared vacantly past his amorphous table partner. He was unresponsive to her comments about Samuel Clemens. "Peter, I thought at least you'd ask me to define blatherskite."

"Sorry, Lillie, I drifted off. I really was paying attention to what you were saying, but then it suddenly hit me. Here I am involved in a intimate relationship with an actual Twain contemporary. Do you know how valuable I could be to the staff at the Mark Twain Project at Cal Berkeley. Not that they'd ever believe a word I said."

"I know it must seem very confounding," she said, feeling a warm glow fueled by his positive remarks regarding their unusual bond.

Peter closed the Kindle and leaned forward narrowing the gap between them. "That's just it, Lillie. I don't find any of it confounding. I've said it before. Being with you feels like the most natural thing in the world."

"I'm glad for that, Peter. Really, I am," she added emphatically.

He fell back in his chair and folded his arms. "So am I. But there are times when I feel like I'm giving short shrift to the spiritual importance of this experience. I mean here I am with someone who is proof positive that life does, in fact, continue after death."

Lillie drifted closer to him. She spoke slowly, picking her words with care. "Peter, you are right in your assertion there is life after death. I am certainly evidence of that. I daresay, though, that you've been exposed to anything that hints of immortality. We talked about this before. Neither you *nor* I have any knowledge of what will happen to me when I leave your pleasant company. For that we still must rely on our faith. I must say, though, that this experience has done nothing but strengthen and reinforce my belief in God and the existence of a blessed eternal life. I hope it does for you as well."

"Yes, it does. I suppose I was taking myself to task for not taking all this too seriously," he explained clumsily.

"Nonsense," she countered. "We are doing exactly what we should be doing with our time together and that is extracting from it all the joy and happiness we can. Let theologians, philosophers, academicians and other heavy thinkers handle the sacred, the profound and..." Running out of words an exasperated Lillie thought a moment and finally added, "the complicated."

Peter paid close attention to Lillie and saw the sense in her views. "I like the idea of keeping it less complicated. I'm not a particularly wise man and by nature I would find it difficult, if not downright impossible, to proselytize."

"What am I to draw from that odd explanation?" Lillie asked.

"Well, let's say all this is happening because the Almighty decided it was time to find someone to go out and find a rock again and build another church. I'm just saying I'm not the ideal candidate for the job."

Lillie's laugh was exuberant and, frankly, so was mine. I particularly enjoyed Peter's self-deprecating supposition. Let me weigh in on this before we move forward. Please know that each and every one of you is a perfect spiritual creature. No one is less or more of anything spiritually. God does not create nor play favorites. Now having said that, let me make room for Lillie's response to her companion.

"I can assure you, Peter, if that were the situation, I would not be His or Her appointed messenger either." Oh, what am I am going to do about these two kids and their silly thinking?

Peter shook his head and stared at Lillie. "As I said, it is astonishing to me that in this high tech Kindle, I have the thoughts and recollections of Mark Twain digitally stored and at the very same time I am seated next to someone who knew him in the flesh. Enough so to call him a blatherskite or a blowhard. Boggles the mind, doesn't it?"

"And that thought, Peter, inspires me to think that there just have to be more of my contemporaries wandering around. Why I wouldn't be surprised if the ghost of William H. Seward isn't taking a stroll in Sitka this very minute. Think of it, Peter, isn't Alaska the perfect place for him to hang. Or should I say chill, given our glacial location."

"Your affection for modern day slang amazes me. However, I must say that hang seems apt for a spirit."

Peter and Lillie behaved as would any couple that afternoon on the Lido deck. In fact, they had become so engrossed in their conversation they soon forgot they were in a public place. So it was that Peter, replying in a louder than usual voice to something Lillie said, noticed odd glances coming from tables that were now filling up with returnees from their Sitka. "Probably best we head back to the penthouse," he said.

"Peter, are you going to tell people about me? About us? About any of this?" Lillie asked, genuinely curious.

He signed the check, turned off his Kindle and then before rising, leaned in toward the lavender form across from him and whispered, "Lillie, you are going to be my most treasured secret."

It took them a few minutes to wade through the Poseidon Grill dining area of the Lido Deck as members of his group stopped him to chat about this and that. Fortunately, for Peter, the this and the that were all favorable comments on the cruise, the ship, the food and the ports of call. There was a part of him – what he called one of his major character flaws –that was always waiting for the other shoe to drop. At each table that stopped him, he steeled himself for the worst. Thus, he was delighted to know that everyone seemed to be having the best of times and there wasn't a grouch in the bunch. He made one final stop and that was Dave and Mary Pat Flannery's table. Fueled by the congeniality of the other guests, Peter looked down at the pair with a huge smile and said cheerily, "My two favorite dancers. How was Sitka?"

An obviously annoyed Dave looked up from his overly garnished hamburger which he held firmly in his two paws and snapped, "Sitka was fine. Now, Ramsey, say goodbye. I want to enjoy this while it's hot."

"Peter, smile nicely and walk away," Lillie commanded.

He did as instructed. As they walked to the penthouse, he told Lillie that rather than being upset at Flannery's rudeness, he admired his candor, churlish as it was. "If I was hungry and that hamburger was six inches away from making me the happiest of men, I hope I would have the grit to say the same thing."

"No, you don't, Peter. You would return the hamburger to the plate and make the visit even longer and the hamburger even colder by your graciousness," she said.

That evening, Peter met up with Liz for a cocktail in the Covey where they joined the Flannerys. While unrepentant, Dave felt Peter deserved to know why he was so abrupt with him earlier in the afternoon. Thus, in his no-nonsense manner, he explained, "It's like this; nobody comes between me and a good hamburger."

"Dave, I completely understand," Peter said. "Heck, you ought to see me bristle when someone tries to delay my first bite of a just-delivered, piping-hot mustard flower fritter with Tardivo chicories and herb salsa. Just ask Liz."

Dave put his single malt down and stared hard at Peter. "Knowing you, I could almost believe that."

"Well, don't," Peter said. "I don't even know what I said."

"I do. It's from one of your radio bits. He does a great Julia Child," Liz informed the Flannerys.

Before anyone could request a sampling, Peter added hurriedly, "I *did* a good Julia. Now she's in the great Kitchen in the Sky and I am retired from being a professional cute guy."

Dave checked his watch. Inching away from the table. he said, "Ramsey, much as I love this good-natured banter, I have a date to do a little pre-dinner dancing with my lovely wife."

As Mary Pat walked toward the exit, Dave stayed back to talk to Peter. "Ramsey, a couple of people in our group told me they observed you talking to yourself. They said it looked like you were talking to someone who wasn't there. I told them it's a thing radio people do and not to worry. So what really gives?" he asked bluntly.

"Dave, you couldn't have given them a better answer," Peter replied. "I get some good thinking done by talking out loud."

Howard Newton's timing was impeccable. He arrived at Peter's penthouse door a few minutes after midnight. Just as he was about to ring the doorbell, he heard Peter's voice. It sounded like he was talking to someone in an excitable manner. At this point, most people, feeling a bit awkward, would wisely walk away, making a mental note to seek out Peter the following day. Howard, however, was not most people, particularly on this night. Thus, this most oafish of gents rang the bell; not once, but twice.

"Howard!" Peter managed to infuse that one word with a heavy dose of surprise, anger and frustration.

It had no effect on Howard at all. "That's me. Actually, it should be 'it is I,' but that sounds so damned silly," he said, edging past his robed host with the flushed face and taking a seat on the small sofa. Putting his feet up on the small coffee table, he looked around, grinning lasciviously. "What's going on here, my friend? Who are you hiding?"

Peter took a seat at the foot of the bed. "I am not hiding anyone," he snapped.

It was the truth and nothing but the truth. Firstly, Lillie was right there beside him. Howard just couldn't see her. As to Howard's first question, that requires a bit of an explanation. You see, Lillie had come up with a decidedly daft idea. She had got it into her head that a ripping – her expression – way of topping off the day was for her and Peter was to demonstrate to him that she was, indeed, capable of pleasing him in a physical way, even though she knew it would be a one-sided affair. Thus, nestling close to Peter while he slept, she began to huskily and lustily describe in tantalizing detail what she would do to him were she more than a spirit wrapped in a lavender aura. Peter slept on his left side, leaving his right ear exposed to Lillie's breathy, erotic utterances. After years of wearing a headset, his left ear was so damaged, had he been on his right side, he would have slept through the entire seduction. In this case, that might have been better. As it was, it didn't take long for her stimulating oratory to work its magic. At once awakened and aroused, he bolted upright and exclaimed, "Lillie, what on earth are you doing?"

Not the least embarrassed, she explained that she had overheard a young couple talking about their personal experience with phone sex. "Peter, I'm sorry and a bit disappointed that all I ended up doing is startling you," she said.

"What did you expect me to do?" he asked.

"You could have at least lent a hand," she giggled.

Howard looked suspiciously at Peter. "All I know is it sounded like you were talking to someone named Lillie, or maybe it was Billie or Willie. I can scratch the last two unless there's something you want to tell me, Big Guy," he teased.

"I talk in my sleep," Peter said brusquely

"Well, it must have been one hell of a dream."

"Howard, it's twelve-twenty and I want to go back to bed."

Swinging his feet off the table, Howard got up and set a course for the small refrigerator. Peter noticed a swagger that he'd never seen before. Grabbing a Heineken, Howard returned to the sofa. "I think you're going to want to hear what I have to say."

"Howard, are you on medication?"

Laughing loudly, his former boss, fashionably attired in an expensive black cashmere sport-coat with black slacks and a black silk mock turtleneck, responded obliquely, "It's the new me; the M.I.B. look, darker hair, the uber confidence and ... I don't know, maybe a...."

"Swagger," Peter suggested.

Howard brightened. "Yeah, perfect! A swagger."

"You lost me with the M.I.B. look."

"It's short for Man in Black," he answered. "I took a picture of me on my iPhone and sent it to Naomi. She texted back that I look like a priest from a wealthy parish." He frowned slightly and added, "Of course, she hasn't seen the swagger yet. That will change her mind."

"Howard, finish your Heineken and let me go to bed."

"I will, but first I want to tell you about my new best friend."

"And who is that?"

"Charles Van Woort."

chapter 28

I AM MINDFUL OF the fact that after the telling of Lillie's amusing attempt at lovemaking, idiosyncratic as it was, I let slip a splendid opportunity to expound on the utterly fascinating topic of sex and the important role it plays in one's corporeal life. I should have done so if only because there is a veritable gold mine of colorful words with which one gets to play. A few of my favorites are *salacious, lewd, prurient, lubricious and technodynamia.* Got you on that last one, didn't I? It refers to the procreative power of women; a meaningful but tricky word to insert in a casual conversation or if, let's say, you're on the timer during a round of speed-dating. Then, of course, there are myriad imaginative but archaic expressions that caught my attention like *cupid's kettle drums* and *gate of life.* The former I'm sure you can work out. If you need a hint, think Dolly Parton. As to the latter, it refers to that body part which for the large part of a woman's day is modestly covered by what Lillie would have called knickers. It is rumored Robert Burns first called it such. If so, it would prove the handsome poet had more on his mind than Scottish republicanism when he sat down to let his moving finger write.

So, as much fun as this topic can be, it is also a thorny subject for me to sink my teeth... Oops, here we go again. I dealt with this in an earlier chapter but it's worth another mention. There seem to be no end to the number of clever and appropriate metaphors that are impractical for me as they all deal with human body parts, none of which we spirits possess. I will, however, continue to use them and, I promise, without further complaint. Anyway, I must approach this subject carefully because anything I say might be construed as being the official party line from On High and I simply can't have that. Besides, there are already way too many sexperts – I won't name names – who are ever so eager to force feed you their diverse, sometimes frighteningly odd interpretations of the moral, physical and spiritual do's and don'ts of sex, regardless of the rightness or wrongness of their pronouncements. Thus, I will leave you with just one Theodomicles' observation regarding this subject. It is glaringly obvious that sex is always and without exception a consensual act with life-altering consequences. Respect that and I see no reason why you shouldn't happily rev up your libidinous engine and enjoy this beautiful, evanescent gift.

Thanks to Howard Newton's insistence that Peter join him in a beer, he opened a Heineken and settled in to hear his account of the unexpected meeting with one of the male-factors in our story, Charles Van Woort.

"It couldn't have gone better," Howard began, rubbing his hands together excitedly. He was thrilled to be playing such a pivotal role in Peter and Lillie's scheme to recover the stolen painting. "It turned out that Van Woort was at the table next to us in the Italian restaurant. During dessert which were these giant dollops of tiramisu, he came over and joined us. There was some small talk but it wasn't what you'd call happy chatter. The atmosphere was definitely frosty. I don't think the captain and the hotel director like him much. Anyway, in a matter of minutes, Jenni and Fritz split." Here Howard paused. Looking directly at Peter, he lowered his voice to what one might call standard gossip level and whispered, "You know, I think there's something going on between those two." Peter smiled but didn't respond. "Right after that the captain got up to... I don't know. What do captains do after dinner? Go steer the boat or something, I guess. Anyway, Van Woort and I stayed at the table and talked until they threw us out."

"Were you able to bring up the painting?"

Howard took a slow sip of his beer. Wiping his lips with the back of his hand, he replied, "I sure was! What amazed me was how quickly he accepted me as a fellow felon. I must admit, though, I did a good job of convincing him I wanted to continue the seedy relationship he had with my mother-in-law." He looked over at Peter and grinned. "So, how about a little round of applause here for your former boss? Better yet, how about another beer?"

Peter went to the small fridge. "All I have are a Guinness and a Corona."

"Corona, please. A Guinness is a meal and I've already eaten."

Peter returned to the cramped sitting area. He noticed Lillie hovering at the foot of the bed. She said nothing to distract him.

"So here's what I know. Actually, it's quite a bit because Van Woort has this incredibly loose tongue. He told me he's hosting some of his best customers to this cruise as a thank you for buying so much stolen art over the years. I don't think this ship has a brig big enough to hold all of them."

"How many?"

"Five. Well, actually four now that Philipa is no longer with us. But then there's me. So I suppose it's still five. Of course, I haven't bought anything yet..."

"Howard!"

"Okay, okay, back to the story. According to Van Woort, the cruise was meant to be pleasure only, no business.

Then he learned, and I don't know from whom, that he could get his hands on the Millais painting and have it in time for the cruise. He said he couldn't resist doing a little business on the side. Knowing of Philipa's affection for works like this, he contacted her first. They agreed on a price and he instructed her as to how he would transfer the painting to her. After her death, Van Woort wasted no time trying to work up interest in the painting with the remaining four. Only one was keen on buying it. This Russian guy..."

"Anatoly Plushenko!"

Howard lifted the Corona in a mock toast. "That's him."

"I imagine a transaction like that, nasty and illegal as it is, can be pretty easy to pull off."

Howard shook his head. "Except for the fact that Van Woort doesn't do easy."

"Did he tell you how he plans on unloading the painting?"

Smug and immensely proud of the way he had handled the auctioneer, he replied, "Of course, but only after apologizing profusely for refusing the late offer I put on the table. He said he has a deal with Plushitski... Plu..."

"Plushenko."

"Yeah. Anyway, I think Van Woort is terrified of him. He said the Russian was not someone who would take kindly to being jerked around. I think that's why he declined my offer."

"So how's he going to get the painting to him?" Peter asked, anxious to get the rest of the story, send Howard on his way and slip back into bed, perchance to dream, this time without the assistance of Lillie.

"The same as he would have with my mother-in-law. That's why she had that note with the numbers on it. Van Woort thinks he's being awfully clever. Plushenko will get the Millais painting by buying another during the ship's first auction, namely, catalogue number 48 376."

Peter recalled his earlier conversation with Freddy and Benjamin in the hallway stacked with some of the auction art. "I know that painting! It's by a Carmel artist, Dewitt Masterson, and it's called *The Lone Cypress*. Why does Plushenko have to buy it?" he asked.

"Because *A Jersey Lily* resides behind that canvas."

"That makes sense. Plushenko buys the Masterson painting at auction, gets a valid receipt, leaves a shipping address and no one is the wiser."

Howard nodded.

"What about the missing digit? I believe it was a three."

"Van Woort figures the bidding on the Masterson won't top three grand. It was his way of letting Philipa and now Plushenko know what it might cost."

Peter stood up and stretched. "I remember someone telling me it wouldn't go for much at auction. Howard, you are my hero."

"Of course, I am," he laughed, finishing the last of the Corona.

"Well, heroes need their sleep and so do we who admire them. Let's get together tomorrow to figure out where we go from here?"

Standing up slowly and grimacing throughout the short exercise, Howard groaned off-key, "*Oh, dem bones, dem bones, dem dry bones...* All those years of sitting on my ass behind a desk, I suppose. Well, all that's going to change, my friend. Tomorrow I am up early and walking briskly around this battleship for an hour or so, boring as that sounds."

Peter escorted him to the door. In the quiet hallway, Howard looked in both directions. Confident they were alone, he put a hand on Peter's shoulder. "Speaking as a former suit whose responsibility was to keep the company image pristine at all times and at all costs..."

"Where are you going with this, Howard?"

"The captain and the hotel director may wear uniforms instead of suits, but they are no different. My feeling is they have no interest in filling their brig with miscreants from the art world. Particularly if one of them is their auctioneer."

"I can understand. By the way, there's something you ought to know. I didn't learn about this until after we talked on the phone the other day and I forgot to mention it to you."

"What's that?"

"The painting Van Woort has agreed to sell to Plushenko is a fake."

"You're sure?"

Peter nodded.

"Man, this just gets better and better," Howard exclaimed as he turned on his heels and headed for his penthouse.

"I liked you better before the swagger," Peter shouted after him.

The new Howard, the strutting, stylish, seemingly fearless Howard, without turning around, thrust his left hand into the air and extended his middle finger.

"You two have a most interesting relationship," Lillie observed.

Closing the door, Peter replied, "*That* is not the man I used to work for."

Lillie dismissed his reply as her mind was on other things. "If I had been blessed with opposable thumbs, I would have happily cleared the beer bottles away and straightened the room while you were seeing Howard to the door. However, I am what I am," she sighed. "Please, Peter, come sit down."

"I'd rather lie down. The new and improved Howard wore me out," he said, yawning and stretching his way back into the penthouse.

"Just for a moment, please."

Peter heard the seriousness of her plea and did as requested. For the second time that evening he sat in the stateroom's small but comfortable easy chair staring covetously at the bed. He wondered if Lillie wanted to continue their brief chat about her bedroom behavior before Howardus Interruptus.

"Peter, indulge me. I want you to imagine our time together as a two act play."

"Do we have a name for this dramedy?"

"Dramedy?" she asked.

"Drama and comedy all wrapped up in one production."

"In our case, that is certainly a fitting description. As to a title, I never considered one," she said with a light laugh. As ideas came easy to this clever wraith, it was but a mere second before inspiration struck and she exclaimed, "I know! We shall call it *The Ghost and Mr. Ramsey.*"

"There are only two acts?" he asked.

"Yes, but there are many scenes. Now stop asking me questions and listen." Lillie's beautifully-modulated voice was always a pleasure to listen to. As truth was her strong point, there was no artifice in it. After shushing Peter she kicked it up a notch. Befitting a woman of the theatre, she filled the room with her dramatic resonance. Note that I instructed my amanuensis to put the R before the E in theater. While it really says nothing about anything, I like it visually, and, after all, it is my story.

"Peter, the curtain is about to rise on act two," she intoned, each word getting its special moment in the spotlight. "It is here that we will have the opportunity to redeem ourselves as the first act was so foolishly and clumsily performed, notably by me. I must say, though, you did rather well."

Peter waited a moment, cautious more was forthcoming. After a suitable silence, he ventured to speak. "Lillie, I think you're being too tough on yourself and too easy on me."

"I am, but for good reason. From the very beginning, you were much better at accepting me as a ghost than I was being one. I have been giving that considerable thought."

"So you're playing a ghost with an identity crisis," he joked.

She shushed him again. "Peter, I'm serious. Now let me finish what I have to say. In my seventy-six years as flesh and blood, I was an incurable romantic. Even though I now exist in this amorphous form, it seems I still am. I reasoned that an infusion of romance might make me feel more like the Lillie I was. I think that explains my flirtatious manner, my suggestion we be more than just friends and my imprudent behavior tonight." Lillie paused and moved across the room to the sofa. Getting that off her chest improved her mood considerably. She was her high-spirited, cheery self again. "You will be happy to know, Mr. Ramsey, I have now come to terms with who I am, what I am and who we are. While disparate beings, we are true partners, but not of our choosing. Something far more powerful brought the two of us together for a reason. There is no randomness in any of this. I feel truly blessed to part of this unique pairing, and from this moment on I promise to be a better spirit and a better partner.

Peter listened intently. This wasn't the first time he'd heard Lillie reflect on why they were together and what it all meant. Theirs was a relationship that seemed to him to require constant tuning.

"I know you wish to retire, Mr. Ramsey. Let me just finish by saying it is very satisfying knowing I am the only spirit in your life."

Peter stood up and grinned at his nebulous companion. "And I can say unequivocally, Mrs. Langtry, I'm thrilled you're the only one in my life."

His satiric response was not lost on her. "Just imagine the fun you would have had earlier tonight if I did have opposable thumbs," she cooed in a sultry, mischievous voice.

"Time to say good night, Lillie."

chapter 29

IF THERE ISN'T a song called *June in Juneau*, there should be. Why? One excellent reason is it's a much better month than, say, January to visit this Alaskan capital. Of course, this anthem would have to pay homage to Juneau's natural assets and that could prove a creative challenge. Imagine a singer warbling their way through a song whose lyrics contain Mendenhall Glacier, Gastineau Channel and Tongass National Forest.

Once again, the captain did a sterling job of parallel parking. Fortunately, for Peter and Lillie the port side looked out on the city and its alpine background. This morning, the more distant, towering Mt. Juneau still had its majestic head in the clouds while the more diminutive Mt. Roberts, just steps away from the ship, was already showing off its dewy mountain greenery and the many scattered patches of snow in the higher elevations. From his verandah, Peter could see the tramway that shuttled visitors to the Mountain House complex. It held his attention as Liz was on the phone suggesting they hike up and ride the tram back. She had jumped ship early that morning and asking around for a good place to hike got directions from a friendly resident to a trailhead that was the start of a path to the top. Of course, she failed to add that it was a narrow, hazardous trail that was often unmarked.

Not taking his eyes off the forested mountain, he said warily, "Looks more like a rigorous climb than a pleasant hike, Liz."

"I checked. There's a restaurant and bar at the top. I'll buy the beers," she said.

"You're buying? Then I'm in. By the way, what was that beer we had in Sitka?"

"An IPA with a weird name, but it was very good."

They left the ship a little after nine. Lillie said she'd meet up with them in the restaurant. As the sky was azure blue with nary a cloud in sight and all indications showing the temperature was sure to rise, they both wore running clothes better suited for a jog along a beach in Hawaii. Peter was in lightweight, black nylon shorts and a threadbare 1992 Bay to Breakers' tee-shirt and Liz wore pink shorts and an oversized Oakland Half-Marathon shirt. As they strolled through downtown Juneau, they drew curious stares from the residents who knew their Alaskan summer weather could change on a dime. One simply didn't venture too far in such meagre attire. They soon reached a quiet residential neighborhood called Star Hill. On 6th Street, they walked up to the Mt. Roberts' trailhead with its aged, worn signage. At the entrance, Peter first looked into the thick forest and then down at the grid of streets and the busy city. "We take one step in that direction and we leave our comfort zone, Liz," he observed, feeling leery about what they were about to do.

Liz was not the least hesitant: "Tio, this is no different than hiking in the Berkeley Hills or the Marin Headlands. Plus, the lady said there are lots of hikers on the trail, and remember I'm buying the beers and you don't want to pass up that once-in-a-lifetime opportunity."

Fifteen minutes into the hike they discovered the Mt. Roberts trail was far more primitive and unforgiving than the ones they were used to. Plus, due to recent heavy rains, the canopied path which saw little sunlight was wet, muddy, cold and at times downright dangerous. Still they plodded on, excited by the adventure of it all. Approximately forty minutes in, they realized that turning back was not an option as the downhill would be murder on their knees. Plus, both had slipped once going up and logically concluded that going down would mean more slipping and sliding. In better circumstances, the solemn quietude of the Mt. Roberts' hillside trail would have been restorative, calming; something to enjoy and celebrate. This morning, though, it could only offer an unsettling silence in part due to the absence of the promised hikers. Not that they were alone. All around them hidden amongst the Sitka spruces, alders, pines and other flora were the full-time residents of the Mount; marmots, wolverines, ptarmigan, grouse, fox sparrows and bears among others. Neither Peter nor Liz relished the idea of being the only ones out there in what they considered total wilderness, even given its close proximity to civilization. One problem with the trail was its many switchbacks which sometimes made their direction hard to identify. In the beginning, they kept their concerns to themselves, but each had a moment or two when they feared they'd gone off the path.

"Tio, I will feel a whole lot better once I see evidence of a building, preferably one with a bathroom and a bar," Liz said, slowly but deftly stepping around a fallen log. Like her uncle, she was sore from an earlier fall. "Do you realize the only person who knows we're out here is Lillie. How on earth can she sound an alarm? By the way, what time is it?"

Peter glanced at his bare wrist. "I didn't bring a watch."

Liz stopped in her tracks. Astonished, she shouted, "You don't have a watch?"

"I don't work in a time-sensitive world anymore, so I'm trying to wean myself off them."

"Well, you picked the wrong time to start weaning," she complained.

Peter stopped and looked behind him at his frightened niece whose long legs were scarred with mud as was pretty much all of the rest of her. He was sure he was in an equally cruddy condition. "Liz, we are filthy, tired and worried."

"No shit," she muttered. Looking up, she took notice of her uncle's sorry, soiled state and laughed. "Tio, you look like you've been mud wrestling. I'll bet I do, too."

"If it's any comfort, I'd guess we've been out here hiking and climbing for about an hour and a half. We have to be close."

"If we're still on the trail."

"You go ahead of me. I want you to be the first to cross the finish line."

A few minutes later, through the trees and filtered sunlight, Liz spotted a horizontal flat object. Ten steps later she saw it was the eave of a metal roof. Did Edmund Hillary feel this way when he neared the top of Everest, she thought. She was immensely relieved and joyous, and whatever fright she had been carrying was left behind on the muddy, unmarked trail.

Peter was just as ecstatic. It had been a silly adventure. Was it truly fraught with danger, though? Perhaps not for the average Juneau citizen, but he knew they were ill-prepared to be on the Mt. Roberts trail and, as a result, they deserved all the mud they wore.

Even after a cleanup, Peter and Liz came down off Mount Roberts still wearing some of the grimy evidence of their wet, muddy trail experience. However, I'm happy to report they did not descend downhearted and depressed. Of course, I must confess if they had come down off the mount exhausted, dejected and wondering if they had the will to live, I would still be exultant. The reason being perfect bliss is the default condition in the Hereafter. That said, it is my distinct pleasure to announce that the newly retired broadcaster and his soon-to-be anthropologist niece were in fine fettle and all was right with their world, or would be just as soon as they showered and put something warm on. The reason for this buoyancy, this lifting of spirits, was they had come up with a game plan, or at least the beginnings of one, hatched over giant-sized hot dogs and Alaskan beers with a funny name in a distant corner of the long bar in the Timberline Bar and Grill in the Mountain House complex.

Once they had stepped off the pine-needled trail, discarding what fear and apprehension they acquired on the hike, Peter and Liz made a beeline for the public restrooms. This meant an embarrassing sprint through a crowd of people who had wisely taken the tram up the mountain, These visitors from the three large ships docked in Juneau for the day, while not fashionably attired, were clean as whistles. They were also wrapped in jackets and scarves as by late morning it had begun to cloud over and turn chilly. In this temperamental environment, Peter and Liz looked decidedly out of place.

Even though both tried their darndest, their rinse-off wasn't good enough to pass Lillie's inspection No sooner had they settled in at the bar with the cold beers in front of them, than Lillie addressed their still grubby appearance. "All I can say is just from looking at you, I'm glad I don't have an olfactory sense," she said.

The charge bothered Liz more than it did her uncle. "Lillie, we can't smell that bad."

"Then why did the bartender slide your glasses along the bar rather than delivering them to you personally?"

"It's probably a routine of his, part of the theater of bartending," Peter replied. As if to confirm his speculation, the bartender approached their party and asked if they wanted to order food. Both ordered the Denali Dog, a longer than usual wiener on an oversized bun with heaps of one's choice of toppings. Peter requested chili and onions and Liz chose the sauerkraut.

While they waited for their food, Peter attempted to explain to Lillie how they got the way they did, but she would have none of it. Shushing him, she reminded the pair of how unprepared they were for their ill-fated hike: "While waiting for you happy trampers to come up the hill, I chanced upon an instructive pamphlet someone left open to the page on hiking Mount Roberts. Did you know they recommend you start here at the Mountain House and then hike *up*? No, of course, you didn't. The reason is the lower trail, which you took, is often hazardous and unmarked. They also suggest that you let people know what your route is. Yes, you did tell me, but I don't count as I am not people. The writer then goes on to suggest appropriate clothing and proper hiking boots. Finally, they say, and I will emphasize, Alaska trails are unforgiving."

"Lillie, Liz always carries her iPhone," Peter said in a weak defense of their preparedness. "We did have a link to the outside world."

Jumping off her barstool, Liz opened her arms wide as if awaiting a pat down from airport security. "Tio, do you see anywhere on me where I could carry an iPhone?"

Her movement didn't go unnoticed by the young bartender who said a quiet prayer Peter would take his sweet time responding. Much to his dismay, Liz sat down as fast as she stood up.

Peter was incredulous. He was convinced his niece was surgically sewn to her smartphone. "You really didn't bring it?" he asked.

"No, I didn't. I thought it might be nice just for once to be in touch with where I was and out of touch with everything else," she replied. "Besides, you didn't bring your watch."

"Enough, you two," Lillie ordered. "You are both safe and sound and that is what matters most." To show she was not totally unsympathetic to their post-hike condition, she added, "You must be freezing. Look at you with your goose flesh. It's not surprising as you practically have nothing on. I think we ought to head back to the ship."

They were, as Lillie correctly observed, goose-fleshy. However, they were also hungry and had no intention of going anywhere until they'd eaten.

"I have an idea," Peter said. "There's a souvenir shop next door. I'll bet I can find a couple of sweatshirts. Lillie, catch Liz up with Howard's late night visit while I'm gone. I'll be back in five minutes."

"Tio, get me an extra large, please," Liz hollered after him. "And no funny writing or pictures on it, if that's possible."

He returned with two grey hoodies, the tags already removed. He handed Liz one while he slipped the other over his head. Emblazoned on the front of his in bold black letters were the words *SLED DAWG*. "Sorry, Liz, these are the best I could find," he said. "They'll warm us up, though."

Liz held her sweatshirt in front of her and stared at the large, multi-colored letters. "I heart my Alaskan Malamute," she read aloud in a derisive tone. "Tio, firstly I don't have a Malamute as you well know, and secondly I cannot abide using a heart as a verb. Come on, I'll trade you. I know they're the same size."

Peter, having no such fashion concerns, doffed his and handed it to his niece. No sooner had she put it on than the bartender showed up with their Denali Dogs. Both were awestruck by the sheer size of the serving and the excessive amount of sauerkraut and chili.

"Tio, we could have split one of these and still have some left over."

"Eat what you can. And try to keep from getting food stains on your stylish new sweatshirt," he teased.

"I appreciate you buying these, but I want you to know that I look upon this as a giant, warm bib. Like my napkin, it will stay here when we leave. There is no way I'm getting on the ship in this thing," she said, as portions of sauerkraut escaped from one end of her Denali Dog to further decorate her hoodie.

Lillie had of late been entertaining premonitions that her tenure as the Ocean Glamour's ghost-in-residence might be coming to an end soon and because of that she was anxious for the three of them to get to the task at hand, namely, recovering her beloved painting. Still she waited patiently as they ate. Then she would insist they head back to the ship. Liz and Peter surprised themselves by almost finishing their designer dogs, and before Lillie could protest, he had ordered another Alaskan beer with the funny name for the two of them. Even though it was lunchtime, the bar was quiet on their end and since Liz had draped herself in an extra large sweatshirt, even the bartender kept his distance. To make it look more like just two people were carrying on a conversation, Lillie had positioned herself between them and behind the bar.

Figuring they were going to be atop Mount Roberts a bit longer, Lillie decided they could talk there as well as on the ship. "Peter, do you have any new thoughts as to what we do next?" she asked. "Considering what we now know after Howard's visit last night."

"Actually, I have," he said, putting his beer down and looking at the lavender vision in front of him. "But I need to ask you something first. Do you remember what you wanted to tell me after we left Freddie and Benjamin's penthouse the other evening?"

"I do, indeed," Lillie replied. "Because of their intriguing tale of the Sprottle twins' larcenous behavior, I concluded that the Millais painting was hanging on a wall in their Mayfair mews clubhouse. As we were just getting to know each other and I was enjoying our time together, I didn't relish a quick resolution. Then it was decided that if I didn't tell you what I thought, we couldn't act on it."

"Even if you're right, Lillie, it wouldn't be that easy to make your case against them," Liz offered. "By the way, I hope we can drag this out a while longer, too."

"Thank you, Liz. However, we are no longer the keepers of the schedule. The pace is now being set by other forces and we must adjust to them."

"I couldn't agree more," Peter said. "Thanks to the new and arguably improved Howard, we know Van Woort is going to sell what we think is the fake Millais to Anatoly Plushenko. We also know this will occur in the early part of the first auction which is scheduled for the day after tomorrow. Somehow we have to get our hands on that painting first."

Liz looked aghast. "You're kidding?"

"Liz, we need to know if it really is a forgery. We only have Benjamin Lytton-Crisp's word, and he's the first to admit he's not an expert, just a fan of that particular painting. I'd feel a lot better if we can get a real honest-to-God authenticator to look at it."

"And just how do we go about getting this valued second opinion? And from whom? We're on a ship, you know," Liz observed.

Peter smile confidently. "I know an expert. In fact, he's part of our group. His name is Malcolm Fitzroy and he owns a gallery in San Francisco. More important, though, he's a respected art authenticator and historian."

Liz finished the last of her beer. "Okay, but how do you plan to steal the painting so he can check it out?"

"I have no intention of stealing anything," Peter replied. "Let me explain."

When he finished, genuine kudos flowed from Liz and Lillie. Their verbal high fives were not surprising as it was an excellent idea. As it will unfold in front of your very eyes in a few pages, there's no reason to detail it here.

chapter 30

PETER AND LIZ rode the tram alone as Lillie, complaining that she always found "those hanging pods" claustrophobic and a bit frightening, opted to spirit herself down Mount Roberts. Wisely, both kept their hoodies on. While self-conscious about its cheesy style, Liz was comforted by the fact that her sauerkraut-stained *Sled Dawg* sweatshirt was not as silly as her uncle's which had inspired a fellow passenger to ask if he, in fact, had a Malamute. Peter not only provided her with a detailed bio of his fictitious four-legged friend named Nanookie, but he even imitated the unique bark the dog used to wake him up mornings. He would have gone on except for a hard nudge from Liz.

Once they arrived at sea level, Liz announced she was going to pop into a nearby tourist shop to get a small gift for a university colleague who once lived in Juneau. Peter bid her adieu and made his way to the ship, anxious to set in motion the plan he'd laid out for his two companions atop Mount Roberts.

"You must be the only person in Juneau wearing shorts." Turning around to see who belonged to the warm, friendly voice, he found himself gazing into the equally warm, friendly eyes of Samantha Whitby. Hers, however, were focused on his chest. "You have a Malamute?" she asked.

This time Peter told the truth. "No, I am Malamute-less. Liz and I set off hiking Mount Roberts this morning when it was warm and sunny. The weather turned, so I bought it in a tourist shop. They had a very limited selection."

They were in a short line of guests who were anxious to board. Both stepped out of the queue to continue their conversation. Looking around, he asked, "Where's your sister?"

Samantha's smile widened. "You won't believe this but Isabelle is somewhere in Juneau visiting art galleries with her new gentleman friend."

"That's great news!" Peter exclaimed.

"Yes, it is. She's certainly a delight to be around now. Only trouble is she's no longer around," she said, happy to have run into Peter. So happy, she realized she wanted to see more of him than just this chance meeting. If only he would hang around for a few more sentences, she might find a way to give form and voice to some kind of invitation to join her for drinks, dinner, chess in the moonlight, napkin folding class... Anything, she thought giddily, as long as they did it together. Then she remembered she'd done the asking the last time. That recollection took some of the edge off her giddiness.

"Is this, dare I ask, a budding shipboard romance?" Her laugh, which Peter thought was delightful, suggested otherwise. "I take it it's a bit more complicated."

"You may know him. He's a member of your travel group. His name is Malcolm Fitzroy," she said.

"I do know him and he is a member of our group. Personally, I wouldn't mind having someone like that show me around a gallery. He has quite a reputation."

"They have art in common," she explained. "What they don't have in common is age. However, it doesn't seem to bother either one of them, so I'm not going to let it bother me."

"Wise of you," Peter noted. As much as he wanted to stay and visit, he had calls to make. "We better get aboard. I'm anxious to shed and then probably shred this Malamute hoodie." Then an inspired alternative popped into this head. "Better than that, I know just the person I can give it to. Her name is Gertie Florian and, trust me, she'll love it."

They rejoined the line. After a few seconds of silence while they searched for their card keys to get past security, each voiced the other's name simultaneously. After a polite round of "No, please, you go first," Peter volunteered to lead off. "Would you join me for dinner this evening?" he asked impulsively.

"I'd love to!" she exclaimed. Samantha was so grateful he saved her from having to do the asking, she realized she'd replied with more zing than was necessary.

"That's wonderful. I have a window table for two in the dining room, late seating. It's French night and the menu looks inviting. We could meet for a drink first. Say the Covey at seven-thirty?"

"I'd like that. By the way, it's a formal night. Will you be in a tuxedo? I ask because some men opt for suits or even sport-coats and I want to dress appropriately," she said, grabbing her bag which just went through the ship's X-ray machine, passing with flying colors.

"I brought along a vintage white dinner jacket. Now I have a reason for breaking it out. I can fantasize I'm James Bond," he joked as the security guard swiped his key and welcomed him aboard.

"Bond movies are one of my guilty pleasures," she confessed. "I always thought of James Bond as being the Archie of the spy world."

"You mean Archie of comic book fame?"

"The very same. Archie had Veronica and Betty who to me represent the two women who always find themselves in Bond's embrace. There's the exotic, sultry, tough-as-nails villainess who routinely gets dispatched in some imaginative fashion. That's Veronica. Then there's the fresh-faced, perky and innocent ally or colleague who acts like she's never been kissed before. That's Betty."

"What a fascinating comparison. You should offer a course in Bondology," Peter said as they climbed the stairs to the lobby deck.

"So tonight, Mr. Bond, would you prefer Veronica or Betty as your dinner companion?" The question was now in full view of the man standing close to her on the landing and no one was more surprised by it than Samantha. "Of course, I can always dress like M," she added hastily, hoping to tone down whatever sexual inference the flirtatious inquiry suggested.

"If you do, I'm coming as Q."

Explaining she was dangerously close to being late for a manicure appointment,

a florid Samantha left Peter to climb the stairs while she took the elevator. Alone in the mirrored capsule, she looked carefully at her hair and decided it would have to do. Continuing to stare at her image, she began a conversation: "What on earth were you thinking? You've never, ever flirted like that before." When the image didn't answer, Samantha smiled and watched her reflection smile back at her. "Maybe it's not about what were you thinking, Samantha. Maybe it's more about what were you feeling." The mirror image offered no comment. It didn't matter as Samantha knew how she would respond.

While the college professor prepped for their dinner, Peter went about the task of building his team of players who would be vital to the success of his crafty plan. As money would play an important part, he sought out Howard Newton first. He caught up with him in the gym where

Skip, a muscled personal trainer from New Zealand with carrot hair, was teaching him how to do a proper pushup. After a sweaty rant, more theatrical than anything, and three almost successful pushups, a red-faced, out-of-breath Howard agreed to open his wallet when the time came. Skip was clueless as to what they were talking about. All he wanted from his client was one more pushup, a gift Howard was unable to give him. Next, over iced mochas in the Portside Bistro, Peter pitched his plan to Petra Dosynk, explaining the major role the Kwyrki would play. Petra was touched Peter had thought of him and enthusiastically signed on the dotted line. Peter still needed to contact Malcolm Fitzroy and the two neo-Victorians, Freddie and Benjamin, but that could wait until tomorrow.

Lillie was waiting for him on the penthouse verandah, a favorite spot of hers. "I believe we're getting close to sailing. A flurry of activity below us indicates we aren't staying much longer in Juneau. I truly enjoy these sail aways."

"I do, too," Peter said. "As for this particular port of call, Liz and I will take a few special memories with us, plus some indigestion from those Denali Dogs."

"Where's your sweatshirt?" she asked.

"Gertie Florian is now the proud owner. I saw her by the elevators on the eighth deck. Right off, she commented on the sweatshirt. She said it just didn't seem to be something I'd wear. I explained why I got it, took it off and offered it to her. You'd have thought I'd given her a gown by Balenciaga."

"What are your plans for this evening?" Lillie asked, even though she knew.

"I'm having dinner with Samantha Whitby," he answered directly,

"How convenient," she said. "Liz and I have decided to spend some time together. It will be an evening of girl talk," she laughed. "By the way, I think your niece is a bit disappointed there's not a more active role for her in your fanciful scheme."

"That sounds like Liz," he said, shaking his head. "Actually, Petra Dosynk is the featured player in the first act. The rest of us stay just off-stage.

"You better get ready for your evening," Lillie advised. "I'm anxious to see you in your white dinner jacket, Mr. Bond."

Peter walked into the nearly empty Covey a few minutes before he was to meet Samantha. He felt particularly natty in his vintage tuxedo jacket, mainly because of Lillie's approving words when he put himself up for inspection before leaving the penthouse. To keep this image of a debonair gentleman going throughout the evening, he knew he would have to do his darndest to not play with or adjust either his bow-tie or pocket-square, gestures that would definitely put a dent in his dash.

Dave Flannery was at the bar, one hand hugging a glass of a very special single malt called Oban which had been aged well into its teenage years. Because of its exorbitant price tag, it was to be his one and only tasting on the cruise of this unique West Highland elixir with its suitably smokey flavor. Dave's wardrobe choice lacked the sophistication of Peter's, dressed as he was in a dark pinstriped suit that had seen better days, a food-stained tie and his regulation Hermes pocket-square. Seeing Peter enter, he reluctantly waved him over. I say reluctantly as he would have preferred to sip the Oban with only himself as company. Letting go of the glass to feel the satin lapel of Peter's white dinner jacket, he said, "I remembering wearing one of these to my senior prom. I threw up all over it thanks to too many Seven and Sevens. It was a rental and my dad was so pissed he made me return it without first getting it dry cleaned."

"Ah, yet another touching moment from David Augustus Flannery's early years," Peter crooned.

Grinning, Dave said, "It turned out okay. I married my date."

Peter looked at his watch. "Mind if I join you?"

"If you don't mind losing me to this sweetheart of a drink every once in awhile. This obscenely priced Oban and I are in the midst of a passionate love affair and each sip, think of it as a lingering kiss, requires my undivided attention."

"Maybe I better leave the two of you alone," Peter said, making a motion to leave.

"No, take a seat. I'll be going shortly anyway. Mary Pat is putting her face on. I'm meeting her in Club Glamour for some pre-dinner dancing. As to this," he said, holding up his glass, "I promised myself one before the cruise is over. So what are you up to this evening?"

"I'm meeting Samantha Whitby for a drink and then dinner in the dining room."

"Be careful, Ramsey. She's extremely bright," Dave warned. Then seemingly out of nowhere he asked, "Have you ever heard of la passeggiata?"

"It sounds like it could be an Italian anything from pasta to a sports car. I'm guessing it's a dessert."

"Loosely, it means a little walk. It's an age-old custom where Italians dress up and go for a stroll in the early evening hours with maybe a stop for ice cream or wine. They emphasize the pace is slow and gentle. What I call real exercise."

Puzzled, Peter asked. "And just what does that have to do with what we've been talking about?"

"I like the word and I like what it means. I read about it in the cruise catalogue for next year. Mary Pat and I decided we are going to take a Mediterranean cruise that leaves from Rome, and when we're in the Eternal City, we will dine sumptuously and then take la passeggiata on the Via Corso."

"Dave, you're a constant surprise."

Flannery and Oban kissed. Peter waited for him to return to the conversation. "Sometimes I even surprise myself. I like life on a cruise ship, Ramsey. Nothing ever happens that I don't want to have happen and that suits me."

"I thought you'd think cruising too sterile and uninteresting."

"I can explain it this way. See this scotch?" he asked, holding up the glass of amber liquid. Peter nodded and Dave continued, "Do you know what goes well with it? And don't you dare say soda."

"In that case, I better eliminate nuts, cured Italian meats and arancini."

"Contemplation, Ramsey," Dave said in a raised voice that even caught the bartender's attention and the other guests who had wandered in during their conversation. "Contemplation," he repeated again, sotto voce. "When I'm in a bar at home, I'm usually in a deep sulk, thanks to having spent a day dealing with reporters who can't report, editors who can't edit and columnists who can't think." Realizing his sweeping comment on the sad state of his paper's staff was patently unfair, he toned it down. "Well, it isn't that bad, but you know what I mean."

"The day's labor weighs heavy on your mind when you should be enjoying yourself and thinking beautiful thoughts," Peter observed.

"Exactly. On the ship, I can give my entire attention over to the tasting of this Oban. In fact, everything gets my undivided attention. When I dance with my wife, it becomes a true romantic experience."

"You certainly proved that the other day with your award-winning tango."

"Harmony, Ramsey," he emoted, once again drawing stares from the ever growing crowd. "Here, I don't think of our petulant teenage children, the newspaper, the silly antics of city government..."

"*The oppressors wrongs, the law's delay. The insolence of office,*" Peter inserted.

Dave stared at him and raised his right eyebrow. "Hamlet?"

"Hamlet."

One sip of Oban remained. Dave put a beefy hand up and halted any further conversation. Peter watched as he slowly raised the glass to his lips, eyes closed, going somewhere where he wasn't allowed. He had considered using some of their time together to tell Dave of his adventures, but Dave's contentment with the calm, untroubled environment of the Ocean Glamour persuaded him otherwise.

When Dave went to reach for his check, Peter reminded him that Symington was picking up all his onboard expenses. "And that includes all the Oban you can drink."

"I forgot all about that," he laughed. "Ironic, isn't it? Part of the enjoyment was the rationing. Knowing I can now drink as much of it as I want changes things and not for the good."

Flannery edged off the stool to make his way to Club Glamour for an hour of fox-trotting, waltzing and what else. He made his exit just as Samantha Whitby made her entrance. She wore a black sleeveless cocktail dress by Escada. It was the most expensive and extravagant item in her limited wardrobe. Around her neck was a strand of pearls given her by her parents when she received her doctorate in literature. Her only other piece of jewelry was a modest silver bracelet on her left wrist. Peter watched from the bar as Dave kissed her on the cheek and whispered something in her ear. He then turned to look into the dark clubby confines of the Covey and shouted, "Ramsey, your prom date is here."

chapter 31

PETER ESCORTED SAMANTHA to a corner table which allowed them to sit at an angle to each other. He much preferred this arrangement over sitting across from each other; a position he always associated with sober business interviews. After seating Samantha, he began to ramble: "I'm curious. Whatever it was Dave whispered in your ear made you blush. I hope he was telling you how radiant you look. Then again, if he did, I'm sorry he got to tell you before I did." Before she could respond, he added, "Listen to me! I'm already talking too much and we just sat down."

"I'm a professor of English literature, Peter. I have no problem with anyone using one hundred words when ten would do. Particularly, if the additional ninety entertain or, in this case, make one feel very special." Seated, she automatically grabbed the hem of her dress to pull it forward. Then just as quickly she let go. Like Peter with his rule of not playing with his bow-tie or pocket-square, she had her own rules of conduct while in polite society and she had just caught herself about to break one. Samantha's personal commandments were inspired by a strong sense of modesty and inexperience in being out and about in fancy dress. This evening's list of no-noes included the aforementioned skirt-tugging along with pearl-fingering and strap-adjusting. Now one would think all this mindful attention to what not to do in each other's company would make for a labored and distracted conversation. Not so with our compatible pair. Both were able to give their undivided attention to each other and still mind the store, if you will.

After their Martinis arrived and they toasted, Samantha revealed what it was Flannery told her: "It was a warning of sorts. He said and I quote, 'Be careful, Sam. He's not very bright.'"

Peter, pursing his lips and placing his hands on the table, responded, "It seems, Ms Whitby, we both have been warned. His exact words to me were, and I quote, 'Be careful, Ramsey. She's very bright.'"

"Then I consider it your duty to prove him wrong and my duty to prove him right," she quipped, lifting her gin Martini to toast again. "Here's to a lovely evening."

With one dinner under their belts and propinquity not a problem, both were eager for conversation. Regrettably, any colloquy was put on hold as visitors began appearing at their table with stunning regularity. First on the scene was a frail couple in their late eighties from San Francisco. Soft-spoken and diffident, they seemed hesitant to interrupt but did so nevertheless. Peter stood to greet them. Samantha was impressed but not surprised at how deftly he put them at ease, listening attentively while they

commented on this and that. Watching the couple drop all pretense of shyness, she realized that Peter's gentlemanly manners worked for him and against him. As the pair droned on, he finally made a motion to sit down. To their credit, it was a cue they understood and respected. On their heels, Howard Newton was next to crash their party. One couldn't find a better verb than crash to describe his heavy-handed, bumbling arrival. This time Peter did not rise, and judging from his stern expression, he was not about to be as accommodating.

"Yo, Peter," Howard said loudly, "I got up to five pushups. This trainer is really good. He's gay, but so what." Dressed in one of his somber-grey business suits, he looked more the radio station manager than the comical hipster-in-training who boarded the ship in Sitka. The new uber-Howard, however, showed itself when he nodded with a certain arrogance in the direction of Samantha, his clumsy signal he wanted to be introduced.

"May I present Samantha Whitby," Peter said formally.

"*May I present,*" Howard mimicked. "Anyway, nice to meet you," he said to Samantha, sending his right hand in her general direction. "I'm Howard Newton. I'm his former boss and current ATM machine. So what do you do? It must be important. I mean, Peter introducing you like that as if you're a senator or a judge or something."

"Samantha is a professor of English literature at Cal Berkeley," Peter answered.

Putting his hand on Peter's shoulder, Howard kept his attention fixed on Samantha. "Well, you're certainly a step up for my former morning man. Peter here usually dates TV anchors who need a teleprompter to carry on an intelligent conversation. Howard looked down at an unamused Peter and realized he may have stepped out of bounds with that last comment. "Anyway, I've, uh, got to go. I'll see *you* tomorrow," he said to Peter in a bossy tone. Looking over at Samantha, he added, "Nice meeting you..." Her name had escaped him.

"Samantha," she said softly. Then pretending to read from the cocktail menu, she recited in a monotone, "It was very nice meeting you, too, Mr. Newton."

Clapping soundlessly after Howard slunk away, Peter said, "You deserve a standing ovation, Professor Whitby. That was inspired. I'm not sure I can properly explain Howard. He is unique among our gender. My only hope is this encounter is the only social damage he'll do tonight."

"What did he mean by his being your ATM machine?"

Peter, not wanting to lie, explained, "Howard has come into some money. In fact, a lot of it. He thinks I want to hit him up for a business venture." He felt it was a response that wouldn't send the truth-meter too far into the red zone.

"Would I recognize any of these TV anchors he mentioned?" she asked altogether too casually. She surprised herself by how curious she really was.

"One anchor. Just one," he replied, his left index finger confirming the count. "And that was very brief as she was unable to win Liz's heart or approval which at the time was a requirement."

And just like that, Liz was standing on the same spot Howard occupied just a moment earlier. "Did I just hear my name?" she asked, bending down to kiss her uncle on the cheek. She had squeezed into the tiny, slinky red outfit that Lillie so admired. Both Peter and Samantha told her how stunning she looked in it. Actually, Peter used the word stunning and Samantha worked effulgent into her compliment.

"Thanks, I appreciate the kind words. I mean I'm hoping effulgent means something positive." Glancing back at a departing Howard, she added, "I see he got to you before I did."

"He did indeed. And he used your line about my date requiring a teleprompter," Peter noted. "Does that ring a bell, young lady?"

With a sheepish grin, Liz explained that she'd run into him in the lobby bar. "He was talking to two women who were peppering him with questions about your private life. He said you were a real Lothario who bounced from one media cutie to the next. That's the part I heard anyway."

A Lothario!" Peter exclaimed, more puzzled than offended by Howard's charge. "I don't think he even knows what the name means. I hope you set him straight." Samantha sat quietly, fascinated by their exchange. "You did, didn't you?" he asked again.

"Yes, I did. I told him and the two women how you spent most of your time raising poor pitiful me." Dropping her voice, she added with a tinge of guilt, "Okay, I might have mentioned the line about the teleprompter." Her uncle's nettled look prompted her to come to the defense of her actions: "Come on, Tio, you know how it is when you're going for a laugh. And it is one of my better lines."

As guests waiting for the late seating in the dining room entered the Covey, many thought a stop at the Ramsey/Whitby table was de riqueur. With everyone, Peter remained patient and congenial. In between these visitations, he muttered apologies to Samantha for the interruptions. She waved them off. If she was anything, she was amused by it all but a bit disappointed they were denied their own company.

Professor Whitby would have no complaints about dinner. So engrossed were they that no one except the wait staff paid them the slightest attention and even they treaded lightly. To boot, the ship's photographer, a perky young lady from New Zealand, hell-bent on ordering every single diner to smile, left them alone. And just what was so enthralling that an entire dining room gave them such a wide berth? It was a bit of everything, actually. They way they ate; slowly appreciating every bite. They way they sipped their wine; frequently reaching across the table to clink glasses before raising them to their lips. The way they talked; animatedly. Because Peter was so used to talking to Lillie, he had forgotten how valuable physical expression was to dialogue. They were in such perfect harmony that if Charles Darwin had observed them in action, he'd rethink aspects of his theory of sexual selection. Please don't give that analogy a lot of thought. I don't wish to lose you to page-flipping through

The Origin of Species just when things are heating up here. Anyway, I'm sure you get my point: They were a natural pair, a perfectly matched set. While this was a conclusion neither Peter nor Samantha entertained yet, it was palpably clear to everyone else within viewing distance.

While waiting for dessert, lacking forethought and naively thinking the time was ripe to inform Samantha of his on-going otherworldly adventures while on the cruise, Peter asked her if she remembered their earlier conversation about Lillie Langtry.

Fortunately for him, Samantha, taken aback by the inquiry, steered everything in a different direction, "Do you know this is the second time thing evening, Peter, that you and I have been thinking the same thing at the same time."

"Stop me from saying great minds think alike," he joked.

"Perhaps, not great minds but certainly ours. This is amazing. I was just now thinking about that very conversation and I was about to bring it up," she said, leaning back in her chair.

Peter found this amateurish clairvoyance utterly romantic. "You first then. Why did you want to talk about it?"

"I was worried you might have come away from that evening with the impression I wished to be a Lillie Langtry knockoff."

Knowing Lillie would love that expression, he made a mental note to tell her later. His next thought was he'd just been given the opportunity to shelve his desire to talk about Lillie. He was much relieved. Finally, as regards Samantha's concern, he understood why she thought the way she did. "Ah, my off-the-wall question about who among famous Victorian women impressed you. Except I used the word emulate and that probably got you thinking in the that direction. So the answer is no, I didn't think you were ready to trade in your life for a black mourning dress and dalliances with royalty."

"I'm delighted to hear that," she enthused. Raising her glass for what was to be their twenty-third toast of the evening (Yes, I was keeping count.), she added, "I just want to assure you that I am one hundred percent Samantha Whitby."

"No doubt certified organic."

"I'm from Berkeley. Do I have a choice?" She entertained a quick thought of what her colleagues at the Cal Faculty Club might think of this conversation.

Peter grinned and looked across at the trim, handsome well-dressed woman. Raising his glass (Yes, they were going for number twenty-four.), he said, "And let's not forget fat-free and very attractively packaged."

Samantha's reaction was to laugh and turn pink at the same time. "Peter, I think I've blushed more in the last few days than I have in many, many years. Not that I don't appreciate it, but I hardly deserve all this flattery."

"I think you do," he countered.

"And there's another thing," she said.

Placing his left palm on his forehead, Peter closed his eyes and announced in a seriocomic voice, "Besides reading your mind, I bring out the silliness in you."

With a pout he found appealing, Samantha whispered across the table, "Something like that, yes."

Peter looked at his watch. "Shall we try to catch the show in the Monaco Lounge. It's a tribute to Cole Porter and it's supposed to be pretty good."

"I'd love that." Her response was filled to the brim with unbridled enthusiasm, her warm perfect smile was back where it belonged and her raised glass indicated they would end the dinner with their twenty-fifth toast.

After just two dinners together, it was apparent Peter and Samantha were extremely well-suited. Now I,

Theodomicles, understand that a lot of you have mixed feelings as regards the role compatibility plays in a relationship. For story-telling purposes, many find it unromantic and devoid of any passionate intensity. I can understand that. For example, Katherina and Petruchio in *Taming of the Shrew* are great fun. There is fiery argument, the throwing of dishes and furniture, sexual tension and a running fervency of passion. While I can't offer you similar dynamics, I can assure you our pair will not find themselves on a completely trouble-free, flower-strewn path to living happily ever after. Their difficulties, however, will not add up to anything that entertains if you hunger for the provocative or titillating. Before I leave this topic, I must say, having observed you temporal beings in action over the centuries, it is apparent to me there are untold blessings and benefits of compatibility. As for here in Eternity, it's simply part of the culture.

An affection for the music of Cole Porter, while a trifle in the similarity category, was yet another affinity shared by our nascent couple. When they arrived at the Monaco Lounge, the show had already begun. It was a full house except for two seats near the exit. They would have been easy to slip into except their neighbors would be Charles Van Woort, Anatoly Plushenko, his bored-to-tears girlfriend with the long last name and, surprisingly, Howard Newton. All were behaving foolishly; paying no attention whatsoever to the stage show where the gaily costumed singers and dancers were doing their best to keep the majority of the audience awake. Peter saw nothing but trouble if they stayed. Fortunately, another striking similarity between them was neither possessed the night-clubbing gene.

Their evening ended at the Whitby sisters' stateroom. It was an affectionate parting, both confirming they had a wonderful time and each looking forward to seeing the other soon. Then Peter gave Samantha a quick peck on the left cheek. The shy professor, anxious to show him that it was, indeed, a truly special evening for her, extended her arms for a welcoming hug. They fit, he thought. So much so, that if hugs were a commercial product and available at the local hug store, this was the one he would purchase.

He again found Lillie on the verandah. "I was going to ask if you were sleeping, but you don't, of course."

"You had a lovely evening?" she asked.

"I did. Samantha and I seem to have mutual interests. It was a comfortable evening," he replied. "I know that doesn't sound very romantic but there you are." He was still thinking about their parting embrace. It felt to him that the most natural place in the world for her was in his arms and he in hers. The Hug, as he would later refer to it, was the first physical evidence that there was a special chemistry between them.

"I was thinking about tomorrow. Is there much we need to do?" Lillie asked.

"I still have to talk to Malcolm Fitzroy and then check in with Freddie and Benjamin," Peter replied. "Mostly, it's just waiting for the following day and the auction."

"Then I think we all ought to go sightseeing," she said. "That would please me immensely. I missed your company this evening."

"And I yours," he answered honestly. "So it's a date. You, Liz and I will wander around Vancouver. Maybe we'll find a store where I can buy a muzzle to put on Howard."

Lillie laughed. "What did he do now?"

Peter mentioned Howard's oafish visit to their table and then later seeing him cozying up to Van Woort and Plushenko. "My main concern, Lillie, is he's treating this as if it's some kind of game. Anyway, I'll rein him in tomorrow."

"Before you retire, Peter, could you indulge me for a moment?"

"I'd be happy to," he said, taking a chair opposite Lillie's chaise lounge.

"I worry that you are going to make a big mistake," she said with genuine concern.

"Mistake?"

"Is it safe to say you are developing feelings for Samantha?"

"Yes, I am," Peter confessed. He liked hearing that said aloud, so he said it again. "Yes, I am."

"I wonder if it might be best to keep a distance from Professor Whitby until we're off the ship and your life has more or less returned to normal," she advised.

"Why?"

"One of your most admirable traits is your innate sense of honesty. I fear you'd be inclined to tell her about us, the missing painting and our efforts to get it back. I daresay, no matter the feelings she has for you, I'm convinced she'd find it all so fantastical and unreal that she would quickly distance herself from you."

"Odd that you should mention that. I was about to tell her tonight," he admitted. "I didn't, though. The thing is, Lillie, I always thought honesty to be the sine qua non of a healthy relationship."

His spirit companion interjected, "It is, Peter. However, your situation is exceptional. How do you explain to Samantha that you're currently communicating with a woman whom she wished to emulate?"

"Whoa, Lillie, I don't remember Samantha saying anything about wanting to emulate you."

"I may have missed a word or two in your earlier meeting with her but I do believe she told you she'd love to have the social daring and spunk of a Lillie Langtry but her natural timidity forbids it."

"You were there! I don't believe it. You've been eavesdropping on us," he charged.

"Peter, don't excite yourself," she said calmly. "I enjoy making a turn through the ship's social meeting places. It's something I do regularly. I just happened to float by you two when I heard my name mentioned. By you, as a matter of fact."

"I did bring you up and Samantha admitted to admiring you greatly, but I didn't hear her say anything that amounted to her wanting be a Langtry knockoff."

Lillie laughed heartily. "What a marvelous expression. In my limited time here, I must find a time and place to use it. Anyway, dear Peter, I have said what I wanted to say. We have a big day tomorrow and you need your rest."

Climbing into bed is an archaic expression to be sure. It was, perhaps, applicable when beds actually required one to climb up and onto them, but the berth in Peter's penthouse barely came up to his knees. Thus, rather than climb, he sat on the edge and threw his muscled but spindly legs up onto the bed and under the duvet. Only then did he allow his upper half to fall backward. Once flattened, it was his nightly custom to remain stock still, gaze at the ceiling and see where his mind takes him. This night, his musings began with Lillie's warning to not share all with Samantha, something he wished to do even though he knew it wasn't wise. Then, remembering a line from a murder mystery he'd recently read, he said aloud, "Maybe the old woman was right. Truth *is* a luxury."

"I heard that," Lillie shouted from the verandah.

"I wasn't quoting you," she shot back.

"Of course, you weren't, my dear. So who was this shrewd woman?"

"A Sicilian woman. She was talking to a detective in Venice."

"What was a wizened old Sicilian woman doing in Venice?" she asked.

"Buona notte, Lillie," he said sweetly but emphatically, moving his head this way and that until his buckwheat-filled pillow was perfectly shaped for a night's sound slumber. Then he prayed. He prayed in his own words, in his own way. Which is to say,

he was easily distracted by sundry thoughts that seemed to take a perverse delight on intruding on his orison. There was one particularly unwelcome notion. Peter found himself again questioning the identity, even the existence of the Entity to whom he was making his appeal. However, as he was getting more adept at taking on the role of a spiritually buffed bouncer when it came to dealing with these kinds of unwanted interruptions, he was able to easily eighty-six the meddlesome thought forthwith. His mind now cleared, he returned to his prayer, only to be interrupted by a sweet memory of his dinner with Samantha, then a moment of wondering what Liz got up to that evening and finally a thought about the warm satisfaction he felt in knowing that Lillie was settled on the verandah wondering what an elderly Sicilian woman was doing in Venice talking to a detective. In those instances he saw no need for a guard at the door of thought. As a result of Peter's myriad cerebral meanderings on this placid Alaskan night, it was a good ten minutes before he finally said, again out loud, "Amen and thank you, God."

"I heard that!" I'll let you guess where that came from. If you suspect there were two possible sources, pat yourself on the back.

chapter 32

VANCOUVER IN THE summertime is a gathering spot for cruise ships, and all of them covet a parking space at Canada Place Cruise Terminal as it is conveniently located just baby steps from the city's vibrant downtown. Noted for its architecturally provocative quintet of nine-story high white sails, the complex also houses the city's convention center and a luxury hotel. The Ocean Glamour was lucky enough on that glorious morning to tie up on Canada Place's more scenic west side.

From his penthouse verandah, a well-rested Peter had a splendid view of the high-rise condominiums and apartments that dotted the Vancouver Harbour shoreline. In the distance was Stanley Park, considered one of the finest urban parks in the world. Even at this early hour, with binoculars, he spied joggers, dog walkers and cyclists scooting along its many paths. It was as fine a morning as one could wish for; clear blue skies, kindly breezes and a teasing hint of an afternoon warmup. Peter wondered if he could talk Liz into a morning run to the park. Remembering Lillie wanted to spend the day with them, he asked, "Lillie, how fast can you go in that sporty aura of yours?"

"If you're thinking of taking a morning run, I don't think I'll join you," replied the atmospheric figure that hovered above the chaise lounge. "You get your exercise and then we'll meet back here and go ashore together. Meantime, there are a few things I wish to tend to here on the ship."

"Anything I need to know about?"

"In due time."

Peter called Liz, who agreeing they had docked in a runner's paradise, said she'd be at his door in twenty minutes. Peter was dressed in ten which was fortuitous as a trio of phone calls took up the remaining minutes.

Caller number one was a grouchier than usual Dave Flannery: "Ramsey, what is about bosses? I thought I was stuck with the looniest of the bunch. Then I met yours last night in the Covey. He was drinking some froufrou cocktail and trying to get the piano player to play *You Light Up My Life,* that mawkish hit by Debbie Boone. You remember it? Anyway, we got to talking and he told me that you and he are up to something that will be a guaranteed page one story. Then he went all coy on me. So what the hell is going on?" he boomed. Without answering, Peter arranged to meet him at the Covey and gave him a time in the late afternoon.

Caller number two was a buoyant Samantha. "Peter, what a wonderful evening! Thank you for being such lovely company. I hope you slept well," she cooed with a flirty sincerity that pleased Peter immensely. When he asked what her plans were for the day, he learned she would be keeping her sister company as Malcolm Fitzroy was meeting old friends at the Vancouver Art Gallery. Peter then arranged to meet her at the Covey and gave her a time in the late afternoon.

Caller number three was a hungover Howard Newton. "Peter, my head hurts. In fact, all of me hurts." he groaned. After Peter told him he was delighted to hear that, he arranged to meet him at the Covey and gave him a time in the late afternoon.

Lillie had left her verandah chaise to join Peter in the penthouse. While he triple-knotted his running shoes, she reminded him of his odd scheduling. "No problem," he said confidently. "Dave won't stay long because he'll have to go dancing. Next up is Howard and he won't stay long because Samantha intimidates him. And If I'm lucky, when Samantha arrives, she *will* stay long,"

"The professor has really cast a spell over you," she observed, not for the first time.

Peter looked up from his well-worn running shoes. "She's..." He shook his head and smiled at his spectral companion. "Yes, Lillie, I believe she may have done exactly that," he said, not for the first time.

In what they called their touring pace, Peter and Liz jogged along the Vancouver shoreline and into Stanley Park. When they reached a turn around point, Liz spotted a bench under a shade tree that afforded them a splendid view of the Burrard Inlet and Vancouver Harbour with its busy traffic of float planes, small and large water craft and the SeaBus that ferried people to the City of North Vancouver and Grouse Mountain. Opening her water bottle, she first offered it to Peter.

"Tio, I'm having second thoughts about this hair-brained idea of mine about you adopting me," she said, staring at a seaplane taking off.

Feigning shock, Peter threw his arms in the air and exclaimed, "Oh no! Don't tell me you found someone more qualified to take my place? Liz, I'm in a very vulnerable place right now after losing my job and all. I don't think I can handle more disappointment."

Liz tapped his arm with the water bottle. "I'm trying to be serious here."

"Okay," he said, turning toward her to give her his full attention. "First of all, it was not harebrained. I thought it was very touching. However, it's a step we don't have to take. We're just fine as uncle and niece. We don't have to change things. And as regards your wedding day, just like any father of a bride, I will walk you down the aisle with just as much, if not more, love, pride and tears." Liz leaned in and kissed his cheek. Grinning, he added, "Besides, avuncular advice is more my speed than fatherly,"

Tapping his knee with her water bottle, Liz said, "Here's some niecely advice: We better head back. Remember we have a date to see Vancouver with our mutual ghost."

Both rose. Liz went behind the bench to use the back to stretch her legs. Peter waited patiently, preferring to run out any stiffness. As she stretched she said "Tio, in a couple of days, we're going to be off the ship and back home in Berkeley. What do I tell my friends when they ask about the cruise?" An expert in Handlery-speak, Peter offered no reply. His silence was rewarded as she continued. "Are these twelve days with Lillie going to be our little secret?" Still he waited. "And what about Lillie?" she asked, stacking yet another query on top of the first two. "We know the painting is with that Sprottle guy in London and will eventually be returned to the Tate. So what happens to Lillie now that the mystery's solved?" All this time the top of Liz's ponytail was all he saw of her as she had kept her head down during the entire stretch. Pushing back from the bench, she looked up at her uncle. "I wish she could stay with us a while longer. I've grown really fond of her. "

"We both have," he inserted quickly.

"What's so odd is we are living in this bizarre twilight zone and I am totally accepting of it. It seems weird. That I'm so unperturbed, that is."

Peter sat back down. Liz finished her stretch and came around to join him. They were quiet for a moment. It was now his turn. "I feel the same way. As to the weirdness factor, don't give it a second thought. I don't."

Liz leaned forward and put her head in her hands. "I almost googled *ghosts and goblins* last night to see what would come up. Then I figured that would be about as rewarding as searching for on-line medical advice." Sitting upright again, she turned to her uncle. Gone was the contemplative frown she'd been wearing. In its place was a wide smile and dancing eyes. "The truth is I'm having the time of my life. You know when you first asked me to come along, I thought I would be staring down twelve days of excruciating boredom. Wow! How naive was I?" she chirped, bounding off the bench, eager for the run back and seemingly anything else that would come her way on what she decreed to be a spectacular day.

As they waited for their post-run coffee drinks in the Portside Bistro, Liz nudged her uncle and asked if he'd given any thought to the questions she asked when they were on their run in Stanley Park.

"There were three. What are you going to tell your friends about the cruise? Is Lillie to be our little secret? Finally, why is she is with us here when the painting is in London, a million miles away," he replied.

"Answer the last one first."

"I know this will sound weird but I think it is as simple as this; if Lillie is here, the painting is close by."

"That could be, I suppose. But where? You know, Tio, I just realized it's a blessing I can also see and hear Lillie. If I couldn't and you kept insisting she existed, I would seriously wonder what the bartenders were putting in your martinis."

"There's your answer to the middle question. Lillie stays our little secret."

"I suppose she has to be if we want to keep the friends we have," she wisely observed.

"And I'm not so sure I could easily embrace the people who would believe us," Peter said, aware of the prejudice in his comment.

"So what *do* I tell my friends about my twelve days on the high seas?"

Lowering his voice, Peter said, "If all goes well, you can tell them how you helped smash an international stolen art ring. You can also tell them how a man from Kwyrkistan wanted to seduce you until he found out you were right-handed. Of course, there's the extreme makeover you choreo-graphed so someone could win a dance contest. Then there was your innocent dalliance with a shipboard butler which you can always enhance. Oh, and let's not forget your blistering verbal attack on a boorish celebrity chef who tried to force himself on you."

Liz looked at her uncle in amazement. "If I tell them all that, I might as well throw Lillie into the mix."

As they were leaving the bistro, both noticed the subject of their conversation hovering near a table where Anatoly Plushenko was engaged in earnest conversation with his Russian girlfriend with a name as long as her legs.

Liz nudged her uncle and whispered, "What's Lillie doing?"

"My best guess is eavesdropping," he replied. "Let's go get cleaned up. I'm anxious to find out what she's been up to while we've been running."

By twelve-thirty, our merry trio of tourists, having already added Gastown, Chinatown, Granville Island Public Market and the Vancouver Art Gallery to their list of sights seen, were standing at the busy and noisy intersection of Hornby and Robson Streets in downtown Vancouver. They looked down Robson over a sea of bobbing heads toward what they had been told was an appealing neighborhood called the West End and where two restaurants recommended to them were located. Liz had her laminated Streetwise map opened, trying to determine how many blocks of the humanity-filled Robson they needed to traverse before reaching Denman Street, the West End's major but quieter artery. Instead, inspired by a hunger pang, Peter recalled a block back was the historic Vancouver Hotel where he remembered peering into the windows of their restaurant named Griffins. It boasted tile floors, two-story high ceilings, ochre walls with dark wood wainscoting, arched windows, and square columns through the center of the large dining room. Ask Peter Ramsey what he likes to see in a restaurant decor and he'd probably mention all six. Liz and Lillie were easily won over as Griffins was inviting and remarkably subdued, offering a temporary sanctuary from the frenetic activity outside. They settled in a corner of the dining room by a window with Lillie between them. The hostess handed them each two menus, one leather bound and the other a printed one sheet. Liz picked it up, perused it and with eyebrows arched remarked, "Wow! This beats anything I've seen in Berkeley, and that's saying a lot." Peter gave it a quick glance, shook his head and put it aside.

A curious Lillie asked, "What is so unusual about it?"

"It's for people who are on special diets like DASH, Diabetic, Vegan, Raw, Macrobiotic and Gluton Free," she explained. "DASH, by the way, is an acronym for Dietary Approaches to Stop Hypertension."

"How do you know that?" asked Peter who readily admitted to being a Luddite when it came to matters of diet and weight-watching.

"Gertrude Horstwick from the Folk Lore Archives is on it. She's a nervous little bird who chatters on incessantly about her health. I know more about her colon than I do my own."

While they were talking, Lillie read Peter's discarded menu. "If I *had* an appetite, I would surely have lost it reading this nonsense,' she harrumphed. "I'll have you know that in the prime of my life, at five feet eight inches tall, I maintained a weight of nine point three stones, and I ate heartily and happily, eschewing few dishes placed in front of me."

"What's nine stones something in pounds?" Liz asked, reaching for a bread stick the busboy just delivered to the table.

"One hundred thirty," she proudly stated.

":How did you keep your weight in check?"

"I jogged," she said matter-of-factly.

Liz looked askance at the lavender vision who now weighed as much an angel's breath. "GET OUT," she squealed, ready to take a bite out of a well-buttered end of the doughy stick.

"Ah, another of your fascinating colloquial expressions, no doubt. Yes, Liz, I jogged. It was quite a popular exercise at the time."

Liz pursed her lips and moved them from side to side as she lined up all the questions she wanted to put to Lillie. Sensing what was coming and being in no mood to ramble on about diet and exercise in the Victorian Age, Lillie quickly changed the subject. "You two are, no doubt, wondering what I was doing this morning in the Portside Bistro. After they nodded their assent, she added lightheartedly, "My guess is having a cup of coffee won't satisfy your curiosity."

Liz laughed. "No, it won't."

Peter quickly added, "I'd also like to know what you do and where you go in the early morning hours."

They had to wait for their answers as a rosy-cheeked young woman approached the table, introduced herself as Maggie and announced she'd be their server. She was an outdoorsy, stocky blonde with a smile as big as British Columbia. When she asked for their drink orders, each requested something made locally; a white wine for Liz and a beer for Peter. They left it up to Maggie to choose. After explaining Griffins' buffet and ala carte dining options, she skipped away, giving the floor back to Lillie.

"I'll answer Peter's question first. My morning routine varies. I always visit the computer center to see if someone is reading the news of the day. I do try not to look at people's e-mail, though it is a constant temptation. Sometimes, I'll visit the bridge to watch the ship's officer's in action, but I have avoided visiting the crew deck. I will often visit the dining room just to listen in to conversations. As these people are in a public place, I don't feel as if I am snooping. Having said that, though, I never enter anyone's stateroom during my forays. One must draw the line," she said firmly.

"So what were you doing at the Russian's table?" Liz asked.

"Snooping, of course. Anatoly Plushenko plays an important role in our search for the missing painting."

"Did he say anything of interest?" Peter asked.

"Alas, he spoke Russian," she sighed. "While I couldn't understand him, I did hear him say Howard's name twice. When he did mention him, he sounded agitated."

"Howard has that effect on people," Peter remarked. "I'll talk to him this evening and find out what he's been doing to unsettle Plushenko. Anything else come out of your eavesdropping?

"I'm convinced Mister Plushenko is not who he seems. I'm also confident that he and that woman with the long last name are definitely not a couple. More likely they are colleagues or possibly relatives."

They fell quiet as Maggie returned with their drinks. For Liz, she chose a Howling Bluff Estate Sauvignon Blanc, admitting to a bias for this particular Okanagan Valley wine as she had family who worked in the winery's tasting room.

To demonstrate what Peter and Liz thought was the depth of her fealty to the place, she spun around and bowed slightly to reveal *Howling Bluff* tattooed just below her waist.

Next she placed a bottle of Attila the Honey – No, I am not making this up – from the Mt. Begbie Brewery in front of Peter. She had nothing at all to say about it nor did she display another body marking.

If I had equipped Lillie with a jaw, she surely would have dropped it after witnessing the server's performance. Peter and Liz's reaction was a mild bemusement. In this era of weird, zany human interactions or antics, mostly inspired by the odd chance they'll be captured on video that hopefully will go viral on the Internet, they did not consider her behavior outrageous enough to earn a full-sized jaw drop. As Maggie sped away with their lunch order, Peter lifted his glass and mumbled, "Let's see if this beer is as original as its name." Indeed it was and he declared it to be a fine brown ale.

Liz swirled, sniffed and sipped her Howling Bluff and declared it to be a fine example of a Sauvignon Blanc. "That was a very funny tramp stamp," she observed.

"I gather you are referring to her tattoo," Lillie said.

"Yes. It refers to tattoos on the lower back. Some think it's sexy and others feel it suggests promiscuity, thus the term *tramp stamp*." Liz explained. "By the way, I don't have one. I can't stand needles,' she said as her body involuntarily shuddered at the thought.

"In Germany they are called *Arschgeweih*," Lillie observed. She hit the word with a bang-on Teutonic accent. She had no idea why she knew this.

"That's a mouthful. What does it mean?" Liz asked.

"Ass antlers."

Now if I held a handkerchief over each expression – *Ass Antlers* versus *Tramp Stamp* – and asked you, the reader, which is the more imaginative and colorful of the two, I'm sure the former would win hands down.

Of my Employer's many inspired creations there is one that is, and will remain so, an utterly intriguing, often baffling work in progress. It is the species called Homo sapiens. You gave yourself that taxonomical moniker. It comes from Latin, a language once used by men in togas, meaning *knowing man* or *wise man*. That presumption alone should prove that marketing and self-promotion have been a part of the human comedy for millennia. This species is, by the way, a magnificent enterprise inside and out. If it were an automobile, I would suggest you open the hood and peek in, as there is an abundance of complex corporeal parts that if kept nourished and well-maintained will last a goodly number of years. Eventually though, even with regular servicing, these parts, like autumn leaves, will decompose. If that sounds like the bad news, here's the good news: There's much more to this human machine. I refer to that perpetual part which is incorporeal. Included at no extra cost is a human being's spirit self equipped with marvelous elements that include reason, free will, intellect, choice, feelings... Well, you get my drift. My point is you have the ability to work things out. As regards this story, it was Lillie who began working things out when she sighed mightily and said, "I am growing weary of these limitations of mine."

Peter, who was adding a tip to the bill, looked up from his accounting duty. "I'm not surprised, Lillie. In fact, I'm glad to hear you finally admit it. I would be frustrated, too. Of course, if you had more senses, it would start costing me," he joked, holding up the restaurant bill.

Before Lillie could respond, Liz added her empathetic two cents: "I would be weary, too. I know how much you want to wear my slinky red dress."

Lillie's laugh was sharp and short. "No, no," she exclaimed. "You both misunderstand me. It's quite the opposite, my dears."

Their befuddled expressions suggested that a detailed explanation was in order. To that, Mrs. Langtry recommended they leave Griffins and return to Peter's penthouse where she would explain all and Liz could react volubly and impulsively without embarrassment.

chapter 33

PETER AND LIZ sat on the cream-brown sofa, backs straight, hands in laps and quizzical expressions on their faces. They were perched there at Lillie's behest. To insure their complete attention, she had Peter first draw the curtains, thus eliminating any tempting distraction a bustling Vancouver afternoon might offer. The stage was now set for her to share with them what she'd learned in her recent ruminations, even though they might not fully grasp what she had to say. For that matter, she wondered just how sure a grasp she had on any of it.

"At lunch I told you I am weary of my limitations. You quite naturally assumed I yearned to have the complete human package; eyes with flirty lids and lashes that winked and blinked, ears from which decorative jewelry could hang from lobes, et cetera. Well, my dears, the truth is I don't crave *more* corporeality but rather *less* of it. Well, actually, *none* of it. I'm sure it sounds confusing, but it will all become clear. I promise," Lillie assured them. Then with a sigh, she muttered, "Or perhaps not.

"As you both know, since I arrived here, I have given considerable thought to the mystery of me. You must agree it is a strange, singular world I inhabit. In an attempt to give it or me some definition, some clarity if you will, I began to focus more on that period of darkness from my death in 1929 to when I woke up on this ship ten days ago. How is it I have no memory or recall of that expanse of time. One can't *be*, then not *be* and then *be* again! I steadfastly refuse to accept such an ill-framed concept. First I thought I might have been in some sort of spiritual coma, a limbo, if you will. I quickly discounted that. My dears, I now firmly believe, that prior to arriving here in this odd form, I was, in fact, a complete spirit; blissfully aware, happy, fulfilled and dwelling eternally in God's realm. Presently, as you fully well know, I am a ghost. Not some run-of-the-mill ghost, mind you, but one with enough human equipment so that I can communicate with you both. Remember, Liz, you told me once you thought ghosts were here to settle things or haunt people?" Liz nodded. "There may very well be some truth to that. I don't really know. What I do know, though, is that I have nothing to settle and nobody I wish to haunt. I have been sent here solely to help you recover my painting."

"Lillie, you came to that conclusion hours after we met for the first time," Peter reminded her.

"I know. But at the time it was guesswork on my part. Now I am absolutely certain that once the painting is in the right hands, I will bid adieu to this restrictive existence, shed these ghostly constraints and return to whence I came with my spirit privileges fully restored. I will return to life without limitations. I might add it is something I greatly anticipate," she exclaimed.

Peter stared at the lavender revenant. "You have no doubts about this?" he asked.

"Of course, I do," she exclaimed. "Who was it who said *Doubt is not a pleasant condition but certainty is absurd?*"

Liz quickly reached for her iPhone and tapped the Google icon. "Hang on, Lillie, I'll have the answer for you in no time."

"It was Voltaire," Lillie said drily.

Liz continued to run her finger down the small screen. "That's right. Hey, here's a fun doubt quote from Mark Twain."

Peter signaled her to put the phone away.

"Why did I know it was Voltaire? I was never a fan and I knew little of his writings. Peter and Liz, I think these involuntary outbursts of esoterica are more evidence that I truly am a spiritual being currently trapped inside the body of a ghost." Hearing herself, Lillie laughed uproariously. "I do surprise myself!"

She may very well have surprised herself but Lillie had, in fact, hit on it. As we've already covered the myriad restrictions that are put on returning spirits, I won't go into them again. Suffice it to say, ghosts have their limitations. In Lillie's case, her deductive reasoning improved greatly when she let her spirit mind play a stronger role. These two unique minds are fascinating, indeed. Both are marvelous creations. First there is the mortal version with its operation's center located in a body part called the brain. This warm, buttery, biodegradable mass is necessary for all sorts of human functions. I will use my amanuensis as an example of how this all works. It has been so long since I mentioned my mortal assistant, you may well have forgotten I require one. Anyway, his name is Michael and when he is not taking dictation he enjoys long runs and walks with his wife. He is a voracious reader and likes to work on easy-to-medium crossword puzzles. Michael values knowing where he left his car keys, the words to a couple of songs by Cole Porter, a smattering of Shakespeare and his mother-in-law's birthday. For all of the above, he relies heavily on niftily-named parts of this complicated organ; names like hippocampus, hypothalamus, cerebral cortex and cerebellum. An added note: He prides himself on knowing these anatomical pieces just like he knows the names of the five Great Lakes and the six wives of Henry VIII. He's never mastered naming all seven dwarfs.

At the same time, Michael is a proud owner, like Lillie, of a spirit mind. Vastly different from that marvelously conceived physical device he lugs around with him causing no amount of neck pain, this mind is dimensionless, spaceless and weightless. It is nothing that holds everything. It is, I humbly submit, perfect! Some among you refer to it as a Divine Mind and we are grateful for all that implies. In a nutshell, your spirit mind, or soul if you prefer, is the eternal and perfect you.

It amazed Peter how quiet the Covey with its darkwooded, clubby atmosphere could be once the sun was over the yardarm. It should have been the reverse, he thought, with early diners queueing up for a libation before heading to the dining room. Where do they all go, he wondered. Such a question, of course, never occurred to Dave Flannery, the bar's only occupant, as he reveled in the pleasing solitude the bar's emptiness provided.

"Am I fated to always be the late arrival when we meet for a drink, even when I'm on time?" Peter said, taking a barstool next to the rumpled newspaper editor.

Flannery took his time responding as he had been staring intently into his single malt scotch, this time a decently priced eighteen year-old Highland Park. Once he found out that he could drink all the pricey Oban he wanted because his publisher was picking up the tab, all the fun had gone out of it. Tearing himself away from his devoted scotch, he turned and gave Peter his attention which came complete with a menacing frown that would have made Ebenezer Scrooge proud. "I make a point of arriving thirty minutes before any appointment or meeting that takes place in a bar. So put away that dream of arriving first," he said.

"There's something to be said for that, I suppose."

"Of course, there is. I started it last year. At first, I did it to force myself to take a much needed breather. Originally, I was going to stay after meetings, but I reasoned I'd still be thinking about what had just been discussed. So I chose instead to be ridiculously early. Now these recesses have taken on a life of their own."

"What do you mean?"

"They have evolved, my friend. They are subject specific. Dare I say, even themed," he said, grinning and returning his attention to the scotch. After a small sip, he continued, "For instance, sometimes the break becomes a memorial service where I lament the death of traditional journalism, civility, political bi-partisanship and language with elegiac prose. Sometimes, I spend the time trying to get my head around this thing called social media asking myself questions like what exactly is it and can it work for the common good. That's a challenge," he snorted.

Putting his hand on Peter's shoulder, he leaned closer and in a low growl added, "This isn't for public consumption as I don't want to ruin my reputation as an insensate SOB, but I will sometimes spend the half hour thinking about all the blessings and joy in my life; my wife, my kids, my health, my passion for news reporting and, let's not forget, my devotion to single malt." He lifted his glass to toast and realized Peter hadn't ordered. "What are your drinking? I'm buying. Rather, Symington is," he laughed.

It didn't take long for Peter to bring him up to date on all that was happening regarding the missing painting. Within minutes, David had the whole story minus, of course, Lillie's very real participation.

"How did you get involved in this all this?" Flannery asked.

Peter told him about Howard Newton's mother-in-law's death and his subsequent discovery of stolen art and her connection to the shipboard auctioneer. "Then one of our guest's son approached me. He and his partner had brought the stolen painting aboard. They were wrong to do it and they understood that," Peter explained. "They were scared and wanted help."

"They're the well-dressed gay couple, right?" Peter nodded. "I've seen them around. So what's this about the painting possibly being a forgery?"

"Freddie's partner owns an art gallery and is pretty knowledgable. He's also a huge fan of the subject of the painting?"

"Lillie Langtry."

"That's right."

"I'd have thought he would have preferred Oscar Wilde."

"He's even confused by the crush he has on her. Anyway, he's sure it's a fake. We'll find out for sure tomorrow," Peter said confidently.

Flannery ran his hands through his shock of uncombed hair. "I don't know, Ramsey. It seems to me this could go a lot of different ways. Be careful. And I mean it. That Russian looks like he plays by a different set of rules than you do. Remember, there's a wide range of people who deal in stolen art and many of them aren't gentle souls like you and me," he said.

"I'm trying my darndest to do all this from the sidelines," Peter told him.

"Just be careful," he repeated. "Oh, and by the way, your old boss is a strange duck. Can you trust him to behave himself?"

"I'm seeing him right after you. I can get him to tone it down."

Flannery grabbed the check and with a flourish signed it, leaving a fat tip for the bartender who was wise enough to know when the newspaper editor drank alone he wanted to be left alone. Edging off the stool, Dave checked his watch. He'd be a few minutes late for drinks and dancing with Mary Pat in Club Glamour but he had one more observation to share with his cruise co-host. "You know, Ramsey, you constantly amaze me. First you choreograph our victory in the dance contest with a support team make up of your niece and two whacky Eastern Europeans who can't abide right-handed people. Obviously, not content with one zany, off-the-wall accomplishment, you now want to add snagging an art thief to your resume. Anyway, having said that, count me in. I wouldn't miss this auction for anything. Plus, it could be a hell of a story," he said, patting Peter on the shoulder as he began to leave. Just as suddenly, he stopped and added, "Don't you think you should have someone at the pier who can take charge of this mess."

"Who do you suggest?"

"I have a close friend. A captain in the police department. Let me call him, explain what's happening and tell him to meet us at the pier as we might have a newsworthy miscreant or two for him to arrest. If the whole thing blows up, I'll promise to take him to the Buena Vista for several rounds of Irish Coffees. He'll have forgotten the whole thing after three of those creamy delights."

It's a phrase I hear thrown around a lot, so I'll use it here. Peter had no end game. Thus, he was grateful for the suggestion. "Call him, Dave. I'd appreciate it. And let's keep it between us."

Howard was walking into the Covey just as the male half of the Flannery dance team was exiting to trip the light fantastic with the female half of the team. Their collision was mild; no dents, no scrapes. Still, they exchanged manly glances. Brushing the exchange off his black cashmere sport-coat, Howard strode toward Peter. He looked like an ad for a department store in his pressed designer jeans and crisp white shirt opened to reveal a hairless chest. There was a newness to everything. He was grinning ear to ear and even that was new.

"Peter, I was just on the receiving end of a terrific compliment," he trumpeted, his face aglow. "On the way here, a lady stopped me and said, 'You, sir, are one of the snappiest dressers on the ship.'"

"How old was this admirer of yours?"

"What do you mean how old?" Howard asked edgily as he mounted the barstool on Peter's right.

"She used the word snappy. I'm betting she's in her eighties."

"Shit, Peter, you really get a kick out of throwing nails on one's highway to happiness," he said sourly.

"Howard, never use that expression again."

"Why? It's one of Naomi's favorites."

"What are you drinking?" Peter asked, figuring it was best to move on.

Howard reached across the bar and grabbed the Glamour Martini Collection menu. Catching the bartender's eye, he waved it in his direction and hollered, "Jurgen, what number am I on in this book of yours?"

Jurgen put down the glass he was drying and approached the pair. Taking the menu from Howard, he scanned it and deadpanned, "Number seven, Mister Newton. The Itsy Bitsy Teenie Weenie Yellow Polka Dot Martini."

"You gotta be kidding," Howard scoffed. "Doesn't seem right; drinking something with itsy bitsy and teenie weenie in its name." He motioned for Jurgen to return the menu. Confirming that number seven was so christened, he muttered to himself, "Okay, I set myself a goal. By god, I intend to reach it even if I have to drink a martini named after a bikini." Waving to the bartender, he ordered him to make it up.

"Dare I ask what this is all about?"

"When I first came in here, I told Jurgen I wanted to order every martini listed in the collection. After this one, I have three to go." he said proudly. "Aha," he exclaimed after looking at number eight, "the next one is the Davy Jones Lockertini and the one after that is the Poseidon Tridentini." Throwing his shoulders back and lifting his head high, he commented, "Now those are drinks that have a manly swagger.

That did it. Fed up with Howard's bumptious behavior and the overuse of the word swagger, Peter said, "Howard, you are behaving like a character in a TV sitcom."

Figuring another compliment was headed his way, Howard exclaimed, "No kidding! Which character? What show?"

A frustrated Peter shook his head. "Forget the sitcom. What I'd like to know is why are you not yourself? Since you've been on this ship, your behavior can only be described as buffoonish. What's going on? Who is this new Howard?"

Just like that, all the air went out of Howard's over-inflated swagger. Dispirited, he leaned forward, put both elbows on the bar and rested his head atop his clasped hands. Peter waited patiently. Finally, Howard raised his head. Looking straight ahead at the row of bottles behind the bar, he answered, "The new Howard should tell you to go fuck yourself." While it was a poisonous little comment, it lacked grit, anger or menace. "However, the old Howard really needs to talk," he mumbled. "And he apologizes for what the new Howard said."

"Let's just call him the real Howard."

That lifted his mood. "How about the authentic Howard? I read where being *authentic* is all the rage." Before Peter could throw water on his suggestion, Howard quickly added, "Okay, okay. No more bullshit."

Before he could begin, Jurgen appeared with his number seven martini. It was neither itsy bitsy, teenie weenie nor polka dotty. However it was a citrus yellow color thanks to the addition of lemoncello. Howard lifted his glass and toasted no one in particular. After a cautious sip, he declared it was not a disappointment.

"Peter, this extreme makeover thing; the new clothes, the strutting, the boasting, the tough talking... Jeez, even the drinking is all because of Naomi. We're, uh, having problems."

"Howard, you and Naomi are peas in a pod."

"We *were*. Now there's this emotional distance between us," Howard said glumly. "There's nothing I can put my finger on, but Naomi's been acting differently. I originally chalked it up to everything that's been happening since her mother's death. It's been a pretty frenzied time, you know. Of course, the matter of the stolen paintings didn't sit well with her."

"I'm sure it didn't."

"No, you don't understand. She had a tough time letting go of them. She never told me why exactly and I didn't push it. Then there were other things. For instance, a simple discussion of what of her mother's things to keep and what to put to auction or give to charity would set her off. I recently brought up our wanting to move to Hawaii and she said we ought to shelve that idea for awhile. The funny thing is we talk everyday. Still do. She takes a genuine interest in what's been happening on the ship. I bring her up to date and then try to steer the conversation around to us. As soon as I say something remotely romantic, she shuts me down and ends the conversation." Howard took another sip of his funnily named martini. "It's just plain weird, Peter, and I really don't know what to do? You have any ideas?"

"Perhaps it's the effects of menopause," Peter offered, thinking Naomi was of that certain age.

Howard shook his head. "No, that all started more than a year ago. She handles it like a champ. She even laughs off her hot flashes."

Peter checked his watch and realized Samantha must be on her way. Having listened carefully to what Howard had to say, he offered what he could which, regrettably, wasn't much. "I'm not very good at this sort of thing, Howard. Never have been. I'm pretty good at trying to make people feel better. As for diagnosing their problems and finding answers, though, I'm out of my league," he admitted.

Howard slumped a little and muttered, "Oh, that's great. I spill my guts and you want to tell me a joke."

"If I thought it would help, I would," Peter said. "However, I do have a thought. I don't know Naomi all that well, but I do know this; all mothers and daughters have a unique bond. It's very strong. My guess is, as you pointed out, Naomi might be having a tough time emotionally dealing with the loss of her mother."

"Could be as simple as that, I suppose," Howard remarked. "I was a mess when I lost my mom and I was a son."

Always the optimist, Peter said, "I have a good feeling you two will get past this."

"Well, if we do, it won't be because of my personality makeover which obviously isn't working, considering you gave me two stars for buffoonery. As I told you earlier, Naomi is the reason I went down this bad road. I thought if I spiced things up a bit and showed her a little dash and daring..." Howard suddenly interrupted himself and asked, "Remember you said we were peas in a pod?" Peter nodded. "Well, I thought if I were more of the swashbuckler type, she might jump back in the pod with me. It was foolhardy, I know."

Peter patted Howard on the back, admiring for a second the elegant feel of his newly purchased cashmere coat. "Don't beat yourself up. Oh, and keep the clothes. They look great on you. Just drop the swagger part. Like I said, I'm sure this thing with Naomi will blow over."

"You're right, Peter. From now on, the old Howard in his new duds will just relax and enjoy the rest of the cruise. By the way, what the hell is a swashbuckle?"

Just then Peter saw Lillie hovering to the right of Jurgen behind the bar. In that familiar know-it-all voice, she explained, "Archaically, the term refers to a less than talented swordsman who disguises his ineptness by making a lot of noise hitting an enemy's buckler or shield with his sword. Thus, a swashbuckler was a noisy, boastful, oafish sort. Only later did it mean someone who is a lion-heart and full of derring-do."

Peter wasted no time in repeating that to Howard who was suitably impressed. Peter also wondered how long Lillie was going to remain behind the bar. To that, he looked at his watch and said loudly and dramatically, "I'm expecting Samantha any moment now."

"You don't have to shout, Peter. I'm sitting right next to you. This Martini has not affected my hearing," Howard joked. "Hey, let me ask you before I go. You want me to contact the agents who investigated Philipa's stolen paintings?"

"No, not just yet. There's a chance nothing's going to come of this." Peter did not tell him of his conversation with Dave Flannery.

Samantha Whitby was right on time. Her quiet entrance was loud enough to make Peter's heart skip a beat. That he welcomed her arrival was written all over his face. Howard looked at his bar mate with the beaming smile, then at Samantha. Nudging Peter, he whispered, "Oh, you do have it bad, my friend."

Peter glanced behind the bar and saw no one except Jurgen who had returned to his corner post at the bar. Lillie had gone. Howard, meantime, took a final sip of his Martini and slipped off the bar stool, ready to make his exit. Peter put a hand on his arm and said, "You don't have to rush off."

"Yes, I do. However, I'd like to stay long enough to repair the damage done by my clumsy first encounter with your college professor," Howard explained. "Now get off that stool and let's welcome her like the two gentlemen we are."

Samantha wore the same black sleeveless Escada with the same minimal jewelry she wore for their last dinner. While it was of some concern to her, it mattered not to Peter who was so taken by her that if she chose to wear it every evening they dined together in the future, he would post no complaint.

Steps before reaching the two men at the bar, Howard stepped forward. Offering his hand, he said, "Professor Whitby, I'm Howard Newton."

Samantha's first thought was Howard might have forgotten their last meeting. Thus, she accepted his hand and reminded him gently that they had, indeed, been introduced in that very bar.

"I know. However, I'd like you to meet the real Howard Newton. When we last met, I was trying on different personas and, unfortunately, I was wearing one that didn't fit."

"In that case, it's a pleasure to meet you, Mr. Newton," she said cheerfully.

"Please, call me Howard."

"And I am Samantha."

Checking his watch, Howard said, "Now that we've met right and proper, sadly I must leave. Although, that will come as good news to the man who is standing beside me." Samantha eyes shifted to Peter and she smiled warmly as Howard continued, "I should warn you that you can expect a short delay before my gimlet-eyed companion here speaks. He seems to be in some sort of stupor. A simple peck on the cheek should bring him around. By the way, if you're inclined to order a Martini, I would recommend number seven on their menu. Now, if you'll excuse me." With that the real Howard Newton shook her hand for a second time, gave Peter a parting glance and took his leave, this time with a well-earned swagger.

Peter and Samantha remained at the bar. She ignored Howard's advice, instead ordering what Peter was drinking, a straight ahead vodka Martini with olives. It is enough for the moment to say the evening went swimmingly. Right after I do a recap of the evening's activities involving the rest of our principal players, I will report on their late night, life-altering experience. After Lillie popped in on Peter and Howard at the Covey, she wandered off to join Liz in her stateroom. Liz was finally going to get her long-awaited interview with Mrs. Langtry who was her usual talkative self. Liz dined in her stateroom on Zen Tao sushi and sashimi, a repast that horrified her Victorian guest. Meanwhile, the good-natured, gluttonous Dosynks happily ate their way through four courses in the main dining room, further impressing the wait staff by topping the meal off with prodigious amounts of Baked Alaska and Italian grappa. Dave and Mary Pat Flannery, after dining early, caught the evening's featured movie, a mawkish romantic comedy. After thirty minutes, they escaped to their stateroom for a spirited evening of marital canoodling. Anatoly Plushenko, perceived bad guy, and his alleged girlfriend with the long name, bounced from one game of chance to another in the casino for the evening. This after an early evening cocktail and an intriguing briefing from Charles Van Woort regarding the next day's auction.

Finally, a last word, at least for this chapter, on our two love-birds. The evening ended with both sleeping fitfully because their last vocal exchange was so surprising, astonishing and extraordinary.

chapter 34

PETER AND SAMANTHA spent most of the evening discussing their respective tomorrows, not knowing at the time that over the course of a Martini and dinner, it would evolve into *their* future. However, I'm getting ahead of myself. In the early goings of the evening, both shared their thoughts on a variety of topics. It seemed no matter the subject, each found common ground with the other. For instance. when Peter brought up the subject of travel, each mentioned places they wished to visit, whereupon the other happily agreed they were locales they, too, wished to plant a temporary flag someday. There was an ease about them that was, perhaps, best expressed during those moments of silence which befall all couples. Neither found the quietude to be awkward or uncomfortable. It was during dessert and such a lull that Peter casually observed, "Samantha, our dreams, or how we see our lives playing out, are so scarily similar, when I hear us discuss them we sound as if we're already man and wife." A flushed Samantha quietly nodded, incapable of any sensible verbal response. Feeling the need to do something constructive, she dove back into the creme brûlée they were sharing. It was then that it had become abundantly clear that whatever the future held, it looked more promising when it involved both of them.

Their physical parting at her stateroom door involved a lingering kiss and another of those hugs that Peter had come to cherish. It was when they were both in their respective bunks, heads spinning from the romance of the evening that Peter decided to turn one particular notion –a doozy of a what-if – into action. Minus any sense of trepidation, he phoned Samantha and without so much as a preamble, blurted out, "Samantha, will you marry me?" On the other end, he heard the extremely sensible and intelligent professor gush, "Yes, Peter, I will!"

There you have it. Look up words like rash, trigger-happy, incautious and extempore, and you'll see a photograph of Peter and Samantha spoon-feeding each other from an extra large serving of creme brûlée. To further discuss this spur-of-the-moment, seemingly reckless proposal is my amanuensis, Michael Patrick Cleary.

I turn this over to him because he acted just as impetuously as Peter did. I have instructed him that he has the rest of this exceedingly short chapter to explain why Peter and Samantha acted as they did. Meantime, I will look forward to seeing you in the Covey tomorrow afternoon for a most unusual auction. The dress code is casual.

* * *

What a pleasant surprise! I say that even though Theodomicles made it perfectly clear he wanted an "exceedingly short chapter." Really, I don't mind following his orders. He is, as taskmasters go, easygoing and good-natured. Admittedly, there was a time in the early going when I thought he came off a little smug. Well, perhaps, really smug. Then I reminded myself that even though he knows everything, he never exhibited excessive pride in that fact nor did he show delight in his know-it-allness, the primary ingredients in classic smugness.

I must say this taking dictation for a spirit is one for the books. As schedules go, we're not on one. No nine-to-five for us. There are times when I open my MacBook and wait for the words to come pouring forth from him. When he's not there to deliver the goods, I check e-mail, read a few on-line versions of newspapers, even get up and go for a run sometimes. He always knows how to find me. As regards our relationship, I've probably said too much already. Perhaps, another time and place, I can explain the mystery and wonder of this unusual experience. This much I will say: It is common knowledge that one should write about what one knows. Thus, if you give that any weight, it should be proof enough to validate the last thirty-one chapters as coming from someone other than me. As I, too, am anxious to know the rest of the story, I will, as ordered, keep this chapter succinct.

Before I attempt to explain what I perceive to be the sound reasoning behind Peter's hasty offer and Samantha's split-second acceptance, let me take a few words to establish my bona fides in such matters as speedy marriage proposals. Like Peter, I found myself in the exact same romantic position. If there is a key word to describe what drives such an imprudent action, it is certitude. When I proposed to Mary Ann, I was certain beyond all doubt. There is one glaring difference, though, between Peter and me. I was younger by twenty years, thus making my impulsive offer of marriage seem really foolhardy and his less so. However, it wasn't. To date, my wife, Mary Ann, and I have been married 360 months. We chose early on to celebrate monthly. It's just one of myriad wise decisions we made over the years. Others include embracing silliness, saying "I love you," "please" and "thank you" ad nauseum, never wearing matching outfits and defending our mutual harmony with all our energy. Our story is, like my sudden proposal, a short one as there really was no courtship.

We met through a mutual friend, a woman I ran with on a regular basis. One day we were suddenly three for the road, as Mary Ann had joined us. At the time, all I knew was she was married and the mother of two young adorable girls., Kelly and Amanda. The more we jogged and chatted the more charming I found her. After a time, my friend, Nancy, informed me Mary Ann was divorcing her husband and wished to keep it as quiet as possible. Far more important for her was dealing with her youngest daughter's fragile cardiac health. So it was, that I was able to observe first hand this strong, courageous woman as she bravely confronted the challenges of a seriously ill Amanda and the emotional rigors of a divorce. Through it all, she remained resolutely cheery and an absolute joy to be around. The good news was Amanda's eventual heart surgery was a success and she was soon back to being a high-spirited four year-old and today a talented and enchanting thirty-three year-old.

Almost instantly, or so it seemed, the clock began to run on the six months until Mary Ann's divorce was final. In May of that year, we ran together in a festive and crazy San Francisco event called the Bay to Breakers. In the midst of some eighty thousand runners, some costumed, some naked, we were lost in our own little world. The day was simply magical and I thought utterly romantic. When I dropped Mary Ann off at her car after the run, we parted with a hug. While I only know so much about Peter's feeling after embracing Samantha for the first time, I can say unequivocally that I came away from our clinch absolutely convinced I had found the love of my life. I left the following morning, off to a golf tournament in Reno and a few days in Hawaii. Mary Ann and I spoke by phone every day. Like Thedomicles' couple, we talked about our interests and the future. Four days into my holiday – like Peter to Samantha – I remarked that if we were to do everything we talked about doing, it would work better if we were married. The phone call ended on that flirtatious note. An hour later, right before dinner with my best friend and radio partner, Frank Dill, and his wife, Mary, I called Mary Ann back and asked her to marry me. Like Samantha, she said yes immediately. When I returned home, we met at my condo and talked for half an hour or so about some of the practical aspects of getting hitched. Then it was that I asked my fiancee if she liked Italian food. Learning she loved it, we went on our first date.

Why? Why rush it? Would you advise your own children to be so rash? You mean you never slept with her before? I've heard all the questions, mostly from men, some, who when they found out I was getting married, strongly urged me to get a prenuptial agreement. Generally, women found our story incredibly romantic and instead of asking questions, simply oohed and aahed and fanned themselves.

So let me tell you what I thought and felt and what motivated me to formalize our relationship so quickly. From the moment I met Mary Ann, I wanted to be with her. I longed to be in her company. Not being with her was no longer good enough. It was not a life I wanted. When we were together I felt complete. I might add better, too. It's really as simple as that. I think Peter came to that same conclusion. Of course, being older, perhaps he felt an urgency to be as closely connected as he could be to this woman who so captivated him. On that, I can only speculate. What about Mary Ann and Samantha? That's perhaps a bigger puzzlement. What prompted them to say yes without hesitation. As for Mary Ann, she told me that prior to my proposal, she had asked Nancy if I could be trusted. Nancy gave me a thumbs up and, thus, Mary Ann gave me an upright thumb. As for Samantha, again I can only speculate. Here's my thought: Peter had opened a new door for her. His charm and easy manner were something new and exciting for her. She also felt safe with him. Quite simply, I think she felt like the other three of us in this strange quartet of characters. She was much better with him than without him.

And now back to our story.

chapter 35

CRUISE LINES LOVE statistics, and they serve them up in all flavors. These stalwart, sea-going record keepers track everything from nautical miles sailed on a particular cruise to the number of garlic cloves used in the gazpacho served up at the Latin Fiesta Buffet. It is common practice at the end of a cruise to publish this data for the guest's entertainment and edification. On this particular Alaska cruise, the Ocean Glamour's records also included four wedding proposals; two while the ship was sailing under the Golden Gate Bridge, one while the ship was hovering near a blue and white glacier in Glacier Bay National Park and, finally, one on the second formal evening during early seating. Considering the dining room was full of children behaving badly, it's a wonder that one came off at all. Of course, you and I know, through no fault of their own, the ship under-reported the actual number of proposals.

On the morning of the penultimate day of their cruise, Peter, Lillie and Liz were having a breakfast of orange juice and croissants in his penthouse. Liz, outfitted in workout clothes, was reading the ship's paper when she spotted the story on the cruise's statistics. Putting her coffee down, she reached for one of the flaky, buttery treats. "Hey guys, listen to this," she said, "there have been four proposals of marriage on this cruise. Four! One of them a same sex couple. That's so cool."

"Actually, five," Peter mumbled through a mouthful of the French pastry.

Lillie, of course, knew of his rash and romantic actions of the previous night. They had talked at length about it after he ended the call. Surprisingly, she was not at all disapproving. In fact, she thought it a wise decision. "I'm sure Liz would love to know about the fifth, Peter," she teased good-naturedly. "Or would you prefer *taking* the fifth?"

"From the look on his face, Lillie, I think he *wants* a fifth," Liz innocently joked.

Best to get it over with, he thought. Peter's main concern was what Liz would think about his bringing another woman into their close-knit, almost insular family of two. On the one hand, it was Liz who paired them up. In all their years together, she had never played matchmaker. Thus, the proposal, he thought, might come as good news. On the other hand, he knew how passionate Liz was about keeping their domestic routine intact. In that case, the news would not be so welcoming. Thinking it best to just tell her and accept the consequences, Peter took a deep breath and explained the events of the prior evening.

Liz's reaction was muted and subdued. In fact, she was remarkably well composed, sitting primly on the small sofa. When her uncle finished, she rewarded him with a loving smile and a long silence. Finally, in a soft, even voice, she asked, "You didn't *really* ask her to marry you?"

"I did and she accepted," he replied. "I know it sounds crazy but it didn't take long for us to realize we are a very good thing. And I should point out that among her many impeccable references was one that mattered greatly to me"

Liz looked puzzled. "Which one was that?"

"Yours," he replied.

She stiffened a bit, put the croissant down and said defensively, "Well, yes, I thought the two of you would hit it off, but this wasn't what I had in mind. I figured when we got home, you might occasionally meet up for coffee at Cafe Strada or maybe a dinner on Shattuck. You know, go on real dates for awhile like most people." She ran her fingers through her hair and looked up at the ceiling. "Jeez, I honestly can't believe Sam said yes. Hell, I can't even believe you asked her."

"Well, he did," Lillie inserted. "And may I say we are looking at a classic case of a rebound romance. Think about it, my dear. When I dumped him, he took it very hard. Hard enough that he immediately chased after the good professor."

Liz looked from one to the other, trying to decide who was saner. "This is too much." Turning her attention to her uncle, she said, "First, you tell me you're marrying someone you hardly know." Next she looked over at Lillie. "Then you, Lillie, start to explain his actions as if you're some actress in a soap opera. Those aren't the words of an eloquent Victorian lady."

Lillie laughed. "No, they are not my words, Liz dear. I was only trying to lighten the mood. By the way, you came awfully close to identifying the source of my humor. Last night, the movie theatre was showing a romantic comedy. I peeked in to see what they are all about. I must say the format seems simple enough: put vapid dialogue in the mouths of extremely good-looking actors playing witless, self-absorbed characters and, voila, you have a modern romantic comedy. That said, I do plead guilty to stealing the rebound romance line." Lillie then inched closer to Liz and changed her tone entirely. "Now let me be serious, young lady. Neither your uncle nor Professor Whitby are capable of acting incautiously, particularly if such an act results in their lives being changed forever. Therefore, I applaud these two mature, intelligent people who were quick to recognize there was something truly extraordinary happening between them and decided to act on it."

Liz pretty much ignored Lillie's serious utterances. Instead, she fired several questions in the direction of her uncle. Peter assured her there were no further details other than he asked Samantha and she answered in the affirmative. Seeing the dazed, confused look on his niece's face, he moved over to the sofa and sat next to her. Taking her hand, he said, "Liz, I am not going anywhere soon. You and I agreed that we'd stay together through your graduation. I have no intention of changing those plans. We are family today and we will be family tomorrow."

Liz treated him to a short grudging smile and nodded in agreement. "I know, Tio, but, darn it all, we've been a team for so long... A great team. I don't know that I want to see that come to an end."

"It won't end," he reassured her. "I promise you. The team will just get a bit bigger. And if all goes well, it will grow even more down the road."

"You're not planning on having children," she exclaimed, shocked at the thought. "No, of course not. You're both way too old," she muttered to herself. "Oh, I see! It's *me* you're talking about."

Peter patted her knee and rose. Looking down on the young woman whom he loved like a daughter, he realized, if the situation were reversed, he'd have just as difficult a time accepting her betrothal. Liz looked up at him and from the look on her face, he swore she had read his mind.

"Tio, I know you well enough to know you are acting out of a genuine feeling for Sam, and I know I should be showering you with congratulations and best wishes and all that, but there's just a lot to digest right now." Letting go of Peter's hand which she held tightly during her little speech, she grabbed another croissant, wrapped it in a napkin and dropped it into her large carryall. "Okay, I'm off to the gym," she announced. "And if I think there's any kind of brain inside that buffed trainer from New Zealand, I may ask him to marry me and we can have a double wedding."

Peter offered no response, only a tight smile and a nod, a subtle acknowledgment of her clever sarcasm. Not so Lillie who merrily riposted, "Oh my heavens, that alone makes me to want to stay here longer than I care to."

Peter added sweetly, "If that's what it takes to keep you around Lillie, then Liz has my blessing."

"Remember, young lady, we are meeting here in the penthouse at two-thirty to go to the auction together," Lillie said. "The game will soon be afoot."

"Right, Mrs. Sherlock," she said to Lillie, heading for the door. "Tio, are you going to tell Sam about our this afternoon's adventure?"

"I haven't figured that out yet."

An hour later, Samantha knew everything. Well, almost everything as Peter made no mention of Lillie's vital role, much less her existence. But I'm getting ahead of myself. After Liz left for the gym, Lillie decided to visit the computer center and then check the movements of the many players in our little mystery. Left alone, Peter was hesitant at first to phone Samantha. Their relationship had changed so drastically is such a short time, he wasn't certain how to proceed or what to say. Samantha, of course, was feeling much the same. Nevertheless, he called and was immediately set at ease when he heard the warmth and cheeriness being broadcast from the other end of the line. Peter suggested a walk around the promenade deck as the seas were unusually calm and the winds gentle enough. Twenty minutes later they met on the seventh deck stairwell. There was an amusing awkwardness about their first physical encounter since last night's phone call. What they needed was an uniformed official to flip a coin to determine who would kick off the conversation and who would return it. As it was, they both spoke at once, then each went mum. This occurred two more times before Peter finally put a stop to it by placing a finger on Samantha's lips. He then came close, removed his finger and gave her a gentle kiss.

"Good morning, Sam," he gulped.

"Good morning, Peter," she gulped back.

Relaxed now, he opened the door to the mildly breezy promenade deck. They waited by the stairs to allow a platoon of serious exercise walkers to rush by before turning left to begin their walk. For about half a lap, they simply breathed in the fresh air, each quietly enjoying the excellence of the day. Walking side by side, Peter's right hand and Samantha's left hand soon found each other. It seemed the most natural thing to do. They continued to stroll, neither speaking for awhile.

It was Peter who broke the pleasant silence: "Last night I called and asked you to marry me. Then the most remarkable thing happened. Instead of telling me I was crazy and to go to sleep, you accepted."

Samantha steered them to the ship's railing, her hand refusing to let go of his. Occasionally, she would nervously squeeze it. Her expression was one of concern and there was a hint of fear in her voice. "After your call last night, I was so excited I couldn't sleep. I was at once deliriously happy and a bit fearful. I mean here we were talking marriage and we hardly know each other. It did seem crazy. However, Peter, I know enough about you and my feelings are such that somehow your offer of marriage simply made sense. It turned out saying yes was the easiest thing in the world. Then when I woke up this morning, I had this horrible feeling that maybe your proposal was one of whimsy and, like you said, I was supposed to laugh it off and tell you to get a good night's sleep. Peter, I hope I didn't embarrass myself by accepting your proposal?"

Peter brought her hand up and kissed the back of it. "No, Sam, you didn't," he said emphatically. "You made my heart sing when you said yes. What prompted *me* to do what I did was the simple fact that I saw no reason why we should waste another minute not being together as it seems it's our destiny. It certainly wasn't whimsy."

So it is that Peter and Samantha arrived at one of those physically electric moments where two bodies can't stand being apart. Eyes meet and melt into each other, lips yearn to meet lips, torsos try to fuse into one and noses politely move to one side or the other to accommodate all this closeness. This is where our couple found themselves. Regrettably, just as their magnet-like bodies were closing in on one another, the band of chirpy, high-stepping exercise walkers came to a halt, joining them at the railing as one of them had spotted a school of playful porpoises frolicking in the ship's wake.

Too excited to continue their walk, Peter and Samantha found a quiet corner table inside the Portside Bistro where, over large frothy cappuccinos, they decided that while they were resolved to marry, it would be best to not publish banns anytime soon. Samantha explained she'd rather wait until her sister returned to the East Coast to tell her, knowing if she said anything now she'd have to put up with Isabel's relentless attempts at dissuading her from marrying.

"She wouldn't be happy for you?" Peter asked.

"Other people's happiness doesn't make Isabel happy. Besides, given the suddenness of our engagement, she would think I was acting rashly and naively."

"I'm afraid a lot of people are going to share your sister's opinion. Fortunately, most of them will keep those kinds of thoughts to themselves," Peter replied.

"You said you told Liz and she was taken aback."

"She'll be okay, Sam. We have an unusual relationship," Peter explained. "We've been caring for each other ever since she was eight. I say caring for each other because Liz got it in her head early on that it was her responsibility to look after me."

"She thinks the world of you, you know. It was something she told me that convinced me I wasn't making a mistake falling for you."

"Uh oh, just what did that niece of mine say?"

"That you're hot," she replied in as seductive a manner as she could muster, given she was new to that kind of thing.

Peter laughed, remembering Liz's eccentricities. "Oh yeah, that's from when she was going through her acronym phase. I was HOT as in honest, organized and trustworthy."

"That's what she told me it meant."

"Did she also tell you that when I snapped at her to clean up her room, she'd change the O to ornery?"

"No, but if honest and trustworthy were a constant, that's a good thing."

"When did she tell you all this?" he asked.

"Early on in the cruise when she was scheming to get us together. By the way, should I be concerned about you being too organized?" she asked teasingly.

Peter continued to stir his Italian coffee. "We... I mean Liz and I are both a couple of fussbudgets, but in a good way. There must be a better word than fussbudget."

"Prissy?" she suggested.

"Ah, Mr. Trollope would be proud of you. Let's just settle for neat, but not to a fault." He caught himself brushing some crumbs off the table as he defended himself. "This isn't a deal breaker?" he asked jokingly, even though he was a bit concerned.

Samantha shook her head and grinned. "Not at all. I fall into the same category, though I do have a messy closet. Just be glad you're not marrying Isabel. All in all, Mr. Ramsey, I'd say you're a lucky man as I am very low maintenance."

So it went for another half hour; gentle explorations into how the other half lives. At some point, Peter found the opportune moment to put the spotlight on the afternoon's auction and his anomalous involvement. Samantha listened intently, wearing no expression that might give Peter a hint of what she was thinking or feeling. Suddenly he wondered if he was doing the right thing by including her in this loopy mess. Those last two words were his, not mine.

Before Samantha spoke, she put her coffee down and reached across the table for Peter's hand. Oh, that's a good sign, he thought. Then just as her lips began to form what would be the official first word of her response, Peter heard a shrill voice coming from behind him. "Oh my! Will you look at those two lovebirds. I told my husband... Freddie, I said, those two were meant to be. You are sooo cute together."

Samantha let go his hand and looked up while Peter pivoted in his seat to stare at Gertie Florian whose largesse was modestly covered by the Alaskan sweatshirt he had given her in Juneau. In her left hand was a plate overflowing with a sampling of the bistro's sugary morning treats. Fortunately for them, her husband was just two steps behind her. Freddie Senior, an old hand at rescuing others from Gertie's many unwelcome intrusions soon had her seated several tables away where she happily tucked into breakfast, keeping one eye fixed on the romantic couple.

Professor Samantha Whitby gave the attentive Mrs. Florian a tentative wave and then turned her attention to Peter who had just finished telling her what he'd told Dave Flannery the night before. This time, though, he felt deceitful not including Lillie in the telling. Perhaps later, he thought. He assured himself he'd find the perfect moment. Now he waited nervously for Samantha's response even though her calm demeanor and warm smile were an indication all might go very well indeed.

Fearing another interruption, Samantha checked to see that the coast was clear before she finally spoke. Leaning forward, she reclaimed Peter's free hand and began: "There's something you need to know about me before I remark on what you just told me which, by the way, was rather extraordinary. Before we met on that hike in Skagway, I sought out adventure by immersing myself in a good book. Between the covers of a book, I could safely lose myself to all sorts of daring and danger and not be the worst for it. In the real world, I would resist doing anything I considered the least bit chancy or unsafe, and that was pretty much everything. Unpredictability was a downright scary notion. This may sound crazy, Peter, but since I've known you, I find myself do things and thinking things, I never would have in the past. Frankly, I am sometimes astonished by my behavior. I suppose it's a positive but I seem to be more accepting of life's myriad vicissitudes and, who knows, even the occasional caprice." Hearing herself, her eyes crinkled and she laughed gaily. "My god! If I want proof of this marvelous transformation all I have to remember is I'm now an engaged woman."

"Attitude inspires action. We Ramseys and Whitbys move fast," Peter joked.

"Uh oh," she said, sounding the alarm that Gertie Florian making her way over to their table again. This time, her husband grabbed her before she was halfway. Fortunately, it was by the bistro's food station, so Gertie was able to reload before heading back to their own table, her head constantly turning to not miss a moment of the soap opera that was at the corner table.

If Peter required further proof he was dealing with a changed woman, he needed only to consider her response to his tale of the missing painting. It was succinct, sincere and nervy. "Peter, I really, really want to come to this auction with you. May I, please?" she pleaded.

chapter 36

IF THERE WERE any language so ideally suited to be the official lingua franca of Heaven, it would be French. This is not my opinion. The world in which I reside requires no such thing as language. It was, though, a view held by Lillie Langtry who, while thinking about the final phase of her ocean-going adventure, chanced upon the word *denouement.* She loved the term and relished saying it aloud as its mellifluousness was not lost on her. Nor will its musicality be lost on you. It is meant to be spoken. Pause here, if you like, and try it a few times. The accent-less pronunciation is *day-new-mahn.* Have fun. I'll wait.

Aha! I have you back. I can understand. One can only play around with three syllables for so long before it becomes tiresome. Now the reason Lillie had landed on that pretty French word is she realized we are nearing the end of our narrative. Well, *my* narrative about *her* paranormal adventure. It is a perfect term to describe the wrapping up of things. Etymologically, denouement comes from the verb *denouer* meaning to unknot, and I do plan on unknotting things. As for dear Lillie, she was at that moment blissfully unaware of just how many knots would require untying before she could slap a *Happily Ever After* on her temporal journey and return to her Eternal domicile, a home she strongly and rightly believes awaits her.

Now I would dearly love to pull out all the stops and present you with a riotous denouement. I'd enjoy nothing more than rewarding you for your devotion to this story with an edge-of-your-seat, emotion-wrenching, sweat-inducing auction. Oh, but that I could. Alas, the afternoon auction aboard the Ocean Glamour was no more exciting than a bingo game at a community senior center. In fact, in many respects, it was quieter and more sedate. There were, though, in the early goings a few entertaining moments, and as they are germane to our story, I will detail them for you.

The ship had given the dapper Charles Van Woort and his two equally well-dressed assistants the Covey for their art sale. Tables were removed from the clubby saloon and the chairs placed in rows with the bar serving as a backdrop for the auction action. At first glance one would think it too small a space for such a popular activity as a shipboard auction. That was not the case, however, as only thirty or so guests were present and accounted for at the first drop of the gavel. Peter noticed that front and center were Petra Dosynk, in his cruise uniform of a wrinkled white dress shirt, grey slacks, brown socks and sandals. His wife, Inka had put more effort into her fashionable attire of designer jeans, a crisp white blouse and gold jewelry. Anatoly Plushenko, in his regulation tight black tee-shirt and jeans, stood alone by the entrance looking angry. The rest of the guests can best be described by an observation uttered by Liz to her uncle when they first arrived. "Tio, what we have here is a room full of grandparents," she whispered to him as they found three seats nearest the exit.

Indeed, there were more paintings than potential bidders which, no doubt, explained why Charles Van Woort charged out of the starting gate, setting a pace designed to sell all in the short time allotted him. It took him less than a minute to welcome one and all and explain some basic rules before putting the first piece of art up for sale. In less than another minute, a painting of a curly-headed little girl on a swing was sold to an excited couple in the last row. Now don't take me to task for not putting more oomph into my description of the work. It was, in fact, titled *Curly-Headed Little Girl on a Swing.* Peter recalled a charity auctioneer telling him the first item was always a loss leader, the idea being to show other bidders that deals could be had. Van Woort was now moving things along so swiftly that Peter and his gang didn't have to wait long before painting 48 376-3 was in the batter's circle. After selling a splashy abstract for a hefty price, Van Woort nodded to his assistant to bring the plein air to him.

"This, ladies and gentlemen, is by the popular Carmel artist, Dewitt Masterson," he announced, his blue eyes sweeping the room. "I'm sure there are among you many who would love to see this extremely pleasant painting hanging in your home. Let's start the bidding at five hundred."

Plushenko gave the auctioneer a perfunctory nod. Van Woort returned his nod and said, "Thank you, sir. We have five hundred, do I hear...."

"One thousand skurls," Petra Dosynk hollered, half jumping out of his chair.

"Squirrels, Mister Dosynk?" chuckled the auctioneer, winking at the audience to encourage them to join him in his little fun with Petra.

"So sorry, I mean dollars. I was using the name of our currency. It is called a skurl, not a squirrel. Besides, my room safe is not big enough to store one thousand squirrels," he said with a hearty laugh. Judging from the audience's reaction, they found him funnier than the auctioneer.

Even though Van Woort wanted to move the auction along, he slowed to offer Petra some advice on bidding.

"Mister Dosynk, the last bid was five hundred dollars. I have no idea how much that is in skurls or squirrels. The point is I was about to ask for six hundred, raising the price in one hundred dollar increments to see who is interested in this piece. You shouldn't have doubled the bid so soon. It shows your too eager to get this painting and that can work against you."

Petra might have smiled, thanked him and taken heed of his counsel if Van Woort hadn't served it up with an extra dollop of condescendence. Instead, he sat, quietly stewing and contemplating his next move. It was not wise to bully or patronize a Kwyrki, particularly if you're right-handed.

"All right, ladies and gentleman, our last bid was one thousand dollars. Do I have eleven hundred?" Van Woort asked.

Plushenko nodded again while grinning at Petra. Angered, Dosynk stood up and said, "Two thousand! And I don't mean skurls *or* squirrels."

"Mister Dosynk, I..."

"You, Mister Auctioneer Person, will accept any bid as long as it is over the previous one. Now, let's get this over with." He turned and glared at the assembled. "Is there anyone else who wants this painting?" he barked, wearing one of his many fearsome expressions.

After a pause, a gentleman of advanced age sitting directly behind Petra tapped the back of his chair. "Would you mind if I asked Mister Van Woort a question?" he inquired, his voice scratchy and feeble.

Petra shrugged. "Be my guest."

"Sir, is it true that Clint Eastwood owns a couple of Masterson's paintings?"

Van Woort had no idea but if it would kick up the price, what was a harmless lie. "Actually, he bought his first Masterson after filming *Dirty Harry*."

"Then I am interested in it," the man said eagerly. Squeezing his wife's hand, he cooed, "I'm going to make our day, sweetheart."

"And you, Mister Plushenko? Still interested?" the auctioneer asked, looking in the direction of the sullen Russian still standing at the entrance.

"Make it three," he growled.

"I'll bid thirty-five," squeaked the gentleman who relished owning something only a degree or two from Clint Eastwood.

"Four thousand," hollered Petra.

"Gentlemen!" Van Woort shouted, his face purple, his oily composure rattled. "There is an order to all of this. Will you please allow me to be the auctioneer." He scanned the room which fell quiet. "All right. Let me see, the bidding was, I believe, at four thousand. Do I hear forty-five?" He looked at the three interested parties. The Clint Eastwood fan's head bobbed up and down slightly. Van Woort smiled and said, "Good, I have forty-five from the gentleman in the second row."

"You most certainly do not, young man," the elderly gentleman snapped. "I had a stroke recently. I nod a lot. If I want something, I'll say so and I don't want it at that ridiculous price."

Van Woort apologized for his assumption and thanked the man for his participation. He then glanced at Plushenko who signaled he was still in the hunt.

"Good. I have forty-five..."

Petra jumped up and shouted, "Five thousand."

Frustrated as he was and eager to move the auction along, Van Woort realized he was going to make a pretty penny out of this particular lot. Again, turning his attention to the Russian, he said, "It's fifty-five to you, sir."

This time, Plushenko merely winked. Van Woort waited a few seconds, convinced Petra Dosynk would up the bid without his asking. When it didn't happen, he cast a glance in his direction and said, "It's six thousand to you, sir."

"See, I am behaving myself," he said, smiling and crossing his arms. "I waited for you. Yes, I will bid six thousand."

"Seven thousand dollars," the Russian said with a nasty smirk.

Charles Van Woort was ecstatic. This time he didn't wait for Petra. "Do I hear seventy-five?"

Petra shook his head and said, "Let's wrap this up. Eight thousand."

Van Woort couldn't believe his ears. "Mr. Plushenko, it's nine thousand to you," said the auctioneer, looking to see if he would issue one of his trademark winks or nods. Alas, there would be no winking or nodding to further enrich Charles Van Woort as there was no Anatoly Plushenko standing at the entrance. He'd slipped out unnoticed.

"I have eight thousand," Van Woort announced. He paused, looked around the room and then, readying his gavel, sang, "Going once, going twice and sold to Mister Petra Dosynk."

Petra kissed his wife, rose and approached the auctioneer. He spoke to him in a low tone. Van Woort's response was to wave an assistant over. He instructed him to take payment for the painting and give the plein air to the buyer as he wished to keep it in his penthouse and then take it ashore on his own. Van Woort and Petra shook hands and parted genially.

That's the only portion of this auction that involves us. The rest went smoothly for the next forty minutes. Then, regrettably, no matter how much drama, flourish, and energy Van Woort put into trying to sell his large inventory, he was challenged by the fact that a third of the audience was happily napping, another third were headed in that direction and the final third were woozy from too much of the free champagne.

Peter, Lillie, Liz and Samantha knew it had not gone as planned. Van Woort showed no hesitation whatsoever in allowing Petra to take the painting with him. Plus, Anatoly's only interest in the painting seemed to be in jacking up the price just to irritate Petra Dosynk. What had gone wrong? Still, the plan was to assemble in the Dosynk penthouse within the hour to dissemble the painting.

Before we join them in the penthouse to examine painting #48 376-3, let me quickly comment on how Samantha Whitby and Liz Handlery got on as they found themselves sitting together at the auction. While Liz was slow in warming to the idea of their marriage plans, she thought the world of Samantha. Given the attention the auction demanded, few words passed between them regarding topic A. However, a promise was made to get together later and talk about it.

Everyone Peter invited to the meeting in the Dosynk penthouse arrived en masse at the assigned hour. Positions were quickly taken. Peter, Samantha and Liz opted to stand along the sliding door to the verandah. Freddie Florian, Junior and Benjamin Lytton-Crisp sat on the edge of the bed bolt upright like the good Victorians they were. Petra and Inka were squeezed together on the stateroom's small sofa. Standing by the stateroom's vanity was Dave Flannery and Howard Newton. The estimable Malcolm Fitzroy stood near the head of the bed where the Dewitt Masterson plein air was propped up on a couple of pillows for all to see. Lillie Langtry was opposite Fitzroy and close to Peter so she could speak to him when needed. He had earlier assured her he would remember the ear tug to acknowledge what she said.

It was a quiet room until Howard huffed, "Well, Mister Dosynk, you were certainly free and easy with my money.

It's a good thing Plushenko left before you got any deeper into my wallet."

Petra removed his hand from Inka's knee and glared at Howard who immediately feared he'd been a tad too impertinent and that might not have been a good idea. "Mister Newton, I did not spend *your* money. I spent *mine.* My darling Inka really likes this painting. We plan to take it home with us. So you are, as they say, off the hooker."

Before anyone could correct him, Peter moved away from the verandah door and asked for everyone's attention. Pointing to the painting propped up on the pillow, he began: "As you all know, it was our plan to buy this at any cost because we were lead to believe a very valuable painting, *A Jersey Lily,* stolen from the Tate Museum in London, was reportedly hidden behind Masterson's painting. According to what we were able to learn, Van Woort's original plan was to sell it to Howard Newton's mother-in-law. When she died unexpectedly, he quickly found someone else who was interested. That person was Anatoly Plushenko. To further complicate matters and without going into too much detail, we had every reason to suspect the painting that Van Woort was selling was a forgery. That's why I invited Mister Fitzroy to join us. My hope is he will be able to tell us what's behind this canvas. What troubles me, though, is neither Van Woort nor Plushenko seemed the least concerned that this painting went to someone else."

"There's a very good reason for that," Malcolm Fitzroy interjected. While Peter was speaking, the noted art restorer and historian had picked up the painting to examine it more carefully. It had taken him no time at all to realize that his quick, knowing glance was all he needed to file his report. "Unless Sir John Everett Millais painted *A Jersey Lily* on tissue paper, I assure you there's nothing underneath this canvas. There's no reason to even look," he said, placing the painting back on the pillow.

Flannery was the first to respond: "Well, there you are. Looks like the final score is Van Woort one, you guys nothing. Game over. You lose. So how about we turn this somber little gathering into a party. Petra, any champagne in that fridge?"

"Dave, what makes you think this is over?" Peter asked, irked by his friend's sarcasm.

"Ramsey, you don't have the painting, do you? Look, if you're convinced this auctioneer is up to no good, share the information with the ship's officers and be done with it."

"I don't want to do that," Peter replied stubbornly.

"If Van Woort is truly up to some nonsense like you claim, I guarantee you it's going to be a lot more difficult for you to discover just what it is. This proves he knows something's up," Flannery argued, pointing to the painting.

Liz had another thought. "Tio, maybe he found out the painting he was going to sell was a forgery and he thought better of it. I certainly wouldn't want to do wrong by that Russian goon."

Flannery came up to bat again: "Liz has a good point. Someone could have told Van Woort not only about your snooping around but that he's fencing a forgery. It's certainly worth considering."

The gentlemanly Malcolm Fitzroy held his hand up. "I suspect, Peter, if that is, indeed, the case, you can be assured the fake is probably sitting in some trash-bin in Vancouver."

The prescient art historian's speculation was right on the money. Van Woort had, in fact, upon learning of the questionable nature of A Jersey Lily, unceremoniously stuffed it into a waste receptacle in the lobby of the Pan Pacific Hotel where a maintenance worker, always on the lookout for castaway treasures, found it and brought it home to his wife. A talented woodworker, she built an appropriate frame. Within a week it was part of a neighborhood garage sale where a young set designer from the Kitsilano Kommunity Players bought it for just under two hundred dollars. It was a hefty price to pay for the penny-pinching, century-old theatre company, but they were ecstatic about their acquisition, not, as you may think, because it was a painting of a famous British actress and beauty. No, the set designer was convinced the painting was that of Printha Marie Pennington, the wife of a wealthy Canadian Pacific Railway executive, who in 1909, provided the seed money for the then fledgling company. It turned out that Lillie and she were dead ringers. So much so, that to this day the painting hangs in the lobby of their small, cramped upstairs theater; a brass inscription affixed to the lower part of the frame identifying the lady in the painting as that of Printha Marie Pennington, generous patron of the Kitsilano Kommunity Players. Artist unknown.

Conversations broke out between the eleven people present in the penthouse. Their murmurings were loud enough that they missed the first buzz of the doorbell. A second longer buzz eventually worked its way into the room and got everyone's attention. Petra asked Howard to welcome the mystery guest.

Shocked at seeing who wanted in, Howard mumbled weakly, "What the hell are you doing here?" Without waiting for an answer, he hurriedly backed into the room to his place by the vanity, seeking safety by inching closer to Dave Flannery.

A transformed Anantoly Plushenko stood before them in the tiny foyer. Eschewing his trademark, muscle-emphasizing black attire, the now dapper Russian wore a honey-brown cashmere sport coat with a yellow and blue paisley pocket-square, white button down shirt and designer jeans. Usually he wore a trademark scowl. Now a shy smile had replaced the bullying frown.

"Is there something we can do for you, Mister Plushenko?" Peter asked brusquely.

"Do for me? Oh my, what haven't you done," he replied, chuckling. "Are you going to invite me in?"

Flannery answered for the group. "Come on in, Anatoly. I'm guessing you don't want a rematch of our dance contest. As I'm still trying to figure out what this crowd is up to, maybe with your help, I'll learn something."

He walked to the foot of the bed where the two pretend Victorians were sitting. Freddie nervously pushed his partner to move down so the Russian could take a seat.

"Thank you," he said to the rattled Minnesota dentist. Than he addressed everyone. "I came here because we have something in common. You and I want something Charles Van Woort has. Perhaps, we might be more successful if we work together. Before I say more about that, though, I should tell you a little bit about myself."

"I know who you are," barked Petra angrily. "You like to tease people from my country. You stayed in the auction only to see me pay more for the painting than I should. You are a gangster."

"It was all an act, Mr. Dosynk. I am not a Russian gangster, nor am I interested in buying a stolen painting. Far from it, in fact." he said with a Chamber of Commerce smile that erased his familiar surly mien. It was a look no one in the room had seen him wear before.

"I am trying to figure out why you look so familiar to me," a curious Malcolm Fitzroy remarked, staring intently at Anatoly who was sporting his debut smile.

"Okay, now that we know who you are not, tell us who you really are," Petra demanded gruffly.

"Let's start with what is true. I do own a restaurant in Moscow and it is hugely successful. My regular customers include politicians, oligarchs, celebrities and, yes, gangsters. From all these people I learn many things. As busy as I am, I still try to find time to devote to a passion of mine which is iconography. Lately, I have taken a great interest in searching for missing or stolen icons. Often, I am commissioned by museums to help in their searches."

Malcolm wagged a finger at Plushenko and said, "Now I know who you are. You wrote a book called *Yes Icon, Yes Icon, Yes, Icon.* I just read it and it was thoroughly delightful!"

"I hope you were reading it to your grandchild," a kinder, gentler Anatoly remarked.

"Indeed, I was, but to my great grandchild," Malcolm responded proudly. Glancing at the others, he noted they were clearly both amused and puzzled by their exchange and, no doubt, the book's offbeat title. "I should explain. The book Mr. Plushenko wrote and illustrated is an excellent children's book that, in my estimation, introduces icons and their rich history of image writing to youngsters in a clear and understandable way."

"Thank you, Mr. Fitzroy. I might add, I had nothing to do with that American title. By the way, you and your reputation are not unknown to me," he replied.

"Now perhaps you ought to continue your explanation of why you're here."

"Recently, two very valuable icons went missing and I have been asked to find them. It is a sad reality, my friends, that these national treasures continue to disappear from our churches, museums and galleries, ending up in unscrupulous hands the world over."

"And two of those dirty hands belong to Charles Van Woort," Dave Flannery speculated.

"Yes. Thanks to the magic of coincidence, I found out they were in his possession and he was looking to sell them to interested collectors in the United States. It is my wish to get them by whatever means possible and return them to the museum from which they went missing."

"So you became Anatoly Plushenko, Russian gangster," Dave Flannery said.

"It was easy," he said, shrugging. "I'm around these types of men in my restaurant all the time. I'm a pretty good mimic with a little amateur theatre experience and I'm a very good listener. So I created Plushenko the gangster. I earlier mentioned the wonders of coincidence. Through a chance encounter at the restaurant one evening, I not only learned Van Woort has the icons but that he was going to be on this cruise. Knowing that, I found someone who had done business with him before to vouch for me. There you have it. End of story."

"I'll tell you one thing. As a gangster, you were definitely intimidating," Howard noted with an involuntary nervous shudder.

"I'm afraid, Mr. Newton, I'm all bark and no bite," he confessed. "My bite, if I ever need one, is Svetlana. She is skilled in any number of martial arts. It comes in handy when you're a beautiful young woman in Moscow."

"Anatoly, you said you needed our help," Peter said.

"More to the point, ladies and gentlemen, what I need is your assurance that none of you will do anything that would prevent Van Woort from leaving the ship and flying back to New York."

"I think I speak for everybody when I say I don't think that's going to be a problem," Peter responded glumly.

"I thought as much" he said. "Still I need your assurances."

"So now we know you want the icons, and you know we want the painting," Peter said. "We can help you by letting Van Woort skedaddle back to New York. What can you do to help us?"

"Maybe it will help if I tell you what I do know about your painting. Just before the auction, Van Woort called me and said the sale of *A Jersey Lily* was off. When I asked him why, he said it was in his and my best interests that no business be conducted on the ship. I played tough guy with him warning him about what happens to people who renege on a deal with Plushenko. It scared him enough that he finally admitted he'd been given a fake and he knew what trouble that would cause him if he sold it to me and I subsequently found out. He swore he didn't have the real painting. At that point, I told him I hoped he wasn't planning on backing out of our deal regarding the icons. He assured me that was not the case and we agreed to meet in New York the day after the cruise."

"So where is the painting?" Peter wondered aloud, refusing to believe it still may be in London.

"Why is this particular painting so important to you to you all?" Anatoly asked pointedly.

"Great question. I propose my co-host for this cruise answers that. So, Ramsey, why is it so damned important?" asked Dave Flannery snappishly, growing ever so impatient with the fact that this gathering was, and looked like it would continue to be, non-alcoholic.

Peter was stumped. There was no explanation that would suit. Of course, he could tell them the truth; that hovering next to him was the subject of the Millais painting and it was because of Lillie that he was duty bound to help her return it to its proper wall space in the museum. A saner thought prevailed, though, and he decided to dodge the inquiry altogether by responding to his question with a question: "Anatoly, you're the unexpected guest. You go first. Why are these icons important to you?"

"I think I've already answered that," he replied tersely. "However, perhaps you are wondering if there's any special significance or importance to the icons Van Woort has. Have any of you ever heard of Ludmilla Fukin?" To a number, they shook their heads. Freddie Florian tittered. "Yes, Dr. Florian, it is a peculiar name. Ludmilla was a famous opera star.

When Catherine the Great came to power in 1762, Ludmilla became a regular visitor to her court. The reason for this was the Czarina was an amateur opera librettist and wanted the mezzo-soprano, Ludmilla, to sing her songs. While it was a time of enlightenment in Russia, it was also a time of promiscuity, and Catherine was as promiscuous as they come. One of her paramours was a young ballet star that Ludmilla was desperately in love with. When Catherine ordered the dancer to her bed, Ludmilla was devastated. She never sang again either on stage or for the Czarina. Ludmilla, who was quite wealthy, moved to the country where she lived a spartan life until her death in 1800. When she died, a Moscow relative inherited the two extremely beautiful icons which Catherine had given her. Almost two centuries later, they were donated to the museum I represent."

"So you're on the hunt for the Fukin icons?" Flannery asked, if only to hear himself say it aloud. Thus, we will declare him the winner of this chapter's punchline.

"I am. Now all I have to do is wait patiently until I arrive in New York where I will take them from the dirty hands, as you so nicely put it, Mr. Flannery, of Charles Van Woort and return them to whence they came."

"So your intent is to buy these icons from him?" Flannery, ever the journalist, inquired. Without waiting for an answer, he quickly added, "Okay, forget I asked."

The Russian slowly looked around the quiet room to see what reaction his story received. Then he let his gaze linger on Peter. "So, Mr. Ramsey, that's my story. I believe it is now your turn."

chapter 37

"DON'T ANSWER him, Peter," Lillie warned. "There's something not quite right about all of this." Hearing her, Liz nudged him slightly to signal she agreed with their ghostly companion.

Peter first acknowledged his niece with an approving glance and then gently tugged on his ear to let Lillie know he had heard her. Now he had two excellent reasons to brush off Anatoly Plushenko, the other being he didn't appreciate the blatant mischief in the Russian's voice.

"I'm afraid I don't know how to answer that."

"Or you won't," the Russian fired back with what seemed to Peter to be a disingenuous smile.

"I don't mean to offend you.."

"For chrissakes, Ramsey, it's impossible for you to offend *anyone*," Flannery snorted, still irked because no one had suggested drinks for everyone besides him.

Ignoring him, Peter continued, "Honestly, I don't know that I have an answer that would satisfy. Yes, the return of the painting matters to me. Perhaps we can just leave it at that," he said with a little bite in his voice, his antagonism toward the Russian returning.

Anatoly grinned at him and shook his head. Standing, he checked his watch and smoothed the front of his jacket. "Well, I must go. Thank you all for your time..."

Petra raised a beefy hand. "Wait a minute. I'd like to know why you kept bidding that painting up when you knew it wasn't worth much more than three thousand."

"I assure you, Petra, I was only trying to further ingratiate myself with Van Woort," he explained. "I figured if I could put some extra change in his pocket, it would further strengthen our relationship. I'm sorry you had to be the victim of my little ploy."

"I certainly wouldn't have minded being your victim, as you so nicely put it," Malcolm Fitzroy said, picking up the painting again, but this time to admire it.

"I don't understand," Anatoly and Petra sang in accidental unison.

"You actually came out of this exceedingly well, Mr. Dosynk," the gallery owned replied. "You see, there are two Mastersons, Dewitt and his older sister, Dianne. Both sign their paintings D. Masterson. I should say one still does. Sadly, Dianne died of breast cancer in 1994. She was a far, far better artist. Her paintings had a depth and vitality that Dewitt could never achieve. Painstaking in her work, she only painted a few pieces. This," he said, holding the painting up and showing it to everyone, is unquestionably a Dianne Masterson."

"So how does that change things?" a confused Petra asked.

"How much did you pay for this at the auction this afternoon?" he asked.

"It should have been three thousand, but I ended up paying eight," he replied, glaring at Plushenko who glared back.

"Mr. Dosynk, your painting at a respectable auction would sell for at least one hundred thousand dollars. My heavens, I have clients who would line up for it and probably pay that and more."

"You are not joking with us?" Petra asked, grabbing Inka's hand. Ecstatic, she was bouncing up and down on the sofa like a prize winner on a TV game show.

"I assure you I am not."

"Perhaps I better get your business card," Petra laughed.

Need I spend anytime on the barely disguised sour reactions of Anatoly Plushenko and Howard Newton. Everyone else, though, was thrilled for Petra and vocal in expressing their feelings.

"Excuse me, ladies and gentlemen," Malcolm said over the happy din, "I must go. Before I do, though, please allow me a few words as regards this sordid business of the missing painting and the two Fukin icons. Dear me, that's an unseemly name for them. Anyway, let me point out that if Mr. Van Woort cannot tell the difference between a Dianne and a Dewitt Masterson painting, I doubt very seriously if he could spot an excellent forgery of *A Jersey Lily*. Therefore, someone had to tell him he had a fake. That someone might very well be in this room. As for the real painting? I seriously doubt he has it. He may know where it is, but I'm sure you can see the difficulty in trying to detain him based solely on that supposition. As for the two icons; being the iconographer that you are, Mr. Plushenko, you should have no problem authenticating them. Thus, it behooves you to continue your relationship with him. As you noted, Peter, you had other thoughts about who might have stolen the Millais painting. It might be wise to contact the authorities and let them know. Then I strongly recommend you all try to enjoy what remains of our cruise and let go of all of this."

"Hear, hear," shouted Dave Flannery, delighted to know he was just minutes from a single malt.

Malcolm's statement was also met with approval from Anatoly who was next in announcing his departure.

"Mr. Fitzroy is a wise man," he observed. "I hope you take him seriously about enjoying the rest of your cruise and let the auction be a forgotten experience."

"I doubt if Petra and Inka will ever forget it," Peter said, nodding to the happy pair.

First Anatoly scowled, then thought better of it and laughed. Stepping toward the sofa, he extended his hand to Petra and said, "I'm sincerely happy over your good fortune. It has taken some of the pain away from my having put you through what I did at the auction."

Uncertain of Plushenko's sincerity, Petra shook hands and mumbled, "It's in the past. I let it go."

Anatoly made for the door. Before departing, he turned and looked into the penthouse. "I appreciate you not standing in the way of our getting the icons back. I'm sure I have no need to worry or concern myself that you will let things be as they are. As for Van Woort being sorted out, I will see to that after I get the icons back."

That last sentence was delivered in such a menacing tone that Peter realized the kinder, gentler Plushenko was waning and the thuggish, bullying Plushenko was waxing, causing one to wonder which one was the real Anatoly.

His departure was followed by declarations of innocence from the three people most likely to have had a reason or opportunity to inform Van Woort about the painting's legitimacy. The first two were Freddie Florian and Benjamin Lytton-Crisp. They insisted they couldn't have said anything because they were scared stiff of the auctioneer and wished to avoid any further involvement. Looking around the room and seeing their questioning glances, the third person, Howard Newton, needed no prompting to plead his case. Admitting to having a talent for conversational faux pas, he swore on all things precious and holy to him that he would never have alerted Van Woort to the fake he was trying to peddle.

Their statements made, Peter decided to close the meeting. "Show of hands. Who believes the Anatoly Plushenko we just saw?" Not a hand went up.

"Maybe he's a little bit of both," Flannery suggested. "I can't explain his little act, but his message came through loud and clear. He wants us to stay away from Van Woort."

"Like I said before, it looks like that is going to be the case," Peter said glumly.

Liz, who had been busy with her iPhone, jumped in. "Amazing what this little thing can find. Turns out there really was a Ludmilla Fukin." she said. "So, Tio, what do we do next?"

"Malcolm's right. I think we make the best of the little time we have on the cruise. Meantime, Howard, you and I will put this adventure to bed by calling your FBI contact in New York who deals in this sort of thing and tell them what we know about the missing painting and where they can find Jasper Sprottle."

Petra rose from the sofa. "Okay, I am now kicking everyone out. Before you go, though, I propose we all meet tonight for dinner. Of course, all drinks are on me. We have lots to celebrate: that painting over there, the dance contest and, most important, our friendship. How about the Italian restaurant at eight? I will make the reservations."

As the guests departed, each gave the Dosynks their RSVP. It was unanimous. They would all come together again later that evening over plates of pasta and heaps of roasted garlic at Va Bene. Once out the door, they scattered to various parts of the ship; Peter, Lillie and Howard to Peter's penthouse to make the phone call, Dave Flannery to the Cove for his beloved scotch, Freddie and Benjamin to their stateroom to preen and Liz and Samantha to the Portside Bistro for their much needed chat. As the two women watched Peter walk down the narrow corridor with his easy, relaxed gait, Lillie floating beside him and Howard bounding ahead, Liz wished Samantha could see the Lavender vision. It would certainly help explain matters. However, Samantha was satisfied just admiring the backside of her future husband.

After pouring two fake sugars into her cappuccino, Liz began to stir away, a nervous whisking that got Samantha's attention. Finally looking up from her coffee, Liz glanced across the table at her positively beaming table mate. "You're really happy, aren't you?" It was not the way she intended to start the conversation.

"Oh, I am, Liz. Terribly so."

"I should be, too," Liz sighed, continuing her stirring. "I mean it's not like we're romantic rivals fighting over the same man. It's just that my uncle and I have been..."

Samantha leaned across the table and put her hand on Liz's stirring arm which prompted her to finally remove the spoon from the deliriously dizzy coffee drink. "There is no need to explain. Yours is a rare and wonderful partnership. I only hope that by entering Peter's world, I will be allowed into yours as well. In all the best ways."

Liz took a spoonful of the cappuccino's froth and held it aloft. "I swear this is the only reason I drink these things. I love the foam."

"I do, too," Samantha said, lifting her cup in a toast to what appeared to be a blossoming rapprochement between the two.

Liz raised her cup and without looking directly at Samantha said, "I'm sure you can understand what a shock it was for me to hear about you and my uncle."

"I think I can. It was as much a shock for me and I was part of it."

"Sam, I know I'll warm to the whole idea," Liz said with a convincing smile. "You do realize my uncle doesn't have much of a history when it comes to romantic relationships."

"We have that in common."

Liz sat back and folded her arms. "I have to shoulder much of the blame for that. Growing up, my middle name was precocity. Plus, I was creative, and that's a dangerous combination. The result was I spend a good part of my childhood thinking up devious ways to send potential girlfriends scurrying. Not some of my prouder moments."

"Now you're being too hard on yourself."

Liz frowned. "Perhaps, but truthfully I didn't make it easy for him to be a bachelor uncle. Much of that was because I simply didn't want to share him. I loved our time together. He was in so many ways the best father a young girl could have." When Samantha didn't respond, Liz, noticing the professor's calm demeanor, was inspired to add, "That's probably why he'd make the best husband a woman could have."

"What about you?" Samantha asked.

"What about me?" Liz returned.

"You're an extraordinarily beautiful woman. I can't believe your romantic history is similar to Peter's."

Liz leaned forward, put her elbows on the table and planted her chin on her folded hands. "I had the usual number of elementary school crushes, then two steady boyfriends in high school, both of whom are still good friends. Since then, I've dated a few men but I have pretty much concentrated on my education. I learned early on, Sam, to separate the boys who are only interested in the packaging and not the content from the ones who are interested in both. Unfortunately, the latter are a rare breed."

"I know Kevin and you got on pretty well."

"Did," Liz replied. "Kevin turned out to be emotionally needy and that's the last thing I want in a relationship."

Sam checked the time and realized she needed to get ready for the evening. "Liz, if it's any assurance, your uncle and I have no intention of rushing up to the bridge and demanding the captain marry us. Any plans we make would certainly involve you."

Liz nodded her head and muttered, "I know. I think much of my negative reaction is based on the fact that your wedding proposal happened on this cruise."

"I don't understand."

"Sam, I am not exaggerating when I tell you this has been the oddest, strangest, weirdest, life-changingest eleven days of my life. And there are two more nights and one more day to go. Heaven knows what can happen between now and when we get off this ship. I don't know that I can properly explain the craziness of it all. However, I do know this: Things will be better once we all set foot on terra firma. I think because your marriage proposal came amidst all this madness, I just lumped it in with the other stuff."

"From what I witnessed this afternoon, I dare say you have had some strange experiences," Samantha said, eager to learn more.

"Yikes, look at the time. We'd better go," exclaimed Liz as she popped up from her chair and walked around the table to Samantha's side. She seemed in that short time and distance to have reached a decision on her uncle's impulsive proposal and and figured the best way to announce it was with an affectionate hug.

As the two stood in the walkway near the arcade of shops, Sam said she was off to freshen up for the evening while Liz said she was off to do a little shopping. As they separated, Liz, looking to have the last word, said over her shoulder, "You know, professor, it's a good thing you don't teach at Stanford. That *would* be a deal breaker."

However, the last word would not be hers. As she walked into the sundry shop, from a distance, she heard a resonant voice accustomed to addressing a gallery of students, shout, "Go Bears!"

Considering the lateness of the hour in New York, Howard was still able to reach agent Sheldon Gibbs in New York without difficulty. Rather than nervously muddling through an explanation of what he considered an already muddled situation, Howard explained to the FBI agent that he was handing the phone to his friend. For this Gibbs was grateful. While he appreciated the cooperation the Newton's had given him in the case of Philipa's stolen paintings, he nonetheless found talking to Howard tedious. Thus, even if Peter spoke pig latin, it wouldn't disappoint him. But to the agent's surprise, this stranger explained all in a clear and concise manner, dotting every I and crossing every T. Peter even remembered to tell him Sprottle also had in his possession *Carrying Corn* by Ford Madox Brown and *Nocturne in Blue and Gold* by James McNeill Whistler. It was enough to happily set agent Gibbs into action. He assured Peter he'd contact his English counterpart immediately, even though, given the time change, London was fast asleep. Before hanging up, Gibbs promised to update them by e-mail the following morning.

"I can't explain it, but I'm uncomfortable talking to him," Howard mumbled. "Thanks for handling that."

Peter shrugged. "Actually, it felt good handing it off to someone else."

Now Peter's former boss had been busy these last few days assiduously working on his merit badge for swagger, an effort that called for total self-absorption. Thus, you can imagine Peter and Lillie's surprise when Howard suddenly asked, "Peter, why is it you act like there's another person in the room?"

It is a fact people do behave differently when the number of company present exceeds two. That Howard Newton noticed wasn't lost on Lillie. "Such acuity. I'm impressed," she said, causing Peter to turn his head in her direction.

"I don't know what you mean," he replied, looking back at his mortal guest.

"There!" Howard said excitedly, pointing to a spot to the right of Peter. "Just now, before answering me, you looked to your left as if somebody had said something."

The good news about dealing with a question put to you by Howard Newton is that eventually he will come up with his own answer. This time was no exception as he waved a finger at Peter, smiled smugly and said, "Oh, I know what it is. All those characters you did on radio are probably still running around in your head. So, which one am I competing with for your attention?"

"You are not competing with anyone," Peter replied sharply. "I was just distracted by something."

"Anyway, it's no big deal. I'm off. Naomi said she'd call about this time. You know she wasn't over the top about me giving you a hand in this."

"Really."

"She'll be glad to hear we turned it over to the authorities," he said, making his way to the door. "Now maybe I can talk my way back into her good graces."

Peter and Lillie decided to get some air. They headed for the promenade deck where a stiff wind, cold and bracing, waited for them on the starboard side. The headwind slowed Peter's pace. Fierce as it was, though, waiting for him at the bow of the ship was an even stronger gust that further slowed him. As he fought his way to the port side, the same wind, now at his back, pushed him toward the stern. Lillie floated alongside him, impervious to the weather. While the wind and cold made it a more challenging stroll than he would have preferred, Peter felt good being outside where he and Lillie could talk undisturbed. There were no other walkers or runners, only the occasional smoker who stood on the stairs at the entrances.

"Peter, do red flags go up when you hear the name Naomi?" Lillie asked.

"They do, indeed," he replied. "I remember Howard once telling me that he talks to Naomi every night. Remember when he said she takes a keen interest in everything he's doing?"

Lillie replied, "That, of course, means everything we've been doing."

"Exactly."

"Of course, her interest might just be a wife's natural curiosity."

"I hope that's the case. Howard would be devastated otherwise. The thing that's bothersome is she knew the painting was a fake," Peter said. "Howard also said something else that makes me suspicious of her. It seems Naomi wasn't as eager as he was to turn over the stolen paintings that her mother had acquired. He said he never questioned her about it. Lillie, it's entirely possible Naomi knows Van Woort from his past dealings with her mother."

"Thus, it's possible she knew all along about her mother's larcenous purchases," Lillie speculated. "Peter, we may be on to something."

"Anyway, I was glad to hear Howard say he was going to tell her we have all lost any interest in Van Woort."

"And your reason for that?"

"If Naomi is feeding information to Van Woort, he will soon learn we are no longer any threat to him. It might cause him to drop his guard and do something foolish."

"I don't think we are much of a threat, Peter," Lillie muttered.

There was a water fountain located in the stern of the ship out of the wind. Peter took a few sips, sat down on a nearby bench and stretched his legs out. Looking up at the now familiar and welcoming lavender vision that was his friend, Lillie, he said, "I believe we still are."

"To that, do you have a plan?"

"No," he said, shaking his head. "I have a feeling."

"A feeling?"

Emboldened by a confidence that was almost heady, he said, "Yes, Lillie, a feeling. I know this may sound crazy but I am more certain than ever that wherever you are, the painting is close by. I'm convinced of it." He rose from the bench and began to walk into the wind of the starboard side. "Let's wait and see what Gibbs stirs up in London in these next few hours." Then with an extra dollop of vehemence that, to be frank, looked silly on him, he added, "Mrs. Langtry, I'm willing to bet you many pounds sterling they won't find the painting in London."

chapter 38

PETER'S ARRANT CONVICTION that only they could recover the missing painting positively thrilled Lillie. While no definite plan of action emerged from their chat on the promenade deck, she, too, felt that by keeping their eyes and ears open, their next move would serendipitously find them. Meantime, there was a dinner to attend.

It was the last formal evening of the cruise and everyone was dressed to the nines. This fascinating stock phrase was voiced during a most unusual conversation involving my favorite threesome. It is, indeed, one of those old chestnuts that gets dusted off and used on occasion. This was one of them. Liz, already attractively packaged in her favorite red slinky thing, had joined Peter and Lillie in his penthouse. Their plan was to meet Samantha at the Covey and then go on together to the Dosynk-hosted dinner at Va Bene. Peter had just put the finishing touches on his bow tie.

"Tio, you make the knot so perfect, people will think it's a fake," Liz observed, glancing up briefly from her iPhone. She wondered how many times over the years she'd alerted him to what she perceived as a fashion faux pas. "Think of Rumpole when you tie it." She'd not used that line before and was impressed with it. I can certainly use that again, she thought, perhaps on his wedding day.

"Is this Rumpole person someone I should know?" Lillie asked.

Without looking up from her small device, Liz replied off-handedly, "Um, not really. He's a fictional barrister who is rumpled, terribly bright and witty and a fiend for justice for all."

"He sounds utterly fascinating. I wonder what he looks like naked," Lillie said matter-of-factly.

Liz looked up at her from her perch on the sofa, her round eyes growing even rounder. "Did you just say what I think you did?"

"I did, dear. I wanted to see how much of your attention I had."

"I'm sorry, Lillie, I was adding something to my list," she explained. "Let me just finish this last entry. Is bow tie one or two words?"

Peter, who considered himself a human spell check, replied, "Two words."

"Thanks," she mumbled, her thumbs busy on the small screen's keyboard.

"What are you doing?" he asked.

"I'm writing a list of things Samantha should know about you."

Peter gave another obstinate tug on his bow tie. "Whatever for?"

"I know you'll think I'm getting ahead of myself, but weddings do that to women. Anyway, I started thinking it might fall on me to throw a bachelorette party for Sam. I figured reading a list of some of your quirks and eccentricities was just the ticket to get some laughs. You'd rather that than a male stripper teasing her, wouldn't you?"

"I have a feeling Sam is more a bridal shower person," Peter said. "Anyway, care to share what you've written so far?"

"Sure," she said eagerly. Returning to her iPhone, she studiously surveyed her list. "Okay, here's one. They're not in any order of importance. This one concerns your hair."

"What about my hair?"

"Tio, you haven't been to a barber in twenty years because I cut it. By the way, lately that involves trimming your eyebrows and cutting the hairs on your nose and ears. Now I can continue to do it, but what if I can't because I'm traveling to some far off exotic place to do anthropological things? I probably should give Sam a lesson or two in barbering."

"Whoa," Peter exclaimed. "Liz, if you want this to be entertaining, let me give you a couple of pointers. First, shorten it up and don't be afraid to exaggerate. Go for the laugh. Something like, 'Samantha, my uncle is so cheap, he won't go to a barber. You'll have to cut his hair like I do. By the way, he doesn't tip.'"

Liz's thumbs once again attacked the keyboard. "Please note I am accepting your help in good humor," she said with an unconvincing smile. "Okay, let me find another. Oh, I like this. Sam should know how much you love to vacuum and you have this thing about spotlessly clean floors. Also, you like doing the laundry and insist on folding your own clothes. That's fine as it is, isn't it?"

Her self-appointed comic mentor shook his head. "Not really. Again, keep it short and go for a punch line like 'My uncle loves to vacuum and do laundry. By marrying him you're not just getting a husband. You're getting a live-in housekeeper with benefits.'"

Before Liz could react, Lillie spoke up: "While there's an air of crisp professionalism in Peter's rewording, Liz, I must say I am enjoying the charming clumsiness of yours. Please, do go on."

Warmed by Lillie's approbation, Liz thanked her and began to scroll in search of another entry. "I think you'll like this: We only have basic cable in the house because my uncle can't abide commercial television. I'm okay with that, but what if his bride-to-be wants ESPN because she's a closet sports' freak?"

"Now *that* was right on the money," Peter responded. Buttoning his tuxedo jacket, he fussed with his pocket square and sneaked a final glimpse in the mirror, a glance that confirmed it was appropriately rakish. Taking one last tug on his tie, he walked over to the sofa where Liz made a place for him. "More like that last one, my dear niece, and you'll lose that charming clumsiness."

Liz's response was to hold her iPhone up so Peter could follow her actions. At the bottom of the screen was an illustration of a small trashcan. With a light tap on it, she was asked if she wished to delete that particular content. Another light tap and the list was gone. Putting the phone in her purse, she gave her uncle a peck on the cheek and said, "Maybe it's best Sam learns about you all on her own."

"You'll get no argument from me," he said, rising from the sofa. Peter turned and offered his hand to Liz, a gentlemanly gesture, to be sure, except this time there was an ulterior purpose to his gallantry. Standing beside her, he kissed her cheek and said, "And I will forget that list I was making of your peculiarities to read at your graduation party."

"Trust me, they are already known to everyone."

"Excuse me, you two, as entertaining as this is, I believe we are all expected in the Covey to meet your fiancee," Lillie said. "Well, two of us anyway. May I say you all look very dashing and glamorous, dressed to the nines as you are."

Peter and Liz were notorious for asking about the origin of an expression, hackneyed or otherwise. However this time, pressed to move along, they passed on inquiring about this particular one. You, though, may be curious. Why the number nine? Why not dressed to the eights, the threes or, for that matter, any number? Some say it's from the nine yards of cloth needed to make a suit. Not much there, I think. Of course, nine has always been used as a superlative, i.e., cloud nine, the whole nine yards, etc.. There is, of course, a very real and rich history to this expression and the other sayings that employ the number nine but I think I will leave you guessing. My reason? To give you something else to look forward to when you are headed my way. You see, you are by nature a curious being. Upon ascension from your temporal address on earth to an eternal one, your curiosity will be left behind because upon your arrival all will be known to you. So imagine: There you are just a few breaths away from the end of your mortal existence. The family is there, gathered around you, as they had been alerted that you took to your California king size bed with its 1500 Thread Count Egyptian Cotton sheets ready for the big moment. Isn't it nice to know you will be further comforted by the thought that in just a blink of an eye (or a bright light), you'll know the back story to *dressed to the nines*. Now a word of caution: You may very well think that, but do not say it aloud. First off, it's not worthy of last word status. Also, if there's a bit of internecine warfare going on between factions of your family who are eager to get their mitts on your earthly possessions, including those fancy, high-priced sheets, you might give them cause to dispute your last will and testament.

There were twelve who gathered that evening in the plush Italianate confines of Va Bene. This convivial bunch was primed for conversation; their spirits lifted and their tongues loosened by the steady flow of delicious Italian wines. Petra was a marvelous host; full of good cheer and blustery bonhomie and, judging from the wines, generous to a fault. Anxious to address them before the first course, he signaled Yurk to get their attention. Petra could have done it himself, but he had his reasons for employing his brooding, stand-offish grandson who was generally unresponsive when in the company of others. His favorite activity when part of a social gathering was to watch his massive biceps expand and retract. Like his grandfather, he sported a menacing mug, but unlike his grandfather, he didn't know his own strength. Thus, when Petra ordered him to quiet the crowd, Yurk picked up his empty wine glass and, taking his knife, struck it mightily. The idea behind this popular attention getter is the repeated tinkle of the silver against the glass would get the table's attention, quieting them down. However, Yurk didn't understand the subtly required to create a tinkling sound, a move that demands a sensitive touch, and, as a result, the glass exploded in bits and pieces. While a crew of Va Bene servers quickly and efficiently cleared the table of the glass fragments, Petra rose to address his guests who included his family along with Lillie, Peter, Liz, Samantha, Dave and Mary Pat, Freddie, Benjamin and a quieter, humbler Howard.

"I just want to welcome you here tonight for this dinner of celebration," he said. Pointing to Peter, he continued, "I met that gentleman at the start of the cruise. He was drinking this wonderful coffee drink which he introduced me to. I will say this about him: if you came on this cruise to have a quiet, uneventful twelve days, he is not the man you want to meet." He waited for the laughter to subside. "Now I want to thank him for letting me part of a..." Petra paused. Looking around the table, he pleaded, "Please, what would you call what we've all been through? I don't have the words."

Dave Flannery was first up with a response. "How much time do I have to answer that?" His wife slapped his knee to silence him.

"I will call it an amazing adventure and leave it at that" Petra said, effectively closing the floor to any more creative suggestions. Suddenly, he was aware that he'd lost the attention of his audience who were now looking over his left shoulder. Petra didn't have to turn around to know who was sneaking up on him. His bulbous, pink nose instantly recognized the distinctive, cloying Eau du Cologne of Charles Van Woort. He turned to face the auctioneer who was holding an empty wine glass.

"Good evening, Mr. Dosynk, Pico Enea tells me you are pouring an excellent Barolo," Van Woort said with his salesman's smile. "I wondered if you might let a tired auctioneer try a taste?" The request made, he thrust his glass forward.

The wine stewart at the time was refilling Mary Pat Flannery's glass. Petra waved him over to pour some of the expensive Tuscan wine into Van Woort's glass. "Is there something I can do for you?" he asked warily.

Van Woort's response was to hold his glass up to admire the Barolo's ruby red color. Then, after swirling the wine in a well-practiced motion, he brought the glass to his nose. Aware he was being observed by all, he lowered the glass to his mouth and took a sip, swishing it noisily about this way and that before swallowing it. Only after this performance did he answer Petra. "No, there's nothing you can do for me. A taste of this elegant wine is more than enough. However, there is something I might be able to do for you."

"And what might that be?" Petra asked with a baleful stare.

Baleful as it was, and believe me Petra was the master of the sinister stare, it failed to intimidate or frighten the dinner party's intruder. The truth of the matter was, if looks could kill, what really shivered the auctioneer's timbers was not the amiable Kwyrki with his incongruous scowl. Rather, it was Anatoly Plushenko, particularly now that he had been briefed on Plushenko's strange appearance at the Dosynk penthouse. What worried Van Woort most was the Russian's scary comment that after he took possession of the icons, he would sort him out. Van Woort, almost from their first meeting, wondered why he ever agreed to do business with this venomous man, threatening as he was. This was truly to be a pleasure cruise for his better customers, meaning those who were as miscreant in their everyday behavior as he was. However, on this cruise he had no intention of selling anything to anyone until the Millais painting fell into his lap. Knowing of Philipa Crumley-Figg's passion for that type of art, Van Woort decided to put it in her lap for, of course, a hefty price. No sooner were they on board that Plushenko started cozying up to him, citing references of mutual Russian acquaintances and armed with the knowledge that Van Woort had two valuable Russian icons to move. A naturally greedy man, Van Woort approached him about also buying *A Jersey Lily* after learning of the accidental death of Philipa. Plushenko was not pleased when he learned it was a fake and Van Woort witnessed first-hand just how angry and potentially violent Anatoly could be. Now, not at all appreciating the nasty innuendo of *sorting him out,* Van Woort arrived at a decision. While it would necessitate taking a financial loss on the Fukin icons, he would take Plushenko at his word that he was buying the icons to return them to the church and simply give them to him along with a wish he had a nice trip back to Moscow. He felt this charitable gesture would thus remove any threat to his physical well-being. Once, in a macabre mood, Van Woort tried imagining what method Plushenko would use to sort him out. It made his skin crawl.

Now here he was standing beside Petra Dosynk in full view of the man's guests facing another yet another intriguing task. This one, while not life-threatening, was going to be far more challenging. Indeed, the gelled, perfumed and manicured auctioneer doubted he could pull it off but he felt it was worth the try. His goal? To try to persuade Petra Dosynk to return the Dianne Masterson painting to him. He was beside himself after learning he had in his possession a painting that valuable and didn't know it. But what really upset him the most and, he had to admit, embarrassed him greatly was the pleasure he derived from foisting it off on Petra Dosynk for eight thousand dollars. As improbable as it was, he was now going to try and talk it back into his possession. Striking an apologetic tone, he addressed Petra: "I have thought long and hard about the manner in which you were treated at the auction this afternoon. You ended up paying way over price for a painting that should have sold for no more than three thousand. What did you pay, by the way?" he asked as if he didn't know.

"Eight thousand," Petra grumbled.

Van Woort took a sip of the elegant Barolo. Issuing his trademark smile that was charming to some and smarmy to others, he continued, "Ah yes, I remember. That's the amount. Now, Petra... I may call you Petra?"

Dosynk shook his head and muttered, "Sure."

"Petra, there is nothing unusual about people at an auction paying more for a piece of art than it is worth. The size of their wallets doesn't always govern people's actions when they fall head over heels in love with a particular piece of art. However, after thinking back on the sale of the Masterson to you, I realized that you were victimized by your own inexperience, the fast pace of the auction and the boorish, bullying behavior of Mr. Plushenko. I would like to make things right."

"Let me guess, you want to buy it back," shouted a laughing Dave Flannery who felt strongly that Van Woort must have gotten word of the painting's true provenance. Before he could say anything else, his wife slapped his knee again.

"As a matter of fact, Mr. Flannery, that's exactly what I aim to do," he said with the oozing charm of a TV game show host. Turning to face a still scowling Petra, he continued in the same oily manner, "I will take back the painting and return your eight thousand dollars to you." That said, he flashed a beaming smile at his audience as if to expect applause. However, there was no one there behind the imaginary cameras to flash the imaginary applause sign. Thus, a strange silence hung over the large table in the Va Bene dining room until Peter decided to bring Van Woort up to date, even though he, too, felt Van Woort had been tipped off.

"That's a generous gesture, Mr. Van Woort, but I'm afraid it's too late. The painting turns out to be a Dianne Masterson and eight thousand dollars isn't enough to even make a ten per cent down payment," he said.

Spirits have no expressions nor do we require them. You air-breathers, however, are cursed or blessed by them depending on the circumstances. In my estimation, astonishment is the hardest to effectively convey if, in fact, you aren't truly astounded, perhaps by prior knowledge of that which is meant to amaze. Whatever Van Woort managed, he hoped it was a passable expression of astonishment. From here on out, he realized he had to play this very carefully if he was to get his hands on the painting. Turning his attention away from Peter, he looked directly at Petra, scrunched his face into a look of mystification and uttered, "That's... That's impossible." Feeling his reaction needed an extra something, he added a dismissive laugh for good measure.

"No, it is not," Petra insisted. "Mr. Fitzroy examined the painting earlier this afternoon and told us it is a Dianne Masterson."

The auctioneer shook his head. "Well, Malcolm certainly knows his business, but I seriously doubt Carmel plein-air artists are his stock in trade. He may very well think you have a Dianne Masterson. It's even possible you do. I deal with such a large inventory, I usually leave it to my very capable assistants to deal with the provenance of the paintings. Believe me, if a Dianne Masterson was somehow missed, heads will roll."

There was no response. As Petra had nothing to say and even Flannery and Peter were quiet, Van Woort kept on talking. "Say, why don't I take a look at the painting. There's always the possibility that Malcolm was wrong in his appraisal."

Dosynk remained stone-faced. He moved his malleable mouth from side to side.

"And what if you say it's not a Dianne Masterson?"

"Then I will return your eight thousand dollars to you and put the painting up for auction tomorrow afternoon. Of course, whether it is or isn't, you may still wish to keep it. After all, a deal is a deal."

"And if it is?"

"I'd be the first to congratulate you."

Petra Dosynk looked over at his grandson. A simple nod and Yurk bounded out of his chair and approached him. In a low authoritative voice, Petra said, "Take Mr. Van Woort to our penthouse and show him the painting. It is still on the bed. We will wait dinner until you return."

Van Woort beamed. This actually might be working, he thought. "This won't take long, I assure you." Glancing at the Dosynks' guests, he added jovially, "In the meantime, enjoy the wine everyone."

"I think I will join them," Lillie whispered to Peter and Liz who watched as the lavender aura known lovingly to them as Mrs. Langtry floated toward the exit behind the two men visible to know one except them.

The auctioneer kept his promise. It taken't long at all. Just enough time, though, for Petra to make one phone call and receive another. The threesome returned to the table not two minutes after Van Woort had called Petra from the penthouse. In a most sympathetic tone, he explained that it took him no time at all to sadly refute Malcolm Fitzroy's assertion that it was a Dianne Masterson. It most definitely was not, Van Woort insisted. His was a confidence born of that earlier hunch he was going to get away with it. Chicanery is so much fun when it means huge profit, he thought.

Stone-faced, Petra returned to the table, signaling the servers to begin taking dinner orders. Sitting down, he leaned in and whispered something to his wife. The assembled watched with anticipation to see what Inka's reaction would be. When he left her ear to reach for his wine, she smiled broadly, took her glass and giddily toasted him. While it wasn't noticeable, one could sense a collective sigh of relief.

When the trio returned, Lillie edged in between Liz and Peter. "This is going to be a very entertaining evening," she said gleefully. "Now you two, just keep quiet and let everything unfold."

Van Woort, who'd left his wine glass on the table beside Petra, leaned over to retrieve it. "As we discussed on the phone, I've made arrangements to have someone pick up the painting. Your shipboard account will be credited with eight thousand dollars," he explained in a low voice that was heard by all.

"Oh shit!" Flannery hissed. While everyone was shocked and dismayed by what they heard, the newspaper editor's expletive was their only vocal reaction. Van Woort paid Flannery no heed. Instead, he held his glass up and bid the table adieu. "You are all invited to the auction tomorrow. Thanks for letting me dominate Mr. Dosynk's time for awhile. However, I think everything has worked out to everyone's advantage. I'll leave it to Mr. Dosynk to explain matters." Then, like a peacock in a full feather spread, he marched to his table by the window.

As the Dosynk dinner party progressed, the earlier air of joviality sadly gone, scattered attempts on the part of his guests to elicit some kind of explanation of what just transpired were met with failure. To every question, Petra's only response was a promising, "All in good time. All in good time, my dear friends."

That good time or, to be more exact, the people who brought the good time with them arrived sometime between il secondo and il dolce (It is an Italian restaurant, after all.). Samantha was the first to spot them. Her sister, looking radiant in a dress she'd purchased that day in one of the ship's boutiques, was arm in arm with a smiling, seemingly more youthful Malcolm Fitzroy who wore his classic, double-breasted tuxedo with a casualness and suavity that impressed everyone at the table. The handsome pair stopped by the corner housing Petra and Inka.

"It is done, Mr. Dosynk?" Malcolm asked decorously.

"It's done, Mr. Fitzroy," Petra replied solemnly.

"What the hell's done?" barked a frustrated Dave Flannery.

"All in good time, my good friend," Petra said with just a hint of a smug smile.

chapter 39

WHILST THINKING ABOUT how to approach this thirty-ninth chapter, I considered a quick mention of yet another of the myriad benefits of taking up residency here in Eternity. Then I realized that in doing so, I might sound like a sales-hungry realtor who talks up a neighborhood's walkability factor, high-achieving schools, nearby parks and the local coffee shop that features an out-of-this-world double mocha latte with soy milk and a sugary morning bun for just two dollars on Wednesday mornings; all in the hopes of putting a family in an adorable Arts and Crafts two-bedroom cottage with a newly remodeled kitchen, hot tub and man cave. As there is such a thing as oversell, I decided to go in another direction. Still, it seems I piqued my amanuensis's curiosity and as a result he pestered me so that I abandoned the new direction and returned to my original plan. After all, when one is promoting an eternal Eden, there's no such thing as oversell.

In what I, Theodomicles, lovingly call home, supreme happiness reigns... Well, you guessed it: supreme. And let's not forget ad infinitum. The absolutely marvelous aspect of this particular blissful state is no slipping in and out of it as can happen so often during your mortal tenure. Thus, sustained happiness is something to look forward to. Meantime, my advice is to grab all you can during your temporal stay on planet Earth. While lots of people will tell you otherwise, that is certainly what is intended for you.

And just how does joyfulness relate to our story? For the moment, as regards the Dosynk dinner guests, it had been usurped by a dark cloud of consternation that hung over the table like a thick fog. Why, thought everyone, would Petra relinquish his painting for a mere eight thousand dollars to that jackanape who dares calls himself an expert on art? Gloom prevailed.

It was the newly arrived Malcolm Fitzroy in the company of the glowing Isabelle Whitby who would transform the general mood. After informing Petra that he had a brief bit of business with Van Woort and would Petra be so kind as to look after Isabelle in the interim, the dapper, elderly gentleman made his way to the auctioneer's window table.

While he was gone, Samantha nudged Peter and asked, "Would you mind if I stole Isabelle away for a moment?"

"Not at all," he replied, standing up to see her off. "By the way, she looks beautiful, Sam."

"I know. I know. I'm so excited for her," she gushed, giving his hand an affectionate squeeze.

The meeting of the two gallery owners was, as Malcolm promised, short but not sweet. Whatever words were exchanged, they were potent enough to prompt Van Woort to storm out of the restaurant, red-faced with clenched fists. Furious at how they had turned the tables on him, he headed directly to the Covey bar where he ordered a double Remy Martin. Meantime, Malcolm Fitzroy, with the confident stride of an aging, handsome movie star, returned to the dinner party where he was immediately welcomed back and given the floor so as to bring everyone up to date.

At the same time, Samantha and Isabelle returned to the table with Lillie following a discreet distance behind them. When Peter spotted the lavender vision, he could only shake his head and wonder what Lillie was up to. Fortunately, his face did not register exasperation, as Samantha would have seen it as well as Lillie. How would he explain that?

After Malcolm seated Isabelle, he turned his attention to the other guests who were anxious to hear what had transpired between the nefarious auctioneer and him. Raising his glass, Malcolm's eyes calmly scanned the table until all had raised theirs. "First, I would like to offer up a toast to the Dosynk family. It also comes with my sincere apology for misleading them as regards the real value of the painting they acquired at the auction." Petra looked up and acknowledged his apology with an affectionate nod. "Would you mind if I sat down to tell my tale?" Malcolm asked his audience. With a murmur of general consent, he took his seat and began his story.

"Shortly after leaving the Dosynk's penthouse this afternoon, I suddenly remembered that a wealthy collector of local Carmel artists named Leland Messner who lives in Pebble Beach owned the very painting that I had, minutes earlier, identified as a Dianne Masterson. I was troubled because I couldn't imagine him selling it. Fortunately, I was able to reach him by phone when I returned to my stateroom. He assured me the Dianne Masterson painting in question was hanging not five feet from where he was sitting. When I explained I'd just seen a masterful forgery, he told me a fascinating story."

"Wait a minute," Flannery said, raising his hand. "You're saying Petra's painting *isn't* a Dianne Masterson?"

"That's correct, Mr. Flannery. Ironically, her brother, Dewitt, painted it," he replied. "Perhaps, you should all listen to my story as it will explain all."

Chastened in the gentlest of ways, Flannery pouted while his wife became his spokesperson: "Forgive my journalist husband. He always thinks he's at a press conference. I will see he remains quiet throughout."

"Thank you," Malcolm responded. "Now according to Leland, after Dianne died, her brother contacted him and asked if he might borrow the Lone Cypress painting as he wanted to study it and then attempt to copy it. It was his intention to find in this exercise just what it was that his sister could do with a canvas, brush and paints that he couldn't. I daresay he ended up creating a marvelous reproduction. It certainly fooled me. Anyway, he eventually returned the original piece to Leland and kept his reproduction in his studio. Leland said Dewitt told him the painting had became in an odd way a muse for him, and there was no way he would ever sell it."

"Then how did..." Flannery began out of habit. Mary Pat shushed him.

"How did it end up as an auction item on a cruise ship to Alaska, you wonder. It seems Dewitt enjoyed the occasional company of some of the itinerant surfers who drift in and out of Carmel who are of his sexual persuasion. He often took them to his Monterey home and studio for varying length of stays. Dewitt is convinced one of them took it, no doubt thinking it a sort of payment for services rendered. Evidently, it wasn't the first time one of these bleached-blond rent boys felt justified in taking what they could. How it ended up here is a mystery not worth solving. Suffice it to say, Leland is delighted it was located."

This time Peter spoke up. "So somebody got word to Van Woort that he'd sold a true Dianne Masterson for eight thousand dollars. That explains why he made that feeble attempt to buy it back."

Petra then interjected, "What Mr. Van Woort didn't know was Mr. Fitzroy called me right after he talked with that gentleman in Pebble Beach and explained everything."

Malcolm continued, "Mr. Messner commissioned me to buy the painting and send it to him. It was his intention to return it to Dewitt with specific instructions that from now on he take his surfers to a hotel room and not his studio."

At this point, the cloud of consternation began to lift and a resolute cheeriness returned to the table. Mary Pat who was doing a fine job of keeping her husband quiet, blurted out, "So, Mr. Fitzroy, finish the story. I love it when the bad guy gets his comeuppance."

The debonair elder smiled. However, much as he loved the attention, he was anxious to wrap things up as his entree had just been placed in front of him and he was ready to attack it. "To sum it up, I offered Mr. Dosynk $5,000 for the reproduction. That's as much as Leland wanted to spend. I thought it a more than fair price. Petra's wife was out and he wanted to talk to her first. We agreed he'd call me sometime this evening and let know of his decision. You can imagine my surprise and delight when Petra phoned just a few minutes ago, informing me of Van Woort's ridiculous scheme to buy back what he thought was a valuable Dianne Masterson. Mr. Dosynk and I agreed that he should accept Mr. Van Woort's offer of eight thousand dollars. When I arrived at the restaurant and learned that that had been accomplished, as you all observed, I approached Mr. Van Woort, first complimenting him on his discerning eye that saw the painting for what it was, a Dewitt Masterson. You could tell from his abrupt and angry exit how that was received. However, before he bolted, I was able to persuade him to sell it to me for five thousand dollars, explaining he'd be lucky to get three for it at auction tomorrow."

Petra clapped his meaty hands together and the others followed; all of them heartened and cheered by the art historian's actions. Malcolm acknowledged the applause with a subtle wave of his hand. Then he looked lovingly at his plate of linguine con vongole, a glance that everyone took as a cue to begin eating.

When the plates were finally cleared and the tiramisu made its entrance, Petra rose to address the crowd: "This has been a very special evening. Thank you all for coming. I know some of you want to go to the show. Mr. Flannery, I know you and your lovely wife will go dancing. As for Inka and me, we are going to bed. Pasta makes us sleepy."

"Let me guess, Petra, you want to rest up so you can have another go at the auction tomorrow," David Flannery teased.

Petra laughed heartily. "No! No more auctions for us. At least not on this ship. That is not to say we Dosynks don't have any interest in the visual arts. Inka and I collect a very special kind of art, Mr. Flannery."

"And just what is that?" Dave asked warily.

"Ice sculptures," he answered drily. Signaling the waiter for the bill, he added, "If you are a person who looks to art as an investment, it isn't for you. The downside is how quickly they depreciate in value."

"I deserved that," Dave said, patting Petra Dosynk on the shoulder.

Before we continue, let me add my own "Bravo!" to Mr. Fitzroy's summing up. As you go through life, you'll find there's nothing more satisfying and entertaining than a tale well told. A good yarn elicits no yawn says I. Rather, it lifts the spirit and energizes the mind.

Now let us finish this fascinating evening in the company of Peter, Samantha and Lillie. An innocent gaffe on the part of the male of our merry trio forced said gentleman into taking decisive action regarding something that was heavy on his mind at the time but for which he was totally unprepared to deal with. Deal with it he did, though, and I feel it's

worth knowing what came as a result of his extemporane-
ous actions. It fascinates me that very often sticky situations
such as the one I'm about to share with you are resolved only
because a clumsy miscalculation forces one to act immediately and forthrightly.

Here is how it happened: As the dinner party broke
up, over the friendly din of people parting company, Lillie
gave Peter a hurried, brief account of what she overheard
when she followed Samantha and Isabelle into the empty
card room adjacent to the restaurant. It seems the two big
pieces of news involved Isabelle gushing to Samantha that
she was joining Malcolm Fitzroy on a week's journey to Florence for an art symposium where he would be speaking and
Samantha, who after seeing her sister so ebullient and cheery,
decided to tell her about Peter and their marital plans. Lillie assured him that Isabelle was ecstatic, giving her sister a
warm hug and tearfully thanking her for insisting she come
on the cruise. It was a brand spanking new Isabelle and Sam
couldn't have been happier, Lillie reported.

Now all of the above is obviously chirpy news. Interestingly, the evening would not have taken the curious life-
changing turn it did if Peter had only waited for Samantha
to tell him about her meeting with Isabelle. Instead, we get
to put my gaffe or, as it is sometimes known, the Oops theory to the test.

Huddled together at a quiet table in the Portside Bistro,
Samantha, ignorant of Lillie's presence, began to describe to
Peter how thrilled she was to see her sister so over the moon.
"I'm so glad we got a chance to sneak away, Peter. It's truly
remarkable. Isabelle is a changed woman," she said, giving
her future partner one of those joyous smiles she could so
easily produce.

At this point, Peter should have done nothing more
than to rustle up a happy face, squeeze her hand and wait

quietly for his beloved to continue with more of the details regarding their sisterly meeting. Instead, he blurted out, "What do you think of her going to Florence with Malcolm?" It never crossed his mind that he wasn't supposed to be privy to that information. Well, it did cross his mind, but only after the words were uttered.

Lillie reacted with a soft, "Uh oh."

"How did you know Isabelle's going to Italy?" Samantha asked innocently, the tone of her voice expressing both amusement and amazement. It was as if she'd just heard a magician identify the card she was holding. "I must have told you," she said, convinced there had to be a sensible reason.

Thinking she'd just given him a way out, Peter was about to confirm that she was indeed the source, but before he could respond, Samantha spoke up again, "No, I'm sure I didn't. I couldn't have."

There you have it. Peter was cornered, all thanks to a guileless blunder. In an instant, he realized the moment to resolve the perplexing issue of whether or not he tells Samantha about Lillie had been forced on him. In a way, it's a good thing, he thought, as he was terribly uncomfortable with the idea of keeping his supernatural experience from her. Plus, how could he possibly broach the topic months or years from now, particularly as their relationship had blossomed during the time Mrs. Langtry was so prominent in his life. More correctly, both their lives. Conversely, he was convinced that telling Samantha he was keeping company with an historical figure from the Victorian Age would put an immediate end to their relationship. Fortunately, a server came by with their cappuccinos, giving him some added time, limited as it was, to figure out a good way, if there was one, to introduce her to the other guest at their table. Yes, he said to himself, I will take my chances with telling her. Still, Peter stalled even more by taking his sweet time adding sugar and stirring his coffee.

"Sam, I'm in somewhat of a bind," he finally began, his voice which faltered a bit gave no hint he was about to drop a bombshell. "I do want to tell you how I came to know about Isabelle's plans. I respect you too much to do otherwise. However, I fear that by telling you the truth, I may lose you."

Samantha quickly reached across for his hand. "I can't imagine that happening."

"Oh, I think what I have to say could do it."

As a result of his seemingly casual manner, Samantha found the seriousness of his sober response amusing. "Peter, how extraordinary can it be?" she asked with another one of her high beam smiles.

"Extraordinary enough that you might jet-eject from that chair and hightail it out of her as fast as those beautiful legs of yours can carry you."

Letting go his hand, Samantha sat back in her chair. With a determined look, she placed each hand on the opposite forearm. "I'm sure you know how difficult it is to rise from a chair with your arms folded. It takes time, balance and effort, particularly on these ice cream chairs. I hereby promise to remain like this throughout your explanation." She was enjoying what she perceived to be nothing more than playful banter. "So, let me start things off," she emoted like a lawyer taking a deposition. "Mr. Ramsey, how did you learn about Isabelle's plan to go to Italy?"

Sotto voce, Peter replied, "Lillie told me."

"I thought I heard you say Lillie," she said, laughing. "You'll have to speak up."

"Lillie told me," he repeated, adding a decibel or two to his response. "She followed you into the card room. Later, while the dinner was breaking up, she gave me a brief account of what she heard including the news of Isabelle's trip."

Still not worried enough to unfold her arms, but becoming slightly unsettled, Samantha said, "Peter, I assure you there was no one in the card room with us. We would have seen her."

"You can't see her. I can, though."

She dropped her hands into her lap. "Is this a preview of what it will be like living with a radio personality? I might remind you, kind sir, that I don't have the same experienced comic imagination you have," she said sweetly. "

As parceling out the explanation didn't seem to be working, Peter, wisely in my opinion, opted for the tell-it-all-in-one-fell-swoop approach. Taking a deep breath, he dove in, his first words a desperate plea for her not to be frightened. After receiving a tentative but tremulous nod from Samantha, he worked his way from his first introduction to Lillie in Philipa Crumley-Figg's penthouse to the present. He left nothing out and, like Malcolm, I give him high marks for detail.

Samantha didn't bolt. Nor did she appear all that visibly rattled after he put a finis to his story. In fact, if you were at an adjacent table and observed the two of them, you might very well think they were talking about the price of cheddar cheese in Wisconsin rather than the existence of someone long considered dead. There was a moment right after Peter explained things when Samantha seemed to go deep inside herself. Peter was wise enough to not ask for a response. He simply waited and hoped for the best.

"Is she here now?" Samantha asked in a furtive whisper, looking to her left and right. Peter nodded and pointed to his left. "And you truly can see her?" Peter nodded again. "Oh God, Peter, this is all so incredulous."

"It is," he agreed solemnly, "but I had to tell you, Sam."

"I know," she mumbled.

"I won't blame you if you want to leave, Sam. If I was on the receiving end of this story, I'd make tracks. I know how utterly preposterous it all sounds."

"It does, but I am not leaving. Not yet anyway."

A silence fell over the table. Even Lillie was quiet. She was glad Peter had taken such a decisive step, impulsive and awkward as it was initially. Now she was fascinated to know just how accepting Samantha would be of her existence. That she stayed, Lillie thought, was a huge first step.

Peter broke the silence. "Sam, I want you to know there is no one else who knows about this. No one," he repeated emphatically. "There never will be. But if we're to be husband and wife, I don't know how I could keep such a thing from you."

Samantha squirmed a bit in her seat, her mind dizzy with a thousand thoughts. She did so want to be believe him as she so strongly believed *in* him. "Could I, uh, talk to her?" she asked hesitantly. What am I thinking, she asked herself.

Peter was startled. He looked at Lillie who happily agreed.

"Where do I look?"

"Lillie is on the chair to your right."

"I want to believe Peter, Mrs. Langtry," she said sweetly and softly. "I really do. But I need to understand."

Peter held up his hand. "Lillie's interrupting. I have learned she's very good at interjecting." Sam stared at him while he apparently listened to, at least through her eyes, what was an empty ice cream chair on his left. Nodding, Peter addressed Samantha, "When you spoke of understanding, Lillie was reminded of a a relevant quote." He turned toward his spirit friend. "Tell me and I'll pass it on."

Suddenly struck by the absurdity of this bizarre scene, Sam snapped, "Peter, please tell me this isn't some sort of sick joke?"

"No, Sam, it isn't," he said with vehemence, perhaps too much. Turning his attention back to the empty chair, he signaled Lillie to continue.

"Did you take Latin in school, Peter?"

"I did."

"Good. You will need it," she huffed. "It was Anselm of Canterbury who said, *'Neque enim quacro intellgere ut credam, sed credio ut intelligam. Nam et hoc, quia, nisi credidero, non intelligam.'* Considering the circumstances, I think it is most apt."

"Lillie, do you know what it means?"

"I haven't the slightest idea. However, I am certain it applies."

Peter turned his attention to Sam and shrugged. "Her, uh, quote was in Latin. I'm afraid I'm too far removed from my high school days to translate. She said it's from Anselm of Canterbury."

Sam's eyes brightened as she recited, *"'Nor do I seek to understand that I may believe, but I believe that I may understand. For this, too, I believe, that unless I first believe, I shall not understand.'"*

"How do you..."

"Know that particular quote?" she finished for him. "Growing up, family dinners always came with a course called discussion. These conversations often focused on faith. One evening, my father recited that passage. And not in Latin," she joked. "Well, Isabelle and I were intellectually precocious teenagers and we found the overuse of the word *believe* hysterical and felt it had all been said in the first sentence. Dad agreed and we all had a good laugh. However, it stuck with me all these years. I suppose because I find it wise." She reached across the table to take his hand. "I truly want to believe you, Peter."

"You're not ready to write me off as some off-center, whackadoodle fantasist."

She grinned and said, "Not just yet."

"Hey!" This modern day greeting, much like the "Salve" that the toga-clad Romans shouted to each other two thousand or so years ago, came from the mouth of Liz Handlery, clad in jeans, sandals and a faded red t-shirt. She was a sharp contrast to the other bistro patrons in their suits, tuxes, cocktails dresses and the occasional gown.

"I just sneaked down to get a coffee, she said, eyeballing the dressy crowd. "Pretend I'm not here."

"Care to join us?" her uncle asked cordially, but hoping she'd go on her way.

"Are you sure?" she asked, looking not only at her uncle and Sam but Lillie as well.

"Of course, we are," Sam generously said, pointing to the chair on her right where Lillie was roosting. It was not mischief on her part, merely forgetfulness that it was already occupied. Samantha simply saw an empty chair and it was closest to their new guest. When Liz, though, walked around to the other vacant seat, Sam suddenly remembered Lillie's position and wondered why Liz didn't take the proffered chair.

"So, what have you two been talking about?" she asked, putting her elbows on the table, her hands under her chin and her eyes darting back and forth between her uncle and Samantha.

"Oh, this and that," replied her uncle casually.

"Just reviewing the evening," added Samantha nervously.

Hands still propping up her head, she again glanced first at Peter and then Samantha, her eyes telling her far more than the cryptic answers they gave.

"OH MY GOD! You told her, didn't you?"

chapter 40

WHAT GOES HAND in hand with the warm, cozy decor of the Parisian-style Portside Bistro where our quartet of players were gathered is a welcome quietude. People read or, aware of the intimacy of the setting, keep the volume control of their conversations set on low. Thus, when Liz realized Peter must have told his future bride all, she forgot where she was and *OMG! You told her, didn't you?* exploded from her mouth; an impetuous action which caused heads to turn and a generated a rise in the level of what might best be called murmuring.

It was apparent to Peter that he was now in the company of two nettled women; Samantha who thought she was the only one who knew of Peter's spirit friend and Liz who assumed her uncle included her in the telling. Peter, clearly innocent on both counts, now saw it as his duty to unnettle the pair. Or do you denettle them?"

He first tended to his niece. "Liz, you're right. I did tell Sam about *my* involvement with Lillie."

His emphasis on my was not lost on Liz who asked, "You mean you didn't tell Samantha *everything?*"

Not a good question to ask aloud in Sam's presence, he thought. Samantha thought so too, asking abruptly, "What do you mean *everything?*"

Liz slumped in her chair. Why didn't I just get my coffee and scurry back to my stateroom, she asked herself. Well, I didn't, she thought, and now I have to deal with the consequences. Sitting up straight, she leaned in toward Samantha. WIth an earnest voice, she began to speak on Peter's behalf. "My uncle is telling you the truth when says he can see and hear a spirit called Lillie Langtry. However, I want to assure you, Sam, he is not crazy. He is not delusional. He is not mentally unstable. He really truly sees and hears her," she said, her eyes betraying her as she automatically glanced in the direction of Lillie, a gesture Ms Whitby duly noted.

Mrs. Langtry had been quite content to be the quiet observer, but now she was anxious to move things along, if for no other reason than she found being the object of their conversation and not being able to participate somewhat frustrating and tedious. Time to stir the pot, she decided. To that, with what one might call her Langtryian flair, she aired, "My dear Liz, you might as well fess up. I do think it best. Samantha strikes me as someone you can trust implicitly."

"I was just about to do that," Liz said with a subdued crispness. She wasn't snappish or brusque in her response, as Peter and Liz never rose to that level of irritation with their ghostly companion.

Samantha, having already been told by Peter that Mrs. Langtry was somewhere in the general vicinity of Liz's gaze, still asked, "To whom are you speaking?"

With a sheepish grin, Peter's niece replied, "I have been advised to explain my role in all this, Sam."

"By whom?"

"Lillie."

"You were advised by Peter's Lillie?" Samantha asked calmly, pointing in the direction of where the formidable fourth member of their table was perched.

"Yes! I'll get to that but first you should know everything my uncle has told you so far is the truth, Sam. You really are the first, and I'm sure knowing him as I do, the last person to know of his fascinating foray into the world of the supernatural," she promised, impressed with the manner in which she described her uncle's unique spiritual experience. "As for me, he didn't have to tell me about Lillie because she is someone I can see with my own eyes and hear with my own ears. He was tight-lipped about my involvement because he feels as I do, that's it's up to me to deal with it as I see fit. Frankly, as a doctoral candidate with plans of working at UC, I figured it would be wise to keep my own foray into the world of the paranormal to myself."

"I couldn't agree more," Samantha responded, knowing full well how her fellow professors, eccentric and wild-minded as many of them were, would react to such extraordinary news. "I assure you, your secret is safe with me."

Interestingly, the revelation that Liz also had a working relationship with Mrs. Langtry was far more impacting than Peter's earlier admission of ghostly goings-on in his life. With both admitting to the same mystic experience, Samantha was now more inclined to believe Lillie was there in their company. Like many, she had always been entertained by stories of the supernatural, even fascinated by them, though she thought it all speculative, suppositional and not deserving of serious consideration. Now though, after hearing the testimony of Peter and Liz, if those same notions were not now totally manifest in her mind, they came pretty darn close to being so.

Peter and Liz sat patiently, while the professor mulled. They did not have to wait long for her to return to them. Before words were exchanged, each looked at the other with warm affectionate glances; small smiles decorating their faces.

Samantha broke the silence with a question. Oh, to be sure, she had many but for the moment only this one seemed timely and important. Shifting in her chair and straightening her back with her handsome head held erect, she looked first at Peter and then his niece. Then, capturing both of them in her professorial gaze, she asked, "Is this an example of what I have to look forward to by marrying into your family?"

Their answer was immediate and louder than appropriate for the bistro's subdued environment. In unison, their heads shaking, Peter and Liz shouted, "No!"

Liz quickly added, "Trust me, Samantha, we're the world's most boring family."

"I don't know if I would call us *that,*" Peter said. "However, I can assure you that what has happened on this cruise is an anomaly." Pausing, he thought about their pleasant, unruffled Berkeley routine and finally admitted, "Well, maybe our lifestyle is somewhat undistinguished."

"Would you consider putting in your wedding vow a promise to keep it that way?" Samantha asked with a tone that was at once mischievous and serious.

"If that's what it takes to marry you, then yes, I promise you a life of quietude and a less than exciting routine," Peter replied, lifting his cup in a toast.

"I must admit, though, there's been something seductive about these last few days," she mused. "Perhaps, you can amend your vow to include the promise of an adventure every once in awhile."

"Certainly. Would you like them served up quarterly, semi-annually..."

Sam held up her hand. "No fixed schedule. We'll take them as they come."

"Well, don't rest up just yet," Peter advised. "This escapade is not over."

Liz laughed. "Will you listen to you two lovebirds. Look, I seem to have done enough here, so I'm off." With that, she sprang up, leaned over to kiss the top of her uncle's head and then gave Samantha's flushed cheek a peck. "Nightie night, Lillie," she sang, weaving her way through the bistro.

"Strange, isn't it? Now that I am aware of Mrs. Langtry, I'm disappointed I can't talk to her," she remarked wistfully.

"Of course, she can talk to me," Lillie huffed. "And that's exactly what I would like her to do. Peter, please inform Mademoiselle Whitby that I would like to take a stroll with her. We will have a tete a tete. Well, I suppose in our case, merely a tete. When we return, you can act as my spokesperson and I will respond to her teting," she said, giggling at her own cleverness.

Judging from the repeated nodding of his head, Samantha determined that Peter must have been listening to an obviously voluble Lillie. Her curiosity piqued, she finally decided to interrupt them. "Peter," she said sternly, "I find it very frustrating not to be part of whatever is going on between you and Mrs. Langtry.

"I'm sorry, Sam. I know it must be awfully annoying. Sometimes, I think it was preordained that Liz would be part of this experience for just that reason."

"So what was Mrs. Langtry going on about?" she inquired.

"She was responding to your comment about not being able to communicate with her. She finds it vexing as well and wants to do something about it. She was telling me that she would like the two of you to go off and have, in her words, a tete a tete."

"And just how on earth are the two of us supposed to have a talk?"

Peter gave one of those internationally known "I dunno" shrugs. "Sam, just go for a walk with her. Talk to her. Ask questions. Lillie said when the two of you return, she'll use me to give you her responses. Go on," he urged her. "Take a few minutes and see what happens. I'll wait here. If you're unable to get anything going, come right back. Just try it, please."

Professor Whitby rose slowly and hesitantly. Straightening the front of her desk, she let a smile slowly blossom. Looking down at Peter, she said, "I can't believe I'm doing this."

"Lillie is right there beside you. She says she'll remain on your left throughout."

I find it remarkable how readily accepting Peter, Liz and Samantha were to having a famous phantom in their midst. While they were wary, confused and questioning initially, all three became quite comfortable with their new reality in a relatively short period of time. I daresay, if I had signed them up for the Famous Ghost of the Month club and delivered a celebrity specter for just $21.95, they'd not only sign up but they'd roll out the welcome mat for whomever hovers at their front door on the first of every month. But, of course, there is no such company. I have made it clear that Lillie's visit had purpose and that was that.

The reward for Peter and Liz's speedy equanimity was the immediate companionship of a fascinating woman of another time and place. In earlier chapters we saw how their fondness for Lillie blossomed almost instantly. Now it was Samantha's turn, albeit, with a more difficult challenge as she could neither see nor hear Lillie to help her form that kind of immediate intimacy. However, to Samantha Whitby's credit, she gave it her best shot and was soon rewarded.

A stiff, bitingly cold wind welcomed the professor to the promenade deck. "I suppose these conditions mean nothing to you, Mrs. Langtry, but I'm freezing. Let's take our chat indoors," she suggested, shivering. It felt clumsy talking to Lillie. Until now, not counting the endless childhood chats with her favorite dolls, Samantha had only conversed with corporeal beings. She soon realized talking to someone you can't see, hear, smell or touch takes some getting used to.

Once back in the welcoming temperature-controlled environment of the Ocean Glamour, Samantha's goose bumps vanished as the pair made their way to the same card room where she and Isabelle just an hour ago had their sisterly love fest. Finding a corner table away from the door, she sat down where she could spot anyone entering or leaving. "Mrs. Langtry, Peter assured me you would remain on my left throughout, so I assume you are here," she said, pointing to the chair next to her. "So this is where I will direct my conversation."

There was an ensuing silence as Samantha was quite naturally programmed to pause for responses. Receiving none, she continued. "I would like to think it's appropriate for me to now call you Lillie. It appears my wish to talk to you has brought us to this place. Thank you for recommending we do this, Lillie. I promise I shall not waste it," she said determinedly.

And waste it, she did not. Samantha Whitby spoke for ten minutes; an outpouring of words thoughtfully and eloquently arranged. Lillie was impressed by her keen mind and touched by her sensibilities. In this articulate and delicate manner, Samantha first described to Lillie the mad onrush of extraordinary experiences to which she had recently been exposed. She then spoke lovingly and sweetly about Peter and her feelings for him. Finally, she explained to Lillie how she was doing her darndest to try and come to terms with it all, particularly the suddenness of their relationship. The more Samantha spoke, the more comfortable she became talking to Lillie. It was her lifetime love of literature that helped make it so. Just like she would form images in her mind of the characters in a book she was reading, Samantha created her version of Lillie Langtry. Soon, instead of seeing nothing but an empty chair on her left, she envisioned a beautifully gowned Victorian lady sitting next to her.

Lillie was quite taken by Samantha. She wished she had the same communicative skills she enjoyed with Peter and Liz. As she didn't, she realized it was imperative they return to the Portside Bistro where Peter could pass on her thoughts to her new friend.

Just as anxious to return to the bistro was Samantha who pulled away from the table and stood up. "Lillie, thank you again for suggesting this. I don't know whether there was anything I said that should remain between us. However, if I did, I trust you to know what Peter should or shouldn't know," she said in parting.

As she started to leave the quiet card room, an idea came to her which stopped her in her tracks, forcing her to return to the table. "Lillie, would you mind terribly if I asked you to do something for me?" Looking in the direction of where she last thought Mrs. Langtry to be situated, she continued in a halting manner: "I don't want you to think ill of me for this... It's just that if I...." Just like that, this articulate woman who spoke so fluidly and flawlessly for ten whole minutes was now hemming and hawing. "Let me see, how can I put this?" she asked aloud, embarrassed at her faltering, stammering manner.

Samantha might not have known how to properly or politely frame her inquiry, but Lillie knew what it was she desired. I assume you, the reader, do too. It was incontrovertible proof that a spirit was in her company. How better to verify Mrs. Langtry's presence than to have Peter repeat back to her something Samantha had only shared with Lillie.

Rising again, she smiled at the empty chair to her left and apologized for being such a shilly-shallier. Checking her watch, she was shocked at how long they'd been gone. "Oh dear, Peter's going to wonder what we've been up to," she sighed.

Peter, in fact, didn't give their lengthy absence a single thought as he was quite busy dealing with two visitors to his table. First to arrive was Dave Flannery who plopped down on what was Lillie's chair. He was now so well known by the ship's wait staff he needed only to use a prearranged sign language to order his beverage of choice. In this case, he caught the server's eye and, raising his left arm, made a fist and mimed removing a cap from a beer bottle.

"Why are you here all alone?" he asked Peter, wiping perspiration from his brow.

"I could ask the same question," Peter replied.

"A dancing time out was called," he said, his formal shirt wet from his rhythmic exertions. "Mary Pat, Malcolm and Isabelle are downstairs paging through this year's cruise catalogue. Did you know Malcolm's on his way to Italy with Isabelle in tow and they're planning to head to Venice for a Mediterranean cruise after they leave Florence? I'm impressed. Anyway, Mary Pat is bending his ear about what cruise we ought to take this fall." Dave grabbed the bottle off the tray before the server could place it on the table. A glass was not necessary. "God, I love this life. Hell, I don't even mind wearing this penguin suit," he exclaimed, dusting fake lint off his tuxedo jacket wherein was planted his catch-all Hermes pocket-square. Eyeing Peter staring at his bow-tie, he added, "I know what you're thinking, Ramsey. The answer is yes, I tied it myself." After a healthy gulp of an Alaskan pale ale, he asked, "So, I'm here for refueling. The bar's too crowded. What's your reason?"

"I'm waiting on Samantha."

"Not that you look lonely, but I'll keep you company until she gets back," he said magnanimously. "By the way, I get an e-mail back from my friend, Tommy Sullivan."

"Is that the police captain you talked about?"

"That's him. Anyway he promised me he'd be at the pier when we disembark and ready to act in case he's needed. Look, I hope you can somehow nail this Van Woort and get your painting, but if you don't, and there's a good chance of that, then like I told you earlier, I'll whisk Tommy off to the Buena Vista and treat him to a few Irish Coffees. I'll send you the bill, of course." he joked.

Visitor number two was their favorite Russian who seemed to have trouble staying in character. One moment he might be a well-connected, menacing mobster. Yet another, he cast himself as a good-hearted Moscow restaurateur with a love for iconography. For this supposed chance meeting, Anantoly Plushenko decided to be the former. Unlike Dave Flannery, he did not sit down, choosing instead to stand close enough to both men that they had to crane their necks to see his face. It was either that or stare into his taut, formally-attired midsection. It was obvious Plushenko knew the discomfort he was causing.

"You certainly have a way of messing with Van Woort. He just told me about the Masterson painting cockup," he said with barely a trace of a Russian accent. His cup of smugness was full to the brim. "Can't you just leave the guy alone?"

Flannery, rubbing his neck, glared up at his former dance opponent and barked, "Plushenko, either sit down or take a few steps back. You're giving me a headache."

Anatoly smiled widely, displaying two rows of professionally whitened teeth. He chose neither of Flannery's suggestions, preferring to remain noses to belly with them. "I will give you both much more than a headache if anything untoward were to happen to Van Woort before I get my icons. I thought I made myself clear on that point earlier today."

Flannery's reaction to Plushenko's threatening response was to lean back, a dangerous and risky thing to do on an ice cream chair. Folding his arms, his face flushed, his voice angry and full of sarcasm, he said, "Let me guess, Anatoly. We've come to that point in our relationship where you tell us you know where we live, where our kids go to school and what time our wives leave for the gym. I always thought that was a threat with a lot of meat on it."

Plushenko said nothing. Perhaps it was because the newspaper editor was teetering slightly, his chair now on its rear legs. Anatoly, along with Peter, realized that Flannery's balancing act was a precarious one.

Worked up, puffed up and his dander up, Dave continued his provocation: "Wait a minute, Anatoly, here's another one that gets tossed around in situations like this. You let us know in an almost comforting way that we have no idea what we're getting ourselves into."

"Um, that's very possible," Plushenko said in an almost comforting way.

"Yeah! Well, here's the deal," Flannery barked, wearing his best menacing scowl, "we don't care a fig about your Fukin icons. So there's no reason to keep threatening us."

The last word of that sentence didn't come out of Flannery's mouth sounding the way it should have. Instead, of being a staccato one syllable burst, it was a high-pitched, panicky wail inspired by an unplanned backwards descent. Peter jumped up and leaned across the table to retrieve him but to no avail. Flannery had only the Russian to prevent him from introducing the back of his head to the tile floor, a meeting rife with dire consequences. With lightening fast reflexes, Plushenko grabbed a fistful of Flannery's tuxedo jacket and effortlessly righted him.

Safe and sound but sporting a bruised ego, the embarrassed newspaper editor adjusted his tuxedo jacket and mumbled a curt thank you without looking up at the man who had just saved him from serious physical injury. Peter gave a little more voice and sincerity to his thanks. Plushenko returned their gratitude with an aw-it-was-nothing shrug.

Mrs. Langrty and Ms Whitby Lillie arrived back in the Portside Bistro just in time to witness Plushenko righting the newspaper man. By the time they reached the table, some semblance of order greeted them. Samantha commented on Anatoly's fast action which elicited another aw-it-was-nothing shrug. "I think it's best you not let these two gentlemen out of your sight," he advised before taking his leave. Peter rose and pulled a chair back for Samantha.

"There's much we need to talk about, Peter. Please eighty-six Mr. Flannery. Besides, he's sitting in my chair," Lillie huffed, prompting an immediate left ear tug from a somewhat flustered Peter who had just seconds ago come to the conclusion that he was simply to old for all this nonsense.

Fortunately, Dave decided to leave. "Sorry to be so inhospitable, Samantha," he said, slowly easing his way off the small chair, "but I need something stronger than a beer after dealing with that Russian pisspot."

"What has been going on here, Peter?" Samantha asked once Dave was out of earshot.

"I can tell you what happened, but I can only guess at why it happened," he replied. "In short, Plushenko stopped by the table to remind us that we better not do anything that would prevent him from getting his hands on his precious icons. He did this in a rather threatening manner. Personally, I think he enjoys playing the Russian gangster. When he saw us in the bistro, he decided to have some bully-style fun. However, he riled Dave who had some pointed things to say to him. Unfortunately, Dave in his ham-fisted way was leaning back in his chair while delivering them and... Well, you saw what happened. I'm not going to make too much of it, Sam. Our only aim is recovering Lillie's painting. I have no interest in Plushenko or the icons. I'm pretty sure he knows that."

"Thank you, Peter, for the explanation," Lillie said. "Now before we talk about the painting, I have a few things to say to Samantha."

Peter held up his hand. In a soft voice meant to not be heard beyond their table, he said, "Let's go to my stateroom. It'll be more comfortable and we can talk less surreptitiously."

Just outside the bistro was located a large map that charted the ship's progress. Checking to see what part of the Pacific Ocean's rugged coastline the ship might be sailing by were a colorfully attired and animated Dr. Freddie Florian and an understated, dour Benjamin Lytton-Crisp. Hoping to avoid a conversation, Peter put a finger to his lips, requesting Samantha not speak while they made there way past them.

Alas, stealth would not work. Just as they passed the pair, Freddie spun around and, with a veddy English accent, whooped, "What ho!" Benjamin, rolling his eyes, merely nodded to them. Peter waved a greeting and kept walking but to no avail as Freddie had stepped out, arms extended and rounded them up like an Australian sheepdog herding two errant sheep back into the fold.

"Peter, I'm so glad I found you," he said breezily.

"Hello, Freddie. Hello, Benjamin. You remember Samantha," Peter said. Looking to his left, he added cheekily, "And, of course, you remember Lillie Langtry?"

Freddie did a double-take that would have made a silent film director proud, his fleshy jowls shaking like jello. After a short pause, his florid face lit up even more. "Oh, you rascal. You remembered our little game. Well, I'm sorry to say we haven't any of her contemporaries with us at the moment. However, let me wish Mrs. Langtry a very good evening," he said, graciously bowing in her supposed direction.

Samantha was shaken and visibly so, a contrary reaction to the silliness that was going on. Peter immediately understood his mistake. With this current mischief, she probably thought everyone on the ship knew of Peter's relationship with the ghost of Lillie Langtry.

The buoyant dentist saved him. Placing his hand on Samantha's arm, he said, "Walk with me a bit. Judging from your reaction to Peter's introduction of Lillie, I'd say that naughty man hasn't told you about his attending one of our Victorian Happy Hours or our pretend friends. I will do that while Benjamin brings Peter up to date with the the latest news from London."

While they strolled toward the shops, Freddie jabbering away, Benjamin pulled a copy of an e-mail out of his inside coat pocket. As he unfolded it, he said, "Freddie and I just received this e-mail from Jasper. Actually, it was sent out to all the members. May I read it."

"Please," he said, taking his eyes off the two strollers and giving Benjamin his full attention.

Clearing his throat, a wooden Benjamin began to read. "'Dear boys, I have been entirely too lax in my duties as the resident member of our small club. So I thought I would let you all know that I finally got off my cute bum – At least, Reginald thinks it so – and gave our enchanting mews hideaway a thorough tidying up. My goal was to return this place to a condition where we could host *any* sort of visitor. I hope you don't mind but I also decided to replace some of the art that has recently decorated our walls. I know some of you said it made you feel uncomfortable. I'm confident you'll like what I've found to replace them. I can't stress enough that our clubhouse is now spotless. And just in time, as it turns out. It seems some museum officials and Scotland Yard plan a visit tomorrow. No doubt, it has to do with their on-going investigation into the missing Millais. All routine, I'm sure. Although, I do so wish I could help them. However, I fear they will go away knowing no more than they already do.' He ends it by writing, 'Desperately miss your company. Love and kisses, Jasper.'"

Peter realized that while the FBI wasted no time in contacting Scotland Yard, it wasn't soon enough. So who gave Jasper the heads-up, he wondered. "Sounds like there's nothing left in your clubhouse that can get anyone in trouble," he observed.

"I'm assuming he figured out how to put the originals back on the Tate's wall without being caught. Of course, if anyone can do it, Jasper can," he noted.

"The e-mail also suggests he doesn't have *A Jersey Lily*," Peter said. "At least, not in the house."

Benjamin cast him a sympathetic glance and said, "I suppose there wasn't much in the e-mail that will help you in recovering the painting."

"On the plus side, we now know one place where it isn't," he joked. "However, you must be pleased to know your clubhouse has been... What's the word? Ah yes, sanitized." Benjamin's stiffness loosened and he actually produced a smile, albeit, a small one. It was not lost on Peter who decided not to make too big a deal out of it. "I assume, though, somewhere down the road, Jasper might still face charges."

"It doesn't matter. Freddie and I have decided to resign. By the way, we have every intention of being accountable if it comes to that. We personally feel like a great weight has been lifted off our shoulders. Now Freddie and I can go back to being our jolly selves." Peter's bemused expression prompted Benjamin to add, "Sorry, this is my version of jolly. Best I can do. Believe me, Freddie has enough in the mirth department for both of us."

Freddie, still chattering on, returned with Samantha. "Peter," he hollered, "You're bride-to-be is absolutely enchanting. We have one more night aboard this luxury tub. Please, please, bring Samantha by about five for cocktails. You don't have to stay long. I know there's lots to do."

Peter, glancing at Samantha who gave him her thumbs-up to the invitation, replied, "We'd be delighted. See you at five."

As they walked to the steps, Freddie hollered after them, "And please bring Mrs. Langtry. It wouldn't be a party without her."

chapter 41

WE CAN NOT yet bid goodnight to that penultimate evening aboard the Ocean Glamour. So why a new chapter? Firstly, my amanuensis and I agreed that what follows demands it's own act, if you will. Besides, except for a few fuddyduddys, I doubt there will be much ruffling of feathers because I have played loose and easy with this chaptering business. As for my amanuensis, he will have to live with what ever biting critiques come his way. Thankfully, I'm immune from such excoriation as one of the blessed benefits of residing in this eternal community is complete imperviousness to criticisms, barbs, insults and other forms of opprobrium. As for you, the reader, a chapter change shouldn't be too big a deal. After all, the only physical labor involved on your part is turning a page or clicking a button or swiping a screen should you be on a Kindle, Nook or some other type of e-reader. That said, I do understand and respect the argument that a chapter's end is a convenient place for a reader to put a book down and get on with, as you like to call it, other stuff. Nevertheless, what's done is done here and there is no going back.

That said, let us now board the Ocean Glamour as it plies its way through moderately choppy waters northward along the Pacific Coast. It is time to give Lillie her due. She had been itching to present her side of her tete a tete with

Samantha ever since they returned to the Portside Bistro, only to be interrupted by first the foolhardy actions of Dave Flannery and then the chance meeting with Freddie and Benjamin. Now, finally, the three are settled in Peter's penthouse and she's raring to go.

"Peter, how fortunate you are to have Samantha in your life," she said, kicking off her official response to their earlier one-sided conversation. "As regards our chit-chat, I found it interesting that Samantha did not ask me any questions. I thought she would have have had dozens at the ready. She did talk to me, though, and at some length. She also spoke quite eloquently and passionately about her feelings for you."

Watching her beloved's head bob up an down while listening to Lillie, Samantha grew ever more curious. "What is she telling you, Peter?"

"Something I already know," he answered.

Samantha was sitting straight and proper on the sofa, nervously rubbing her hands together. "And what is that?" she whispered nervously.

"How very lucky I am to have you in my life. Lillie also seemed surprised you didn't have any questions for her."

Still a bit raw from her hurried introduction to the spirit world, Samantha's perturbation was evident in the her pointed tone, "Yes, as a matter of fact, I did dominate the conversation. It's a very easy thing to do when you're unable to get a response from the other person to whom you're addressing. In fact, it's quite maddening."

"Lillie said you spoke eloquently and passionately."

"Well, I did, I suppose," she admitted. "Because I trust you, Peter, I chose to believe Lillie was beside me. Still, it's not the same as knowing she was there." Samantha looked about the room and continued, "Peter, it's fine for you because you can see and hear her. You know for certain there's a third person in this room. I have to take it on faith she's here and, frankly, sometimes that's difficult."

Peter's response was thwarted by Lillie who said, "As regards that very subject, Samantha did have one question for me, but she had a difficult time framing it."

Peter repeated Lillie's observation to Samantha. "Oh, that. Yes, I had this idea that if I told Lillie something I knew you couldn't possibly know about me, and then she told you and you repeated it back to me, it would serve as a test as to her legitimacy."

"Legitimacy!" Lillie huffed. "Whatever does she mean by that?"

Unaware she was speaking, Samantha barreled on. "It was a crazy notion and I had a difficult time trying to ask it because I seriously thought it might offend Lillie."

"Why would you think that?" he asked.

"Lillie has every right to expect that my belief in her should be all that is required to know she exists," Samantha replied.

"That might work for God, but I'm another matter entirely," Lillie remarked. "Peter, go take a walk for sixty seconds. Before you go, though, instruct Samantha to tell me something you couldn't possibly know about her."

"Why? Samantha truly believes you're here," he argued, looking over at his future bride who was vigorously nodding her pretty head to indicate that was indeed the case.

"Indulge me," Lillie said.

After a minute's worth of pacing in front of the elevators, he returned and took a seat on the sofa next to Samantha. Taking her hand, he asked, "Did you work something out?"

"It is I to whom you should speak," Lillie said sharply. This was her game and she was going to play it her way. "Yes, Samantha has given me something. A warning, though;

tread carefully. Do not laugh." Peter nodded, signaling for her to continue. "She told me the name of her teddy bear, which, by the way, is with her on the cruise."

There was absolutely no fear of Peter laughing as he was no stranger to stuffed animals and the important role they play with some adults. One of his niece's most precious possessions was Beatrice the Bear, a scruffy, eight inch butterscotch bear, silky to the touch, that he and Liz found in the gift shop at the Globe Theater in London a few years ago. Liz's love of *Much Ado About Nothing* inspired her to name the bear after one of the play's main characters. He knew Beatrice the Bear was onboard as he discovered her stuffed in his suitcase when they boarded.

When Peter reported to Samantha that she had given Lillie the name of her teddy bear, she beamed, her winsome smile lighting up the penthouse. Just knowing Peter knew they talked about the bear was proof enough for her. The name would just be icing on the cake. Still, she was a little curious. "Did she mention my bear's name?"

"Not yet," he said. "Lillie has a sense of the dramatic and she's milking this for all it's worth."

"Of course I am," Lillie said nonchalantly. "Well, here it is then. The bear's name is Lavender. I'm nitpicking, I know, but I thought our professor could have come up with a more creative name."

Ignoring Lillie's disapproval of the bear's moniker, Peter turned to Samantha and announced, "His name is Lavender."

Thrilled that he knew, she nevertheless felt it necessary to point out a small error in his response. "Lavender is a she," she said gently. Little did she know this would be just the first of countless corrections as Peter was hopeless in his use of pronouns applied to anything other than humans. He was one of those who grew up thinking a dog was a he, a cat was a she and all stuffed animals were either he or it.

"Got it. Lavender is a girl bear," he said aloud hoping it would stick in his memory. "Well, I'm looking forward to meeting hi.... Her."

"This isn't a deal breaker?" she asked sheepishly.

"What isn't?"

"Lavender."

"Absolutely not," he said. "Unless, of course, you drive around with forty or more stuffed animals in your car's rear window. Then we might have to talk."

She laughed. "No, Lavender is an only child. I was in Sonoma one weekend a few years back and in the hotel's shop there were these adorable, lavender bears. They even smelled of lavender. I couldn't resist getting one. Now there's not a scintilla

of a lavender scent and her color has faded, but she's mine and she's wonderful company."

Pointing to Lillie, he said, "Speaking of lavender, Sam, that's Lillie's hue. How appropriate you decided to use your bear's name for this experiment."

"I don't mean to quibble, Peter, but I do wish we could devise a more suitable way of conversing," Lillie said. "I'm certain it's a nuisance for you, having to repeat everything I say, and I'm certain it's just as frustrating for our dear Samantha. Consider that the poor woman is now forced to talk to the mere idea of someone rather than the real thing. Or at least someone who has a few parts of the real thing," she giggled, aware of her minimal physical accessories

Like Lillie, they wished for the very same. However, no one had a clue as to how to make that happen. But I, Theodomicles, did. I saw no reason why I couldn't expand her minimal list of mortal companions from two to three as it required no heavy lifting on my part. Just a snap of the fingers, so to speak. I should admit that, besides helping Lillie, there were other reasons I got involved. Firstly, the last day at sea and the morning of disembarkation will see our group in constant contact with each other. Indeed, how inconvenient and irksome it would prove to be with Samantha as odd man out. Secondly, it's important, I think, for Samantha, Peter and Liz to leave the ship with a shared experience. I don't think I'm ruining the storyline by telling you that they will, as you say in fairy tales, live happily ever after, and Liz will remain close to them for all those bliss-filled years. Imagine how difficult it would be if one of them did not have the opportunity of having known Lillie in the flesh, metaphorically speaking. Finally, this action would save my amanuensis from dealing with the challenge of having to first pen Lillie's lines and then repeat them via Liz and Peter. I did, though, decide this time to pay more careful attention to the timing of their introduction. If you remember, Peter had to deal with a room full of the ship's officers when he first met Lillie, and Liz, you may remember, rocketed out of the Italian restaurant making every effort to hit high C when I brought them together. This time, I wished to make the meeting less dramatic, less emotionally messy.

It was getting late and Samantha was winding down. With sleepy eyes, she glanced at her watch; the first action one usually takes in suggesting their departure is imminent.

Her gesture didn't go unnoticed by Peter who wasn't ready to part company. "Sam, you're welcome to stay here," he whispered, even though he was aware that it was an awkward offer, particularly if you buy into the theory of two's company, three's a crowd. Thus, knowing the invitation would not be accepted, he decided to get silly. "You know how dangerous these hallways can be late at night, especially on a rowdy ship like this one."

"Oh, really," Samantha said, grinning and wondering what was coming next.

"Yes, really. You never know when you might encounter a gang of drunk octogenarians eager to corner you and force you to look at pictures of their grandchildren."

Shaking her head and laughing at what she imagined a scene like that might look like, she countered, "I'm relying on you, my dear sir, being the consummate gentleman and escorting me to my stateroom."

A yawn she could no longer stifle prompted Peter to prepare for her exit. Standing in front of her, he extended his hand to help her rise from the sofa. Peter's heart sang when he looked at her. He loved everything about her; her understated but confident manner, the dextrous way she moved and her inexhaustible inventory of extremely pleasant facial expressions. It seemed as if there was one for every occasion.

There was plenty more about this university professor that had Peter swooning so. Samantha Whitby was an intelligent, solicitous and resolutely cheery woman whose sense of wonderment was fine-tuned. Let me assure you there is not a cosmetic enhancement on the market – over-the-counter or prescribed – that will improve a woman's looks more than the aforementioned qualities. That is not to say skin-deep doesn't have its place in your temporal world. Peter, of course, understood her transcendent attractiveness and appeal. But he also found her physically fetching and very sexy; assertions she would immediately pooh-pooh, as she did not consider herself sexy. In fact, she felt awkward and almost little girlish around the topic. That said, though, she couldn't wait for them to get beyond mere kisses and hugs. Dare I say Peter had her beat in that department by aces and spades.

As they stood together by the sofa, hands clasped, Samantha leaned in with closed eyes and kissed Peter. It was a sweet, lingering peck. When they separated, he nodded his head in Lillie's direction. "We're not alone," he pointed out.

"Don't let me stop you. I'm really enjoying this," Lillie said. "It's so much better than late night TV."

Peter's reminder they had company made Samantha cringe with embarrassment. "Sorry, I forgot. Out of sight, out of mind. That's my only excuse. I should say a proper good night to Lillie before I leave." Surveying the penthouse, she asked in a hushed voice, "Where *is* she, Peter?"

He peered over his shoulder. "On the edge of the bed, directly behind me and in front of you."

I took that as my cue to do what I could to make these last few hours on the Ocean Glamour more accommodating for all. I counted on Samantha's tiredness to help lessen the shock. Even so, it was a visibly rattled Samantha staring open-mouthed at Lillie that proved the deed was done.

Peter was aware something odd had happened as Samantha suddenly nudged closer to him, her body trembling, her moist hands squeezing his to the point of discomfort. And just as fast, she let go his hands and backed away just enough to, as I mentioned, stare over his right left shoulder at Lillie. Pointing, she asked, "Didn't you tell me Lillie is this amorphous form with a lavender hue?" Her voice was tremulous and she was shaking.

"Yes, that pretty much describes her," he replied, looking into her eyes that were wide with alarm. "Sam, what's wrong?"

Taking a deep breath, she whispered, "Peter, I *see* her! There is this triangular, cloudy mass right where you said Lillie was positioned. And it's lavender!"

That shocking discovery sent Samantha scurrying once again back into the safety of his arms. She hugged him tightly, comforted by his physical support.

Lillie, while initially taken aback by this unexpected development, was ecstatic about the possibility of having a new friend with whom to play. But, she thought, there was one more hurdle to jump before that could happen. "You can see me," Lillie said aloud. "I am overjoyed. Now I pray, my dear, you can you hear me as well."

Her caring, warm voice, rather than creating another aftershock for Samantha, did just the opposite. Hearing Lillie's words calmed her; enough so that she relaxed her hold on Peter and lifted her head from his shoulder. WIthout a word, she moved around him, sitting down on the edge of the bed next to the lavender apparition that was Lillie. "Yes, I *can* hear you," she said timorously. "I can see you as Peter sees you and I can hear you as Peter hears you. I am..." She paused, unable to find any word in the English language – and she knew many – that could properly describe what she was feeling. Finally, selecting one, she gushed, "I am overwhelmed."

"As am I," Lillie seconded.

"Me too," Peter thirded. This now unanimous vote signified I did something rather extraordinary in their eyes, and just like with any successful magic trick, after the oohing and aahing subsided, their thoughts were focused on the wizardry behind it.

"How did it happen?" LIllie marveled. "I certainly have no powers that could have made it so. I wished it, of course, but I've had that wish before and nothing happened. And as to the why of it, I'm rendered speechless."

"You speechless. I don't think so," Peter joked.

"Regardless, it is very perplexing," she repeated, ignoring his teasing. "You see, Peter, there is a definite purpose to our relationship. I am here to see that *A Jersey Lily* is returned to the Tate. I can't do it alone. You have hands with opposable thumbs to hold it. I don't. Thus, we have been paired."

"I understand that," Peter said. "But then how do you explain Liz?"

"Ah, your niece," she sighed. "A purpose there as well. Liz's involvement, I believe, was meant to assure you that you weren't going mad; to relieve you of thinking you were hearing voices and seeing things others didn't. Please, don't misunderstand me. I am more than delighted to have made Samantha's acquaintance. It's just that her unexpected arrival into our intimate clique is altogether baffling."

Even though the novitiate of this intimate clique, as Lillie dubbed it, Samantha shook off the usual newcomer's hesitancy to participate. "Growing up, my mother would often explain the unexplainable by telling Isabelle and me that it was God's plan in action. It was one of several Momism's I thought would forever remain in my childhood. Now I hear myself using all of them," she laughingly admitted with a shrug and warm smile. "So my response to this... This miracle, if you will, is God's plan in action."

Peter undid his bow-tie, opened the top button on his formal shirt and leaned back into the sofa. Stretching his arms, it was his turn to stifle a yawn. "I think it's as simple as that."

"And I, my dears, agree with you both," Lillie said happily. "If it isn't God's plan, then one has to ask whose is it, and I don't wish to consider that."

"Not at this hour anyway," Peter said, rising and approaching Samantha. "Do you mind being escorted back to your stateroom by a man with his bow-tie undone?"

"I can't guarantee he'll get the same passionate parting I would reserve for someone fully attired," Samantha replied with what was to Peter's eyes a beguiling grin.

"I have heard enough romantic silliness for one evening," Lillie said as she floated toward the verandah. "Peter, before you leave, there's one bit of business that needs tending to. You were going to phone Howard and let him know just how disengaged we are with anything that has to do with Charles Van Woort."

"I thought I left him with that impression the last time we spoke," he said into the mirror while making a half-hearted attempt at knotting his bow-tie for the second time that evening.

"This time, perhaps, you need to be more emphatic. Oh, and you must convince him to pass whatever you say on to Naomi."

Giving Samantha the just-a-sec signal, Peter went over to the bedside table and picked up the phone. Luckily, the sometimes swaggering but always bald Howard Newton was in residence. "Oh, it's you."

"Have you talked to Naomi tonight?" he asked directly, noticing Lillie was now close to him and his phone ear.

"No, I was just about to call her. Why?"

"I have a huge favor to ask. I know you have a big SUV," Peter said. "Liz and I need a ride. She broke up with the guy who brought us to the ship, so he's out. Before I try to make other arrangements, I thought if Naomi was picking you up, we might bum a ride."

"No, she isn't," he said glumly. "She's still in New York. Says she'll be there for another week. Visiting old girl-friends, she said."

"Sorry, Howard. I know you were hoping to put a lot of things right when you got home."

"I may fly out to New York and surprise her," he said with little if any enthusiasm.

"When you talk to Naomi, tell her I'm sorry for dragging you into this," Peter said, quickly trying to rustle up something extra to more strongly suggest he was through with Van Woort and the art world in general. Then it came to him. "Listen, Howard, tell your wife when we're all back on dry land, we'll go to dinner and I'll explain my wrong-headed decision to..."

"Your bone-headed decision," he interjected.

"All right, bone-headed..."

"Might as well throw in idiotic, uninspiring, puzzling..."

"HOWARD!"

"Easy does it, Peter. It's fun finally being able to mess with you."

"As I said, I feel bad I got you involved in all this. But I feel good knowing that what I thought was something turned out to be nothing."

Lillie whispered in his ear, "Oh, that's good, Peter."

"I have admit, though, I have had a good time," Howard confessed. "A little weird but nevertheless enjoyable."

"I'm delighted to hear you say that," Peter said. "I know, Howard, I kidded you about this, but I have to admit you did acquire some real swagger. Some, dare I say it, aplomb."

"What's that second word?" he asked, always suspicious of Peter.

"Much the same as the first. It's another way of saying poise or self-assurance."

"Well, I'm definitely a changed man," he boasted, the tone of his voice less woebegone and now more authoritative. "Now I think I will try some of that new aplomb stuff on Naomi and see if I can woo her back into the kennel."

"Howard, you should really stay away from metaphors."

"Up yours, Ramsey."

Upon hearing the phone's click, Lillie muttered, "There's that strange goodbye again. Is it unique to your radio profession?"

"Something like that," he said.

That bit of business complete, Samantha bid Lillie goodnight. "I have no idea what my dreams will be tonight, but they certainly can't top this. I so look forward to seeing you tomorrow. Good night, Lillie," she said affectionately.

With equal warmth, Lillie replied, "Up yours, Samantha."

chapter 42

EVEN ON THE last full day of a cruise, a luxury liner, expressly designed to spoil its passengers rotten, happily rolls out its usual excess of pleasurable pursuits, gastronomic treats and the cocktail of the day. Guests, however, are forced to moderate their intake of these indulgences as they must also make time for those unpoetic tasks unique to the day. This is the time when they, willingly or unwillingly, must prepare for the following morning's no-nonsense, please-get-off-the-ship disembarkation. Guests get into all sorts of stuff on this final day on the high seas, and none of it is what you might call fun. For example, many – perhaps too many of them – will try to get one or more loads of wash done. There will no doubt be a few laundry room dustups. This is because group laundering, much like any democracy, is a messy, uncivil business. Another grim activity involves a guest's charges. As the ship sends out a preview of what they have already spent, many will scurry to the front desk and dutifully stand in line with other comrades, anxious to settle or dispute their account. Could I really have had all those Pina Coladas by the pool, they will ask themselves. Still others, realizing they have unused shipboard credits; funny money that disappears if not spent, will hit the shops and spa in a last-minute, frantic attempt to use them all up. This means buying, while not necessarily kitschy items, stuff they really don't want or need and will probably foist off on a friend or family member as a gift when they get home. In most cases, those recipients will probably re-gift them. In the end, this stuff may change hands four or five times before finally finding a permanent home. Finally, as a cruise is not carry-on, everyone will pack rather large suitcases. Packing is a complex operation, calling for considerable strategizing as all luggage except for what one lugs off the ship must be outside the ship's staterooms before midnight.

You must agree there's not a lot there to warrant our further attention. However, this particular day was not without its curious moments as regards our cast of characters. The first curious and extended moment came about because of Liz Handlery's choice of how to start her day. Fresh from a dreamless night's sleep and anxious to burn some of the calories accrued at the previous evening's Dosynk-hosted Italian feast, she made a bee-line for the Ocean Glamour's well-equipped gym. Her plan was forty-five sweaty minutes on a treadmill and then a breakfast of fruit and a soft-boiled egg with Lillie, Samantha and her uncle. Her spartan breakfast, while well-intentioned, went awry at the last minute. She was now staring gluttonously at a golden brown waffle slathered in butter and syrup. Ever anxious to dive in, she still waited, as the news she was about to share with the table came first.

"Guess who I saw in the gym working out together?" Barely pausing, she answered her own question, "Yurk Dosynk and that Russian's tall piece of arm candy."

"Arm candy?" Lillie asked.

Samantha, forgetting the spirit's discreet presence, blurted, "It's another one of our modern day idioms, Lillie. Arm candy describes a woman in the company of a man who wishes no more from her than her sexual attractiveness."

"Good God, Sam, that definition is like right out of the OED," Liz laughed. She hurriedly took a bite of the waffle, wiped her mouth and was about to continue when she suddenly looked up at Peter, then Lillie, then Samantha. Slapped in the face with the sudden realization Lillie had a new friend, she joyously cried out, "Wow! I prayed last night for just this. This is so cool for so many reasons."

Samantha Whitby broadcast one of her wider smiles. "I'm thrilled. No, more than thrilled, Liz. In fact, there are no words to describe how I feel. Anyway, continue with your story."

Liz let go her hand and directed it back to the fork which was waiting patiently with a generous piece of waffle attached. "So after their workout, looking very serious, Svetlana bent his ear for about ten minutes. After she left, he approached me. Knowing how farouche he is... Don't you just love that word. It means shy around company, if you're wondering." Glancing around the table, it was apparent the word was familiar to all. "Okay, so it's new to me. Anyway, I started jabbering; telling him how impressed I was with their strenuous workouts." Liz looked up from her breakfast plate, her eyes unable to hide the excitement of her next bit of gossip. "You are not going to believe this. Yurk said, and I'm quoting him word for word, 'Thank you. My daily schedule is muscles in the morning, mind in the afternoon and merriment in the evening.' Then his face lit up and he said, "I say, don't you think Svetlana is proportional perfection?'" She sat back in her chair to await their reactions.

"I didn't know he spoke English," Peter said all to casually, taking a bite of a pineapple spear.

"I didn't know he spoke at all," Lillie remarked, understandably not taking a bite of anything.

"The thing is, gang, he is extremely articulate," she explained. "And the odd thing is he sounds like he grew up to the manor born. Tio, remember that radio character you used to. That old English lady. What was her name?"

"You mean Lady Millicent Mountbutton from Piddling-on-Thames?"

"That's her. Well, Yurk sounds like he could be her son. Anyway, he said something to me about wanting our help."

"Our help?" Peter, Sam and Lillie chorused.

"Something like that, yes. Anyway, he said he'd explain everything."

"When does he plan on doing this?" Peter asked, chuckling at his niece's dizzying explanation of her morning adventure.

Liz glanced over her uncle's shoulder and spotted the muscular Yurk headed to their table carrying a tray holding a breakfast for four. "How about right now."

Yurk set his plates down whereupon a waiter immediately scooped up the tray. Taking his seat, he quietly surveyed the eggs, sausage, bacon, fruit, pastry, waffle and yogurt. They could not tell he was saying a well meant grace. Finally, gratitude expressed, the hungry Adonis was poised to attack the first meal of the day. Holding his fork at the ready, he addressed his table mates: "I'm at a loss really. I don't know how to give this breakfast it's proper due and also explain the unusual situation I now find myself in."

Peter marveled at what he'd just heard. As Liz had reported, Yurk did, indeed, sound like the dashing young lord of the manor. "Dig in," he told him. "We all have breakfasts to finish. We'll talk later."

"A smashing idea," Yurk enthused, taking a sizable chunk of chicken-apple sausage. His face confirmed the bite met with his approval.

They ate in silence. Little murmurs of satisfaction emanating from Liz and Yurk prompted Peter and Samantha to head back to the buffet where each grabbed half a waffle.

They all finished in unison. Uniformly, napkins went to mouths and then back to laps. First to speak was Yurk, his voice a rich, velvety baritone. "I think the first piece of business is for me to explain why I have been silent and sullen these past eleven days."

Speaking for the table, Peter said, "Trust me, Yurk, we are all ears."

"Grandfather and I are always wagering on this and that. Because I'm known for my loquaciousness, he bet me I could not go the entire cruise without talking up a storm."

"You mean you don't have to be totally silent?" Liz asked, thinking that if she had met this version of Yurk early on in the cruise, she would have become left-handed on the spot.

"Good heavens, no," he exclaimed. "Merely taciturn. That's tough enough. Inka is the judge and if she determines that I have kept my utterances to an absolute minimum, I win."

"Win what?" Samantha asked.

"The thrill of having bested the other person," he replied cheerily. "Anyway, I decided the way to handle this was to become a sulking introvert. I must say I have enjoyed myself. Although, staring at my biceps, which I thought gave my character some added gravitas, became extremely tedious. But on the positive side, that benign gesture along with a bored but menacing scowl did keep people from chatting me up."

"The cruise isn't over yet," Peter reminded him.

"The bet is unimportant now. There are more important things to deal with," he said. "All will be well, though. Grandfather will win and he'll gloat mercilessly for a couple of days. I'm used to it."

"Yurk, why do you sound like a member of the Royal Family?" Liz asked.

Her question clearly rattled him. "I do? You mean to say it's still too posh?"

"Just a tad."

"I've been working on it, you know. Look, here's the thing. My father and I lived in London for two years when I was a teen. I took to English like a swan to the Serpentine. I just love the language and the regional accents. But it was Received Pronunciation, or the Queen's English as it is commonly called, that won my heart. As regards the poshness, I've been trying to tone it down. You know, get rid of some of the swank. Don't want to be mistaken for a toff," he laughed.

"Liz said you wanted to talk to us about something regarding Svetlana. How did you two meet?" Peter asked.

"In the gym. Eleven days ago. Initially, we were wary of each other. I'm Kwyrki. She's Russian. I was playing Yurk the Jerk. She was pretending to be the supercilious girlfriend to a faux gangster. We'd smile and nod but that was about it. Then the morning after the dance contest everything changed. Feeling genuinely bad about their boorish behavior, she told me who they really were and what at the time she thought they were up to. That's when I confessed to not being who I was but that I wasn't up to anything except trying to win a silly bet. Since that morning, we've become very close," he said, his expression pellucidly moony. "I'd do anything for her."

Liz couldn't resist. "Is she left-handed?" she asked.

Yurk grinned. "Of course she is. That's the first question my grandfather asked when I told him about us yesterday. He's very approving of our relationship."

"What about Plushenko?" Peter asked. "How do you think he's going to feel about you and Svetlana?"

"Actually, if we can get him out of this bizarre mess he's created, he'll be over the moon about it." Looking at three friendly faces all expressing puzzlement, Yurk was anxious to end their curiosity. "I have already admitted to being a rather chatty chap. That said, I will edit this as best I can. However, it's one of those start-at-the-beginning kind of stories."

"How about starting with who they really are," Liz requested, still aglow from Yurk's pleasing words.

Yurk took a deep breath and began: "Anatoly is, in fact, Svetlana's uncle. Her mother, his older sister, was a professional ballroom dancer. A champion, in fact. While there are no other professional competitors in the family, all of them are superb dancers. David Flannery and his wife might like to know they beat two of the best amateurs in Russia."

"I'll be sure to tell him," Peter said.

"Svetlana is a model but hardly financially successful. She supplements her freelance income working as a hostess in her uncle's restaurant. Anatoly already told you she's a martial arts expert and that's true. I've been on the receiving end of some of her practice moves. Finally, as Mr. Fitzroy pointed out, Anatoly is a well-respected authority on Russian icons. Svetlana said Russian icons are to her uncle what expensive shoes are to a New Yorker.

"So, why are they are on this Alaskan cruise, you ask. This is truly fascinating. According to Svetlana, her uncle loves to roll out the red carpet for the Russian mobsters who frequent his Moscow restaurant. One of these regulars, Spartak Kozlov, was always ordering wines with four digit prices. One day, a visiting American tells Anatoly he represents a high-tech billionaire in Silicon Valley who is selling his private wine collection for $500,000. He tossed around names like Petrus, Sassicaia and Domaine Romanee-Conti as well as some valuable New World wines. Thinking he was doing Kozlov a favor, Anatoly offered to act as the middleman if the mobster wanted the collection. It was all a con. Most of the wine was counterfeit plonk. There was about $50,000 worth of the real stuff which Kozlov kept. The rest he gave back to Plushenko with a bill for $450,000. Anatoly has until the end of this month to pay up or Kozlov takes his restaurant instead. That will hurt Svetlana because she has a small piece of the place. It's her only savings."

"I gather there's no such thing as caveat emptor in this case," Peter remarked.

"With a goon like Kozlov?" Yurk laughed. "He probably thinks caveat emptor is a dental procedure."

"Are they in physical danger as well?" Liz asked with concern, her mind imagining all sorts of horrible things that could happen to them.

"You mean the Russian version of knee-capping, cement shoes... That sort of thing?" He shook his head and replied, albeit not too confidently, "I don't think so."

"So how is coming on an Alaskan cruise going to help him come up with $450,000?" Peter asked.

"Just when you think this story can't get weirder, it does. The cruise came about thanks to another of Plushenko's shady customers. Shortly after the wine deal went south, Plushenko was approached by Ilari "Big Wolfie" Volkov who knowing of his love of icons told him a New York art dealer was looking to unload a couple of Russian icons with questionable provenance. Volkov had done business with Van Woort but he had no personal interest in icons. It was rumored their religious meanings intimidated him. Anyway, he told Anatoly he thought the price Van Woort wanted was very low and Plushenko should jump at the chance to buy them. So Wolfie contacted Van Woort who, always on the lookout for the right kind of buyer for the wrong kind of art, told Volkov he was on a couple of Alaska cruises with his auction business. He suggested Plushenko join him on this specific cruise and they could get to know one another."

"So Mr. Plushenko, thinking he can resell the icons and make enough to pay off his debt, comes on the cruise," Samantha theorized, surprising everyone because they didn't expect to hear anything from the new kid on the block.

"Exactly," Yurk replied. "Svetlana said he contacted an acquaintance who was a higher-up at a well-funded museum in Moscow. They agreed on a price that would allow him to pay off Kozlov and still have a few quid to spend as he wishes. As for Svetlana's involvement, the only thing she knew at the time was they were on the cruise to buy the icons. From the beginning, she was uneasy about him playing a mobster, but he explained that that was how he was described to Van Woort by Ilari Volkov. She also knew her uncle was having the time of his life pretending to be a Russian goon. At that time she had no knowledge of the counterfeit wine cockup and the $450,000." Yurk took a sip of cold coffee and continued, "Last night her uncle whom she described as despondent told her everything."

Peter checked his watch. The problem was it wasn't on his wrist. He remembered he was trying to wean himself off the timekeeper. Clearing his throat, he asked what it was that forced Plushenko to come clean.

Yurk tried and failed to suppress a smile. "In a word, Facebook."

Sam burst out laughing. Liz initially looked puzzled, then began to laugh. Peter remained baffled.

"Social media did him in?" Samantha asked.

Yurk nodded. "It did, indeed. Plushenko's Facebook page reveals a man who is far more docile and charming than the strutting, wise-cracking Moscow bad boy Van Woort knew. Svetlana had warned her uncle his fondness for pretending he was a gangster would prove to be his undoing. What I can't understand is why Van Woort waited until last night to do a computer search."

I have an answer. Quite simply, it didn't occur to him. Why it didn't had everything to do with his age. You see, in one's formative years, there is an intuitive embrace of new technology. Had the art dealer been two decades younger, he would have been on-line typing in Plushenko's name seconds after shaking hands with the man. As it was, it wasn't until the penultimate night of the cruise before it even dawned on him to do a search.

This time Yurk checked the time. Fortunately, he did have a watch on his wrist.

"Let me wrap this up. You can imagine Van Woort's reaction when he discovered this Russian fraud who excelled at scaring the bejesus out of him was no more a threat than a TV game show host," he said, smiling at his clever comparison.

"What exactly happened last night?" Liz asked before anyone else could.

"First you must remember Van Woort knew he had to tread carefully because Plushenko came highly recommended by Volkov and he didn't want to do anything to harm their relationship. So last night, he called Anatoly and explained in an evenhanded tone how he'd found him on Facebook. Then he explained to him that if a renowned expert such as he was wanted the two icons, it must mean they are worth far more than what he was asking. He then informed him that he was doubling the price. When a now deflated Anatoly told him he couldn't possibly meet that price, Van Woort told him he wasn't short of potential buyers. Then he added insult to injury by asking if he could friend him."

Peter realized he had now been exposed to three different versions of Anatoly Plushenko and his antics. Firstly, there was the general impression the Russian gave everyone leading up to and during the dance competition. Secondly, there was the new and improved Plushenko who came a visiting to urge them to do nothing that would keep Van Woort from going to New York to sell him the icons. Now comes this account. Peter had a strong feeling Yurk's, or rather Svetlana's narrative, was the most fact-based. If Flannery were here, he thought, he'd probably think it all just another whacko scheme thought up by his dance opponents.

"Peter, you look awfully pensive," Yurk observed. "I daresay, I can't blame you."

"Just trying to piece it all together, Yurk," he muttered. Then in his mental wanderings, he remembered Lillie's painting. "Did Svetlana say anything about the deal her uncle had with Van Woort to buy the Millais painting?" he asked.

"According to Svetlana, that was a legitimate offer and he did have a way to pay for it," he replied. "When he learned *A Jersey Lily* was available, he contacted Ilari Volkov who jumped at the chance of owning it. Volkov instructed him to buy it for him. Anatoly, thinking this was a great opportunity to pad his criminal bona fides, told Van Woort he'd buy it but he never mentioned Volkov's involvement."

"It's quite a story. However, I honestly don't see what we can do to help. It seems to me that Plushenko's life or death problem is... What's the name of that man to whom he owes $450,000?"

"Spartak Kozlov."

"Yes, Kozlov. How can we, short of loaning him money which we don't have, do anything to help?"

Yurk held up a beefy hand and interjected, "As regards that problem, Svetlana is meeting with my grandfather," he said. "He has an idea as to how to get them out of that particular mess."

"Care to share it with us?" Peter asked.

Yurk shrugged. "I don't know the details of his plan yet, but there is one thing my grandfather wants me to do."

Liz, perplexed because to her the only crucial problem seemed to be Anatoly's life-threatening financial difficulty, asked, "And this is something you're asking us to help you do?"

Almost shyly, Yurk replied, "Yes, Liz, it is."

"So, what does your father want you to do that requires our assistance?" she asked smartly.

"He wants me steal the icons."

Again the chorus rose up as one voice. "Steal them!"

Yurk took a final sip of his coffee. Good-humoredly, he said, "Yes, steal them. If you prefer a juicier turn of phrase, we can snatch them, filch them, pinch them, liberate them..." Running low on alternative phrases, he looked at his small audience and said slowly and with genuine sincerity, "How about *recover* them? I'm sure that sounds better and less felonious."

Liz was the first to ask and as soon as she did, she regretted it. "Okay, so what do you mean by recover?"

Yurk laughed and said, "It means we are back to square one. We steal them! Look, her uncle clearly didn't think this through very carefully. Even if Van Woort had never found him on Facebook, his plan still wouldn't work. When he discovered Van Woort had in his possession – excuse my French – the Fukin icons, he knew instantly they were truly valuable and historic. He also knew they'd been spirited out of Russia decades ago, but from whom he couldn't recall. That was the good news. The bad news came when he decided to do an Internet search. Much to his chagrin, he discovered they had been stolen from the very museum he hoped would write him a big check for the icons. Now all he can look forward to is maybe a small reward, a few handshakes and three cheers for he's a jolly good fellow for returning what rightfully belonged to them in the first place."

"So why do you want steal them?" Peter asked directly. "And, by the way, you know as well as I do that in order to steal them, we first have to know where they are.'"

"And they are not on the ship," said a heretofore quiet Lillie. "Trust me, I have looked extensively while searching for my painting."

Instinctively three heads out of four jerked in her direction and then just as quickly snapped back. This strange choreographed group gesture somehow failed to get Yurk's attention.

"They are not on the ship," Peter repeated.

"You're probably right," Yurk grumbled. This time it was his turn to be pensive. After a few second's pause, in a soft, gentle voice that contradicted his muscular physical presence, he pleaded, "I really could use some help here. If my grandfather wants them, it has to be for all the right reasons." He looked at his audience and asked, "Any ideas?"

Peter surprised the table by exclaiming, "Yes, I have an idea."

chapter 43

ACTUALLY, LILLIE WAS the first out of the gate to shout, "I have an idea!" Even though it was delivered with her usual spirited enthusiasm, Yurk was deaf to it. What he did hear was Peter's more restrained, less certain version. For some reason Peter had felt compelled to echo Lillie even though, awash with feelings and hunches, his mental cupboard was bare of clever notions, plots, plans or schemes. Still, he got all the credit from Yurk who was genuinely pleased they were seemingly onboard with helping him put the Fukin icons in Dosynk hands.

Before the young man could ask him to elaborate further, Liz raised her hand and asked for the floor. "I'm not a prude," Peter's niece stated for the record. "Far from it. In fact, I have even been known to use the F-word on occasion, and I might add my timing, tone and delivery are usually impeccable. That said, I have a suggestion. Is it possible we can temporarily rename these icons while they continue to be a topic of discussion among us?"

I found it fascinating that Liz would rather not hear the legitimate name for the stolen icons spoken. Let me assure you that cannot happen here in Eternity for there is no need for language as you know it. All temporal tongues are checked at the door and tossed into a spiritual shredder.

Thus, a Norwegian, a Sicilian and a Bosnian can happily chat away, forever free of the nuances and myriad rhetorical influences that are part and parcel of every tongue. That, my mortal one, is in your future and it is good news indeed. Meantime, though, you must communicate, and communicate you do; jabbering away in languages ranging from Akan to Zulu. To the point, though, it is an incontrovertible fact that within all these languages there are words or phrases that can be disagreeable to the ear, and the more discerning the ear, the more displeasing they seem to be. This distaste can arise from either the word's meaning or simply in the way it sounds. In Liz's case, while Fukin is a perfectly respectable Russian surname that can be sounded out in any roll call without fear of disapprobation, it can for the ears of some speakers of English have a decidedly rough edge.

Liz's request met with instant approval. Samantha was the first to offer a name. "Why not call them Kwyrkicons?"

"Sounds like a game app for a smartphone," Yurk quipped. "However, I think it makes a great substitute."

"Put some content in that app and you might even give Angry Birds a run for its money," Peter joked, even though he felt the idea had some merit.

"If my grandfather got involved, which he no doubt would, the app would only be for southpaws, and he'd figure out a way of promoting his so-called sex syrup," Yurk said in a mildly derisive tone.

Peter was surprised by his comment. "Your grandfather told me being left-handed is what defines you as a Kwyrki. That it is who you are politically, socially and culturally."

When Yurk tensed, little ripples appeared on any exposed muscle. Such was the case as he mulled over his response. After trying to coax one more drop of coffee from his cup, he attempted an explanation. "It is true that left-handedness was passed, of course by the left hand, from one generation to the next. All that slowed a bit with my father's generation and has virtually stopped with mine. For many, it's unimportant and irrelevant." he said, suggesting that most of the many were young and he was one of them.

Remembering the first time he met Petra, Peter told Yurk how his grandfather had asked him to help set up a sexual liaison between Liz and him. "Which I nixed by telling him she was right-handed," he added.

Yurk looked at Liz and Peter and blushed. "I apologize to you both for my grandfather's indelicate approach to matchmaking. Did he tell you I was a bullniki?" Peter grinned and nodded. "You see, one evening at dinner, I told him how lovely I thought your niece was. Still do, in fact. Well, that's all he needed to take matters into his own hands. It seems ever since he met Inka..." Yurk paused. "You've all met my grandfather's new wife?" They nodded. "Need I say more."

"Actually, I wish you would," Sam said gently.

Yurk leaned back and studied his new friends. Yes, he thought, they deserved better than to think his relative was simply a sex-obsessed old man with a young trophy wife. "My grandfather clings to the left-handed tradition, believes his syrup contains a magical sexual stimulant and collects ice sculptures because he truly believes the odder we are as a people, the more likely it is that neighboring countries will take no interest in us other than to, perhaps, ridicule our lifestyle. He believes the best border defense Kwrykistan can have is quirky behavior. I can say positively that Petra Dosynk is a charming, intelligent man, albeit, with eccentricities. Most of which, by the way, I find endearing or entertaining. What I particularly love about him is his ability to do the unexpected. I think you'll see that side of him demonstrated later today or tomorrow."

Sensing that was an end to it, Lillie, anxious to get things back on track, asked Peter to move it along.

Without looking at her, Peter pulled at his earlobe. "Yurk, about this idea of mine."

"Yes, please! I'm eager to know what you think."

"It's actually less of an idea and more my way of saying we'll do what we can to help you." Realizing he'd just volunteered his three female cohorts, he said to all, "This can work for all of us. We want to recover the *A Jersey Lily*. My gut feeling is the painting is in the exact same spot as the icons."

"Yes, but where?" asked Sam, her excitement and enthusiasm for being part of this zany adventure was building by the minute.

"You said earlier you were convinced they are not on the ship," Yurk said.

"I'm certain the Millais painting isn't," he answered. "As for the icons, all we know is Van Woort was already on the ship on the previous cruise when Volkov called to tell him about Plushenko's interest in them. What that means, I don't know. They could be here. They could not be here. I'm betting the latter."

Yurk fell back against his chair and folded his massive arms. Frowning, he muttered, "This is beginning to sound quite impossible."

"No, it's not impossible," Peter said reassuringly. "I have good reason to believe Van Woort and the stolen art will eventually be in the same place at the same time. With any luck this reunion will be tomorrow, and when it happens, we'll be there to separate them from each other."

"Sounds a lot easier than trying to steal the stuff. Now all we have to do is wrest it from him," Yurk joked.

"Wrest implies force," Sam said, inserting herself into their conversation. "I think what Peter means is we are going to persuade Mr. Van Woort that it is in his best interests to turn over to us that which doesn't rightfully belong to him so we can return it to those from whom the art was taken."

"Sam, you are now our official spokesperson. Not only was that well stated, but grammatically correct," Peter said jovially. Not really certain as to the accuracy of the second half of that sentence, he added quickly, "At least it sounds correct."

Liz raised a hand. "Okay, guys, when altruistic people start talking about doing something which sounds suspiciously like a back alley mugging, doesn't someone usually pop up and ask that all-important question?"

Peter grinned. "I'm not sure what that is, but I assume you've decided to accept the honor of popping up and asking?"

"Yes, I have," she smirked. Clearing her throat, she said formally, "As law-abiding citizens shouldn't we contact the captain and tell him what we know about his crooked auctioneer? Then shouldn't we alert the authorities on shore, otherwise known as the police, and let them do their job?"

Peter and Yurk exchanged glances. Both had a long list of substantive reasons for saying that was completely out of the question. Yurk, however, summed it up for both of them. "No, Liz. we should not. At least, not until the stolen art is in our possession. We can move more efficaciously, expediently and efficiently than the gendarmes can."

"Also more discreetly," Peter added.

Liz threw her hands up and said cheerily, "Just thought I'd ask. So where do we go from here?"

Her uncle fielded that inquiry: "First on my to-do list is finding out when Van Woort is scheduled to disembark."

"That's a logical start," Yurk muttered, distracted by an idea that had suddenly popped into his head; an inspiring, or so he thought, notion that made him feel all warm and cuddly inside. His pensiveness, though, produced a contrary physical effect; causing his eyes to narrow and his lips to purse. While squinting and pursing does wonders for people like Clint Eastwood, regrettably it painted a beady, bullying look on his mug. So much so, his table mates wondered what was going on inside the head of this young man who, built like a monster truck, now sported a menacing visage. Thus, you can imagine their surprise and astonishment when, with a sweetness in his voice that was quite becoming, he whispered, "I sense a strong spiritual presence among us."

Lilllie was first to respond: "Oh my! Suddenly, I'm all the rage."

Peter, Liz and Samantha heard her, but nary a one turned in her direction. Instead, bewildered by the contrariness of what they were seeing and hearing, they continued to stare at Yurk. Sam finally found her voice and asked, "This spiritual presence you sense, Yurk, does it have a visible form?"

Yurk's laugh was more a quick snort. "I fear I'm guilty of overstatement. It's just that I suddenly had this crazy notion that there must be spirits among us who wish for our success in recovering the stolen art. I mean, here we are trying to get our hands on two important Russian icons and one English painting in order to return them to their respective museums. These treasures allow all of us to peek into the past. So I started to think it was entirely possible we are surrounded by the spirits of the iconographer, the saints on his icons, the English painter... What's his name?"

"Sir John Everett Millais," Peter replied.

"Yes, Sir John. And let's not forget his model."

"His model!" Lillie harumphed. "Would someone please tell the young man I have a name!"

Liz, barely able to keep a straight face, told Yurk the subject of *A Jersey Lily* was the famous Lillie Langtry.

"So there you are," he exclaimed. "Even your famous Lillie might be among us. Now please don't think me silly, but as I said it makes me feel good thinking they could be here lending moral support."

"One of us is doing much more than that," Mrs. Langtry huffed.

"I think you'll find everyone at this table of well-fed people is more in step with the concept of spirits among us than you can ever imagine," Peter said, raising his orange juice glass. "Now we'd best be about our day. As soon as I can find what Van Woort is up to tomorrow, I will notify everybody. Yurk, is your family scheduled to fly out tomorrow?"

"No, we're staying on for a few days in San Francisco."

"Great! I'll see to it that we leave the ship together. I have a strong feeling Van Woort will lead us right to the paintings."

Jenni Ramirez was, dare I say it, Jenni-on-the-spot. "Peter, you were right," the travel agent sang into the phone. "Your auctioneer has changed his plans for tomorrow. He was scheduled to disembark with the green group at eight-fifteen. These are guests who are headed directly to the airport to catch late morning flights. There are busses to take them to SFO, but he had hired a car. He has now canceled everything; the flight and the limo. Fritz said his two assistants are still in the green group and will fly back to New York as scheduled."

"Let me guess. They take the bus."

"You got it."

"What about all the art? How is that handled?"

"Right after today's auction, his assistants prepare everything for shipping. Then the ship's crew take over. The paintings and other auction supplies are taken off the ship around midday. Then they're picked up by UPS and flown either to his warehouse in New York or wherever the next ATSEA Auction is.

"Jenni, what's Van Woort's new departure time?"

"Let me see." He could hear her rustling paper. "I scribbled everything down so fast," Jenni explained. "Oh, here it is. He is now in the ten-thirty orange group They're the last group to leave the ship. Now here's where it gets interesting. Van Woort is now listed as an independent traveler. Fritz said the concierge asked him if he needed transportation and he said he was taking care of that personally. Fritz thought that unusual because in the past he's always had them do everything for him plus sticking them with the bill. By the way, this is his last cruise on the Ocean Glamour. Fritz and the captain have told him to take his auctions elsewhere. It seems he has always been difficult to deal with, and Fritz said he treats the crew horribly and that is a major no-no. It also didn't help matters that my darling hotel director and the captain weren't exactly thrilled with the caliber of people he brought along on this cruise through his travel agency." As serious as this all was, Jenni's reaction to her report was a burst of laughter.

"What's so funny?" he asked.

"Mein Fritz," she said with a comic Teutonic accent, "gets so mad talking about Van Woort, he reverts to German. When I jokingly asked him how he *really* felt about him, Fritz said, *"Er geht mir auf den Sack."*

"I don't know what it means, but I'm assuming it's not a compliment."

"No, it isn't at all. It means he's a pain in the ass," she said. "I find it fascinating that I can't remember how to say anything useful in any language other than English. But when I hear a swear words, insults or something naughty, I remember them forever."

"Look at it this way; now you can add X-rated polyglot to your LinkedIn bio."

Jenni giggled and then turned serious. "Peter, Fritz is concerned. He's heard some stories and doesn't want anything happening that will cast an unfavorable light on the Ocean Glamour."

"Maybe I ought to talk to him directly."

"He would appreciate that. By the way, I want you to know our group has had a wonderful time. And so have I. If you discount Howard... I'm joking. Anyway, there's not a troublemaker among them," she chuckled. "You and Dave were entertaining hosts and our functions were a huge success. Of course, the dance contest was an unexpected bonus. If you guys want to host another cruise sometime, just say so."

"I'll certainly think about it. As for Dave, he's hooked on cruising. Whether he's up to playing Mr. Congeniality again, though, I don't know."

Peter called Fritz Henning right away to assure him the Ocean Glamour needn't worry about any adverse publicity stemming from any action they might take regarding the auctioneer. The hotel director thanked him and then, like Jenni, effused about the size and quality of their group and the success of their events. He followed that up by asking Peter if there was anything more he could do for him. Now when a gracious and grateful hotel director on a luxury cruise ship tosses a question like that in your direction, it requires some creative thinking on your part as the inquiry implies he's armed and ready to indulge you. Would you like a bottle of Dom Perignon and Russian Caviar sent to your stateroom? How about a Baked Alaska personally marched to your dining room table by the ship's captain while violinists play the Norwegian National Anthem? You need only ask. However, like Shakespeare's King Harry at Agincourt who said to his battle weary troops, *"such outward things dwell not in my desires,"* Peter's interest was solely fixed on intelligence gathering.

"Actually, I wondered if I could bother you for some more information regarding tomorrow's disembarkation?" he asked, sparing Fritz from having to rustle up some costly indulgences.

"Of course," he said.

"I'd like to know if any of the guests who booked through Van Woort's travel agency have changed either their disembarkation time."

"That's easy enough. Anything else?" he asked in a crisp but friendly manner.

"There is, actually. There are a couple of us who would also like to join that ten-thirty orange group. Can that be arranged?"

Fritz chuckled. "I assume all this has to do with the movements tomorrow of our erstwhile auctioneer?"

"We just want him to return something that doesn't belong to him. I promise our actions will be discreet, quick and totally unnewsworthy."

"I'll take your word even though I know you have a newspaper editor on board with you and, no doubt, he's part of all this."

"Fritz, it will be a non-story. I promise you," Peter repeated. "By the way, you've turned Dave Flannery into a real fan. I believe he's booked another cruise."

"I hope we've done the same with you."

"It goes without saying."

Fritz had one last question for Peter which first required an explanation. "I'm sure Jenni told you we have ended our relationship with Mr. Van Woort. It was due solely to his inability to get along with us. Us being the officers and crew. When you live in a confined society like ours, social harmony is all-important. It may seem petty, but we are all delighted to finally see the last of him and his auction gavel."

"It doesn't sound petty to me at all," Peter remarked, quick to grasp how different and demanding life must be on the Ocean Glamour for those in its employ.

"Now I don't know all the details about what you and he have to settle and I'm not sure I want to. However, I am compelled to ask you if you know of any fraudulent behavior on his part as regards the auctions themselves. To our knowledge, they appeared to be aboveboard and run well. Very well, in fact. Do you know otherwise?"

"Fritz, there's the irony. If Charles Van Woort ran all his businesses like he does ATSEA Auctions, we wouldn't be having this conversation. I'm pretty sure, though, from what you've said about his boorish behavior, he'd still get his walking papers."

"At least we aren't making him walk the plank," Fritz said with a tight little laugh that suggested he might prefer that method of termination. "Anyway, I'll get right back to you with the information you requested. As for the people you want put in the orange group, give me their names and I'll see that it's arranged. By the way, just a heads up, but you should know many guests play free and loose with departure times. Many ignore their assigned times and walk off whenever they feel like it."

Looking up at her walking partner as they strolled the port side of the promenade deck, Samantha observed, "You look like Willie Nelson." Because of the stiff wind, Peter had wrapped his head in a blue bandanna which had inspired her comment.

"Willie Nelson," he grimaced.

Capable of spotting a sincere grimace from fifty yards, she leaned in close to him and diplomatically whispered, "Naturally, I mean a better looking version." Peter thanked her by grabbing her hand and squeezing it. Feeling she was now back on solid ground, Samantha added, "Looking like Willie isn't so bad, you know. He does have an appealing earthiness and authenticity."

"Samantha, I'm now convinced you could tell me I look Ebenezer Scrooge and then explain why that's a compliment."

Sam laughed and said, "Speaking of Willie, you also look like your ready to sing a country song about lost love and hard living."

"As well he should," Lillie said, floating alongside them. "Tomorrow is full of so many unknowns."

The trio stopped by the water fountain in the stern of the ship. Protected from the strong winds, they sat on a nearby teak bench and quietly watched a large group of walkers stroll by. Finally alone, he took Sam's hand. "Lillie's right about the unknowns. Even so, we both feel strongly that the stolen art will be at the pier tomorrow, and we're pretty sure we know who will be there to meet Van Woort when he disembarks."

Sam leaned around Peter to look at Lillie who was hovering on his left side. "Lillie, is that true?" she asked.

"It is, my dear," she replied. "The silly thing is Peter and I never talk about it. Around it, perhaps, but never about it."

Samantha's double take confirmed her puzzlement. "I don't understand."

"Of course, you don't," Lillie said sweetly. "We're not sure we do. However, let me see if I can sort this out for you. Early on in the cruise, I spent much of my time wrestling with the dizzying question of why I was suddenly and unexpectedly in a penthouse aboard a luxury cruise ship bound for Alaska. What was the raison d'être, if you will, for my quasi-human existence. I worked through all sorts of theories, but I always returned to the idea that I was here to do what I could to recover *A Jersey Lily*. Then once it was in safe hands, namely back on display at the Tate, I would move on."

"When did you figure it all out?" Sam asked. "I mean about the stolen painting. I assume you're still trying to figure out the why of you."

"How perceptive you are," she replied. "As regards the painting, it was after our first meeting with Freddie and

Benjamin. It didn't take too much figuring. In fact, our detecting skills haven't really been put to the test."

"What was it you learned?"

"That a talented art restorer from the Tate in London, a miscreant named Jasper Sprottle stole my painting from his place of employment. He then painted a most impressive forgery which he sent via Benjamin to Mr. Van Woort who, thinking he was receiving the original, arranged to sell it to Philipa Crumley-Figg. However, she died just two days into the cruise."

Eager to take part in the narrative, Peter interjected, "As Lillie said, we've known that for some time, but we purposely chose not to discuss it between ourselves."

"But why?" asked Samantha becoming curiouser and curiouser.

"I had grown very fond of being here, and as unusual as our partnership was, I loved being with Peter and of course, Liz," Lillie answered. "Frankly, I didn't want it to end."

"*We* didn't want it to end," Peter noted affectionately.

"It's silly, but we figured if we kept whatever we knew to ourselves and didn't talk about it openly, we would continue to... How shall I say? Keep the mystery of the stolen painting alive, and as a result it would keep me here rather than vanishing into thin air. Does that make any sense?"

Samantha didn't answer right away. She stared straight ahead at the foamy, white wake of the ship and thought a moment. Finally, glancing first at Peter and then Lillie, she declared solemnly, "I don't want it to end either. But it will, won't it?"

"Yes," Lillie sighed. "And for that I am grateful. This in-between world has me yearning for a more complete spiritual existence which I truly believe awaits me."

"Sam, it's not just a question of recovering the painting. We need this to end right and that's what complicates matters.

"What are the complications?" Sam asked.

"I'm speaking for Lillie here as well as me. She can interrupt anytime she disagrees," Peter began. "Firstly, we want to see the painting returned without drawing too much attention to ourselves. After talking to the hotel director, we know the cruise line feels the same way. Secondly, we want to resolve this in such a way as to keep Freddie and Benjamin out of legal trouble. Thirdly, now that we've heard Yurk's story, we'd like to see the icons put into the hands of the Dosynks."

"And what about Van Woort?"

Peter shrugged. "Right now, I'm more concerned about the painting. Once we have it and the icons, he can walk away as far as I'm concerned. His day will come without us having to do anything about it."

Lillie was to have the last word before they left the windy, chilly promenade deck: "Before we go in, I have something to say to you both. Let us try to fill these last moments together with as much joy, gaiety and mirth as we can muster. Are we agreed?"

Peter took Sam's hand and offered his other to a space near Lillie. "Like the Musketeers," he proclaimed, "we are one for all, all for one and everyone for some joy, gaiety and mirth."

Sam leaned in and kissed his cheek. "All in good time. Right now, I'm going to pack and tend to things so I can be free to enjoy Freddie and Benjamin's cocktail party and our final dinner together on the ship."

"What about lunch?" Peter asked.

Samantha rubbed what was a full tummy, broadcast a fake groan and said, "Peter, after that breakfast, I am fasting until five o'clock."

He held the door while Sam and Lillie moved past him into the temperature-controlled environment of the

Ocean Glamour. Sam made a beeline for the steps while Lillie remained with Peter in the doorway. She, too, begged off joining him for lunch; explaining she was curious as to how Charles Van Woort was spending his last day at sea.

It was during this conversation that Fritz Henning came marching out of the long corridor of staterooms on the port side almost bumping into Peter. After excusing himself, he looked in the direction of the stairs and then back at Peter. "I thought I heard you talking to someone," he said, mystified.

"You did," Peter replied. "Samantha was just on her way up the stairs."

"I'm glad I ran into you. Well, that's not appropriate as I almost ran you over," he chuckled. "But it saves me a phone call. I checked on the guests who are in Van Woort's group. No one has changed their departure times. They all have midday flights and will be disembarking with the first group."

If I may insert a fascinating side note here: While it is not a sales' record to be proud of – at least from my lofty point of view – Van Woort could boast that over the years this group had purchased forty-seven stolen works of art from him. Exhibiting an obvious disdain for buying anything legally, none of these malefactors attended the shipboard auctions. Fritz's information about their early departures warmed Peter's heart. He now felt confident Van Woort wouldn't be conducting any wharf-side business involving either the painting or the icons.

The hotel director was not the last to literally run into Peter on his way to his penthouse. As he stepped off the last stair on deck ten, Howard Newton bounded out of the hallway, stopping just in time to avoid a collision.

"Peter!" Howard shouted. "Sorry, I didn't see you."

"Don't tell me you were looking for me."

"Matter of fact, I was. Are you headed to your state-room?"

"I am."

Howard put his hand on his shoulder. "I've got something to tell you."

"I'm sort of busy, Howard," he said lamely.

"Naomi wants a divorce."

chapter 44

IT WAS AS if Peter had posted a sign on his stateroom door reading *No sulking, brooding or moping on these premises* and Howard was doing his darndest to obey it. So instead of shuffling into the penthouse with his roundish bald head hanging down and his cherubic face sculpted by, as Will would say, *the pangs of despised love*, he marched in; shoulders back, head held high and his face bare of any emotive expression. Peter watched as he snatched an apple from the bowl of fruit on the desk and tossed it up and down like a baseball. When the apple seemed to pass whatever test he had just given it, he took a seat in the far corner of the sofa and crossed his legs. Looking at him, Peter wondered whether Howard was now into shining his bald spot. Then he realized it was just the way the light of the room hit it. More to the point, though, he wondered why he wasn't witnessing a man wrestling with heartache. He had always thought his former boss had a successful marriage if for no other reason than their mutual love of sea birds and oddly named ice creams.

Feeling obliged to commiserate, Peter said, "This must have come as quite a shock. Then there's the suddenness of it all." Howard offered no response. He just sat there and stared at the apple. Deciding to give commiseration one more chance, he added, "You must feel awful."

That did the trick. Howard glanced up and glowered. "It's damned difficult to feel pissed and heartbroken at that same time," he hissed.

"I can imagine how..."

Howard held a hand up and waved him quiet. "I'm just sorry she asked for a divorce before I had a chance to fire her," he barked.

"Howard, she's your wife. You don't fire spouses."

"I know. I just didn't want to say divorce twice in the same sentence," he explained tetchily and, I might add, illogically.

"Tell me what happened."

Howard took a violent bite of the apple and tossed the rest on the table as if it were forbidden fruit. Uncrossing his legs and folding his pudgy arms, he told Peter that Naomi phoned sometime around eight this morning. "There was no "how are you, what are you doing.' She just blurted out that she wanted a divorce. Oh, and of course she reminded me of our pre-nup."

"You had her sign a pre-nup?" asked a surprised Peter.

"Other way around. I was asked to sign one. The Figg's fortune is monstrous. Naomi is the only heir and they have enough personal lawyers that a deposition would have to be to held in the New Orleans Superdome. I didn't have a chance. It's okay, though. I get to keep what I earned working for the company, and thanks to a good salary and generous stock options which I wisely reinvested because radio is dying a slow painful death, I'm in pretty good shape. Check that. I am in ridiculously fine shape."

"Did Naomi tell you why she wants a divorce."

"She said she was sick of birds and sick of me and not necessarily in that order. That last part was pretty bitchy, don't you think?" Peter shook his head in agreement while doing his best to stifle a laugh. "You know, ever since her mother died, she's been acting just like her. She used to be so easy-going and lovable. Now she's terse and insulting. Her tone with me is downright ugly." He paused, wondering if he ought to bring up the other reason she gave for the split. Deciding it was best, he added in a soft but awkward voice, "Uh, there is something else besides the terse, insulting and ugly stuff."

"Some*thing* or some*one?*" Peter asked.

Staring dolefully out the penthouse window and feeling somewhat embarrassed, Howard mumbled, "Yeah. I think there's another man."

"Do you know who?" he asked even though he had a pretty good idea as to the identity of Naomi's new Prince Charming.

"I'm guessing it's Mr. Smooth-as-a-Baby's-Butt Charles Van Woort," he barked angrily. "Goddam, Peter, you do realize it was must have been Naomi who told him your missing painting was a fake. Worse, you're looking at the idiot who gave here that information."

"We... Um, *I* did sort of figure that out," Peter said. "Did you have a chance to ask her about her relationship with Van Woort?"

Howard shook his head and muttered, "She said it was none of my fucking business. She sounded just like her mother who really loved the F-word. That's the last thing she said to me. We haven't spoken since. Of course, that was just a few hours ago."

Thinking anything he had to say now would be pretty feeble, Peter offered up his version of the international gesture of futility which involved a slow motion shake of the head, a shrug of the shoulders and a smile of resignation.

"Can people change like that so suddenly?" Howard asked. "I mean like on a dime."

This time, Peter felt a voiced response was more fitting. "Apparently," he said, padding it with another quick shake, shrug and smile. "I think, though, most unexpected and potentially ruinous actions like Naomi's, while they may appear on the surface to be spur-of-the-moment, are, in fact, imprudent actions taken by someone who has been slowly changing over a long period of time and in that time there may have been no noticeable difference in the person until they finally decide to act on those ever evolving changes."

"You should have stopped after apparently," Howard grumbled.

"Well, what's done is done. Sounds like she's not one who would agree to marriage counseling."

"That's okay by me. I'm done with her," he said angrily. "I swear if she walked in right now wearing nothing but a garter belt with black nylons and holding a pint of Mabel's Magnificent Munchie Crunchie in one hand and a pint of Sassy Suzy's Swirly Strawberry in another and begged me to forgive her, I'd show her the door."

"Whoa!" Peter exclaimed. "That's quite a picture you painted. Sounds to me like that might have happened once or twice."

"Once," he confessed, his eyes glazing over just thinking about it. "To be exact, November third of last year at exactly nine-thirty. Wearing that very outfit, she stood in the doorway to our bedroom and said in this kinda fluttery and sultry voice, '"All right, Bird-man..." She called me the Bird-man of the Bedroom. 'What's it to be? Mabel, Suzy or me?'"

"And you picked the Munchie Crunchie."

"Ramsey, there are times when you don't joke around. That was one of them."

Peter couldn't remember any partner of his being similarly costumed for a night of romance. They were more the flowing negligee types. He wondered if they might have been more adventurous had the relationships lasted longer than they did. Silly thinking, he told himself. Samantha's now in his life and it's still to be determined how fanciful and creative their love life will be.

"It was a great night," Howard sighed, "but it was a one off. Naomi went right back to wearing this worn-out extra long tee-shirt advertising a *Brideshead Revisited* marathon on PBS. She thought she looked sexy in a comely maiden fashion."

Peter's mind was not on Naomi's nightwear. He was thinking about the Van Woort-Figg connection. If Philipa had been buying stolen art from Van Woort over the years, it was entirely conceivable Naomi knew him and knew about her mother's nefarious shopping habit. He shared this thought with Howard who got up from the sofa and stood by the opened door to the verandah. His pique had peaked. Without turning around, he said in a less acrimonious tone, "I swear to you all the time we were working our way through her mother's estate, his name never came up. In all our conversations after I got on the ship, she never once mentioned him. But you're right, Peter, they must have known each other. Now I suppose if they did, it begs the question how intimate was their relationship."

Peter answered quickly, "Intimate enough for her to become an accessory to a crime."

"That's her problem now."

"I want you to know that tomorrow, we're... Rather, I'm going to... Well, I'm not really sure what's going to happen, but I'm going to try to get that painting back. It might involve her."

Howard turned around and stared quizzically at Peter. "You seem to be having a difficult time today determining whether you're a we or an I."

Peter ignored him. "Be that as it may, there's every possibility Naomi might be here tomorrow, if for no other reason, to pick up Van Woort."

"Doesn't matter to me," he said smugly. "I'm not getting off the ship."

"What do you mean?"

"I'm not getting off," he repeated with a casual shrug and a benign smile. "An hour ago, I signed up for the next cruise. Fritz says I can stay in the same penthouse. I know we're in San Francisco all day and I probably could go home, but Naomi might also be there and I don't want to deal with her just yet. And like you said, if she's at the pier tomorrow, she's there for Van Woort."

"Even if she's in a garter belt and..."

"Don't go there."

"Why are you staying on for the next cruise?"

"Honestly?"

"Of course, honestly," Peter laughed.

"Because I'm having a lot of fun and it's not just being part of your whacko adventure. Since I dropped the idea of trying to become what you called a swaggering sort, I've met some really nice people who sincerely enjoy my company and I enjoy theirs. They know I'm a bit eccentric; my fascination with sea birds and all that, and that's okay. So I'm back to being old eccentric Howard but with a lot of new clothes," he chuckled.

As Howard's gang of nice people would be leaving the ship tomorrow, Peter assumed someone attached to the ship must have played a significant role in his decision to buckle up for another twelve day boat ride. He asked him outright.

His former boss was neither shy nor hesitant in responding. "There's this really fascinating woman, Millicent Duckworth, who teaches watercolor. Under her contract, she has one more cruise. Millie and I have something in common," he explained, a soupçon of sheepishness creeping into his voice. "If you guessed sea birds, give yourself a prize. So far, it's just a warm friendship, but I think..."

Peter walked up to him and put a hand on his shoulder. "Say no more. I envy you another sailing. To tell you the truth, I was daydreaming about Samantha and me staying on for the next one. Back to back cruises has a nice ring to it. Truth is, I'm not really ready to get off the ship yet either."

Howard's eyes brightened. "Do it!" he urged. "Fritz says it's a wide open cruise and you can probably keep this penthouse. Although, they cost a pretty penny, you know, and you won't be cruising on the newspaper's dime."

"I thought about that, too," Peter said, frowning as the air went out of that daydream. "Another problem is Samantha's schedule at Cal."

"At least you're thinking about it," Howard said, making ready his departure. "Hey, I've taken enough of your time. Thanks for listening. By the way, if you're planning a get together with your gang of good guys later, I'd like to be excused. I've done my bit."

"You have and more," Peter said sincerely as his guest slowly moved into the hallway. "Now you better get out of here before I become so awash with empathy, I'll start spouting cheesy cliches like when one door closes, another opens. Or how about..."

Howard cut him off by turning on his heels and walking toward the bow of the ship. At an appropriate distance, he thrust a finger skyward and said crisply, "Up yours, Ramsey."

While Peter watched him fade into the carpet of the long hallway, Lillie sneaked up on him from the other direction. "Do you have a special greeting that goes with that strange parting?" she asked in a manner suggesting an answer wasn't required.

Peter, recognizing such, didn't give her one. Instead, he played doorman, waiting while Lillie drifted into the penthouse where she settled in on one end of the small sofa. Following behind her, he sat opposite the diaphanous lavender vision which he'd come to accept as he would anyone sitting opposite him. "Just so you're up to date, Howard dropped by to tell me Naomi wants a divorce."

"Aha! It is my thought that he should welcome this estrangement with open arms," she replied. "I have reason to believe Naomi is anxious to shed her current husband so she can acquire a new one."

"You sound like you know who the next one might be."

"Yes, I think I do," she said in a breezy confident manner.

"Charles Van Woort?" he asked.

This was one of those moments when Lillie wished she was better equipped physically so to fully express her delight over the success of observing Charles Van Woort go about his day. This ardor would have been more forcefully conveyed with eyes that widened, a smile that broadened, arms that waved and a body that squirmed about, but she had only her voice to express the excitement she felt. "Peter, forget the Newton's marital woes for a moment. I have the best news! My painting and those Russian icons with the provocative name will definitely be on the pier tomorrow morning."

"Lillie, that's wonderful news."

"And yes, Charles Van Woort is the answer to your question," she replied belatedly. "Oh, I had the most interesting time watching our favorite auctioneer go about his day. It was like panning for gold, though; sifting through a lot of valueless matter until, voila, I struck gold."

Lillie went on to explain that after their unusual breakfast with Yurk, she went in search of the auctioneer, finding him in the Covey doing what auctioneers do and that was preparing for that afternoon's auction. He was all business; showing his assistants where the paintings should be displayed, in what order they would be auctioned and directing the ship's crew as to how he wanted the room set up. Lillie described him as gentlemanly, courteous and upbeat. That came as a surprise to Peter who had been told Van Woort was the final word when it came to churlishness. When it appeared all was to Van Woort's satisfaction in the Covey, he returned to his stateroom where he began to pack. Just as Lillie was convinced she would learn nothing except what clothes were going where in his suitcase, his cell phone rang.

"Was it Naomi?" Peter asked anxiously.

"If she also goes by Buttercup, Honey Darling or My Little Sexpot, then it was Naomi. I'm afraid during the entire phone call, he never once called Miss Whoever-It-Was by her Christian name. Oh, there was one other term of endearment in his arsenal, but I will save it for later."

"Why didn't you lean in close to him like you do with me when you want to hear what's being said on the other end of the line?" he asked teasingly.

If Lillie could blush, she would have. "Peter, I know this sounds silly, but even in this spiritual state, stripped of any physical features, I cannot permit myself such intimacies with strangers."

"Start from the beginning and tell me what you can about their conversation and how you found out about the painting."

"They began billing and cooing right from the start. There was an extended period where it was solely an exchange of affectionate words; some of them quite explicit. It was toward the end when things got interesting. First he asked Honey Darling if she had any questions about tomorrow morning. In fact, he asked her twice. I assume she had a good grasp of her duties because he then shifted gears, telling her he'd just checked the weather in Honolulu where it was eighty-two and sunny. He murmured something about naked midnight swims. I definitely heard a girlish giggle come from the phone. It was then that she must have made some comment about the stolen art. Whatever it was Miss Whoever-It-Was said obviously irritated him. In a rather forceful manner, he reminded her that they would be much better off without, and I quote, 'that damned Millais and those silly religious icons.' He said he was glad to be getting rid of them and that then his shelves will finally be bare, whatever that meant. Then, Peter," she said snappishly, her dander up, "Mr. Van Woort said, and I quote again, 'I can't say I'm sorry to see *A Jersey Lily* go tomorrow. Lillie Langtry was never my idea of a beauty anyway. The good news is I now have A *New* Jersey Lily to call my own.'"

Clearly, Mrs. Langtry was stung by that last remark. Peter let her know it upset him as well. "That well could have been Naomi. I remember Howard telling me once the Figgs have a huge estate in New Jersey that was an easy commute to New York."

"Yes, I'm certain it was her. I'm also certain she will be at the pier tomorrow with the art."

Peter's sudden exhalation of a giant sigh caught Lillie's attention and prompted her to ask him what it was that concerned him.

"Everything, Lillie," he confessed, nervously rubbing his hands together. "The wackiness factor of the last twelve days is so off the charts, I sometimes wonder if I have been cast in a surreal dream and getting off this ship tomorrow will be like waking up. Will I set foot on dry land only to discover there is no such thing as a country called Kwyrkistan or that you were just a figment of my imagination or Dave Flannery can't tango or that *A Jersey Lily* still hangs in the Tate?"

"Or that you and Samantha Whitby didn't declare your love for one another on a warm Alaskan evening while three Bald Eagles did a fly by and a whale breached to celebrate the two of you," she added to his list of all things whacky and wonderful.

"Okay, okay! I was just having a this-is-all-a-crazy-dream moment," he said, putting his hands on his knees. "So, back to reality such as it is. From what you heard, it sounds like Naomi is bringing the painting and icons to the pier tomorrow as we hoped. I hope I can convince him to turn them over to us. If that doesn't work, maybe the next best thing to do is to sic Yurk on him."

"That was discussed at breakfast," she reminded him.

"I wonder if I can find out whom he plans to sell them to."

"We don't know that he plans to sell them."

"Lillie, he isn't going to give them away."

"I know. I was just thinking that I never once heard the word sell in his conversation with Buttercup or My Little Sexpot or Miss Whoever-It-Was. Anyway, you need to get about your day. We have Freddie and Benjamin's party at five and you still have to pack. I'll be on the veranda. If you need any advice as to your packing, you need only ask. Mr. Van Woort seemed to be an expert on what should go where."

"Lillie, you're being awfully cool about all of this," Peter observed, noting her buoyant mood.

"That is because I truly believe God's plan is in action, Peter. I'm quite sure He's taken sides on this matter and will direct us to do what is needed to get the painting back."

By the time Lille, Peter, Samantha and Liz were standing in front of Benjamin and Freddie's penthouse door, Peter had learned that one of Van Woort's guests who were flying out to various destinations in the morning had unexpectedly changed his plans. The hotel director told him that Moke "Kona Kong" Kamaka from Honolulu was sticking around. Kamaka, who was big enough to occupy two offensive guard positions on an NFL team, had just called the concierge with instructions to book him into a large suite at the Mark Hopkins Hotel on Nob Hill and hire a very large car to get him there. Kamaka also had him cancel his existing flight and make one for the following day. In Peter's mind, it now seemed logical that this Polynesian behemoth would be the one taking *A Jersey Lily* and the *Fukin Icons* off Charles Van Woort's hands.

"Come on in, dear friends," Freddie chirped, waving his pudgy, manicured hand. "The whole gang's here. Well, now that you three are here, that is. Wait a minute! Did you bring Lillie with you, Peter? Then it's four! But she doesn't drink. Good. More champagne for the rest of us. I do so love to play Let's Pretend," he said with his trademark high-pitched giggle.

When Peter saw everybody standing cheek by jowl in Freddie and Benjamin's Victorian-decorated penthouse, he whispered to Sam, "Now I know what it must be like to throw a cocktail party in a hospital elevator."

"If we were in my stateroom, it would look like we were trying to set a new record for phone-booth stuffing," she whispered back.

If there was a roll call, Dave and Mary Pat Flannery, Malcolm Fitzroy and Isabelle Whitby, Svetlana With-The-Long-Russian-Name, the three Dosynks and the most recent arrivals, Peter, Samantha, Liz and Lillie Langtry, would have all happily hollered, "Here."

It was shortly after their arrival, drinks in hand, that Freddie clinked his champagne flute. The room quieted. Looking resplendent in his and his velvet smoking jackets and surrounded by small, battery-equipped candles flickering not so realistically, Freddie and a surprisingly ebullient Benjamin welcomed everyone to their five o'clock salon. They then explained that Freddie's parents had decided to take a nap before dinner and would not be joining their party.

Normally, this would not be news worth reporting except that it delighted Peter for now his arms would be spared from Gertie's painful clutching and, considering the heft of the two senior Florians, movement in the penthouse would have been severely impeded. Freddie and Benjamin had been generous, pouring Dom Perignon for everyone except Dave who managed to find an Alaskan beer in their fridge. After a final welcome from Freddie, the guests lifted their glasses as thanks for their hospitality. Before everyone drifted off into private conversations, however, Benjamin clinked his glass once again. Once again, the room quieted. Looking directly at Peter and wearing a wry smile, he addressed the assembled: "I'd like to turn the floor over the Peter Ramsey who will explain how he plans to involve us all in being part of what might end up being one of the most unusual disembarkations in the history of cruising."

"I can guarantee it will be for us, Benjamin. Remember, though, the goal is to not call attention to ourselves," Peter cautioned while stepping away from Samantha to locate where he would have everyone's attention. "So here's what I've been able to piece together. Charles Van Woort is scheduled to leave the ship at ten-thirty tomorrow morning. I'm pretty sure I know who will be waiting for him. I'm counting on the painting and the two Russian icons being in that person's car or van. This is speculative but there's the possibility he plans to sell them to one of his cruise guests, a man by the name of Moke Kamaka."

"Hey, I saw that guy down five scotch and waters in the space of ten minutes the other night in the Covey. That's one drink every two minutes. I'd hate to have his bar bill by the end of the cruise," Dave commented, obviously impressed with the big man's ability to imbibe on such a grand scale." Irked, Mary Pat nudged her husband who, understanding his infraction, mumbled, "Sorry, Ramsey. You were saying?"

"It looks like our only opportunity to get our hands on the stolen art will be on the pier tomorrow before Charles Van Woort has a chance to drive away."

Ignoring his wife's displeasure with his interruptions, Dave exclaimed, "*If* they're there, that is. Do you hear yourself, Ramsey? You're using words like speculative, possibility, pretty sure, maybe..."

"Dave, please let Peter speak," Mary Pat interjected, "or I'm sending you to bed without dinner."

Peter realized he'd peppered his speech with ambiguity because he was afraid anyone curious about his certainty would question him about how he got all his information. How would he explain Lillie Langtry's involvement?

Malcolm, ever the gentleman, put him back on track. "What is it you plan to do tomorrow, Peter?" he asked

"I am going to ask him for them," Peter said directly and with more confidence than he felt.

"Why would he just hand them over to you?" Isabelle Whitby asked but not contentiously.

"Tomorrow morning, if his wife allows him out of bed, Dave Flannery will be met by a close friend of his, a San Francisco police captain. Dave has told him nothing about the stolen art, only that he might need his help. They will be on the Embarcadero with the intention of getting close enough to Van Woort for him to notice them when I approach him."

Samantha's sister was now confused. "So you plan on signaling the police captain who will arrest him and confiscate the paintings."

"No. I'm going to offer Van Woort a deal. The art for his freedom. I will tell him that all he has to do is hand over the painting and the icons and I will not cue Dave to bring the police over to question him. Once the art is in my possession, he can go on his merry way."

"Why don't you just let the police handle it?" Isabelle asked with what her sister thought was a patience and niceness she'd not heard from her sister in years, if ever.

With equal patience and niceness, Peter explained, "There are a number of reasons, Isabelle. One is I promised the captain and the hotel director there would be no disruption of the embarkation process. The last thing the ship wants is for the media to get their hands on a story about their shipboard auctioneer and his illegal shenanigans."

"Actually, I can understand your desire to be as discreet as possible," she said, still sore from a couple of incidents that had recently put her university department in an unfavorable and unjustified spotlight. "Still in all, just asking him for them seems weird to me."

"It's only weird if it doesn't work," he remarked. Being an old school broadcaster, Peter felt compelled to give credit where credit is due. "It's from a TV spot. Beer, I think."

Isabelle smile broadly which made Samantha beam. "Well, good luck, Peter. Just tell us how we can help."

"I appreciate that," Peter said, rubbing his hands together. "I've been told the disembarkation process has its own crazy rhythm. The captain described it as orderly chaos. He also said that veteran cruisers often ignore their scheduled departure times and get off whenever they feel like it. Van Woort is in the last group to leave. From what I've been able to learn, there doesn't seem to be any reason for him to get off the ship earlier but you never know. If he does leave early, so will I. Our goal is to stay as close to him as we can. It would help if we all have each other's cell numbers." Peter was glad he'd added that last comment as he realized he still didn't know Samantha's number.

Benjamin raised his hand. "One more item of business. We're going to be stymied a bit by that fact that we all have to first retrieve our luggage and go through customs. You won't be able to just follow him out. The good news is he has to go through the same process. I talked to Peter earlier today and we decided to volunteer Freddie's parents to watch over all our bags. They will be among the first off. When they have their luggage, they intend on turning right just outside the pier and setting up an area to watch everyone's stuff. My parents have a car parked in a nearby garage so they have no one waiting for them. Remember, it will be a madhouse out there. Do any of you have a driver picking you up? If so, they won't be able to hang around while we lollygag on the Embarcadero waiting to see what happens."

As it turned out, everyone was planning on hailing cabs, including Peter who was relieved Liz's old boyfriend would not be there to retrieve them.

"May I take it from here?" Yurk asked as he muscled his way through the small crowd to stand next to Peter and Benjamin. His polished British accent clearly startled Dave Flannery. "Peter mentioned there were a number of reasons why he's going about this in such a..." Here Yurk paused and turned to Peter. "Let's see, weird has been ruled out. How about wingy? That certainly applies," he said with a rascally smile. "Isabelle, one of the other important reasons for all this discretion is that it's imperative the icons transfer from Van Woort's oily hands to mine without police interference of any kind. I cannot emphasize the importance of a swift return of these religious icons to Russia. They will, I assure you, be returned to the museum where they belong. If they are retrieved and held by the police, God only knows how long it would take for them to finally come home. My father and I will take full responsibility for their safe journey. So, my dear friends, let's rally around Peter here and make tomorrow morning's adventure a winning one. As I see it, we take back the stolen art, celebrate being on terra firma and Bob's Your Uncle."

"Why do I feel like I'm in a scene from a Lord Peter Whimsey mystery," Dave said, finally having a chance to weigh in on Yurk's accent and suave manner.

"I'll explain it all later, Dave," Yurk replied with a toothy smile, pulling out his smartphone to set about harvesting the others' numbers.

Just like that, everyone began trading mobile numbers. It made for an interesting parlor game what with Benjamin and Freddie's guests juggling their phones and champagne flutes and dizzy conversations about what tomorrow holds. When everyone was finally wirelessly connected, Freddie and Benjamin began ushering them to the door as early seating dining was just minutes away for some of them.

While they marched toward the stairs and elevators, Petra Dosynk approached Peter. "So after eleven days at sea, you finally got to meet the real Yurk," he said with a gravely laugh. "It's an experience, I tell you."

Looking at this odd, pudgy gentleman from Kwrykistan – if there is such a place, he thought – Peter silently declared him the second most fascinating person he'd met on the cruise. Lillie, of course, being the first. "Yurk told me of your rather unusual political philosophy," he remarked.

Petra smiled broadly. "Ah, he did. Well, it has worked for centuries in our country. Did he tell you that? It is simple. Bizarre behavior triumphs! Always," he declared. "You see, even if it's widely known that what you're up to is not what it seems, it doesn't make any difference. It still intimidates others who now find your embrace of fiction just as threatening, if not more so. Does any of that make sense?" he asked with a wide grin.

"To tell you the truth, Petra, not much that has happened in the last twelve days makes any sense," he replied with a gracious smile. "By the way, what do you think of Yurk's new love?"

"She's too bony for me," he joked. "They are well suited, though. I am happy."

"Yurk told me you met with Svetlana..."

"And her uncle," he added. "He is in a lot of trouble, you know. However, I have come up with a plan that is agreeable to all."

"Care to share the details?"

"I have decided to buy Anatoly's Moscow restaurant for a sum that equals the amount of money he owes. I will let him retain a small share. I have also provided ample shares for Yurk and Svetlana who have agreed to manage the restaurant. Give those two a week on the job and any goon or mobster who was a regular will be looking for another place to dine. As for Anatoly, I will make sure he returns the icons to the museum. I think his fascination with Russian gangsters is at an end.

"You amaze me," Peter said, impressed with Dosynk's largesse.

"Let's hope tomorrow goes well, my friend," Petra said, patting Peter on the shoulder. "It all hinges on you getting the icons back from Van Woort."

"I'm going to bed tonight and fantasize that tomorrow morning, I walk off this ship, confront Van Woort and then before I can say anything, he says, 'Mr. Ramsey, I have something here for you.' Then he gives me the painting and icons, gets in his limo and drives off into the sunset."

And that's exactly what Charles Van Woort did. In his own fashion, however.

chapter 45

REVEILLE CAME EARLY for our erstwhile protagonist. Early, considering Lillie and her three earthly contacts stayed up way past yawning time. Assuming everything would change drastically in just a matter of hours, all of them wanted to squeeze in as much time together as possible. Lillie had insisted they say their goodbyes with a promise to embrace with joy any time they would have together after that late night love fest. Now, like some ornery platoon sergeant, here she was urging Peter to shake off his latest dream, don a robe and come watch as the Ocean Glamour slowly narrowed the gap between the dark, choppy seas of San Francisco Bay's capricious Potato Patch and the Golden Gate Bridge; a span they'd sailed under just twelve days prior. While it was biting cold with a scolding wind, it was remarkably clear for a San Francisco midsummer dawning. Even though the fog horns were quiet, there was still a heady mix of bridge, sea and ship sounds; a cacophonous symphony that drifted up to his eleventh deck verandah. Distant lights added to the spectacle. Peter was glad Lillie woke him.

"I was so befuddled by my sudden resurrection twelve days ago, I never saw us go under the bridge when we departed," she recalled, clearly enjoying the spectacle of it all.

"You would have enjoyed it, Lillie," he said. "It was a different setting entirely with all kinds of activity. There were windsurfers trying to get close, police boats shooing them away, a fireboat spewing water high into the air and lots of kids and adults on the bridge waving to us."

"This, too, is a remarkable sight. It is odd to think there was no bridge when I first came to San Francisco. Oh, Peter, I do so hope I will last long enough to set foot on this memorable piece of terra firma again," she sighed.

"If, as we truly believe, your raison d'être is..."

"...to recover the stolen painting. Yes, yes, I know that," she interjected moodily.

"I was just going to say that as it now appears *A Jersey Lily* is somewhere in San Francisco, it's only logical you'll be joining us on dry land later this morning."

"You're right, of course," she said cheerily, shucking her brief dolefulness. "I must say, though, unlike my previous visitations which always caused a stir, this arrival will be as covert as they come."

"When were you last in San Francisco?" he asked, pulling his robe tight against the early morning chill and wind.

"A little more than a century ago. But it feels like yesterday," she joked. "I starred in a vaudeville production of *Ashes* at the Orpheum Theatre in 1912."

While Lillie enjoyed this early morning stroll down memory lane, she wanted to give her full attention to the present, as short a time as that might be. To that, she asked Peter directly if he was ready to face the day.

"Face the day, you ask," he repeated, making a face signaling he was giving the query considerable thought. "Well, as you know, the experiences I have..."

"This is not a morning to ramble, Peter. There's much to do."

"You're right," he said agreeably. "I'll be brief. Anyway, as you know my experiences on this cruise have been truly extraordinary. In fact, out of this world in so many ways..."

"You're doing it again," Lillie interjected. "Poor dear, you simply can't help yourself."

"What am I doing?"

"Rambling," she replied. "Are you ready to face the day? Yes or no."

"My answer requires an explanation," he said in defense of his windiness.

"Can you get it said before we reach the bridge?"

He looked left, his face slapped by the rush of cold wind and saw there was ample time, as Lillie put it, to ramble. "Look, here's the thing. A cruise allows a person to put their regular lives on hold. Five-star, luxury escapism is what the cruise industry is really selling. It's no wonder some people with enough money under their mattresses choose to just keep sailing."

"No, they choose to keep *cruising*," Lillie said, correcting him. "Sailing is about getting from one place to another. When I sailed, it was strictly a means of transportation, albeit, a rather glamorous one for those of us fortunate enough to afford first class travel. Cruising aimlessly from one port to another is another thing entirely. Anyway, continue with your rambling answer. I'm still not certain where you're headed."

"The answer is yes, of course, I'm ready to face the day, That said, though, I'm sorry I'm leaving this marvelous floating cocoon. Not just because, as I said earlier, my regular life can be put on hold for another twelve days. Rather, I wish we could start this whacky, intensely spiritual and magical ride all over again with the same cast of characters. Truth is, I am going to miss everyone, especially you."

"Peter dear, I know eternal joy and happiness awaits me as a complete spirit. I know it cannot be anything but perfect in every way imaginable. While that is a consoling thought, I, too, rue our separation. What a marvelous friendship we've built. Even so, I can't say I will miss you," she said, her tone not as harsh as her words. "As I see it, there's no room for that kind of yearning in wherever it is I'm headed."

"Aren't you the lucky one," he said glumly.

"Cheer up," she said. "What are you? Sixty-five? Good heavens! In no time at all, we'll be together again."

"You could have gone all morning without saying that."

I was impressed with Lillie's embrace of the notion that perfection reigns supreme here in Eternity. Now you would think that is a comforting thought for all reading this. After all, how worked up can you get over eventually taking up spiritual residence in a place where there's bucketfuls of ruefulness, sorrow, fretting and, as Lillie said, yearning. Still, it's a difficult concept when feelings – good or bad, deep or ephemeral – are such a vital part of your mortal existence.

Disembarkation is an five syllable word describing a most peculiar event; a mass exiting that elicits from its participants myriad emotional responses. How disembarkation affects a person depends on what role they play in this fascinating ship-to-shore production. The captain and crew are the most dispassionate of the bunch, as so much has to be done to properly drain the ship of approximately a grand's worth of humanity in the morning, only to take on another grand's worth in the afternoon. Add to that the fact that they are at this time-consuming, complex task once every seven to twelve days, they generally remain a cool and collected lot. Not so for the I-want-off-this-ship-right-now crowd where myriad emotions run high. Most guests obviously feel a trifle sad or disappointed the adventure has come to an end. For many, though, mixed in with that manageable melancholy is a gnawing impatience and a sense of feeling put upon as a result of the hurry-up and wait rhythm that defines any respectable disembarkation. Some tend to let these potentially volatile emotions take charge which makes them a group to steer clear of if you have a disdain for disruption.

This particular disembarkation started out no different than the others. Prior to opening the one and only exit, somber-faced guests hidden beneath coats and hats, looking for all the world like lost waifs, wandered zombie-like through the ship's public areas lugging bags, carry-ons, backpacks, purses and shopping bags. Meantime, the crew below decks prepared to unload hundreds of pieces of luggage as soon as the ship was cleared by U.S. Customs. On the stateroom decks, recently emptied cabins were readied for the next batch of Alaska-bound travelers by stewardesses in high spirits who wasted no time at their housekeeping chores, hoping to clear enough time in the middle of the day to go ashore to shop for necessities or to simply have a relaxing lunch or a drink in a nearby San Francisco restaurant.

By ten-forty that morning, the captain of the Ocean Glamour was able to put his feet up and rest easy as all the guests, minus Howard Newton and three elderly widows who lived most of the year on the ship, were now ashore. The disembarkation had gone surprisingly well thanks to the promptness of U.S. Customs and the tip-hungry dockworkers who got everything ready a good fifteen minutes before the first group was ready to leave the ship. As regards those of interest to us; the Florians were already at their post surrounded by luggage belonging to their son and his partner, Samantha and Isabelle Whitby, Malcolm Fitzroy, the Flannerys, the Dosynks and, interestingly, a humbled Anatoly Plushenko and his niece, Svetlana with the long last name. Petra Dosynk had insisted they join the party. While Liz left the ship early, she remained inside the pier to watch for Van Woort should Peter lose him.

At ten-thirty, a scant ten minutes before the captain could rest easy, Peter was in the last line of passengers to disembark. "I'm just about to have my card swiped," he said to Liz on his iPhone. Turning around and seeing no one behind him except Lillie, he added, "I think we may be the last to leave. Anyway, Van Woort is about five people ahead of me. Do you have all our bags?"

"I have mine," she said, speaking louder than usual due to the noise inside the cavernous pier. "I'm headed over to the orange section to find yours. I have a porter who will take them all out for us. Oh, don't forget to have your passport and Customs' form ready."

"I will. Van Woort's bags should be with the orange group as well."

"Tio, are we *really* taking a cab home?" she asked nervously.

"Sorry, honey, but it looks that way," he said, remembering Liz wasn't a big fan of taxis since she'd experienced a young Oakland cabbie who, angry over her rebuff of his clumsy, flirtatious advances, scared her witless by suddenly driving recklessly and dangerously.

"We'll look for a van and team up with Samantha. You'll be fine."

"I'm sure I will. Time to grow up," she added with a self-effacing giggle.

"I've got to go," he said, approaching the double-doored exit on the starboard side of the Grand Atrium. Taking one last look, he glanced up at the railing outside the Portside Bistro on the sixth deck where Howard stood with an attractive woman who looked to be near his age. He smiled down at Peter and waved. Then he said something Peter couldn't hear over the piped-in music. Lillie was certain he shouted, "Up yours, Ramsey."

"Have a safe journey home, sir," the security guard said as he swiped Peter's keycard, a plastic card that had been his door key and identification for the last twelve days.

"Don't you want it?" he asked the smiling man in the starched white uniform.

"No, that is yours to take home. It won't open anything, though, and it certainly won't get you into any private clubs." That response came from Fritz Henning who, dressed in running gear, now stood behind him. "The idea is to collect as many of those as you can in whatever time you have left on this planet that I will remind you is about seventy percent salt water."

Peter was now concerned that he'd have this wise-cracking hotel director as company on his way out. Still, he managed a smile and, noticing Fritz's well-worn New York City Marathon tee-shirt, managed to ask, "How many miles today?"

"Not many, I'm afraid. This is a very busy day on the ship," he replied in a rushed manner. "I'm going to try to run for an hour. I love running the Embarcadero and the Marina. Peter, would you mind if I scoot ahead. I'm in a bit of a hurry."

"Not at all," Peter said with a sigh of relief, moving aside to let Fritz go ahead. "Wish I could join you. I need to run off all those wonderful meals I've enjoyed these last twelve days."

With a wave, the hotel director began to bob and weave through those who remained on the gangway leading to the pier. Peter, too, kept a lively pace through the curlicue exit. By the time he had entered the large area reserved for luggage, his mobile rang.

"Shit!" Liz shouted into his ear, panic in her voice. "I don't believe this. Van Woort is headed straight to Customs and the exit. He has only what he carried off the ship; a garment bag and a carry-on. We should of taken that into consideration."

"Did you find my bags?"

"Yes, the porter has them."

"Good. Start for the exit. I'll meet you there," he said, turning on his heels and heading for the exit which was a football field's length away.

"I'd follow him but there's no way for me to inform you as to his whereabouts," Lillie said, feeling quite helpless as she floated beside him.

"Actually, there is. You can be a great help," Peter exclaimed, eyeing Van Woort casually chatting up the Customs' agent who was collecting the immigration forms. "Remember, Liz, Sam and I can see you. Follow Van Woort but stay above him. I'll be able to see you as soon as I leave the pier."

"A wonderful idea," she chirped. "I'm on my way."

Just like that, Peter saw her lavender translucent form hovering above the auctioneer who was now stepping out into the bright sunshine. He called Samantha as he walked toward Customs and asked if she could see Lillie floating over the rush of people on the Embarcadero.

"How can I not," she exclaimed, spotting Lillie slowing moving in the opposite direction of where she was standing with the Florians and others. "It's quite amazing."

"Follow her, Sam. In fact, have everyone follow her... I mean have them follow you. Van Woort is directly below her. She's helping us keep track of him."

"When you come out, Peter, look left. You can't miss her," Sam said.

By this time, Customs' agents were checking their watches, anxious to take a long, relaxing coffee break. As a result, Peter and Liz were sent packing after no more than a cursory inspection. As Samantha instructed, once on the Embarcadero, he looked left where he saw Lillie hovering above the crowd. She was stationary and appeared to be on the street edge of the wide sidewalk some fifty yards south of the Pier 35. Peter asked Liz to take their bags to the Florian's temporary campsite near the pier and then come back to where Lillie was positioned.

Moving through the crowd, he felt someone tap him on the shoulder. It was Dave Flannery. "I thought you were going to take a cab home?" he asked gruffly.

"I am."

"Then why is that rock star limo waiting for you," he said, pointing to a shiny-black, stretched SUV limousine parked some twenty feet away. A husky, black-suited driver was standing nearby holding a large white sign that read "RAMSEY." Leaning against the right fender of the limousine, his arms and legs crossed, Charles Van Woort, smug in his contrived suavity, caught Peter's eye and with a practiced nod of his head motioned him over.

"Dave, can your friend tell the traffic cops to leave us be for awhile?"

Dave nodded. "Tommy's right behind you. He'll take care of it. We'll wait here."

Then Lillie shouted, "May I come down now?"

WIthout thinking, Peter hollered, "No, stay there."

"I just told you we are staying here," Dave said grumpily.

"Sorry, uh..."

"Will you go see what this is all about," Flannery said impatiently, pushing him toward the auctioneer.

"Ah, Mr. Ramsey," Van Woort said as Peter approached. "I gather your eccentric bunch of compatriots are not far behind you. My God! Here they come now en masse. What a nuisance you all have been. That said, though, I suppose I ought to thank you for encouraging me to make a move I've long been contemplating."

"Why is that man holding a sign with my name on it?" Peter asked, even though he knew it was the practice of limo drivers waiting for their customers.

Van Woort flashed his trademark grin. "I took the liberty of hiring a car and driver for you."

"I don't need a car, particularly this monstrosity."

Van Woort grinned again. Only this time it was more a smirk. "Might as well accept it. All Randy there knows is he's been hired by a Mr. Peter Ramsey to drive him and his niece home to Berkeley. He got the order last night, specifying he was to bring the biggest and flashiest limo in their fleet. By the way, he has all your credit card information. Given my unique position as the shipboard auctioneer, it was relatively easy to get that information."

All this time, Charles Van Woort lounged idly against the SUV. Now he moved away from the car and came close to Peter. "This is a loading zone. We don't have much time. Come here."

They stepped to the rear passenger side door which Van Woort opened. "Please, take a look inside. You'll see that a porter has already dropped off some of your stuff."

Peter peered inside the garish interior. Sitting upright on the floor against the back seats were three well-wrapped items, two of similar size and one larger.

"I'm sure you know what they are without having to open them. What you do with them is, of course, your business. I'm confident when the time comes you will have a thought up some creative explanation of how they fell into your hands. Needless to say, I would appreciate my not playing any part in your story." Checking his watch, Van Woort added, "I should be going."

He can't go yet, Peter said to himself. There are too many questions. "I suppose you and Naomi are going somewhere romantic?" he asked, hoping the inquiry would open the door to more questions.

It turned out that was the only query he needed. Casting him an odd look, Van Woort laughed aloud. "Munchie

Crunchie Naomi and me! What an absurd idea. Peter... May I call you Peter?" Ramsey shrugged his shoulders. "Good! Peter, I'm not only lactose-intolerant, I'm Naomi-intolerant. She's a younger version of her mother and that is not a good thing. However, she did her part and more to save my skin and for that I will be eternally grateful."

"Then it *was* Naomi who told you about the fake Millais?"

"Oh, she told me much more than that," he happily admitted. "You see, after her mother's death, when Naomi and her husband were working on the estate, she phoned to give me a heads up about the discovery of some iffy paintings I'd sold her mother. While we were chatting, I told her about the arrangement her mother and I had regarding *A Jersey Lily.* It came as quite a surprise to her. She explained she'd been on the outs with her mother due to Philipa moving in with them in San Francisco and, as a result, she was unaware of what her mother was up to when she booked the Alaska cruise. I believe it was during that conversation I made it quite clear that I had decided that would be my last sale of anything lacking impeccable provenance."

"Why?"

"This is no act of expiation, mind you. But who knows? Atonement might follow. For now my reason is purely business. Like I told Naomi, the clientele has changed. Now it's all Russian or East European mobsters, bosses from the Mexican drug cartels and other equally ruthless, violence-prone types. Gone are the good old days when one could count on dealing with harmless society ladies and egoistic business execs eager to have something no one else has. These new clients are downright scary and I frighten easily."

"So Naomi decided to help you..."

"Clean up affairs," he said, finishing Peter's sentence. "When she learned I had a forgery, she let me know.

Unfortunately, by that time I had already arranged to sell *A Jersey Lily* to Anatoly Plushenko. At the time, I was under the impression he was a Russian mobster who came highly recommended by a really nasty man I met in Moscow. My thinking was if all went well, he'd leave with the icons and the painting and my inventory of questionable art would be down to zero. What a strange web I weaved. Or is it wove?"

"So how is it that the real Millais ends up in the back seat of a stretched SUV?"

Van Woort produced one of those smiles he reserved for people who had the winning bid at one of his auctions. "You can thank Naomi for that. When she realized I had a fake and was in a bit of a fix, she flew to London, met with Sprottle and returned with the real painting. I still can't get her to tell me what transpired between them. She assures me, though, that's the real thing," he said, pointing to the package in the limo.

"She's certainly not the Naomi I met while she was married to Howard."

Van Woort shrugged. "I've known her a long time. She's quirky and unpredictable."

"But she and Howard were together for quite a while and their lives revolved around peaceful, harmless pursuits like sea birds, art and ice cream. You mean to say that was all an act?" he asked.

"I recently read a book where a certain person was described as six different characters in search of an author. That may well describe Naomi. Mind you, she's done me a good deed and for that I'm grateful, but that's as much contact as I want with her." Extending his hand, he said with genuine cordiality, "As pleasant as this is, Peter, I really must go. I'm sure between you and that odd assortment of friends over there, you'll figure out how to deal with your new acquisitions. As for me, I am off to a new life."

"I'm curious. Who is the *new* Jersey Lily in your life?" Peter asked, watching to see what reaction his question would get from Van Woort.

The auctioneer was clearly taken aback. Clearly, Peter had struck a nerve. Then in an instant, Van Woort grinned from ear to ear. "Aha, you mean Darla Lanphier from Jersey City," he replied, pointing with pride to a tall, attractive, well-dressed woman standing next to a black town car parked behind them. "Plushenko must have told you? He's the only one who knows about her."

"You know those Russians. Great gossips," Peter said facetiously. "Well, thanks for making this too easy."

"It was a pleasure. I wish I could stick around to see how you're going to explain all this to that mountain of a cop standing next to Mr. Frumpy-pants," he said, looking in the direction of the perpetually disheveled Dave Flannery and the police captain.

With that Charles Van Woort turned on his expensive Italian heels and headed toward Ms Lanphier and a new life.

While Peter watched him walk away, Lillie asked softly, "May I come down now?

"Sure. I gather you saw and heard all?"

"I did. I must say, Mr. Van Woort has the perfect partner for a naked midnight swim."

Captain Thomas "Tommy" Sullivan was, indeed, a mountain of a man. Tall, broad-shouldered, rock solid, square-jawed, jutting chin, penetrating blue eyes... He had it all to the point of caricature. "So you got me here to see that a friend of yours can overstay his visit in a loading zone," he growled at Dave. Even his voice seemed muscular.

"It's more than that," his friend mumbled. "Be patient."

"Look at that! The other guy's gone and Ramsey looks like he's still carrying on a conversation?" Sullivan observed as he watched Peter chatting animatedly with Lillie.

"Ramsey is, uh, weird. Talks to himself a lot. I think it's a radio thing," Dave said, mounting what you would agree, I'm sure, was a weak defense of his friend's eccentric behavior.

"Well, I want to talk to him," the officer barked.

Almost as if Peter had heard his growling demand, he started toward the pair while his cohorts who were close by also inched closer.

"Captain Sullivan, I'm delighted you came," Peter said, feeling expansive after his unusual experience with Van Woort.

"I'd like to know why I'm here."

"I'm sure you would. Oh, excuse me," Peter said, looking at Petra Dosynk who was to his left. "Petra! You know, the art you bought at auction? They were mistakenly put in my car. You might want to get them and put them with your luggage."

The chunky Kwyrki matter-of-factly made his way to the SUV and just like that, the Fukin Icons were that much closer to going home to Mother Russia. Dosynk's casualness unnerved Anatoly Plushenko who stood directly behind the policeman and Dave Flannery.

"Captain, I have something for you," Peter said. "However, it will take some explaining. Is there somewhere we can all go?"

"Who is all?" Sullivan asked.

"There are a bunch of us," Peter explained, pointing to the group now huddled around the confused police captain.

As it was Dave's rule of thumb that, if at all possible, meetings be held somewhere that has a liquor license, he recommended the nearby Buena Vista. The bar had a sizable back room, and he was confident at this early hour they could commandeer it. He also knew Tommy Sullivan possessed an over-sized thirst for the bar's signature drink and would second any motion to go there.

The Florians were relieved of their duties as guardians of the luggage so they could join the party. Captain Sullivan, using his authority, had their bags stored inside the pier under the watchful eye of a security guard. Cabs were then hailed for those who couldn't squeeze into Peter's stretched SUV. Within minutes, they were all holding Irish Coffees and sporting cream mustaches from their first sips. In a far corner, on a cleared table covered with protective paper was the unwrapped *A Jersey Lily*. Benjamin Lytton-Crisp, the painting's biggest fan, and Malcolm Fitzroy needed mere seconds to declare it the real thing.

While Malcolm stepped away to join Isabelle and her sister, Benjamin remained planted in place, staring lovingly at the portrait. He was joined by another admirer, as the real Jersey Lily had suddenly positioned herself between Lytton-Crisp and the painting.

"My heavens! I swear I have never seen her look so radiant. It's as if I can see her soul," he swooned to no one in particular.

Now you may think from that seemingly prescient remark, Mr. Lyttton-Crisp sensed the presence of Lillie as he had to look through the lavender nimbus to view the painting. That might also lead you to believe I was up to my old tricks. Not at all. As a matter of fact, it was Benjamin's usual practice to utter something fanciful and fantastical whenever he visited the painting at the Tate.

Savoring his first Irish Coffee, a bemused Tommy Sullivan listened attentively as Peter tried to craft a plausible explanation for how a stolen masterpiece from London's Tate Museum just happened to be currently on display in the back room of a San Francisco historic saloon. The challenge, Peter realized, was building a credible enough story in such a way that it didn't implicate anyone. His performance was, in a word, clumsy.

With just a sip or two left of his first Irish Coffee, Captain Sullivan signaled for another as Peter concluded his remarks. His response was to coolly advise Peter that while he most certainly was confiscating the painting, he would appreciate going back to the station with a valid explanation as to how he himself came by it.

Now into his second Irish Coffee, Captain Sullivan decided that if Peter couldn't give him what he needed, he'd appeal to the general population. With his commanding voice, he asked for everyone's attention. Whereupon he asked if anyone had anything more valuable to offer him than what he'd just heard from Peter which he described as vague, ambiguous prattle. Peter initially bristled, but Sullivan's twinkling eyes and impish grin hinted he was just having some fun at his expense.

Now with just a sip remaining of his second Irish Coffee, Captain Sullivan, full of alcohol, caffeine, sugar and cream, felt a warm and embracing bonhomie for his new friends even though they remained less than forthcoming about the painting. Looking around the crowded room festooned with old photos of San Francisco, arms outstretched, he said pleadingly, "I'm looking for some help here, folks."

Liz decide to take him up on his offer. With an air of innocence that is easily assumed by most young people, she asked, "Couldn't you just pretend you found it? Like maybe here in the back room of the BV?"

Before Sullivan could respond, Freddie and Benjamin approached him. As the designated spokesman, Freddie said tremulously, "Captain, I believe we can help. If you would like us to accompany you to the station, we'd be happy to make a statement." They both then put their hands out to be handcuffed.

"What? Did you two steal the damned thing?" he asked.

Horrified, both convulsed at the thought. "No, of course not," they sang in unison. "However, we were unwittingly... No, that's not right. I should have said we were inadvertently involved and it's time we owned up to it," Freddie added emphatically while casting a loving at his partner.

If two Irish Coffees had any effect on Captain Sullivan, it was to bring to the surface his true benevolent nature. Putting a beefy hand on Benjamin and Freddie's shoulders, he guided them to a corner table where they would participate in their one and only police interrogation regarding the matter of the stolen painting.

After five minutes, all three rose. Benjamin, Freddie and Captain Sullivan's impassive expressions gave no hint as to what transpired. Flannery, who knew the veteran police officer better than most, looked at Peter and gave a subtle thumbs up. The room quieted as the tall man with the chiseled face again signaled he wanted their attention. Dave also knew the longtime police officer loved having the floor and would preface whatever he had to say about the missing painting with a personal word or two. He didn't disappoint.

"I'm retiring in a couple of months," he began, his booming voice that of one used to commanding. "Almost made chief. Even had the endorsement of Dave's paper."

"You would have made a great chief," Flannery said of his high school friend, earning a nod from the captain and a nudge from Mary Pat.

Thomas "Tommy" Sullivan paused a moment. "Dave, this is all off the record."

"When hasn't it been with us?" Dave joked.

Tommy cleared his throat. "In a police department, like any bureaucracy, the higher up in rank you go, the more you're expected to go by the book. That said, I have had a few cases where I was more free-wheeling and imaginative than the book allows. There weren't many of these occasions but there are none I regret. Now it appears I'm going to add one more to the list."

"Captain Sullivan reminds me so much of Judge Roy Bean," Lillie whispered to Peter who quickly shushed her. Fortunately, it went unnoticed.

"After hearing what Mr. Lytton-Crisp and Dr. Florian had to say, I venture to say you all haven't exactly been playing by the book either. But here's the thing to remember; by the book or not, the goal is always the same and that is a resolution you can live with. I get the feeling in your case, you've accomplished that. Now, thanks to those two," he said, pointing to the two neo-Victorians, "I have something more substantive to take back to the station along with the painting. Who knows? Maybe I'll get a trip to London out of it," he laughed. Looking at his watch, he debated a third Irish Coffee. The matter was settled as he spotted Lillian, a thirty year veteran of delivering Irish Coffees to customers. Known to her regulars as a lovable grouch, she looked his way and that's all it took. He raised his empty glass. Her scowl was all he needed to know the order was in.

Malcolm stepped forward to shake the captain's hand. He was followed by Isabelle and before you could say, "Sir John Everett Millais," everyone was thanking him effusively for his understanding. Peter Ramsey finally got a moment alone with him.

"Jason Sprottle stole the painting, but you know that now," he said. "Benjamin and Freddie, while not exactly blameless, did come to their senses on the ship and they did the right thing. I am sure they gave you an honest accounting."

"Here you go, Tommy, me boy," Lillian barked, interrupting their conversation."

"It's turning out to be my breakfast this morning," Sullivan said.

"Well, they do contain the four important food elements, so they can't be all that

bad for you," she said with a raspy giggle. "You know, I remember you coming in here as a young street cop from North Beach. You'd say 'easy on the whiskey, my darling.' You were insufferable even them."

"Aye, but I gave up saying that after my first promotion, my darling," he laughed, taking the Irish Coffee from her so she could tend to other thirsts.

"Sounds like you two go way back." Peter observed.

"Lillian? Oh yeah. You know with the business this place does and her tips, she can probably buy and sell us." After taking a sip of his fresh Irish Coffee, he asked, "So the auctioneer figures into all of this?"

"Sprottle was supposed to send him the painting as Van Woort had a buyer. Instead, Sprottle shipped him a forgery."

"I gather Van Woort was the gentleman you were talking to at the pier. Like our couple over there was he also trying to make amends for doing something he shouldn't by giving you the painting?"

"Benjamin and Freddie are truly remorseful and contrite. Van Woort is cleaning up his act for other reasons. I do feel, though, he's out of the business of fencing art and will probably stay out of it."

"Well, he's not my concern right now," Sullivan said in a dismissive tone that pleased Peter. "I'm sure the FBI, Scotland Yard and whatever other agency that handles crimes like these will be able to find him without our help."

"I think he may also have a disgruntled client or two looking for him as well," Peter remarked. When Sullivan gave him a quizzical look, Peter shared with him Van Woort's fascinating take on what the auctioneer called the new and troubling demographic of fanciers of stolen art.

Tommy took a sip, licked his lips and stared pensively at Peter. You got room for one more question?" he asked casually.

"Sure," Peter gulped.

In that nanosecond between the question and his response, Peter's mind was awhirl. What was problematic, he thought, was so much of the last twelve days was unexplainable. He wondered what Sullivan might ask: How did you get involved? How did the real painting get from London to the pier. Who brought it? What about the fake? Where is it? Do you know where Van Woort is headed? Who are all these people and how do they factor into the story? Then his mind brought up myriad images: Philipa's body in the bathroom. Seeing and hearing Lillie for the first time. Petra Dosynk sipping his coffee concoction in the Portside Bistro. Proposing to Samantha. He thought in that instant he saw it all.

Interesting, isn't it? How you can process all that instantaneously. I don't mean to be smug but it's a no-brainer for me and everyone else in residence here in Eternity. We do it all the time. You do it as well, however you probably don't pay much attention to what it is you're doing nor do you give it any weight. Particularly spiritual weight. You should as this amazing ability to assemble so much in an instant is one of my Employer's little gifts. It's a tiny glimpse of what awaits you when you no longer have the ability to leave a carbon footprint. You see, in a timeless spiritual world, life is an eternity of instants. You see all and are all forever.

So Peter gulped, "Sure."

With a furrowed brow, Sullivan asked with a barely restrained laugh, "Is it true Dave won a ballroom dancing competition?"

EPILOGUE

THE TALE IS told, but the story continues. Isn't that always the case? For example, Shakespeare wrapped up *Henry V* with just as farcical an ending as mine. After clumsily proposing to Katherine, Harry dove right into a bawdy locker-room exchange with the Duke of Burgundy and some other French noblemen; behaving as if they were all randy stags at a Las Vegas bachelor party. The Bard certainly spun a ripping good yarn, but it's obvious there was more to the story. Thus, you have this nifty device called the epilogue to help give the author's close a little more weight should it need it. Mine certainly does.

As a true believer in saving the best for last, I will first catch you up on the more nefarious members of our cast, namely Charles Van Woort, Naomi Figg and the Sprottle lads. The suave but oily shipboard auctioneer, after tanning himself silly in Hawaii, returned to New York where he became one of the FBI's best informants when it came to investigating crimes involving works of art. Emboldened by the fact they were never prosecuted for stealing the Millais from the Tate, the Sprottle twins were quick to get up to their old tricks. In a month's time, their luck ran out and they found themselves caught, tried and convicted. After spending a respectable time as guests of her majesty's government in one of her cushier gaols, the two were signed by Naomi Figg, now an executive producer for Figg Broadcasting, to host what would become the most tasteless reality show ever to air in either Great Britain or the United States.

Now it is on to the others. Dr. Freddie Florian and Benjamin Lytton-Crisp returned to Winona, Minnesota; Freddie to his flourishing dental practice and Benjamin to his art gallery. For a brief time, they feared their involvement in Jasper Sprottle's stolen-painting caper would come back to bite them. Then one day a check for the same amount of money they had invested in the Socrates Club arrived with a terse note saying the mews house in London had sold and the club was disbanded. With this unexpected windfall they purchased a lovely condominium near their home for Freddie's parents who, learning their son and Benjamin were serious about adopting or taking on a foster child, decided to move from California and join them to help out as only loving grandparents can.

Dave and Mary Pat Flannery went home to once again deal with their rancorous, and rambunctious teenage children (Their description, not mine.). While they came home bearing gifts, their best present turned out to be their revitalized romantic relationship. Right off, their petulant progeny noticed how kind, loving and supportive each was to the other. It was then that an amazing transformation began. Slowly – after all, they are teenagers – their normally recalcitrant behavior was replaced by one their parents could only call welcoming. While a positive pussycat at home, Dave was his usual irascible, hot-tempered, disheveled, single malt-swigging self at work. His staff wanted it no other way.

Rather than rushing home to their beloved Zneferuk, Kwyrkistan, the Dosynks flew – dirty laundry and all – to Moscow where Petra and his wife, Inka Dinka Dosynk checked into the Ritz-Carlton. Petra promised his wife he could accomplish everything he needed do there in two weeks time. Firstly, he arranged a dinner at Anatoly Plushenko's restaurant, instructing the ever so grateful Russian to include Spartak Kozlov. At evening's end, Kozlov left with the $450,000 Plushenko owed him and Petra took over ownership of the restaurant which he promptly closed; posting a sign announcing a grand re-opening in less than two weeks. In that fortnight, the clubby, masculine interior became floral,frilly and feminine. Pastels abounded. Decorative opened umbrellas hung upside down from a ceiling painted sky-blue with puffy white clouds. Petra named the place *Miss Goody Two-Shoes*. The silly new name and outrageous decor had its desired effect. Anatoly's former restaurant was now mob-free as no self-respecting gangster would ever frequent a place that looked like a teenage girl's bedroom and was called *Miss Goody Two-Shoes*. Petra was delighted to hear from his grandson a month later that the restaurant, thanks to social media, was a huge success. A generous man, he gave a substantial percentage of *Miss Goody Two-Shoes* to Yurk and Svetlana with the long last name for managing it. He even gave a small piece to Anatoly who agreed to work as a host a few days a week. Otherwise, Plushenko spent most of his time as the newly appointed Executive Director of the small museum where the Fukin Icons were now prominently on display in the newly named Dosynk Family Hall.

Malcolm Fitzroy and Isabelle Whitby continued their world travels for a time. The gentlemanly octogenarian art historian peacefully departed your planet; joining us here in Eternity in late October. Isabelle's grief was diminished somewhat by the gratitude she felt for the precious time they had together.

Peter, Liz and Samantha returned to Berkeley where Liz in due time earned her PhD in Anthropology, graduating with honors. She immediately went to work for the university. While not returning to radio full time, Peter kept busy doing occasional voice-over work; a pursuit that earned him a strange celebrity when we was hired to be the voice of Albert the Articulate Aardvark on an award-winning PBS children's show. Samanth continued to teach at Cal. Soon after Liz's graduation, they married. The wedding was held in the library of the Berkeley City Club, a Julia Morgan masterpiece of a building. It was an early wedding with the happy couple sneaking out after a short cocktail reception to head home to catch a rerun of Downton Abbey. Or so Liz keeps telling people.

Finally, what of our dear Lillie? Did she, as filmmakers say, *fade to black* whilst Captain Sullivan was asking Peter that shaggy dog of a question? I couldn't have that. Nor could I have Lillie beckon her three friends to step outside the Buena Vista only to have them watch her disappear on the tourist-crowded cable car turnaround at Beach and Hyde Streets. A cold, insensitive departure to say the least. Yes, I know the original plan was to have Mrs. Langtry come straight home when *A Jersey Lily* was in safe hands. However, once off the Ocean Glamour, all it took was one lingering look at the imposing hills of San Francisco and Lillie"s head – metaphorically speaking – was filled with fond remembrances of The City and its gorgeous surroundings. Her nostalgia was such that I decided to let her stay on for a few days. During that time, she tried as best she could to show her friends the San Francisco of her day. Alas, too many years had passed and she was hard-pressed to find much to point to where she could say, "I was there." Her three companions, though, delighted in showing her the modern day version of The City. They attended a Giants' game and a performance of *Beach Blanket Babylon*. They rode a cable car halfway to the stars and visited the imposing Ferry Building, now a bustling culinary marketplace. Then a day came when the foursome toured the campus of the University of California in Berkeley. In the late afternoon, they ended up atop the Campanile admiring the splendid views. I thought it a most appropriate place and a perfect time for Lillie to catch the drift of the wind off the Bay and sail away. So it was, with their hearts full and their eyes teary, Peter, Liz and Samantha watched as their special friend, Lillie Langtry by name of Emilie Charlotte, Lady de Bathe, nee Le Breton, floated off like a balloon that had escaped a child's wrist. They watched with a mixture of sadness and joy as her lavender presence began to slowly diminish in the bright afternoon sunshine. In that instant she was home. Never let it be said we residents of Eternity don't have a flair for the dramatic.

About the Author

MIKE CLEARY IS a longtime radio personality who is best known as co-host of *Frank and Mike in the Morning* on KNBR. His partner, Frank Dill, said Mike's only responsibility was to make him laugh. He said Mike took the job very seriously. The show was a success and ran for years. In 2007, he was inducted into the Bay Area Radio Hall of Fame.

In 2012, retired from full time broadcasting, he decided it was also time to retire his shortened first name. He once again embraced Michael Patrick which he had shelved, thanks to the threatening manner in which a tough-talking third grade nun used to call on him.

A proud neatnik, Michael Patrick Cleary has a fondness for colorful socks, pocket-squares, Martinis and memorizing Shakespeare. He is a long slow distance runner getting slower.

Mr. Cleary is happily married with two grown daughters. He resides in Piedmont, California.